Hands of the Maker

Book I

By

Robert P. Cox

Enki Publications
Jeanne Shaw, publisher
Denver, CO 80231

Visit us online at:
http://www.handsofthemaker.com

Enki Publications, LLC and design are trademarks of
Enki Publications, LLC
and are used under license by Enki Publications, LLC,
the publisher of this work.

Biblical quotes are from:
The Holy Bible, King James Version
Genesis 6, Verses 13, 5, 11, 12, 7, 3, 17, 1, 2, 4, 8, 9
II Thessalonians 2, Verses 3 & 4
Psalms 82, Verses 6 & 7

The *Epic of Gilgamesh* quotes are from:
The Gilgamesh Epic and Old Testament Parallels, Alexander Heidel
(The University of Chicago Press, Chicago and London, 1946 and
1949)

No trademarks or trade names were used in this novel.

A special thanks to the Hampden Branch of the
Denver Public Library.

The cover art titled: "The Anunnaki" was created by Colorado artist
Tim Petro. Please feel free to contact him at: onenesstp@yahoo.com

Meagan Templeton-Lynch, editor

ISBN 978-0-9727683-3-7

Thank you, Mom, for your unconditional love and spiritual insight.

Max Stiner was awakened by a voice that was harsh and full of condemnation. He lingered in between sleep and consciousness, at first unable to identify the shapes around him.

"'And God said unto Noah, The end of all flesh is come before me; for the earth is filled with violence through them; and, behold, I will destroy them with the earth!'"

Flanked by figures of agony and sanctimony, sweat dripping from his brow, a priest was chastising a packed house full of parishioners.

"'And God saw that the wickedness of man was great in the earth, And that every imagination of the thoughts of his heart was only evil continually!'"

Max was slumped down in the back pew – among the homeless people, prostitutes, and blue-collar workers – wearing an old t-shirt and dirty blue jeans, a month of insomnia evident on his pale face.

"'The earth also was corrupt before God,'" the priest read. "'And the earth was filled with violence! And God looked upon the earth, and, behold, it was corrupt; for all flesh had corrupted his way upon earth!'"

The fire and brimstone that echoed from the cavernous ceiling overhead was breaking through Max's fatigue-induced trance and slowly dragging him back into the conscious world. It was a transition that had become increasingly difficult for him to make.

"'And the Lord said, I will destroy man whom I have created from the face of the earth, both man, and beast, and the creeping thing, the fowls of the air, for it repenteth me that I have made them!'"

Max's first lucid thoughts were not of the fearsome words of judgment raining down on him, but of the obviously fearful notion of God that had inspired those words.

"'And the Lord said, my spirit shall not always strive with man! For that he also is flesh: yet his days shall be a hundred and twenty years!'"

Max searched the faces of the congregation for some sign of religious epiphany. Only like him, most of those who had gathered on that particular day sought neither penance nor damnation.

It was the subject of the sermon: the saga of a great flood, a boat, and a band of faithful climate refugees that had attracted one of the largest audiences the priest had ever addressed.

"'And, behold, I, even I, do bring a flood of waters upon the earth, to destroy all flesh, wherein is the breath of life, from under heaven; and every thing that is in the earth shall die!'

"Noah may have lived a long life before the Flood," the priest said. "But even by Noah's time God had already grown angry with man:

"'And it came to pass when men began to multiply on the face of the earth, and daughters were born unto them, that the sons of God saw the daughters of men, that they were fair, and they took them wives of all which they chose.

"'There were giants in the earth in those days, And also after that, when the sons of God came in unto the daughters of men, and they bore children to them, and the same became mighty men which were of old, men of renown.'"

Max ran his calloused hand over the cover of a textbook dedicated to one of those "men of renown": the *Epic of Gilgamesh*. As he had many times before, he used his finger to trace the pristine photograph of a four-thousand-year-old slab of dried earth.

Brilliantly lit and museum mounted, the fragmented clay tablet was covered from edge to edge with distinctive hash marks known as *cuneiform*. Scholars had discovered among those seemingly unreadable impressions an older version of a great flood, a boat, and a band of faithful climate refugees.

Sitting there on that uncomfortable bench, fondling the scholarly volume, Max had an epiphany of his own. It was his obsession with the origins of Genesis, Chapter 6 that was behind his recent decline, a rather obvious insight that had somehow escaped him until that very moment.

"This was, of course, ten generations after Adam and Eve and the original sin," the priest said. "And it was because of that tainted legacy that in many ways God's retribution was inevitable. The seeds of the Great Flood were sown all the way back in the Garden of Eden.

"But 'Noah found grace in the eyes of the Lord... Noah was a just man and perfect in his generations, and Noah walked with God!'

"It was only because he was a righteous man that Noah was spared God's wrath and rewarded with everlasting life. He and he alone was warned by God of what was to come. Then it was up to him to trust in the 'Holy Word.' He did trust it, and he and his family survived as a direct result of that faith.

"The fable of Noah and the Flood demonstrates two very important lessons. The first is that the pious are always rewarded by God. The Lord may test us to our very limits, but in the end, the man or woman who remains faithful will prevail.

"And the second very important lesson is that God always punishes sin. He may have to send an act of nature to get it done. But wickedness will always be condemned to destruction."

Max had good reason to disagree. He knew from personal experience that "sinners" escaped divine judgment all the time. More often than not, it was the innocent who caught hell.

Feeling every year of his middle age, he got to his feet and stumbled out the front entrance, onto a crowded New York City block. With his book tucked under his arm he merged with the flow of foot traffic.

When Max cut his long brown hair and shaved the patchy traces of beard that dotted his cheeks, he was handsome, defying his age of forty-two by at least ten years. It was just that when he was clean-shaven, he was also a rather "average-looking white guy," a tag he picked up in the army and always hated.

He dropped his head and plunged his hands deep into his pockets, barely watching where he was going. Max could cover miles that way, sliding between people, sensing his way around corners and through crosswalks.

He would roam the length of the island of Manhattan, from the machine shop in SoHo where he worked, to his fourth floor walk-up in Washington Heights, feeling invisible to everyone he passed. Sometimes it was to avoid work, but mostly it was to avoid sleeping.

The gridlock that encircled him that day would have been maddening if Max hadn't become so adept at disengaging from the place in which he had chosen to live. Thanks to the restless time he had spent in cities such as Los Angeles and Miami, he had arrived at Grand Central Station already equipped with the pragmatic ambivalence that came from living in a metropolis like New York. In many ways, his detachment had become complete since his arrival on the island.

In other ways, Max had become far too connected to the world. Somehow he had become so invested in both the past and the future of humanity that it had rendered him unable to find any kind of solace in the present.

After twenty years out of the army without a single change in his habits, the routines of a responsible life now seemed pointless. A resignation had washed over him, as it had his fellow New Yorkers, as it had his fellow Americans.

Now whenever Max walked the streets, he couldn't shake the nagging feeling that he and everyone else was living down some kind of dysfunctional birthright of which they were all completely oblivious, and all completely compliant.

If asked directly, Max would have admitted that he couldn't stand the people around him, or the society they had created. He just couldn't stop thinking about their collective fate.

He looked up at the sign above, "Precision Machining" – his most recent place of employment. He loitered in the doorway, unable to remember how he had come to work there. Though it hardly mattered, he was sure to quit or get fired soon enough anyway.

For Max the choice had always been simple. It was either serve as an admittedly well-paid cog, or sleep in a cardboard box. At one time the answer had seemed obvious. Now he wasn't so sure.

He took his hand off the doorknob at the last moment and hustled away from the front of the building before he was spotted by another employee, or worse, his supervisor. He walked around the corner to a payphone he often used and dial a number from memory.

3

After a conversation of only a few words, he was moving through the New York streets again.

That evening in his claustrophobic bedroom, Max was stretched out on one side of his bed reading, while a brunette woman in her thirties snored on the other. A loud crash from the television in the corner woke her.

Liz was immediately coherent. "What time is it?"

"After six."

"You ass. Why did you let me sleep?" She slapped Max hard on the leg.

"You've got time."

She checked the cover of the book he was reading as she sprang out of bed. "Gilga who?" she said while dressing.

She noticed the piles of books at his bedside. An old Bible, the Kabala, and the Qur'an were among the growing stacks of magazines and newspapers that had begun to clog the walls of the tiny, depressing space. Some were heaped as high as the few pieces of furniture in the room.

"What's going on with you, anyway?"

"Where do I start?"

"Where the hell did all these magazines and newspapers come from?" she said. "That's a start."

The dusk that was descending on the city outside the windows was casting a warm glow over Liz's chilly exit. She was careful not to look directly at him while she prepared to leave. She had never been able to look Max straight in the eye, particularly after one of their illicit rendezvous.

"What's it been, a year now?" he said. "I can't even remember how we lost touch."

"You've always known how to find me. I haven't gone anywhere."

"We were pretty good together, but we just stopped trying," he said. "Oh, now I remember, you couldn't leave your husband. What was it? Couldn't afford it? The kids wouldn't understand?"

"I left my husband maybe two months after we stopped talking."

"You what?"

"Divorce papers were filed over six months ago."

"You never called..." Max's pride was hurt, more than he thought it would be.

She gathered her things. "I've had too much to do lately. I haven't had time for distractions."

"Distractions, huh? Don't you ever want love, Liz, for your life?"

"My kids give me all the love I can handle. They're my heart and my soul, you know?"

"Yeah, I got that message loud and clear a year ago."

"People don't change unless they want to, Max. You're stupid if you think you can make somebody really change their life before they're good and damned ready."

"I'm stupid all right."

"Hey, I'm sorry I didn't call, but that's the way it goes. Right now, all I have time for is making sure me and my kids are taken care of, that they know there's somebody who will protect them."

Max rolled his eyes. "Please, don't start again."

"Because there is nobody else, you know?" She did a fast makeup job in the mirror. "What, are you gonna come over and take them to Little League, or get them to the doctor's when they get sick? I'm responsible for bringing them into this shitty world, and I'm all they've got."

"We all have our excuses, and they're usually always good ones."

"You've always had the luxury of running your mouth because you're alone," Liz said. "Nobody relies on you, and you've always liked it that way."

"It wasn't your kids that drove us apart, or even your husband for that matter. You know as well as I do that I would have moved in with you at any time and taken on that responsibility. You weren't interested in the help. You made it crystal clear that it wasn't my business. That's the thing about trying to do it all yourself, Liz. You turn around one day and realize that you're all alone."

"And it's killing me, really, to finally have all you men out of my life. Now, my children's needs aren't set aside for some asshole's wants. Now *we* come first, and I'll tell you, the kids aren't complaining."

"Shutting out the rest of the world because you believe that you're the only important ones in it is fine, if that's what you want to do. But it's a problem when a billion other people are doing the same thing. I'm sorry to have to break it to you, Liz, but your kids won't be raised in a vacuum. The next generation is going to have to learn how to rely on each other, or it will be the end of us all."

Liz inched her way toward the door. "What do you know about having children? You've never had to take care of anybody but yourself. You're a selfish prick and you always have been."

"You're right. And as a selfish prick, I can say that I have never met a person so loving and protecting, while at the same time so utterly self-involved as you."

"Screw you, Max. We have our little fun and then we go back to our responsibilities. You shouldn't expect any more from life." She jerked the front door open. "Maybe then you wouldn't go through it so damn disappointed all the time. See you around." The door slammed shut behind her.

"No, I don't think you will."

Max stared up at the dingy ceiling over his bed; he was back in the very place he had been trying to avoid. Almost instinctively he reached for the translation of the *Epic of Gilgamesh* on the nightstand, turning to the end of the epic poem.

He was fluffing up the pillows behind him, in preparation for another

5

reading, when it occurred to him that he had already read it twice that day. It was when he recalled that the day before he had read it four times, at least, that he slapped the book shut.

Max groped for the TV remote to turn up the news, staggering into the bathroom. Lying around in bed was out of the question. He weighed his options for the rest of the evening while examining every line of his unkempt face in the mirror.

Would he go on in to work, as was expected of him, or would he play hooky again – easily the tenth time that month. He glanced at the bed in the corner and decided that it was best he get out of his apartment, regardless of the destination.

A splash of cold water on his face braced him. His usual second wind was kicking in, the full effects of which would allow him to stay up for another day before the inevitable collapse.

He drifted back into the bedroom, his head buried in a towel. The din of protest coming from the television caught his attention and he stopped to listen to the obviously irritated anchor deliver her report.

"Most of the area around the United Nations Building in New York City was at a standstill this morning due to a publicity stunt staged by a previously unknown activist group called the Unity Council.

"Acting on what turned out to be a false tip, many of the news operations here in New York City sent camera crews to the corner of 45th and 1st, in front of the UN building. The tipster claimed to be an insider who had vital information about a 'sex and money for influence' scandal currently rocking the UN.

"What the news crews actually found was this environmental and social activist group setting up for a news conference without the knowledge of UN officials or the city of New York. Nor did they have a permit for the demonstration that followed.

"Though it can't be directly attributed to the Unity Council, a traffic jam that clogged streets in a four block radius of the UN for almost half an hour gave the spokesman, Hector Madrano, just enough time for a short address. Then he and everyone else involved began to disperse and eventually all of them disappeared before the police could mobilize any kind of major response.

"The officers that did get close enough found a lot of people leaving the area, but no demonstration. Eventually the traffic seemed to ease up, and by the time riot control made it to the location there wasn't anybody left to arrest. Our camera crew was able to catch the dramatic announcement."

The newscast cut to a replay of the speech, where a stout Latino man in his fifties was speaking behind a makeshift podium. "Well over a decade ago, a study commissioned by the Federal Emergency Management Agency predicted three major disasters with a high probability of impacting America in the coming millennium.

"They predicted a major terrorist attack in New York City. They predicted that New Orleans would be struck by a cataclysmic storm. And the last disaster foretold by these scientists was a major earthquake on the West Coast.

"We've gathered in front of the headquarters of the United Nations in New York City because over twenty years ago it was here that some of the first official – and unofficial – warnings of climate disaster were delivered to the world.

"In 1988, the Intergovernmental Panel on Climate Change was established, publishing its first report in 1990. That was just the beginning of a long line of reports on the impacts of global warming that have become increasingly grim over the years.

"In 1992, a contingent of Hopi traveled here from Arizona to deliver a heartfelt and informed message of alarm over the state of the environment. Their concerns were dismissed as the naïve claims of a victimized indigenous people.

"Obviously, if those warnings had been heeded, if real action had been taken to curb carbon dioxide emissions then, almost a generation ago, we would be in a very different situation than we are now, in the new millennium.

"But those warnings weren't heeded, so now we must deal with the consequences of that inaction together.

"We've disrupted traffic this morning to draw attention to our mission. And to say that if you live on the West Coast, or in an area of the United States that has been devastated by natural disaster in the past, the Unity Council relocation effort may be able to help get you moved out of harm's way. If you contact–"

The broadcast cut back to the vapid anchor before Hector could finish. "Besides the concern for public safety, they didn't even have permits," she said to another anchor. "And a lot of people got caught in the traffic jam they caused."

"An anti-terrorist response was called out. Who's going to pay for that?" another commentator said, his red face flushed with contempt. "They could have caused an international incident with this little stunt to get attention."

"We will be tracking down more information on this group as I'm sure the authorities here in New York City will be as well." Following the appropriate pause, the anchor enthusiastically continued. "Next up: The city of New Orleans owes over $150 million and needs to borrow $250 million more. Should it be allowed to?"

Max frantically scrambled for the remote control, engaging the mute button as quickly as possible. He could no longer tolerate watching the main cable news channels for very long, lest the urge to put his foot through the television became too hard to resist.

He knew what he could do to avoid reporting to the dreaded Precision Machining. He dressed and in no time he was winding his way through the post rush-hour crowds, the translation of the Gilgamesh epic in hand.

He turned a corner at the end of a block that had been his stomping ground for two years: 164th and Broadway, the home of his favorite bar and the coffeehouse where he got on the Internet.

With drinking out of the question, the risk of passing out was too great, he made his way to the café that had effectively become his window to the world.

The stained oak molding and service counter were classic New York, while the computers were top of the line and connected to the World Wide Web. Those computers – along with the double espressos – had been sustaining Max on the many nights he dodged work, and during the many aimless weekends he spent alone. He came through the door and was met by a perky redhead behind the counter.

"Your usual?"

"That'll work, Sherry."

He took his place behind a computer near one of the front windows, his usual spot for surfing the net and keeping an eye on the crowds. He logged on and decided to check his emails while he waited for his espresso. It didn't take long.

After deleting the ubiquitous offers for credit cards and penis enlargement drugs, all that remained was the occasional veterans' newsletter. The sad truth was that the death of his parents and his nomadic existence since had left Max with few personal relationships and fewer friends.

Once again he let Sherry deliver his jolt of caffeine and depart with no more than a polite smile and a thank you. She would have been happy to have a more personal relationship with Max, despite his often ragged appearance. But whenever he came into the café, he buried his head in the computer screen, ignoring everything and everyone around him, including her.

Max opened the web browser and took another long drink from his mug. He could have inputted any number of informative news websites that he used to frequent into the address bar. His intention was to find out more about the incident involving the UN and the Unity Council. But in the end, he typed the words "Epic of Gilgamesh" into the search engine.

A list of websites appeared, all of which he was certain he had visited before. He clicked on one and was soon looking at a picture of a clay tablet, the same museum quality photograph that adorned the cover of the book on the table next to him. He had virtually memorized the short background paragraph that accompanied the photo. That didn't stop him from going through it once again.

"It was one of the most influential books ever written," he read. "It inspired millions throughout the ages with its tales of morality, religious conviction, and divine intervention. Its words would be turned into prayers that would be recited by the faithful for millennia.

"Although the later versions of the *Epic of Gilgamesh* were pressed into wet clay by royal scribes and placed in the grueling Middle Eastern sun to bake around 1800 BC, eight to nine hundred years before the first versions of the Old Testament were to appear, source material for the legend can be traced much further back than that."

The first time Max saw the ancient clay tablets it was hard for him to believe that anyone could have deciphered the jumbled mess. After weeks of looking at the photograph on the cover, he had taken to running his fingertips over it, as if he could feel the indentations of the cuneiform-like Braille, trying to imagine the time in history when such tablets were the prized possessions of the first kings of the first cities in Western Civilization.

He caught himself doing the same to the picture on the computer screen. He closed the web browser, deciding at that moment that he could no longer ignore what was happening to him. He needed to know why he had become so intensely interested in an ancient legend that up until a few weeks earlier, he had never even heard of.

Customers came and went while he deliberated on how he could get more information on an era so remote in time that most only knew of it from myth and biblical parable. Another trip to the library was in order, he decided. He would have gone right then but it would have been closing by the time he got off at the subway station on 42nd Street.

The crowd both inside and outside the coffeehouse began to swell. Max emptied his cup and barely had a chance to look up before Sherry had started work on another one. He knew that soon the influx of people would become too much for him to watch or ignore.

He was over three hours overdue at work, and completely exhausted, but slinking in late was starting to sound better than hanging around or going home.

"That's OK, Sherry, I better get going. But thanks, though. I'll be back later." He dug into his pocket for a twenty dollar bill for a ten dollar check.

Less than twenty minutes later, Max found himself in front of the Precision Machining sign once again. This time he reluctantly entered, doing his best to creep past his boss's office.

"Max! You didn't call in again, damn it! Now, you're late! Again!"

"I know but I haven't been feeling too well lately."

"Obviously, you look like shit!"

Max stepped into the dingy little room and stood uncomfortably in front of his boss's desk.

"Max, when I first brought you on, you were kicking ass. Now you can't even seem to get in on time or pick up a damn phone to call in. I'm getting complaints about defects in your parts, and your production numbers suck!"

"I'm...I'll try to get it together," Max said, moving toward the door.

"You'd better, or you're gone. I'll have no choice. And take a shower before you come in here from now on, hear me?"

Max slipped away to make a beeline through rows of noisy machines, thankful when the deafening racket of hydraulic drills and punch presses enveloped him. Once he reached his rolling toolbox and put on his earphones, the rest of the world disappeared behind a constant stream of rock and roll from his favorite radio stations.

He put on his safety glasses and jumped on a bench in front of his hydraulic bender. He picked out one tiny zinc rod from a bucket positioned beside the machine and placed it in the correct fixture. Engaging the pedal caused the top of the machine to come down with a crunch, bending the rod in half. He measured various dimensions of the part with a set of calipers before throwing it into an empty bucket. Only about two thousand more to go, for that order, anyway.

Working with robot-like efficiency was the point of Max's job. And indeed it was easier to make the ten hours until quitting time pass when he made himself an extension of the machine. All he had to do was forget that he was a human being and just feed the machine.

It worked for the first two hours but it couldn't last. Max hadn't slept all day, since getting off of work at 2:00 that morning, and he had only slept a scant three hours the day before that. With his body running on automatic, the fatigue he had been battling for two weeks was soon getting the upper hand. Five hundred bent rods later he was beginning to nod off.

He was fading in and out of consciousness, while his hands were still moving. He was still bending rods. Every time his eyelids would dip, he would catch them and become more determined to stay awake. Then he would nod off again. This went on for ten minutes, until he finally succumbed.

Slowly the guitar rift in the song he had been listening to faded into the distance, replaced by the clamor of subdued voices coming from behind him. When he opened his eyes again, he was no longer looking at his machine or his toolbox, all he could see was a dazzling blue-green panorama.

The fast-moving clouds below, obscuring a strangely familiar landscape, along with the pitch-black void in his peripheral vision, led Max to conclude that he was hovering high above the Earth.

He tried to turn his head for a better look; as usual he had no control over his body. As had become the norm for his increasingly-vivid dreams, he would be left to make sense of only what was put in front of him.

Deep in reverie, suspended in orbit above the passing clouds, Max finally identified the region of Earth on which his vision had been locked. It was the Persian Gulf. He had identified it but could barely recognize it. It wasn't the same place America had invaded in 1991 or again in 2003.

The brutal deserts of Iraq, Kuwait, and Saudi Arabia, forbidden places where Max had sweltered until he thought he would die, those deserts were nowhere to be found. This Persian Gulf region was green and vibrant with life. The beaches of Kuwait on which Max had landed all those years ago were gone, carpeted over by a thick jungle that extended deep into the Gulf basin and down to the edge of a much smaller Persian Gulf.

Max counted four rivers that, after taking long rambling courses through Saudi Arabia, Mesopotamia, and Iran, converged at the northernmost point of the shrunken Persian Gulf.

Cries of horror came from behind him, cries as disturbing as anything he had experienced in real life. He was unable to turn to the source, though. He was unable to see anything but the lush region at the confluence of rivers.

He heard a collective gasp from the faceless people around him when a pale blue wall of water visible from space approached from the southeast. Funneled by the narrow channel of the unfilled Persian Gulf basin, the tsunami spilled into the thriving gorge, absorbing the existing gulf waters and swallowing up the surrounding jungle.

From Max's God's eye perspective, it all seemed to happen in slow motion. The mighty onslaught of water pushed north, eventually overrunning the swampy delta at the southern end of Mesopotamia: Eden.

It poured over the first city in the world, Eridu. It poured over Shuruppak, the home of the Hero of the Deluge, and over Abraham's birthplace of Ur. It overtook the future site of mighty Babylon. The flood made it all the way to the south of where Baghdad would be built before it showed any signs of diminishing. The entire Persian Gulf basin along with four hundred square miles of Mesopotamia was all, suddenly and unceremoniously, underwater.

Max reached out in his astonishment to touch the cold glass that protected him from the vacuum of space. He looked at the unfamiliar hand pressed against the window and could finally tell that he wasn't floating perilously above the earth after all. He was orbiting safely inside an enclosed room, with air, gravity, and other people.

For the first time Max's view shifted away from the disaster unfolding below. Just for a moment he caught his reflection in the window. Expecting to see his own tired visage, he was surprised by the cruel face that had been haunting his dreams for far too many nights. The shock woke him.

Once again Max was able to hear the music from his headphones and feel the low-grade hum that ran through the floor of the machine shop. He had closed his eyes for only a moment, just long enough to briefly lose control of his arms and legs.

Dazed, he inadvertently engaged the clamp on the bender before getting his hand clear. The closing metal fingers pinched his left glove. He recoiled from the machine as a spot of blood grew from the bottom edge of his hand. Workers from other machines began to gather when it looked as if he had received more than merely a scratch.

Somehow sensing that people had stopped working, Max's boss was on the scene immediately. "All right, all right, break it up. What happened?"

"He caught his finger, may need a stitch or two," one of the other machinists said.

"All right, break it up. Everyone get back to work."

The crowd dispersed leaving Max and his red-faced boss alone. Max extended his lacerated hand for inspection. It was clear a doctor was needed.

"Could've seen this coming."

"I...I–"

"Save it, get your ass down to the emergency room. You want someone to go with you?"

"It's not too far to walk. I should be okay."

"That remains to be seen, Max. The company'll reimburse you for a cab. Take one and call me after they look at it."

He nodded then gathered his things as fast as he could. More affected by his experience in dreamland than he was in pain from the cut, he had to get out of the machine shop and onto the street. After stopping off at the medical kit for some gauze, he was on his way on foot to the hospital.

The instant Max passed through the doors of the emergency room the murmur of suffering hit him like a wave. The rows of injured and downtrodden people reminded him of the combat field hospitals he had seen but had been lucky enough to stay out of. He almost turned around and left, except the gauze on his hand was full of blood and it was obvious that it wasn't going to stop.

He approached a nurse behind the information desk. "Hi, I cut my hand and I need someone to look at it."

"Was it on the job?" she said.

"Yeah, I work for Precision Machining."

"Fill these out completely and come back when you're done."

Max took the considerable stack of paperwork and a pen and cut back through the crowd, unable to find an open chair. He made for the far side of the room, to where he could use the corner of an end table to complete the forms.

Despite being dangerously exhausted and bleeding profusely, it became immediately obvious to Max as he walked through the ragtag assemblage that he was better off than 95 percent of the people he passed.

With one hand and little table space, he did his best to complete the forms and return them to the nurse. He was resuming his awkward place by the table when a clamor ensued, caused by the arrival of a doctor.

The senior physician appeared to keep his head buried in his clipboard as he went up and down the rows of afflicted people. Each man and woman looked up at him hopefully, thinking he had come to relieve their suffering. But he passed by the broken legs and fractured arms, the stab wounds, and concussions without a trace of expression on his face.

Max watched the doctor suspiciously, noticing that he was only pausing in front of the men. And that he didn't seem to be looking at their ailments but at their faces. The doctor had inspected every male in the room before he spotted Max in the corner.

The short, balding man began working his way over, still studying his clipboard and doing a very poor job of acting casual. He stopped out of earshot of Max, acting as if he was receiving a call on his cell phone. He brought the phone to his face as he turned it toward Max. He clicked a photograph that he confirmed out of the corner of his eye before closing the phone and returning it to his pocket.

Max had been watching the doctor the entire time, gripped by a strange urge to run when he finally approached.

"Your name, sir?"

"Max Stiner."

"Follow me, please."

Max felt more apprehensive than privileged following the doctor past patients that had been waiting hours for care. His apprehension increased after they turned down an adjacent hall into a rather isolated examination room.

"I figured I was in for a wait," Max said. "You guys are packed out there." He climbed onto the examination table in the corner.

The doctor dragged over a stool. "Had a mishap, eh?"

"Yeah, I caught it in a fixture at work."

"Let's have a look."

"Damn, that hurts!"

"Looks like you got yourself pretty good. That's a deep laceration."

"Yeah, I've been bleeding like a damn sieve."

The doctor cleared away the bloody gauze and examined the wound. "A few stitches will take care of it. When was the last time you had a tetanus shot?"

"It's been a while, probably ten years."

"We'll have to get you a tetanus shot and an x-ray or two. Just to be sure there isn't a fracture."

"Will that really be necessary, Doc? I'm looking to get out of here as soon as possible."

The doctor acknowledged Max's sleep-deprived eyes and the black circles underneath, before turning his concentration to his medical chart. He searched the admission forms for Max's address and phone number.

"How have you been sleeping?"

"Like a rock, when I do sleep."

"Is it becoming a problem?"

"Well, I know one thing; I can't afford to be falling asleep in the middle of my shift while I'm working a machine that can apply as much as 10 tons of force when you press a pedal."

"I see what you mean. I can prescribe something that will help you sleep. Let's get some stitches in that hand first."

The doctor worked quickly to repair Max's wound. With the help of a nurse, he had sewn the gash closed and injected Max with a tetanus booster. After another half an hour in the x-ray department, Max was back in the claustrophobic examination room, poking at his bandaged hand gingerly and waiting for the doctor to return with the results.

The prolonged quiet had him fighting sleep again. He would have nodded off if the doctor hadn't burst in with the x-rays. He clipped them both to a light box mounted on the wall and turned it on. The inner workings of Max's left hand became visible.

"This looks good, Max, no fractures or breaks. We should be able to get you out of here pretty quick. I just wanted to confirm some information." He found Max's chart, turning to the back admission page. "You work for Precision Machining?"

"That's right."

"And this number is your cell phone?"

"No, I don't like cell phones. Now can I get out of here?"

The doctor produced a bottle of pills and a sheet of paper with instructions on how to change the bandages. "Take two of these at bedtime. They should help you get some real rest."

Max was skeptical but took the pills and instruction page anyway.

"I'll be recommending a few days off work. Go home and get some rest, you'll feel better. We'll see you back here in two weeks to remove the stitches."

Max was already halfway out the door. "Thanks, Doc."

The doctor started dialing his cell phone the moment he was certain Max was far enough down the hall not to hear. "Intra-Guard code 12-457," he said to the man that answered. "This is about the priority one alert bulletin... Yes, I was able to acquire a photograph." The doctor sent the picture he snapped of Max then waited for a reply. "I would like a confirmation number for this report, please." He took out a pen and waited patiently. "Confirmation number 5783, got it. The bulletin says that anyone reporting a lead that pans out will get raised two security levels. Is that true? Well I don't want anybody else getting credit for this... No, I'm not accusing you of anything. It's just—" The doctor closed his cell phone when he realized the line was dead. He clutched the confirmation number with a self-satisfied grin on his face.

At that moment, General Masterson's executive jet was on approach to the largest American embassy in the world: the Green Zone, Baghdad, Iraq. A knock at the door of his plush, oak-lined office roused him. He woke sitting uncomfortably in front of his computer screen.

"What is it?!"

"We'll be landing in twenty minutes, sir," his bodyguard said, without opening the door.

"Make sure the helicopter is ready! I don't have the time or patience to deal with delays! Not today!"

"Yes, sir!"

Masterson punched a button on his desk that brought a screen beside his computer monitor to life. His top scientist Doctor Hasline appeared, catching the gawky, graying man in his fifties by surprise.

"Report, Doctor."

"General, you must give me more time. I believe my earlier assessment was correct, considering the complexities of psychic surveillance, there is no guarantee this approach will give you the kind of results you're expecting. There are real reasons why the Russian research hit a dead-end. But despite my reservations, I am working to carry out your orders."

"I want the system deployed immediately."

"If there was some kind of specific threat, maybe we could–"

"I don't need a specific threat to expect total and complete security, on every level necessary. Test your microwave emitters and email me the results. If they're effective, I want them installed in all CIG facilities and on my personal vehicles, including this airplane."

"I still need to run some tests on the implications of operating the emitters in flight, sir."

"I'll be waiting for the results, Doctor, on all of it."

Masterson ended the teleconference with another stab of his finger. He groped for the coffee pot, still waking up. He used a silver flask from his jacket pocket to spike his cup, then he returned to his computer screen.

Although the general's unquestioned authority kept speculation about anything as personal as his age to a minimum, the assumption from his salt and pepper hair and experienced face was that he was in his early sixties.

He was always draped in the finest clothes and surrounded by opulent luxury. Nevertheless, as was often the case with men who wielded the kind of power Masterson did, he was constantly dissatisfied. That condition had only worsened recently, making him more than merely irritable. To his subordinates he had become downright dangerous.

Masterson's steely gray eyes monitored a constant stream of emailed reports coming in from his vast network of operatives and disciples. With no assistants and few trusted confidantes, he demanded detailed, real-time information on all of his many operations.

On the other side of the computer display, he was scrolling through driver's license photographs. When he wasn't reading reports, he would hold down the arrow key and they would fly by, one headshot after another, for hours.

The emailed updates from his minions rolled in at a steady pace. "Report number 5783," he read aloud. "Maxwell Jeffery Stiner."

He clicked on the email and the photograph of Max the doctor had snapped in the emergency room in New York. It appeared on the right side of the screen.

Initially the general struggled with Max's scraggly face. He had seen so many "average-looking white guys" during his search. Still, there was something familiar about this particular "thirty-something Caucasian male, brown hair, brown eyes, approximately 165 pounds."

"We're landing, sir," the bodyguard said from the other side of the door.

Masterson fastened his seatbelt. "Understood."

The moment Masterson set foot in the most heavily fortified American military outpost in the world, a contingent of mercenaries surrounded him, their automatic weapons at the ready. They escorted him all of a hundred yards before he boarded the waiting helicopter and it lifted off. It was joined by two heavily armed attack helicopters as the formation turned southeast toward the ruins of Babylon.

Masterson traced the Euphrates River through the window of his private compartment, deep in thought about his return to the city the ancient world had once considered the jewel of Mesopotamia. He knew every bend and curve of that famous river just as he knew every chapter of the storied history of Babylon:

From Nebuchadnezzar's fabulous Hanging Gardens and the exile of the Jews, to the plans of Alexander the Great to make the city the capital of his vast empire, before his abrupt death while fighting back the encroaching waters of the Euphrates; to two thousand years later and the despotic Iraqi ruler Saddam Hussein, who spent millions of his people's dollars rebuilding Babylon, in a vain attempt to recapture the glory of ancient Mesopotamian rulers like Nebuchadnezzar, Hammurabi, Sargon the Great, and most certainly Gilgamesh.

Masterson knew every historic episode by heart, yet it had been a long time since he had actually seen Mesopotamia. He returned to find most of the region devastated by foreign invasion and civil war.

The areas of Babylon that had once been occupied by American marines – with Saddam Hussein's palace serving as a tent city for soldiers, and acres of crucial ruins being paved over for parking lots – now stood idle and abandoned. Masterson was unprepared for how it all would affect him.

He found the intercom to ring the pilot. "Circle the city." He searched the ruins and the military base for signs of people. By the third pass he was satisfied that both the soldiers and the visitors had been cleared out.

"Set down at the Ishtar Gate."

The helicopter swooped down to land in front of the celebrated main gate of Babylon while the escort choppers continued circling overhead. Masterson was the only one to emerge from the aircraft. Unconcerned by the danger, he wandered toward the walls of Babylon.

"Stay here," he said to his bodyguards.

"But sir, there has been confirmed insurgent activity in the area."

"Stand down! There won't be any insurgent activity here today. I have guarantees. Follow your orders."

The Ishtar Gate Masterson stood in front of may have been a replica that had been reconstructed with bricks baring Saddam Hussein's name, but it was a surprisingly accurate one.

Rich blue and gold tiles covered the colossal arch, as they had more than two thousand years before. Carvings of the dragon and the bull were scattered over the gate and the rebuilt seventy-foot high walls that ran in both directions, which were also authentic recreations of the original.

Masterson reached out his hand with uncharacteristic reverence to touch one of the dragon carvings on the gate. He paused for only a moment before stepping through the main arch and onto the once grand Procession Street.

Once a focus of Babylon's political and religious life, Babylon's main street was now weed-choked and lined alternately with carefully reconstructed walls and fatigued cement barriers. Masterson walked solemnly down the middle of the avenue past scores of crumbled foundations of homes and shops and administrative buildings, interspersed with structures rebuilt by Saddam's work crews.

He stopped to peer through an archway at Nebuchadnezzar's restored palace, just beyond which stood Saddam Hussein's own garish palace. It was quite a distance and Masterson wasn't as young as he used to be. A swig from his silver flask would get him the rest of the way.

Twenty minutes later, he reached the place dubbed Saddam's Hill. It was a mound of ruins on the banks of the Euphrates River that – like much of Babylon – had been repeatedly built over.

The last time it was with a knockoff of a step-pyramid, the iconic Mesopotamian image of power and divinity. Masterson confirmed what time it was before beginning his ascent.

Strangely, Saddam's palace had been turned into a tourist attraction since being abandoned by the U.S. military. There was even talk about developers installing a shopping mall. Masterson had put a stop to that, though, at least temporarily.

He was nearing the top of the hill when he heard the helicopter, right on schedule. Surveying the city below, he used a silk handkerchief to wipe the sweat from his forehead. He frowned with disapproval and disgust, like a landlord returning to a property destroyed by careless tenants. He observed the helicopter land at a helipad close by as he entered the doors of the palace.

Masterson marched past the abandoned gift shop and other meager attractions, directly to a maintenance access that led to the basement. He followed the cement corridors and stairways into the bowels of the palace, straightening his tie and wiping off his suit coat along the way. Once again he was perfectly arranged and focused on his objective.

He turned down two more corridors until he came to a hole in the cement wall. It exposed a skillfully excavated tunnel that led to a descending stairway constructed of dilapidated bricks. The sound of an older man speaking from deep below confirmed that Masterson was in the right place.

"All my life! All my life I've searched! Hurry! Samuel, Hurry!"

At the bottom of the stairs, an aged American professor held a lantern over his assistant while the younger man worked to break through a doorway that had been bricked in. The bricks and mortar crumbling in his hands encouraged Samuel's frantic push into the pitch-black space beyond the barrier. He flung himself recklessly into the breach. Disregarding his own procedures, Professor Reynolds climbed through right behind him.

It immediately became obvious that the lantern they brought was insufficient. The pair had to stay close when they moved, as it only lit the space directly around them. Samuel turned on his flashlight but they were still effectively shrouded in darkness.

"This must be it, Professor."

"We have to find proof."

Samuel let out a loud grunt before falling to the ground. The professor found his assistant cursing and rubbing his big toe. He had stubbed it on the leg of a heavy wooden table. The professor put down the lantern and came to his aid.

"Professor, look," Samuel said upon standing.

Reynolds had shone the light on a miniature model sitting on the table, a reproduction of a Mesoamerican step-pyramid. It was sandstone-colored and surprisingly detailed, with patches of green twigs and leaves painstakingly arranged around the base. Though the professor was certain of its origins from the style, he recognized immediately that it was unadorned, that it had not been decorated with the animal representation of any patron god.

"It's from Central America!" he said. "I knew it! Ancient man traveled the seas! They crossed the oceans thousands of years before Columbus! I told them it was possible, but I never dreamed!"

"But is this the Hall of Records?" Samuel asked.

Reynolds backed into another table and discovered they were in the middle of several models. The lantern illuminated a miniature of a bright white structure, built with gigantic columns and soaring arches.

"It's Baalbek platform," he said. "They cut and set blocks larger than one thousand tons for the platform Baalbek rested on."

"I've got Karnak over here," Samuel said.

"Also constructed with blocks that weighed hundreds of tons." Reynolds recognized three other reproductions as legendary temples or palaces. "They're builder's models. They often made scale models of big projects before construction began."

"But they're from different cultures, even different parts of the world."

"Ningishzidda, Thoth, Hermes, they may have been from three different civilizations but they were all the same builder, the same god."

18

Reynolds gasped upon seeing a prototype of the Great Pyramid at Giza, its sides perfectly smooth with simulated white limestone. He risked the wrath of the gods to reach out and touch it.

Samuel raised the lantern high in the air, shining the light on statues and artwork from Mesopotamia, Egypt, Greece, Mesoamerica, India, and the Holy Land. They moved carefully out of the cluster of tables and followed the statues along the wall.

"It's limestone," the professor said. "The entire chamber is limestone. The closest source of limestone is thirty-five miles away. The Zagros Mountains are even farther."

The faint lantern limited what they saw, while also making each new discovery that much more amazing when it came into view.

"This sun dial, Professor, it's from Peru. Tiahuanacu. Do you think it could be here, the book?"

Reynolds stopped at the end of the dense collection of statues and stele made from various stone. "Here, Samuel, bring the lantern closer to the wall. We need to find Ningishzidda's symbol."

Samuel moved the lamp around the granite facade until Reynolds found what he was looking for: a carving of two intertwined snakes.

"The caduceus," Reynolds said.

"This is it! It's the Atlantean Hall of Records!"

"They all insisted Thoth's Hall of Records had to be under the Sphinx," Reynolds said. "Because legend said so, because a bunch of half-baked occultists said so. But Thoth had many guises, many alter identities. In Mesopotamia, he was known as Ningishzidda. It was as Ningishzidda that Thoth hid his secrets. This is definitely Ningishzidda's chamber. But we can't be sure if it's the Atlantean Hall of Records unless we find the book."

Reynolds's attention was drawn to the darkness farther down the wall. Samuel followed his mentor until the lamp revealed the beginning of a long set of shelves, crammed full of clay tablets, scrolls, and roughly bound manuscripts.

"Samuel, we're going to need the lights."

Samuel handed him the lantern, using his flashlight to find his way back to the jagged doorway. He started up the stairs but another flashlight blinded him.

"Professor!"

A silenced gunshot sent him rolling back down the stairs, onto the granite floor of Thoth's Chamber.

"Samuel? Samuel, are you there?"

Reynolds heard only the busy sound of men carrying equipment. He saw several flashlights come on and scatter into the gloomy distance. One of the flashlights turned his way as an icy cold voice pierced the black.

"No, Professor Reynolds, not Samuel."

"Who the hell are you?"

General Masterson stepped into the glow of the lantern. "Relax, Professor, I'm merely curious about what you've found here."

"All discoveries are top secret. As is this project."

"I'm fully aware of every facet of this project, I assure you."

"Do I know you?"

"No, but I know about you, about your quest to be right, in the face of so many critics. Looks like you were, Professor. Congratulations."

"Where is Samuel?"

Reynolds dropped the lantern after the entire chamber was flooded with bright light. Masterson's men had set up a series of high-yield lamps along the walls and in the corners of the tomb. They turned them on before filing out as quickly as they came in.

Reynolds's eyes struggled to adjust; the first thing he saw was his protégé lying dead at the doorway. He began to tremble, though he couldn't move.

His bodyguards standing by, Masterson turned his back on the professor to wade into the astonishing assembly of history.

He strolled past statues taller than he was, interspersed with pedestals displaying rare Greek vases and striking Indian figurines. Egyptian sculptures and Mesopotamian clay cylinder seals were displayed side by side with fine bronzes and wood carvings from Mesoamerica.

Masterson paused in front of a brightly painted statue from the Aztec empire. "Quetzalcoatl, the plumed serpent god that bestowed civilization on the bloodthirsty primitives of the Americas. The Aztecs were wiped out waiting for him to return 'from the East.' Somebody did show up, but it wasn't their god. His name Cortés and he was one bloodthirsty primitive himself."

"Are you a student of history?"

"Actually I was, for a long time, but nowadays I'm more of a student of the future."

In light of the fallen Samuel, Reynolds decided to take in as much of the room as he could before he joined him. "I expected to find Mesopotamian and Egyptian artifacts, even Indian, Mesopotamia had contact with India very early. But the presence of Greek and Mesoamerican works puts this chamber to much more recent, at least the hundreds BC."

Masterson stopped in front of a full sized statue of a human body with a bird's head. "The god of writing and the arts, the god of mathematics and building, of magic and alchemy, credited with authoring the Egyptian *Book of the Dead*, credited with building the doomed Atlantis from scratch. He was quite a guy. But really, what kind of god is represented by an *ibis*? I mean, what the hell is an ibis, anyway?"

"Of all the gods, in all the major pantheons, very few ever showed any real concern for humans," Reynolds said.

"There was Enki..."

"Besides Enki of the Anunnaki, Thoth in all his forms was the original architect, the original master builder, and Atlantis and the pyramids, and the Baalbek platform, and the Temple Mount were all the result of it. He was one of the only ancient gods of any pantheon that left a legacy generations of humans have longed to rediscover."

"Generations of occult degenerates and wannabe magicians." Masterson reached the end of a row of statues.

He found himself in front of a three-foot by three-foot sheet of solid gold that was sitting on a table and leaning against the wall. "I had forgotten all about that," he said.

At first glance it appeared to be merely a fabulously extravagant piece of art. A closer look revealed that it was also a diagram of the Solar System, with precious stones representing the planets and diamonds representing the Asteroid Belt. The orbits of the planets had been carved into the solid metal, all circling an enormous bright yellow jewel: Sol.

"I can't believe it!" Reynolds said. He rushed toward the artifact until Masterson's guards reacted to his abrupt movements. Masterson waved them off. "This is extraordinary! It's obviously fourth millennium BC Sumerian."

"Very good, Professor."

"It's a startlingly accurate representation of this solar system."

"How do you explain it?"

"The Sumerians possessed sophisticated astronomy, but this is exceedingly precise."

"And what is the academic explanation for the accuracy and depth of this ancient astronomy?"

"Generations of observation," Reynolds said. "But there appears to be a discrepancy here."

"Generations of observations recorded by scribes and scholars." Masterson pointed to the shelves of scrolls and clay tablets that ran down the wall to the corner. "But then that is what this is about, isn't it, a book?"

The ancient library took Reynolds's attention away from the diagram, reminding him of his quest. Again his abrupt movements drew the concern of Masterson's guards and again he waved them off.

Reynolds worked his way down the shelves in search of a specific volume. "It won't be a scroll or a clay tablet," he said. He neared the corner, where a small alcove became visible. What he saw inside stopped him in his tracks.

A wave of Masterson's hand prompted one of the guards to move a light closer to the alcove. Reynolds was too paralyzed to react when Masterson and his guards closed in.

"The *Book of Thoth*," Masterson said.

There, resting on a wooden pedestal was a thick book bound by two pieces of colorfully adorned wood and bulging with wrinkled parchment pages.

"No secret panels or booby traps, no complicated riddles or tests," Reynolds said. "This room was created to reveal all the secrets from before the Flood. They left this for us to find when mankind was ready."

"As you well know, Professor, when Marduk assumed total power over Babylon, he tried to invite the other gods to join him, to become a part of him. Some refused; they were vain and prideful. Others like Ningishzidda and Ishtar chose to join him. This was long after Thoth had been kicked out of Egypt and forced to flee from a sinking Atlantis.

"That's why this chamber is here, because Marduk's Babylon reigned supreme. It was the only place that mattered at the time. And you can trust me, the humans of that time were far too busy serving their gods and feeding themselves to worry about sending cryptic messages down the ages to their spoiled ancestors."

Reynolds stepped up to the pedestal, at first appearing to reach out his shaking hand to open the cover. He stopped short. "Stories say that 'to read the first page of Thoth's book is to gain command of heaven and earth.'"

"And to read the second page 'is to command the universe,'" Masterson said.

"Mystics and magicians have obsessed for millennia about what could be in this book. There's no doubt about it, this is it. Thoth's Hall of Records. The long lost remnants of the god of Atlantis and the real builder of the pyramids. Will we even know what to do with all of this knowledge?"

"He really did it," Masterson mumbled to himself. "He went native and didn't come back."

From their position in front of the pedestal they were able to see that there was an opening in the side of the alcove that led into a small room. A snap of Masterson's fingers brought a guard with a light. He positioned it in the alcove to expose a stone coffin that was translucent white.

"It can't be," Reynolds said. "It's alabaster. The entire thing is alabaster. Amazing!" He rushed around the smooth sided, beautifully crafted casket. "It can't be; it was only a myth."

"What is it, Professor?"

"But it was only a legend, and an apocryphal legend at that."

"You can say it."

"The coffin containing the body of Adam that Noah took on the Ark before the Flood."

"Again, very good."

Reynolds threw up his hands. "But why? Why would Thoth leave these things for us?"

"Just imagine what a modern DNA test on the body of Adam would reveal," Masterson said, shaking his head in amazement.

"I must see the book." One of the guards blocked Reynolds's access when he tried to return to the pedestal.

"Imagine that," Masterson said. "He really did leave you everything you needed to figure it out. And no one will ever know. It's kind of sad really."

"Figure what out?"

"They never believed you, Professor. I was the only one. But you did it, you're vindicated."

"I don't understand."

"Who do you think made it possible for you to dig here? The army and the local militias would have arrested you or killed you a long time ago if it wasn't for me."

"We must notify the State Department and the Iraqi Government."

"That won't be necessary."

"But this is the Rosetta Stone of archeological finds! This knowledge must be shared! It is the real story of human civilization, of thousands of years of missing history, of human creation itself!" His voice cracked as he ranted, all the while two menacing guards were moving in beside him.

"How long have you been waiting for permission to dig here, Professor? Eight years?"

"It wasn't safe and later, with the elections, the bureaucracy became formidable."

"Excuses, nobody wanted to know what was buried here. Not the Americans and not the Iraqis. They were all afraid it would change their neat little version of history. And it looks like they were right."

Another look at Masterson's henchmen kept Reynolds quiet.

"People hate change, Professor, especially change in their perceptions. They've lost their ability to look back and learn. They're only concerned with where they're going, and how they're going to get there. That's where I come in.

"If it wasn't for me, you would still be camped out in Baghdad trying to convince them of your crackpot ideas about the fabled Atlantean Hall of Records in Mesopotamia. I would say that technically all this belongs to me now."

"You have no right..."

"The oldest sayings are the truest. Might makes right." Masterson raised his hands grandly. "All of the primitives who created these works of art understood that better than modern man ever could. They lived it, everyday. But it's even truer now than it was then.

"Get the team in here," he said to one of the waiting guards. "And make sure the shape charges are precise, we wouldn't want to bring down one of Iraq's newest tourist attractions."

"No!" With an adrenalin fueled spryness that defied his age, Reynolds lunged at Masterson for the last time. One of the guards stopped him with a single shot to his back.

Masterson returned to the main room, to the jewel inlaid depiction of the Solar System. "We're taking this and the book," he said. "Leave the rest."

A guard lit the way while Masterson climbed the brick stairs back to the world. He opened his cell phone to type a text message on the tiny keypad. A text that would be sent the moment he regained cell service: "Acquire all background on Maxwell Jeffery Stiner and report."

2

Late for a meeting with his prized confidential informant, Peter Anderson climbed out of the back of a taxi onto the Washington Mall, searching the crowded plaza warily. He threw a twenty dollar bill through the window without a word.

After spending most of the cab ride contemplating his journey from being one of the first African-American journalists at a major Washington D.C. newspaper, to becoming one of the last of an old breed of political reporters still working The Beltway. Peter was quietly itching for a confrontation.

The call from his source had come unexpectedly, as usual. He had over the previous months grown somewhat accustomed to jumping and running when the phone rang. Nevertheless, for some reason this time the clandestine routine had sparked in him a particularly keen bout of self-reflection.

Now that he was reporting as ordered once again, he was forced to consider if he would have been as desperate as he was at that moment if his beloved newspaper industry wasn't dying a slow death, and taking his career with it.

Peter was well-dressed, as always, his graying temples adding a certain distinguished touch. That day his suspicion and doubt made him stick out from the crowds of amiable sightseers all around, however, despite his halfhearted attempt at blending in.

He soon found Mr. Graydin sitting on a bench reading that day's copy of his newspaper. Peter took his place beside the man, without taking his eyes off the people strolling by.

"Mr. Anderson. How have you been?"

"What do you have?"

"All business today, OK. Do you know a man named Phil Simmons?"

"Sure, he's a deputy over at FEMA. I've seen him around The Hill. But I thought you said you had videotape on some cheating senator or something like that."

"This is better, trust me. Simmons is one of the FEMA officials in charge of approving construction contracts in New Orleans."

Graydin had green eyes, a clean-shaven head, and a cat's grin that had always made Peter uneasy. He had been able to surmise from professional experience that Graydin was a veteran of government service. Beyond that, the true identity and background of his informant had remained a mystery.

"So you're talking about greed and favoritism in the contracts bidding process?" Peter said. "Like my old mentor used to say: 'It ain't news if it happens everyday.'"

"According to the information on this CD, there's about eight million dollars involved. With all the talk about the coming hurricane season, and the whining over the New Orleans rebuild, a story of corruption on this scale should generate enough public outrage to sell a few more papers. It may even get you on the cable news circuit for a day or two."

"There is no more public outrage, only gruesome curiosity. But that is enough money to get my editor's attention. It's interesting how well you know just exactly what makes him happy."

"These records can be verified."

"Oh, I have no doubt. Who are you, Mr. Graydin?"

Graydin wagged his finger, never looking directly at Peter. "That's against the rules and you know it."

"Simmons has a good rep on the Hill. He's respected as a straight shooter."

"Isn't that what makes the story that much more salacious? And that's what sells papers, right?"

"Why haven't you gone to the Justice Department? If you're a government employee, you can claim whistleblower status."

Graydin rubbed his smooth, pink skull then laughed heartily. "Yeah and like all the other government employees who've talked about what goes on in this cesspool of a town, I'll be heralded as a hero. Right before they crucify me."

"Nobody sticks their neck out anymore," Peter said, "Including me."

"Follow up in your usual thorough manner. I'm sure you won't be disappointed."

"I'm sure I won't. But maybe I should spend a little time investigating you."

"You know damned well that would be pointless."

"I don't know; it might turn out that my new 'anonymous source close to the investigation' is the best story of all."

"You want this or not?"

"I just want to know who you work for. Whose water have I been carrying all these months?"

When Peter didn't drop it, Graydin placed the CD on the bench in between them. "Just like a reporter to look a gift horse in the mouth. Are you trying to tell me you don't want any more scoops, that our little arrangement is done? Because I find that hard to believe."

When Peter didn't immediately reach for the CD, the experienced intelligence operative became concerned that his asset was wavering.

"You try to put on a good act, Mr. Anderson, complaining about having to go on TV and run your mouth about some story you didn't even uncover. But you and I both know where you would be if I hadn't come along. You would be down at your favorite bar. Ned's Pub, isn't it?

And you'd be drinking yourself into the grave, wouldn't you? That's were you would be."

Graydin acted as if he was taking the CD back, stopping only when Peter put his hand over the disk. Graydin got to his feet, pointing to where crowds of tourists were milling around a tall, narrow span of scaffolding. Inside the lattice of metal and wood stood a hobbled 555-foot tall obelisk known as the Washington Monument.

"Guess they're lucky the whole thing didn't shake apart," he said. "You know, they say we can get earthquakes in this area, but I've lived here my whole life and I've never been in one before. Not like that anyway."

Peter stared at the CD under his hand, full of shame.

"It's funny, too, with all the bitching and moaning about taxes, they'll use as much money as it takes to rebuild it, the next time it happens. And all these taxpaying voters here will approve, right up until their own lives are in ruins. Then they'll come crying about why there isn't any money left to help them."

"It's supposed to be a symbol of America's greatness," Peter finally said. "Never made much sense to me..."

"That's because it's not supposed to make sense to you. Besides being a walking cliché, a dinosaur, you've worked in the halls of power for how long and you still have no idea who controls the United States of America or what they really believe... Much less what they'll do to survive."

"You mean lie, cheat, steal, blackmail, and kill? I think I have an idea of what they'll do. You're not the only one who's lived in this town his whole life."

"And you grew up to be an illustrious 'Inside the Beltway' reporter. Your wife must have been so proud. Did she ever find out, before the 'Big C' got her, that your job consisted mainly of placating the public by busting petty thieves and adulterers, and then writing about it so that everyone thinks justice has been served?"

"What do you know about my wife?"

"I know everything there is to know about you. And I also know that there are plenty of stories out there left to write, plenty of petty thieves and adulterers left to expose. So you can trust me when I say, don't let your obvious disgust for yourself distract you from your very important job. It's far better to be disgusted than dead." He laid his copy of the paper over Peter's lap before disappearing into the crowd.

Peter had provoked the reaction he anticipated from his anonymous source, now he wasn't quite sure what to do about it. It didn't help that Graydin was, for the most part, correct. Nor did it help that Graydin's stories had always withstood extensive scrutiny, whatever his motives.

The prospect that Peter had been getting information from anyone other than a disgruntled whistleblower was something he had previously chosen to ignore. He had come to consider their covert arrangement an easy way to maintain his increasingly shaky position at the paper. Graydin's not-so-vague warning had forced him to question everything.

Peter lingered for over an hour while the visitors to the Washington Monument came and went. He studied their reactions and mulled the situation his own professional vanity had created. The hard-bitten reporter had to consider whether he actually could have been as naïve as the tourists he had been watching.

As he wandered back toward the street and hailed a cab, he decided that he would look into the FEMA deputy and the stolen eight million dollars. If it checked out, he would write the story. Then he would launch a new investigation, one that – it appeared – he himself would be the center of.

Not far from there, down Constitution Avenue, Sylvia Billy sat outside a senate hearing room with her head buried in the ragged backpack she had lugged through fifty different countries. Fresh off an international flight, she was still wearing a well-used pair of khaki pants and equally weathered flannel shirt.

She was drawing looks from the political elite that passed, with her sun-beaten complexion and vibrant red hair barely controlled by a ponytail, but Billy couldn't care less about appearances. The world in which she had been living for the previous seven years had little concern for such things.

Tears filled her eyes when her long time friend and colleague Phil Simmons stepped out of the hearing room. She dropped what she was doing to embrace him, her Southern drawl made more pronounced by her emotions.

"Phil! My Lord it's so good to see you!"

"Billy, what are you doing here?" Phil suppressed his surprise and concern long enough to give his old friend a warm greeting. "It's good to see you too," he finally said.

A tall, balding Swede from Minnesota, Phil usually towered over Billy. On that particular day, though, he was slumped over so far that they could almost see eye to eye.

"I thought you were staying in Japan for another two weeks."

"They moved up the briefing to Thursday. I was just informed..." She struggled to maintain her composure. "That was fine because I just couldn't take anymore, anyway. I had to get out... Now I'm supposed to leave for South Carolina in something like an hour. I promised Joan that I would go and I don't want to let her down..."

Phil led her back toward the window, all the time watching the people passing by.

Although they were close in age, Billy had always walked and talked faster than Phil. Her vibrant nature and indomitable spirit in the face of disaster was what made her his hero. He recognized immediately as she skulked behind him that something was missing.

"I haven't even been to my apartment yet," she said. "It's looking like I won't be able to either. Have you seen Mrs. H. lately? Is she eating OK?"

"She's doing just fine," he said. "What's it been? Six months since you were home?"

"At least." She touched his gaunt face and sunken shoulders. "Jesus, Phil, you look as bad as I feel."

"I haven't been sleeping. What did you use to say? 'You can't let the bastards grind you down'?"

"That was before there were so damn many of them," she said, scowling at the politicians and attendant lobbyists populating the halls around them.

"Let's get out of here; I'll get you to the airport." Phil hoisted her bag over his shoulder and headed for the door, careful not to let Billy see him checking the crowds for pursuers. "I have to admit that I'm a little surprised to see you."

"I can tell. In fact, if I didn't know better, I'd think you were trying to get rid of me. Of course, if you arrange another overseas assignment that you know I can't turn down, you probably will get rid of me."

"I'm not 'arranging' the disasters. They all needed your help."

"How long have we known each other, Phil?"

"It has to be twenty-five years now."

"Then you know that you can't keep anything from me. Not for very long, anyway."

"It's all gone wrong, Billy... You should just catch the next plane out of this city and never look back."

"Where would I go? After Indonesia, Haiti, Chile, New Zealand, Japan, my god, I just want to curl up in a corner for a while and cry my eyes out."

They were forced to part momentarily to avoid several legislators in a tight huddle in the middle of the hall.

"I talked to Dawson," she said when they came back together. "He told me *you* called *him*."

"Like I said, they needed you. You save lives, Billy. Just like how they need you down in South Carolina, to get them organized."

She stopped him with a tug on his elbow. "Dawson didn't call for help; you called him and offered me up. And that wasn't the first time you've done that either. After what just happened in South Carolina, you couldn't keep me from going down there, but I know you've been trying to keep me out of DC. The only thing I don't know is why."

"That's ridiculous."

"What's ridiculous is you thinking you're going to be able to keep from telling me what's going on."

"So, you're not wearing that when you meet with the President, are you?" he said as he kept moving down the hall.

"Now don't go trying to change the subject. You know I'm not playing about this."

"I'm just saying. Wearing the same clothes to the White House that you flew twenty hours in two days before might not be a good idea."

Phil perked up long enough for a wily smile and a wink. Billy could never resist his smile. She decided to let him evade her questions, for the moment. She could always ambush him when she returned from South Carolina and force him to talk.

"So have you met *him*?" she asked.

"Just for a second. His chief of staff is the one you'll have to deal with, and he's a prick."

"They're all pricks. When they first called me about briefing the President on Japan I told them to forget it, to find someone else. Then I figured that if he was crazy enough to ask for my opinion, I was damn well going to give it to him."

"Looks like half the Carolina coast has been wiped out down there."

"It hit at category three. They're going to need some serious federal help."

"Well I wouldn't mention that when you do go to the White House. You're there to update him on the relocation efforts in Japan. In their minds, one doesn't have anything to do with the other."

"My ass!"

"To them, they'll all be a series of unconnected events, every natural disaster that happens, and most of the man-made ones too, until it's all come apart."

Billy stopped at the front doors of the Capitol Building. "The saddest thing of all is that there are still people all across this planet that think we'll come to their rescue. That, out of the goodness of our hearts, America will ride in and save the day. They're learning the hard way what we've already known, huh Phil?"

"You still carrying that old FEMA report around?" he asked.

"Two of the three disasters already happened, I know. Does the third one have to kill thousands for them to say: 'Hey, maybe our priorities have been all screwed up all these years'?"

"That admission will never take place," he said.

Billy's smooth, freckled cheeks stretched tight when she winced. "I'm more worried about the most recent Quadrennial Defense Review. Victims of natural disaster are national security threats now? Really? Those maniacs down at the Pentagon have been looking for a reason to take over for years and Mother Nature is going to give it to them yet. It's happening everywhere else in the world right now. Why not here?"

"Billy, there are some people who−" He suddenly stopped himself. "Come on, I'll give you a ride."

Phil had protected Billy from the cronies and political hack appointees who had come and gone from the crippled Federal Emergency Management Agency since the Department of Homeland Security absorbed the agency years prior. Then the near total destruction of New Orleans changed everything for the agency. Even though she was out of the country during the catastrophe, it changed everything for Billy as well.

"I don't think I can do it anymore," Phil said in the back of his chauffeur-driven town car.

"Maybe you should think about getting out, Phil. You've done more than anybody could have ever expected. Frankly, I don't know how you've made it this long."

"I tried to warn them," he said.

"You did, we all did, but nobody was listening."

He stared long and hard before he spoke again. "And now I have nothing to show for it."

"Don't say that, please."

"I was never as strong as you were, Billy. It's the only excuse I have."

"Excuse for what? Look, Phil, just walk away. Nobody will blame you."

"I talked to Joan in South Carolina and she said she almost quit when she saw the damage down there. Why do you stay?"

"I'm a glutton for punishment," she said in her most playful and endearing drawl. "Besides, who said I'm staying?"

"I'm serious."

Billy was still thinking about how to answer when their car came to a stop near the airport tarmac. The supply plane that would take her to the hurricane ravaged South Carolina coast was warming up not far away.

"You need to let all this go, Billy. You should start living your life, instead of always waiting for disaster."

Billy did her best to hide the tears welling in her deep blue eyes. "Disaster is all I know, Phil. I guess it's just too late for me."

"It's only going to get worse and they won't let you help. You know that."

"I know, darlin'." She hoisted her backpack over her shoulder. "I'll call you when I get back. We'll get together and talk. You know, like we used to before all this started."

"I love you, Billy, I always have. You've been my only real friend. I just want you to know that."

"I love you too, Phil. We'll talk tomorrow."

A short plane ride transported Billy from the ostensibly civilized streets of Washington DC, into the chaotic aftermath of a category three hurricane.

Following a rough landing on a makeshift runway, Billy found herself hanging out the side door of a National Guard helicopter as it skirted along the South Carolina coastline. There was only devastation as far as the eye could see.

Billy searched the endless terrain of sheet rock, roofing, and two-by-fours for something that resembled a house or storefront. She was unable to find even one. Entire apartment complexes had been scrubbed from their foundations, with even the rubble being whisked away by a record storm surge.

It was becoming a disturbingly familiar situation for the seasoned aid worker. The category three hurricane that had ripped through four coastal states two nights before had by then moved offshore and was fizzling out hundreds of miles away in open water, leaving Billy to pick up the pieces.

Though much of the media was downplaying the implications of another major disaster starting off the new hurricane season, seeing it all happening again and knowing it was probably just the beginning was almost too much for her to bear. She had never cried before when she arrived on a disaster scene, but this time Billy was tempted.

Doubt began to overtake her. As the miles of destroyed shoreline became a haze, a deep-seated doubt that she had harbored about America since long before she had embarked on her many years of globetrotting began to return.

Billy had stood witness during those intervening years to the aftermath of what ended up being the deaths of a quarter of a million people in Indonesia. She had seen millions more uprooted by floods, earthquakes, and other disasters.

She had taken comfort during that time in the naïve assumption that America had remained comparatively lucky when it came to catastrophic devastation, despite 9-11 and Hurricane Katrina.

Having that assumption shattered in such startling fashion was instilling her with not only sorrow, but a profound sense of dread as well. Flying over such immense destruction, Billy was forced to ask just exactly how much more her beloved home country could endure before coming completely apart – a question she had had to ask of ten other catastrophe-stricken countries during her travels.

A blazing red cross came into sight in the distance. It was time to pull herself together, she would be the ranking FEMA official on the scene and bawling like a baby wouldn't do much to inspire the troops. She needed the team to believe that they were making a difference, even when she couldn't believe it herself.

Like a doctor who had lost their nerve for surgery, or a veteran coroner who had started throwing up at the sight of blood, Billy's tolerance for traumatizing sights was starting to wane. And there didn't seem to be much she could do about it.

The helicopter closed in on a mass of tents and National Guard vehicles surrounding the enormous Red Cross banner. Billy was instinctively taking note of where the headquarters, hospital, and water trucks were placed as they ascended. She was gratified by what she saw. Her colleague, Joan, had obviously been hard at work.

The helicopter circled an open area beside the main headquarters tent and gently touched down. Billy propped up her courage at the sight of the crowd assembling around the landing pad. After climbing out and clearing the whistling blades, she found herself face to face with a group of overworked FEMA employees. She was deeply relieved to see her old friend.

Joan's long silver hair was falling out from under her FEMA cap. Her jeans, FEMA windbreaker, and ruddy face were covered in mud. She looked to Billy as if she had been personally digging through the surrounding rubble or fighting one of the many fires that had sprung up in the area.

"Welcome to South Carolina, Billy."

"It's a damned shame, darlin'. Are you OK?"

"I'm alright. Reports are still coming in, but it's starting to look like the overall destruction is as bad as Katrina. And this was just the first of five major hurricanes they're saying are coming this season. I tell you, Billy, this is as bad as I've ever seen it."

"I know, believe me, I know. Why don't you get everyone together?"

Billy plunged into the hectic operations center of the rescue effort. Joan motioned for her staff to rally around a cluttered worktable in the middle of the room.

"All right, people, gather around please."

The men and women of Joan's emergency response team formed a circle around the table.

"I know most of you," Billy said. "The rest of you know me and why I'm here. I have a meeting with the President later this week. Even though I've been advised against it, I'm going to talk to him about what happened down here.

"Joan will be getting with the team heads for your damage estimates and condition statements. I'll be delivering all that to DC personally. I won't be here long, but I promise I will get with each of you before I go. Your hard work is much appreciated. Hang in there, guys. Thanks."

"Okay, that's it," Joan said, and the crowd dispersed. "Ready to check out the area?"

"No, I'm not."

"When I saw it for the first time, I couldn't believe my eyes."

Billy located the pile of paperwork Joan had set aside for her to review. She threw her backpack down and began picking through the mess. She immediately found a message that required urgent attention. After a frustrating conversation, she slammed the phone back down.

"Damned bureaucrats!" she drawled at the top of her voice.

"We're bureaucrats."

"Don't remind me, Joani. I swear I don't have a clue what I'm going to tell McCrea, that smarmy little prick."

"It doesn't matter what you report, Billy. It won't be very long until the money will dry up and these people will be fending for themselves."

"All I have to do is tell McCrea the truth, and suddenly I have a bad attitude. Do I have a bad attitude?"

"It used to help you get the job done; now it just gets you in trouble."

Billy threw her phone down. "It's as futile as building a bunch of houses on a stretch of land that's destroyed by hurricanes every few years like clockwork."

"What do you expect? Humans have lived by the oceans since the beginning of recorded history."

"Yeah, but at what cost? So, how early tomorrow?"

"We have a transport lifting off at six o'clock in the morning. It'll get you back in time to get settled before you have to meet the President. Thank you again for coming down. I know you've been gone for a long stretch this time... My God, Billy, thousands of square miles of Japan, completely uninhabitable."

"You know, Joani, we've been at this a while and Lord knows we've seen a lot. But I never thought I'd see that.... We moved thousands of families, hundreds of thousands of people. You would think that after a good third of the island of Japan gets written off, thousands of lives uprooted, somebody would start seeing a pattern here."

"Don't hold your breath on that one."

Joan reviewed her clipboard and the long list of things she felt Billy should see before returning to Washington DC. "The President held a press conference and pledged all kinds of money we will never get for a rescue effort that will, let me quote him now, '... strive to help every single victim of this terrible tragedy.' And he said that unlike before, FEMA – that's us by the way sweetie – unlike before we will get everything we need to fight this battle. So, feel better?"

"Not in the slightest. In other words, we'll be held responsible when these people get dumped out on their asses. I don't imagine you have anything on that little clipboard of yours that won't make me want to gouge my own eyes out?"

"Thanks to early warnings there are only fifteen people confirmed dead so far. There could have been so many more."

"Amen to that."

"And the Unity Council kind of saved our asses. It was a good thing they didn't get turned away by the National Guard because they've been able to send a steady stream of people and materials since the weather cleared. "

"Who?"

"Yeah, you know, from the news?"

"I've been traveling the last few days."

"They just started showing up yesterday, a couple hundred of them. The semis full of materials are still arriving. Blankets, canned goods, you name it."

"So which corporation is fishing for good PR this time?"

"None that I saw. Besides, the quantities of people and goods they've committed are far more than any corporation would ever part with. They said they've been operating food and clothing drives in some of the major cities close to this area and had the stuff stockpiled for when this happened."

"Bullshit," Billy said before she was able to stop herself. "I mean, I don't believe it."

"I got that. Their team leader sent word that she wanted to talk to me. I thought you should come too, after we survey the area."

"Well, lead on my dear. No sense in putting this off any longer."

Billy followed Joan out of the tent into a mob of busy aid workers. Each person who passed was covered in soot from the fires and mud from the rain. Billy climbed into the waiting National Guard vehicle watching a rescue dog sniffing a mound of wood and cement for signs of survivors, yet another sight that had become all too common for her.

The National Guard private behind the wheel had to concentrate on negotiating the four-wheel drive vehicle down the middle of a street littered by periodic mounds of wreckage. Every pile had been somebody's home just forty-eight hours earlier. Tents occupied driveways, while groups of men climbed on mountainous heaps on all sides of the block. Billy wanted to record what she saw, to brainstorm on plans of action later. It was just too much.

Beleaguered and exhausted workers looked out in disbelief from the back of a Red Cross van as it crept by. Billy was working hard to hide from Joan and the soldier that she was again on the verge of tears. She had to choke them back.

They continued their trip down every passable street in the area until they came upon an open four-wheeler full of men dressed in black, high-power assault rifles in hand. One of the men in the back of the vehicle stood up to point his automatic rifle directly at the National Guard truck, and Billy in particular. This incensed Joan and the National Guard soldier.

"What the hell are you doing, God damn it!" the young soldier yelled at the top of his lungs. This startled the man, prompting him to quit sighting Billy's head through the crosshairs of his rifle. "God damned mercenaries!"

"I'm getting their license number!" Joan said. "I'm reporting them to the company who hired them!"

"They're going to kill somebody, for Christ's sake, over a damn pile of wreckage," the soldier said.

"They didn't show up until later in New Orleans," Joan said. "They kept you clear of that one Billy and it was a good thing." A shell-shocked gaze came over her face. "I went in right after, then they kicked me out too."

Billy pivoted for a troubled look at Joan.

"This is how it is now. You lose your home, they can gun you down. See how that works?"

"Damned mercenaries," the soldier said. "Excuse my language, ma'am, but it ain't right. I have a newborn baby at home and I'm losing money to come out here and do my duty. Those assholes are getting paid a hundred thousand a year to come and aim guns at people."

After a long and gruesome ride, they returned to the area around the headquarters.

"What's next, Joani?"

She consulted her clipboard. "Sharon Grant, the site coordinator for all those people from the Unity Council. I told her people that we would be by."

"According to the status reports, they committed a third of all the manpower that's shown up."

"Yes, and more in fundraising and food."

"So how are they showing up out of nowhere with these kinds of resources? What's the catch?"

"I don't know. Some of the usual relief groups have joined with the Unity Council but the Red Cross and some of those haven't even heard of them. The buzz is that they are up to something, though. I personally won't turn down any help from anywhere. That includes the corporations looking for good press. Could you take us over to the Unity tent please?"

"No sweat," he said.

Billy endured another short ride through the devastation until they were finally parked in front of an expansive army surplus tent. Billy and Joan got out of the vehicle almost unconsciously inspecting the arrangement of the Unity Council's foothold of civilization.

"You sure they don't have any FEMA people working with them?" Billy asked.

"I couldn't say. When Wendy briefed me on what they were up to over here, I was just happy to get the help. Washington was trying to give them static but I shut that down."

The ladies entered and were immediately struck by how familiar it felt inside the Unity base of operations. They found a long row of tables displaying pamphlets and announcements from a wide range of sources on one side of the room, while on the other side, at another long row of tables, Unity Council staff were counseling storm victims.

Billy and Joan drifted toward the table with the pamphlets, paging through them skeptically. They found literature that ran from logical and well-researched environmental alarmism, to just plain kooky speculation, none of which gave them a handle on the organization.

They took to eavesdropping from behind pamphlets on what was going on across the tent, where storm victims were talking with counselors and getting information about what to do next.

"We believe that Japan and the mass migration that became necessary there will become necessary here in the U.S.," one of the counselors said. "...at least from our most vulnerable coastal regions. What happened two days ago is just more proof of that."

Both women recognized quickly that the counselors were offering help and services that Billy and Joan knew FEMA didn't have the money or infrastructure to deliver.

Billy's acute mind was rolling over the possibilities when she heard Joan's name. She looked up to find a willowy, African-American woman in her forties smiling at both of them.

"Joan, is it? Hi, I'm Sharon...Sharon Grant."

36

Joan turned to Billy. "This is Sylvia Billy. She came down from Washington to help out. She's currently the senior FEMA official down here."

"It's just Billy," she said, shaking hands. "Nice to meet you."

"I just wanted to say thanks for all your help," Joan said. "Are you affiliated with the Red Cross?"

"Oh, no, nothing like that." Sharon led them out of the tent, onto the street. "Honestly, we weren't sure they wouldn't turn us back, like what happened in New Orleans."

"Did you guys go down there?"

"We tried."

Not one to mince words, Billy cut to the chase. "Look, darlin', it's obvious you guys know what you're doing and you're helping greatly, but I'm concerned about a few of the things your counselors were promising some of those victims in there."

"I'm not sure what you mean, but I'm confident they didn't mention anything we couldn't do."

"But how?"

"I wanted to talk to you personally, Joan. I just wanted to let you know that your team leads have been doing a great job."

"I appreciate you saying that. Billy taught me everything I know."

"Our people who have been here for the past few days, will be moving on," Sharon said. "But more should be showing up. They'll be able to help with some of the cleanup but they won't be involved in any rebuilding."

Billy thought that a strange comment and was about to question it but Sharon continued.

"To be honest, many of our people haven't been very excited about staying in this area for too long. With the new hurricane season starting like this, they know this won't be a very nice place to be this year."

"I probably don't have to tell you," Billy said. "But there have been a lot of real lowlifes coming out of the woodwork to take advantage of people who have already lost everything. Corporations, non-profit scams, petty crooks..."

Sharon just smiled while Billy had her say.

"I took a look at some of the literature laid out in the tent back there. From what I saw, the press could jump on some of that and try to discredit you as being crackpots or alarmists. They could say you're trying to scare people and manipulate them into doing what you want. I heard some of those counselors saying they could guarantee housing for those people. I don't know what you have to gain but–"

"The press accusing *us* of manipulation?" Sharon said. "That's a good one. If the information we're making available to people scares them then I would say good, Billy. Because you know as well as anybody, they should be scared. They need to be scared right the hell out of this area."

"Well sure but–"

"The press will say what it wants, regardless of what we do. But no one around here has time right now to think about anything but water, blankets, and tents. And where these people are going to end up."

Billy was far from appeased.

"So what do you think takes more courage?" Sharon asked. "Staying or moving?"

"I wouldn't exactly call it courage to stay in the middle of hurricane alley," Billy said.

"People are just stubborn," Joan said.

"No doubt about that, darlin'."

Another worker bolted up in a panic, imploring Sharon to follow.

"Like I said, there's no time to think about anything but the essentials. It's been nice to meet you, Joan, Billy." When they shook hands again, Sharon held Billy's grasp, taking an extra long look into Billy's eyes. "Does Phil know you're back?"

"You know Phil?" Joan asked.

Sharon pulled away. "I'm not supposed to say anything. He was adamant about that."

"What? What do you mean?" Billy asked. "How do you know Phil?"

"I have to go. You'll have to talk to Phil."

"You can damn sure bet I'll do just that!" Billy said.

It took the rest of the day for Billy and Joan to spend all the money they were certain would be allocated for the immediate response to that particular disaster. There was no point in making plans to spend any more because chances were it wasn't coming, at least not without an undetermined period of "debate" in congress and the media.

Jet lagged and exhausted, Billy sought refuge in a tent Joan had set up for her near the FEMA headquarters. She sat cross-legged on a cot working on her laptop, in the center of a mass of reports and color displays, munching on a can of beans and some dried fruit from her backpack.

Interspersed among the various pages were computer projections of the East and West Coasts she had received from a friend at the National Oceanic and Atmospheric Administration more than two months prior. They were the results of high-powered machines, high-powered software, and high-powered intellects trying to predict exactly where sea levels would be in ten, twenty, and fifty years.

Billy just stared at the areas where the color blue – signifying sea water – was covering towns and cities that were currently heavily populated. According to the printouts, entire regions where people were now living would be inundated.

She knew that the litany of horrors she witnessed that day would pale in comparison if those projections came true. Her mind reeled at all the different calamities that would undoubtedly occur along the way. She fell asleep there among her maps and reports, thinking about a future that terrified her to the core. The next morning, Joan's voice was the first thing Billy heard.

"Billy, wake up."

Joan fell down onto Billy's cot, tears streaming from her eyes

"What's wrong, what happened?"

"It's Phil. He committed suicide last night. He's dead…"

"What? No, we just talked. There must be some kind of mistake, Joani."

Billy was still waking up but she could see from Joan's expression that there was no mistake.

"He wouldn't just… He wouldn't leave me like that…" Joan wrapped her arms around Billy as the news sunk in and the tears came.

"I don't believe it," Billy said. "He wouldn't kill himself, I've know him for years, he just wouldn't do it. Something is going on here. And I'm going to find out what it is!"

Eventually, Joan rose and wiped her cheeks. "I have to make a call to get some more information. I'll be back."

Billy buried her head in her Red Cross issue pillow and sobbed uncontrollably.

Back in Washington DC, Peter slipped through a teeming newsroom doing his best to make it to his office without getting noticed. His stealth was unnecessary, no one was in a hurry to talk to him that particular morning. They had all heard the news and no one was looking to rub it in.

Peter had broken four major front page stories in a row before Phil Simmons came along. That was cause for adulation from his peers, even if it was jealous and begrudging adulation. On the other hand, having the target of one of your articles commit suicide was cause for a deafening silence.

Only one of his colleagues was crude enough to comment. Of course it was the young upstart reporter that had been the bane of Peter's existence for months.

"Graft in New Orleans, there's a new angle," Calvin said. "That was a nice one."

"And it was still better than your last piece."

"At least my stuff doesn't get people killed."

Peter kept his head down until he made it to his assistant's desk.

"Your mail and overnights are on your desk," she said.

"Thanks, Patty. No calls right now please."

Peter barely had a chance to lay down his briefcase and get settled before his editor barged through the door.

"You're an animal! You are totally out of control!" Ed turned on the television in the corner of Peter's office. Peter cringed, immediately using the remote control to lower the volume.

"What does that make? Four big exclusives in the last five months?"

"Ed, a man is dead."

"Your article was published on the website at midnight," Ed said as he sat. "From what I heard he killed himself as early as seven or eight the night before. You can't blame yourself; he did this because he knew it would come out. Contacted his office for a comment yet?"

"I can't imagine what I would say."

"In a way it's the ultimate validation of your story. Check your make-up, Pete, because they're going to want you on air over this."

If his editor had bothered to stop for a good look at his star reporter he would have seen a hollow and beaten man. But Peter knew that Ed was like so many; he only saw what he needed to see to get what he wanted.

"Turn it up," Ed said. "They're running it again. It's been in cycle since 5."

Peter reluctantly complied.

"Needless to say, after the controversy over their handling of Hurricane Katrina, and their eventual reforming as a cabinet level agency, morale at FEMA had to be low," the anchor said. "The allegations of corruption in the granting of reconstruction contracts have plagued the agency since rebuilding began in the Gulf Coast region.

"It appears that scandal has claimed its first victim with the suicide of Phil Simmons last night. Apparently he killed himself in anticipation of a story that ran this morning accusing Mr. Simmons of receiving eight million dollars in kickbacks."

Ed sprung from his chair. "You're writing a follow-up and I have to make some calls. I'll talk to you later."

Peter turned down the volume on the television, sitting in silence for a moment. He had no intention of writing a follow-up story or appearing on television. Out of habit he reached for his mail. He ripped the end off an overnight package to let a single sheet of paper fall onto his desk.

Stamped with words like "above top secret" and containing document identification numbers which Peter knew were for the strict control of classified material, the page looked much like a spreadsheet. Below all the cautionary stamps were the column headings: "CIG-Operational, WRC Admin., ERC Admin., Construction, Deployment."

Peter didn't recognize any of the departments, but he knew he was looking at a financial summary. Each column denoted a different department or facility; the staggering numbers next to those headings were the amounts of money needed for each department to operate for a month.

Peter checked the sender information to find only the address of a shipping store and a name he didn't recognize on the box. When he lifted the page off his desk, he notice there was something written on the back. He flipped it over to find a handwritten sentence:

"We were pawns, all of us! Barbara used to say that you were a good man. Maybe you can do what I don't have the courage to do. Expose them! Nobody deserves to be a guaranteed fatality!"

At first Peter didn't recognize the handwriting, though he could discern highly classified material when he saw it. He tensed up at merely being in possession of the document. By his estimation, it was either a vital clue to a huge story or a one way ticket to an investigation by the Justice Department.

It all turned over in his head as he watched the muted television in the corner of his office. He focused on the handwritten note on the back of the spreadsheet. The mention of his deceased wife had the intended effect of throwing Peter off.

On the television, the twenty-four hour news cycle demanded another airing of the report of Phil Simmons's demise. It was when a photograph of Phil appeared on the screen that Peter got an idea. He went into the stack of records Graydin had supplied that had damned Phil Simmons as a not-so-petty thief.

He thumbed through the copies of memos and emails for a clear example of Phil's handwriting. Thanks to Graydin's thoroughness, Peter had several to choose from. He held it beside the note on the back of the top-secret document. He was no expert but there were enough distinctive letters to make a match.

Peter quickly flipped the document back over. The headings were what mattered now. "CIG- Operational," he read aloud. "WRC Admin., ERC Admin., Construction, Deployment." They meant absolutely nothing to him.

He typed "CIG" into the search engine on his computer. The results that came back were in the thousands, far too many to sift through.

Since Graydin had become suspect, and none of his other contacts would have called him back, the only place Peter could think to go for further insight was his most highly placed source.

Chances were the assistant to the president's chief of staff Victor Duncan was going to want to talk to Peter anyway. Graydin wasn't the only one who contacted Peter when they had something they wanted the public to hear.

Peter buzzed his assistant to ask her to get a hold of Victor's secretary about a meeting at the White House. Peter expected to hear back with a time; instead she was transferring a call.

"Well, if it isn't crack investigative reporter Peter Anderson. It's been a while."

"How have you been, Victor?"

"Busy."

Peter slid the top secret document under a stack of file folders before reclining into his chair. "I was hoping to get a few minutes with you when you have a chance."

"I don't think that's going to be possible."

"Today or ever?"

"Where are you getting your information, Peter? The President wants to know."

"You know very well that I can't reveal my sources."

"There was a time when *I* was your big source. You never called on the Simmons thing. In fact you haven't called in a while. Apparently, you had all the sources you needed for that one.

"Just a heads up; the evidence you have may have been airtight, but anyone who knew the man couldn't believe he was capable of any of it. It doesn't track. Running with that story could end up being a problem for you."

"The records were authenticated by the Justice Department. They were proceeding on it, before he...uh."

"Your point being? You can quote me on this. The President has no doubt that FEMA will acquit itself admirably during this recent hurricane on the Atlantic Coast. The President has every confidence in the people of that department to weather the storm."

"Nice statement," Peter said. "But I wasn't contacting you about that specifically. Have you ever heard of a government agency that goes by the acronym CIG?"

"With the hurricanes and recent flooding," Victor said. "The fires in Florida and California, I swear this country is going to hell."

"I wouldn't argue that, but have you ever seen the letters CIG anywhere?"

"Continuity in government," Victor said after a long pause. "But it was too classified for you to know about before you became *persona non grata*. Now you can forget it."

"So should I not bother trying to come to the White House in the future?"

"After the job you did on Simmons, I think it would be best that we just stick with the phone for a while. You're the damn kiss of death, Peter."

"I wouldn't argue that either. If you hear anything interesting, I'll owe you a favor if you would call."

"Stay in touch and remember what I said," Victor said before hanging up.

Peter had been on television plenty of times before, with most of his recent appearances involving stories from Graydin. He was now questioning everything he had gotten from the man. Beyond that, he found that being sanctimoniously objective – a seemingly incongruent feat often accomplished by many in television news – was something he could no longer do. He knew it in his bones.

Peter also knew that Ed wouldn't stop hounding him until he did what he had always done and capitulate to the ever demanding television new cycle. There was nothing in Peter's contract compelling him to make television appearances, but to decline offers was ill advised from a career standpoint. He needed to disappear for a while.

It didn't take much more thought before Peter knew exactly where he could go to avoid his editor, except first he had to stash the evidence, and he had a good idea of how to do that as well. He quickly gathered his things . Careful to avoid Ed, he grabbed a copy of that day's early edition and made his way out of the pressroom, the top secret document in his briefcase.

After consulting the movie listings, he caught a cab to a revival theater downtown. He sat down in time to catch the opening sequence of the film *Citizen Kane*. He took a deep swig from a smuggled bottle of brandy as the dying Charles Foster Kane uttered his cryptic opening line.

A gloom Peter had done a lot of drinking to avoid was threatening to return for the first time in a while. Orson Welles's brilliant portrayal of a misguided newspaper mogul flickering on the screen before him, he saw only his wife's name written in the hand of a dead man.

By the time the movie was nearing the end, the familiar buzz of Peter's favorite drink had set in and he was swearing oaths without regard for the consequences. Tomorrow he would try to remember some of the skills that had made him a trusted investigative reporter, he vowed. Then he would use those skills to discover the truth about Phil Simmons and how he knew his beloved wife.

Peter suddenly had a strange sensation. He could almost feel Barbara sitting beside him. He became convinced that they had been to that theater together before. The tears came and with them a flood of inebriated memories. It had been a while for all that as well.

She was the one who had always dragged him to showings of *Citizen Kane* when it came to town, as a cautionary tale to her journalist husband. She never made a single comment about the movie either, Peter remembered; not before, during, or after.

Hector Madrano was summoned away from a rare, home-cooked meal to answer what he knew was an important phone call. He was forced to drag a landline into the bathroom of the busy old house where he was staying for a little privacy.

"Gina?"

"Hector? Did you hear what happened?"

"We heard."

"Where's Ben and John?"

"Sweat lodge, but they heard the news before they went in."

"What are we going to do?" she said. "He was cooperating all the way up to the end. Then his friend, someone named Sylvia Billy, came back into town and he–"

"Sylvia Billy?" Hector said.

"She came back and after that he wouldn't make contact anymore. Then he lost me and went back to his house, of all places. I'd have to do the autopsy myself to believe he committed suicide, but by the time I got there he sure was dead."

"My God, Sylvia Billy."

"I take it you know her?"

"I've known her for over twenty years."

"Well, you better hope she doesn't know anything about all this, because if she does, they're going to either destroy her publicly, or kill her, or both."

"I thought she was still in Japan."

"She was until a day ago. She came back to brief the President on the evacuations. They sent her down to South Carolina, but from what I hear she'll be back."

"Does she know about Phil?"

"Oh, I imagine she has to by now."

"Poor Billy," he said. "Gina, I can almost guarantee she doesn't know anything about the CIG. But she needs our protection."

"Then I need Ben and John out here."

"If I could talk to her, more than a few of our problems may be solved."

"Approaching her directly is out of the question. She'll be under tight surveillance."

"Ben and John are scheduled to leave for New York in the morning," he said. "They got a hit on Stiner, a lead from a CIG *light* informant."

"What's the deal with this guy? Masterson sent out a bulletin for him on the IntraGuard network and no one knows why."

"I don't know, but Ben and David are both convinced that if Masterson wants him, then we want him. At least to keep him from permanently disappearing."

"Well tell them to deal with that situation and get their asses down here as fast as they can. I can't keep tabs on all the players in this little debacle myself. There are too many of them."

"Got it, and please watch out for Billy. She's special, Gina, you don't know."

"I'll keep her alive, but we better figure out what we're going to do if Phil made the video like Ben told him to. Because if he did, it could be out in the open. I know I don't have it."

"I'll brief Ben and we'll come up with something. Be careful out there."

"Always."

Hector hung up the receiver, lingering on the closed toilet seat in contemplation. A knock at the door reminded him he was tying up the only bathroom in the house. He opened the door to find a Native American girl of six with a very concerned look on her face.

"I'm sorry little one," Hector said. "Come on in."

Hector left the phone on the counter and wove his way through a spacious country kitchen that was crowded with a diverse collection of people. A Native American family was hosting guests from all over North and South America. Hector and his Unity Council team were among them. He kept moving through the living room, through the people milling around the front of the house.

He walked out the front door onto the wind-swept Second Mesa, the ancestral home of the Hopi people and the location of the ancient village of Oraibi.

The ground under Hector's feet was craggy and unforgiving, the sky above was endless, and the views virtually infinite. He had spent the previous day letting the enchantment of the place calm him, after a hectic time making the news in New York City.

Oraibi may have become virtually deserted since the schism between Hopi traditionalists and progressive generations, but what Hector saw was a village that was thriving with activity.

A construction crew was completing the final touches on a small stage and podium close to the edge of the Mesa; others were refurbishing several abandoned buildings in the village itself.

He was gratified that things were going as planned for one of the most important publicity stunts he would be attempting on behalf of the Unity Council, but he was also distracted by the news that Sylvia Billy was back in the country.

He wandered to the edge of the five hundred foot drop that punctuated the Second Mesa, where a bright red blanket had been spread out over the opening to a raised dugout in the ground. He stared into the distance, trying to come up with a way to contact Billy without endangering her life.

Wisps of smoke escaped from the edges of the blanket at Hector's feet, and from the subterranean chamber, the ceremonial *kiva*, below it. Shirtless and sweating, Ben Spiritdancer exploded through the blanket and threw it to the ground, letting out a primal roar that echoed all the way down the cliff.

Hector stood back to give the aging but sturdy ex-detective room to shake off his experience. Ben's son John, a tall Hopi man in his twenties, slowly climbed out of the kiva and stretched his lean body until several of his vertebrae cracked loud enough for Hector to hear.

"Gina called," he said.

Ben dumped one of several buckets of water left near the kiva over his head. John bent all the way over until the tip of his nose touched his knee, holding the yoga position effortlessly.

"Is she OK?" he asked.

"She's fine, but she's going to need your help. Sylvia Billy is here in the U.S. She's due back to DC tomorrow."

Ben looked up from his towel. "Do you think she knows?"

"If she knew, she'd be screaming her head off. That's the Billy my wife and I know and love. We need her... alive."

Four Native American men and a much older woman, all dressed in colorful ceremonial garb, made their way from inspecting the construction efforts, to where Hector was talking to Ben and John.

"Are you ready to face our enemies?" one of the elders asked.

"We give ourselves to this fate willingly," Ben said.

"But the question is do the tribes accept that this has to happen?" John asked. "Because we can't do it without their cooperation."

Marta pointed to each of the elders in turn. "We've got the Sicangu Lakota, the Pueblo, the Navajo, and the Hopi, all standing together, as has been prophesied."

"It's long overdue as far as I'm concerned," Ben said.

"Hector and his Council have made it possible for the tribes to forget past differences and look to the future," Marta said.

"It looks like we're just about ready for the announcement," Hector said.

"Renewing the pilgrimage to the 'White Mountain of the East' seems a fitting way to start our alliance," the elder from the Pueblo said.

"We're looking good for affiliates from Phoenix and Flagstaff," Hector said. "We just have to hope the story will pick up steam by the time we reach Colorado. Then there's the alternate news outlets and the Internet buzz. They've been working great for us." Hector nodded to the elder from the Lakota.

"This is going to piss some people off," John said.

"You mean more than New York?" Hector said. "There were bench warrants issued over that one."

Ben pulled his favorite L.A. Lakers t-shirt over his head. "What's with the get-ups?" he asked one of the elders.

"We're bringing back the old ceremonies," the representative from the Navajo said. "And the tribes are agreeing to Pow Wow. We're all performing our ceremonies together, as a show of solidarity."

"Prophecies about tribes uniting or not, I'm just finding it hard to believe they can pull it off."

"There's still some asking why we should care about what happens to people in New Orleans, Los Angles, or anywhere else that isn't on the reservation," the Hopi elder said. "And many more don't believe the White people will survive the Great Cleansing anyway."

"Does that include me?" Hector said with a rye smile.

Marta hobbled to the edge of the Mesa, closing her eyes. "The Unity Council has moved many with their message and purpose. If so many can put aside their differences and work together for the future, then we should be able to as well."

"Many among our people are afraid of trusting outsiders so completely," the Hopi man said.

John shook his head. "But plenty of tribes can cut deals with crooked lobbyists for gaming houses, or with big corporations for mineral rights. They don't seem to have problems trusting outsiders then, do they? And how many of those tribes have gotten screwed out of millions?"

"We don't have any more time to waste acting as racist and bigoted as the rest of this country has become," Ben said. "The other tribes may like to think that what's happening doesn't concern them, but all the casino money in the world won't help during widespread drought, any more than it'll help the people in L.A. during an earthquake."

"Sometimes our leaders don't really represent their people," Marta said.

"Another thing you have in common with us outsiders," Hector said.

The evening was cloudless and pristine, and from their vantage point on the Second Mesa, a good fifty miles of Arizona desert was laid out like a picture in front of the group.

Marta opened her eyes and did what she had done every morning for seventy-three years. Every time she gazed upon the Three Mesas, and the land they rose from, she reaffirmed her covenant with the earth.

"We have lived on this land since the Earth Guardian, Maasaw, entrusted it to our ancestors thousands of years ago," she said. "The Old Ones who lived here before our time– they saw the lakes, thousands of miles wide, that covered our land. They knew the danger of floods. But when the water left, so did they.

"For the generations since the land turned to desert, we have clung to the rocks, the cliff face and the valley wall, safe from predators, enemies, and nature's angry wrath. But before our people found this high ground, we were nomads.

"We can't deny the possibility that history has come full circle and we may actually have to leave our homes again. If the water leaves, so will we. But there are many holy places on this earth. And there are many of our brothers and sisters who will share their land with us if that should happen."

"With all the prophecies and foreknowledge we've had," John said. "It would be pretty stupid to end up getting caught in some disaster that even our ancestors knew was coming."

"What have you seen on your dreamwalk?" Marta asked the men.

"Well, the verdict isn't good," John said.

"And you, my son?" Marta asked Ben.

"All I see is disaster ahead of us. But that doesn't mean we're done."

John patted his father on the shoulder. "It didn't all the times before."

"From the reports David has been filing, a whole bunch of people sure think something is coming," Hector said. "We've had a surge in people coming to our counselors with nightmares about floods and earthquakes. That's besides the psychics."

"There have been stories of widespread dreamwalking among the untrained – the outsiders – young and old," the Hopi elder said.

"We could be looking at a dangerous situation with that," Ben said.

Marta's expression was peaceful and confident. "It's going to be OK, Son. It just means that it's time."

3

Dr. Hasline darted around a glass booth at the far corner of a room the size of a gymnasium. Rows of fluorescent lamps hung the long distance from the roof and lit only two rows of cubicles in the middle of the space, casting the surrounding area in shadow and completely removing any distractions.

The main lab of his innocuous-sounding Institute for Psychological Studies was the perfect setting for his experiments in the phenomenon people in the trade knew simply as *psi*.

To prevent unintentional audio cues, each cubicle was separated by a plastic barrier. Technicians in lab coats were flashing cards to male and female soldiers on the other side of the divider while another lab technician was circling and making notes on a clipboard.

Sterile white light from the hall momentarily illuminated the darkened monitoring booth when General Masterson opened the door and joined Hasline.

"How was your trip?" Hasline asked.

"Report, I need some results and I need them now."

"General, you look terrible."

"What did you just say, Doctor?" Masterson's normally intimidating stare was made doubly so by the swollen red blood vessels streaking his eyes.

"I mean, have you been sleeping, sir?"

"Why do your experiments always start at such odd times?"

Hasline pointed to a clock on the wall showing a time much different than what was on Masterson's watch. "We're at the mercy of sidereal time. It has to do with the constellations and–"

"I know what sidereal time is. Now what do you have?"

"I'll just repeat that this experiment should have been conducted in the WRC," Hasline said. "Considering that that is the primary area you're looking to protect. I understand your prohibition against psychics in that facility for the last twenty-five years, but we're dealing with a special set of factors when we are talking about Mt. Blanca.

"It's the geology, sir. They chose a very old mass of granite for the Western Range Complex. That particular mountain chain dates from 1.7 to 1.8 billion years. As opposed to 250 million years for the chains above and below. We're still unclear as to the affects of granite and water on psi. Initial indications are that they amplify the phenomena."

"Billion year old granite or not, Doctor, this better yield some serious results."

"Fortunately, this is the most powerful batch of remote viewers the government has produced to date. Collectively they boast a ninety-two percent accuracy rating."

Masterson stepped up to the glass and eyed each of the test subjects suspiciously. "Then that's a room full of very dangerous people."

"Most of them are vital assets in the weather and earthquake prediction program, General. This has been a distraction that could delay my most recent report. I don't have to tell you that it's barely a week until the first probable date of disaster."

Hasline received only a cold silence from Masterson that he knew well not to test. He moved on immediately. "This is a standard accuracy assessment test for psi abilities," he said.

Outside the booth, the various technicians were drawing cards from special decks and showing the soldiers only the blank backs of each card. It was left to the test subjects to discern whether the design on the other side of the card was a star, a circle, a triangle, or one of ten other images. The technician would then record the result in his or her computer.

"We've been training soldiers – even random troops off the line – to remote view for years. Soldiers know how to follow orders and pay attention to the protocols. They disengage and become conduits. But these abilities are like any other. Some will excel and some will be prodigies. These are the prodigies."

"So what is preventing them from reading me right now?"

"I've been generating a low-level energy field in the chamber and around the booth, a very specific frequency of electromagnetic radiation."

"And it's preventing them from using their abilities?"

"That's what we're testing. Research in the Soviet Union was promising but they eventually ran out of money to make a leap past what became some very real scientific obstacles. Then there was the incident where they were caught bombarding the American embassy with microwaves in an attempt to drive the diplomatic staff crazy.

"No effect at level two," he said to his assistant. "Step up one level at a time. We need to determine an operational range."

The assistant adjusted a dial on the console in front of him, as Hasline searched the subjects for some sign of a reaction.

"Before the turn of the millennium, the focus of parapsychological research varied greatly by country," Hasline said. "In Russia the focus was remote influencing. The Russians never lost sight of the biological and physiological connections to the psi phenomena.

"Humans interact with the quantum world at very specific locations in our brains, using very specific neurological structures. If we can determine the exact spectrum of electromagnetic energy that will disrupt those structures, then maybe we can disrupt that interaction with the quantum, and thus disrupt reception of the psi 'signal,' if you will."

He looked to a computer monitor when it appeared the psychic soldiers were still unaffected. The results of the ongoing card tests were constantly updating on the screen.

"What about HAARP?" Masterson said. "Couldn't it be adjusted to the right frequencies?"

"Possibly, but then it would work on more than just humans," Hasline said. "That's why it will be so effective for Sunday if it looks like they're going to say something you don't like. One pulse from the array will disrupt communications of all types for hours. We need a scalpel; the HAARP is a twenty-pound sledgehammer."

"Wait, wait, here we go," he said. "These results show a serious drop in accuracy. These two are usually the highest scorers and now they're logging more misses than hits."

Masterson crossed his arms. "But can it repel a remote viewer who isn't within the radius of the energy field?"

"Still undetermined," Hasline said as he nodded to his assistant to continue ratcheting up the intensity of the microwaves.

It was on the fourth and fifth settings that several of the soldiers were rendered unable to continue with the card tests.

"Ingo Swan compared the psi signal to a weak transmission buried in interference," Hasline said. "He eventually ended up working on decreasing the background interference that prevented the psi signal from coming through. Now, he meant mental interference: doubts, conflicts, fears. But we want to increase the field interference, until the signal is completely disrupted."

"That sounds simple enough," Masterson said. "Why the hell isn't it done?"

"Because nothing is simple when it comes to the human mind, sir."

One of the test subjects suddenly keeled over, prompting the technician who had been circling the cubicles to nod to Hasline. Two more of the remote viewers began to vomit uncontrollably before hitting the floor. Half of the soldiers were down but three remained.

The two men and one woman struggled to continue with the psychic test, until finally the two men fell. One convulsed violently while the other became too confused to form sentences.

The only one left was the woman: a plain looking blonde of twenty-eight who seemed out of place in her army fatigues. Straining, tears were running down her cheeks, she refused to give in.

Hasline may have resembled an insurance salesman more than a mad doctor, but he had no compunction about inflicting pain in furtherance of his scientific goals. He tapped the shoulder of his assistant and the man turned the knob even higher.

The suffering woman stood up to face Masterson. She gave him an accusing look that he had seen before, in his dreams. It was the disgusted expression of someone who had peered inside his head. It was intolerable to him.

"Higher!" he yelled to Hasline's assistant.

The pain was obviously excruciating as her defiant stare remained unbroken. She never stopped staring at the shadowy figure behind the glass. She couldn't see his face but she knew what he had done.

Astonished, Hasline had his assistant turn the knob one more time, the highest setting was only one notch away. The rest of the soldiers were heaving and wrenching in pain before the woman was finally overcome and thrown to the floor like the rest.

"Have the first emitter installed outside my office at the WRC." Masterson said. "Begin full-scale deployment immediately."

"Yes sir."

"What is her name?"

"That's Erica Brown, sir, one of the top performers in the remote viewing program."

"Have her detained," Masterson said as he walked out. "I'll question her tomorrow."

A familiar feeling of dread swept over Max when he opened his eyes. He had come to abhor the tunnel vision that now accompanied his dreams. Besides being stifling and claustrophobic, it meant that once again he would be forced to bare witness to somebody else's nightmare.

He felt himself descending to earth as the ground approached quickly from below. The porthole he looked through was narrow, while the view on the other side seemed to go on for miles.

The expansive tract of land between the Tigress and Euphrates glistened in the sun from a thousand feet in the air. Once a verdant plain, supporting the most prolific farmland in the region, Mesopotamia was now a desolate mudflat, scrubbed clean of vegetation from river bank to river bank by a mighty flood.

Max tried to relax and take in everything he could about the experience, in hopes of deciphering the meaning later. It soon became clear, though, that there wasn't much to see. In all directions the terrain was flat, bare, and waterlogged.

Panic came on when Max tried unsuccessfully to move his arms. It was always when he was prevented from exerting his own will during one of his strange dreams, that a deep-seated fear would overtake him.

He could feel it all happening again: the loss of control, the helplessness. But soon something came into his field of vision that was so curious that it made him temporarily forget his anxiety.

There was a lone structure in the middle of the bleak expanse. It was rectangular and dark and it obviously towered several stories above the muddy plains. Max immediately became preoccupied with how it could have possibly survived the flood intact.

Circling the unlikely scene allowed Max to make out campfire smoke trailing up from in front of an opening in the side of the structure. With each pass he descended lower, until finally he could see people gathered by the fire.

The next thing he knew he was on the ground, with the sunlight hitting him in the face. He was in a group of people he didn't recognize and they were all walking toward the colossal structure he had seen from the air.

He was finally getting close enough to determine that it wasn't a building at all, it was a craft. He could tell that it was wooden and at least four stories tall. And he could see that it was windowless, except for a raised portion of the roof where a series of openings ran the length of the boat. A ramp had been propped up to the only door.

Max observed that the people he was walking among were dressed in gilded robes and ornate headdresses from a culture he could not immediately identify. He was momentarily amused by how carefully they stepped through the mud, so as not to soil their finery.

Meantime, the bearded man who rushed up to the group from the craft fell to his knees in the muck, his brown smock already filthy and torn. He raised his hands high in reverence. The prayers he recited were frantic and impassioned.

Max watched the supplicating Hero of the Deluge in awe, wondering if he would remember any of it when he woke. That was when his view was abruptly blocked by an angry man in a business suit.

"Private first class Maxwell J. Stiner, you are trespassing in a restricted zone!" Masterson barked.

The man's booming voice and hateful sneer were so threatening that Max demanded to wake up. He didn't think it would work, but it did.

Max opened his eyes to find a grubby hand reaching into his coat pocket. "Get off me!" he yelled.

He shoved the gaunt, trembling man off the subway bench, onto the floor of the train car. The dazed addict stumbled to his feet and ran through the door to the adjoining compartment.

His fists clenched and chest heaving, Max searched the rest of the mostly-empty car for more threats. The few early commuters that were present were ignoring what was happening. He sat back down after a few moments more of guarded posturing.

He looked for the translation of the epic, irritated when he was initially unable to pull it out of a gap in the seats. He began paging through the book immediately, though his eyes were still adjusting to the harsh fluorescent light of the subway.

He turned to the commentary that accompanied the translation of the Gilgamesh epic tablets, becoming agitated by his brief hunt for a specific passage in the background information. He calmed down considerably by the time he found it.

"Later versions of the flood myth," he read. "...including the account found in the Gilgamesh epic, describe Mount Ararat and other well-known mountains in the region as probable landing places for Noah's ark. Meanwhile the oldest version, the one from the parent culture of Sumeria, told of the ark simply coming to rest after the flood waters receded."

Max struggled to retain every aspect of the dream before it slipped away. The appearance of the threatening man in the suit made it easier. He had never gotten such a good look at him before. Now that he had, he was more confused than ever.

After everything he had been through, Max didn't recognize the man who had been troubling his dreams for weeks. He had never met him, and besides noticing that he had a distinctly military bearing, all Max could say about him was that his head was full of indescribable torments and unfathomable mysteries.

The sun was just rising over the city and he had the street to himself when Max emerged from the 42nd Street subway station down the block from the New York Public Library. He stopped at a corner diner for a coffee to go.

It was still well over a half an hour until the library opened, so Max climbed the steps to the front door and got comfortable near the top. He sipped his coffee, watching the morning shifts of the newspaper stands, the restaurants, and the coffee shops prepare for the impending assault of commuters. He planned on being long gone by the time that assault hit.

Max had originally decided to stop by the library to see if he could learn more about what had been turning his waking life upside down. But as he sat and thought about the man in his dreams with the evil sneer, it was plain that what he needed to do was find out if he was real. A task Max knew was probably impossible.

"You're the one that has that book," a voice said from behind him. Max looked up to find a wiry older man in an electrician's uniform standing over him, pointing at the translation of the Gilgamesh epic on the step. "I've been on the waiting list for that one for weeks."

The man scratched his blonde, salt and pepper beard before deciding to sit down. "You know the first thing Old Noah loaded on that ark?" he said. "Before all the beasts of the earth, even before his own family? His gold and silver, of course. Now that's what I call priorities."

"I remember reading that," Max said. "Hey, I don't think I'm overdue on this but–"

"Wouldn't sweat it. I think I'm something like forty-eighth of a hundred and fifty on the waiting list."

"Really? Damn."

"Yeah, I wouldn't have given the wage-slaves credit for being smart enough to get into the Epic," the man said, his thin, wrinkled face exhibiting his utter revulsion. "And I bet a month ago there wouldn't have been a waiting list at all."

"So what happened since?"

The man waved his arm at the city. "Who the hell knows? They're all a bunch of freaks out there. I'd like to think that after a good ten years of kings and wars and climate change kicking their asses, they're finally waking the hell up."

Max placed his hand on the Gilgamesh epic for reassurance. "I have to admit, there definitely was something familiar about a story that starts with a dictator pissing off his own people by messing around in other countries for his own good, and ends up with one serious flood."

"You're a vet, aren't you?"

Max suddenly became preoccupied with deciding where he would buy a copy of the translation when he had to return the one he checked out. The idea that he would go without the book never crossed his mind. "How'd you know that?"

"I can always tell." The man leaned back and crossed his thin legs, throwing a quick salute. "First Sergeant Richard Schott reporting as ordered, sir! They call me Bud."

"I was about as far from being an officer as anyone could be...PFC Maxwell J. Stiner."

The moment Max spoke his own name and former rank aloud he was reminded of the dream on the subway. And the man who bellowed like a drill sergeant.

"You ever get online and search for other soldiers?" he asked Bud.

"Yeah, there're a couple of websites."

"Any with pictures?"

"I'd imagine, service record photos. Desert Storm, right?"

"Affirmative."

"Is that what made you check that out?" Bud asked. "You know Mesopotamia is where it all went down. What was it? Five, six thousand years ago?"

"I was in a uniform and carrying an M16 the first time I saw Mesopotamia with my own eyes."

Bud shrugged. "It's the damn 'Cradle of Civilization' and it's been blown to hell. People are crazy if they think that won't have some kind of effect on us all."

"If most Americans couldn't have found Iraq on a map before the second invasion, you can be damn sure they could after."

"It's been ugly over there. No doubt about that."

"We marched past the dead bodies. They were half-buried by sand... The wind, it seemed like it would never stop. Oil wells burning all across Kuwait... Cradle of Civilization or not, Mesopotamia was hell on earth as far as I'm concerned. I thought I had gotten by it all, but I guess not."

"Maybe it was seeing them go back in," Bud said. "The second invasion could have dredged up some shit in your head. I don't know what I would have done if all of a sudden they invaded Vietnam again. 'Course, North Korea will be close enough."

Max ran his hand through his stringy hair. "I don't know. I've had flashbacks before. But never like this. I guess I don't know what made me check this out."

"Oh, I doubt that's true." Bud revealed the cover of one of the books he was returning to the library. Max immediately recognized the photograph of more Sumerian clay tablets. "I found this one," he said, handing the book to Max. "It's a pretty good history on Mesopotamia."

Max began paging through the glossy pages intently.

Bud chuckled. "If more people picked up a book about the country they were getting ready to invade *before* they invaded... Well, a lot more people would be alive right now, most of them innocent women and children in the Middle East and in Southeast Asia."

"And South America," Max said without looking up.

"And Africa, miss any?"

"The first Gulf only lasted a few months for me and it was hell on Earth," Max said. "Vietnam had to be worse, if that's possible. Now the war in Afghanistan has been going on longer than both of ours put together, with no end in sight."

"What's been happening over there ain't no war. I wasn't in no *war* forty years ago. Invasions and occupations. We invaded those countries, then we occupied them, then we wonder why the hell everyone there hates us."

Max chuckled. "I couldn't believe it when they started talking on TV about 'winning the hearts and minds' in Afghanistan. I heard that shit when I was a kid in the '70s. I know there're military historians out there, half the shows on TV anymore are about WWII. What, they didn't cover Vietnam in school?"

"And just like in 'Nam, now there's gonna be a whole generation of chopped up men and women coming back. And to what? No jobs and then foreclosures?"

"It was twenty years ago for me and I'm still not right. I think I finally just gave up trying to get right."

"After I came back, 'course I was all twisted up. I did Winter Soldier, confessed the war crimes I did. And then drank for a few years, more than a few years. The ex left over that.

"But it was when I saw all that shit about how the Gulf of Tonkin never happened... I mean, you had Cronkite and Safer investigating, then it comes out that the shit was all a lie! Now we've got how any ex-government criminals who can't go to some countries in Europe without having their asses arrested? And nothing has changed to this day!"

"Yeah, I read the stories about how they sucked Saddam into invading Kuwait so we could go in and smack him down. People barely said anything about it."

"History only repeats itself because the white-guys-in-ties don't have shit for imagination. But then they don't need to be too creative, do they? When the wage-slaves have permanent amnesia, it makes it easy. Now they've made it so people are counting themselves lucky just to have a job. Just to *be* a wage-slave!

"I knew when the Twin Towers were blown up that it was starting all over again," he said. "That train wreck at the polls in 2000 was bad enough: Two spoiled little princes from inbred political families running a rigged election to be 'King of America.'"

"I don't vote," Max said. "I don't think I've stayed anywhere long enough to even register."

"I didn't need any more proof that we don't live in a democracy. You know? I mean, after WWII they did a hell of a job convincing us all that we lived in a real democracy. All that 'American Dream' shit. But the fairy tale got tired pretty quick.

"Just not before me and a bunch of other guys rained death on innocent women and children all over Southeast Asia. I finally started asking myself what the hell kind of country I was living in. Then 9-11 answered that."

"You said 'blown up'? The Towers fell due to fire," Max said with a sly grin, still too involved in the textbook Bud gave him to make eye contact. "Are you some kind of conspiracy nut?"

"They used thermite in the Gulf, didn't they? They sure as hell used it in Vietnam."

"I wasn't in New York when it happened."

"Well I was. We were running cable over on West Twenty-Ninth. I made it to Ground Zero just before they blew up the garages under World Trade Center Two. Turned out people were maimed and killed down there, long before either tower came down.

"I know thermite when I smell it and taste it. And I know the sound of demolition charges when I hear them. And no self-righteous jackass who wasn't there is going to tell me different."

"You've got to be some kind of right wing crazy then."

"The militia wannabes that hang out at the bait shop up by my cabin, now they're right wing crazies. I was an eyewitness to one of the biggest crimes in history and I get called a liar half the time. Pisses me off.

"See, you ain't old enough to remember, Private, but they said that kind of shit when they shot Kennedy too. Oswald killed JKF with one pristine bullet that they just 'found' on a gurney in the emergency room a couple hours later. And *we* were the crazy ones for not believing that shit?

"It's like the story that they just 'found' a passport from one of the terrorists in the rubble at Ground Zero. There was paper and shit blown halfway across Manhattan after they dropped those towers, and they just 'found' one of the terrorists' passports? Then the guy turned out to be alive and living in the Middle East somewhere. Never even been to the U.S.

"The congress finally said the Kennedy assassination was a conspiracy in '77 but by then nobody gave a shit. No wonder it happened again. No wonder they think we're stupid."

"Besides religion, the biggest fights at the shop where I work are about 9-11."

"I don't get it, either. Even the most skeptical people I know, people that usually don't believe a single thing the government says about anything, believe everything the government says about 9-11. Doesn't make any god dammed sense."

"It's too big. Nobody wants to believe that their government would do something like that."

"Screw that! Welcome to the real goddamn world. I've seen commanders sacrifice entire platoons to take a hill that they didn't even need, nobody called that an 'inside job.' FDR sacrificed Pearl Harbor, nobody ever called that an 'inside job' either. They laid up the *Lusitania* to get sunk for W-W-One. Hell, they just made the whole Gulf of Tonkin story up out of thin air. A straight-up false flag operation! Like I said, the white-guys-in-ties got no imagination. When a tactic works, you keep it working."

"I gotta admit, when I turn on the TV now and see grunts killing and dying in that damn desert – again! – after the place ruined my life... I don't know, maybe that is what's been messing with my head lately."

The street was coming to life around the pair and the noise was increasing. Max was oblivious now, lost in the pages of the newly acquired Mesopotamian history. Recognizing that he was enthralled, Bud began thumbing through the other book he was there to return.

"Which one is that?" Max eventually asked.

"This one is *War is a Racket*, by Smedley Butler. At the time he wrote this he was the most decorated Marine ever."

"Sounds like the title pretty much says it all."

"Yeah, Butler broke it down back in '34. Basically, you put on that uniform and you become some wannabe king's attack dog or some money-grubbing banker's source of revenue, most of the time it's both. This one guy called them the Paper Aristocracy. They're the chinless bastards that have got us by the nuts right now.

"They wanted the sugar in Nicaragua and they sent in the Marines. Hell, Butler was killing in China and Mexico for oil back in 1914. 1914! What the hell?"

"What did it have to be like to be a grunt in 1914," Max said.

"Same as it is now: they stick you in somebody else's backyard, with your buddies' lives at stake, then turn you loose on the people that live there. Then act surprised when everyone on both sides turns bloodthirsty." He pulled out a stained and dog-eared paperback book that had been tucked down in the side pocket of his pants. "What did it have to be like to be a grunt in the 1700s?"

"The library's gonna be pissed when you try to return that."

"I checked *Common Sense* out a few years ago. I ended up buying this copy. Paine was talking about how only kings make war; regular people usually aren't interested in killing each other, not wholesale anyway. We'll fight, over just about anything, but it's the pathetic little wannabe kings that get off on warring."

Max motioned to the Gilgamesh epic then turned another page in the history textbook. "You don't have to tell me about kings."

"That's why the last war criminal they had in the White House was itching to invade Iraq again. All those scheming moneygrubbers and religious wackos around him had their own reasons, but being a crowned prince of the American political royalty, and the family idiot, he had to make a name for himself. To prove he was better than daddy.

Meantime people are dying all over the place. But all that's bound to happen with kingship."

"I read about kingship in the commentary," Max said of the Gilgamesh epic.

"That history book gets deep into it. It all started in Mesopotamia...the cracked idea that one man – or a bunch of men – have some kind of God-given right to rule over everybody else.

"That book was talking about how those Sumerians believed lock, stock, and barrel that some higher power laid it down thousands of years ago: there's gonna be masters and there's gonna be slaves, there's gonna be the royalty and there's gonna be the peons. And you can guess which one of those all of us are."

"I know one thing," Max said. "Nobody ever sat around when they were a kid dreaming of being a wage-slave, but somehow most all of us end up being one. If you got a job at all. How'd that happen?"

"And I didn't put on a uniform and kill people so that forty years later the goddamn 'King of America' could take the power to assassinate anyone he wants on the planet without so much as a 'kiss my ass.' Because he can do that now, did you know that? Thanks to 9-11. And he can wage war whenever he wants and on whoever he wants, and he doesn't have to answer to a soul, not you, not me, not even Congress.

"Now when you have some power hungry little spawn of the so-called 'elite' running around screwing us unchecked, and the rest of the 'elite' running around screwing us unchecked, then you're close enough to that old-time kingship that you might as well just call it what it is.

"Why the hell do you think they've been camped out down on Wall Street? They're finally figuring out that it doesn't matter whether it's the Inbred Aristocracy or the Paper Aristocracy, we're all still the peons...

"And Paine and those guys gotta be spinning in their damn graves too, because they were warning us all about this shit a good two hundred years ago. They knew that it was 'The System.' And they knew that system was dead wrong."

Max was obviously looking up kingship in the index of the history textbook, then searching through the four hundred page volume for the appropriate chapters.

"Yeah, if you're getting into the history of Mesopotamia then there's no way you won't be hearing about Sumeria and about kingship."

"I guess that is why I came down here," Max said, finally looking up from the book. "I wanted to get some more stuff on that damn place. But I didn't think it would be all this."

"At first I didn't know a thing about Mesopotamia, never heard of it." Bud cradled his heavily bookmarked copy of *Common Sense*. "I was reading Paine and he was screaming his head off about the kingship setup when he was pitching for the American Revolution.

"He even went so far to say maybe they should have been checking into just exactly where a bunch of swinging dicks so 'exalted' like some kind of 'new species' even came from, and whether they had helped or hurt us.

"Seriously ballsy for him to be questioning the system like that, considering that he lived in a time when crossing the king could get you killed or locked up, no trial, and no one would say shit. He was staring down five, six thousand years of history right there."

"All the way back to Sumeria."

"Those ancient bastards had all kinds of shit we have, it's all in there. It was saying that they were living in the first real cities on the whole damn planet and suddenly they were using the first wheel and the plough. They had courts, schools, and libraries. The first writing, the first advanced medicine, and full-on religion. They had prescriptions, and divorces, and taxes, and beer."

"And kingship," Max said, his nose back in the book.

"Damn right, full-on kingship just like that. They talk all about it in there, but they don't really tell people what it means, or that the Sumerians made the Christian Right look like card-carrying socialists."

Bud crossed his arms and looked over his shoulder at the front doors to the library. There was no activity yet. Max couldn't have cared less at that moment whether the library was opening or not.

"That's the thing about kingship," Bud said. "It's politics, business, and religion all rolled up into one. They can call it democracy nowadays all they want but it's just kingship with elections."

"And that's the problem, the elections," Max said. "False hope is a bitch."

"See, genuine blue-bloods are hard to find nowadays. So now we have the Paper Aristocracy. Our crowned heads of state are politicians and corporate crooks and celebrities and musicians and sports stars and media whores. Most of them are assholes all the time because that's what people expect from their so-called gods."

The street at the bottom of the library stairs began to load up with morning traffic, making Bud restless. Max had become engrossed in a particularly interesting section of the textbook, seemingly unconcerned that the commute was already winding up.

Bud suddenly tensed up and began searching the block in front of the library. He appeared to act on instinct when he eventually stood to scrutinize the entire area.

"You work nights?" Max asked.

"I have to be in by eight. I get into the library early because coming here after work is a bitch."

Max recognized the way Bud was scanning the perimeter. "Everything OK First Sergeant?"

"Ever get the feeling you're being watched, soldier?"

"Every single day I was in Kuwait."

"I was LRRP."

"Long range recon, damn. You guys were legends."

"I can tell you for a fact that people can feel it when someone is watching them. They did scientific tests."

"You in trouble, old man?"

Bud reluctantly sat back down on the step. "Not for a long time. Now I'm a fine, upstanding citizen of the United States of America."

"Yeah, right."

The service people who owned the early morning began to retreat, just as the first men and women in business attire appeared on the sidewalks. Bud was finally unable to contain his well-developed disdain for anyone in a tie.

"Look at them, Max, they're the money-grubbing elite. They're the best and the brightest. Didn't you know we're all supposed to be busting our asses for that magical upgrade to the Paper Aristocracy?"

His disgust grew, as the sidewalks clogged up with commuters, and his general suspicion heightened. "They walk around acting like they don't know that their time is running out. But if you stop and listen, you can hear the truth, because they're always thinking it.

"They paste on their fake little smiles every morning when they look in the mirror, because they think that will get them through, but it won't. It's too late for them. And because of their stupid-ass greed, it's too late for us now, too."

"At least they weren't living a lie back then," Max said. "The Sumerians, all those ancient people, at least they knew they were slaves. They weren't under the delusion that there was hope. They didn't have to live with all the broken promises."

"You're right about that. All they had to do was serve their god and remember their place. 'Course, who knows how many of them died from war and starvation and forced labor."

"Yeah, all that happens right now, everyday."

Still scanning the area, Bud spotted a rushed businessman tapping out a text message on his cell phone. "There's a reason there always seems to be some suit wearing little bastard at the bottom of the schemes that screws us over. It's because that's the way it's always been. They dress in the finest, most cultured threads, to hide the fact that they're really the most uncivilized thugs around."

Bud jabbed his finger at one of the many glass-covered skyscrapers soaring overhead. "We built temples, just like the Sumerians, and we grovel around them waiting for the word from the priests inside. Granted, the temples back then weren't nearly this ugly."

"The commentary in *Gilgamesh* was talking about how each city had a different god, and that the cities warred with each other over those gods. Ever seen a Raiders or a Packers fan at a football game? They can get crazy."

"And that's over a game," Bud said. "Back then everything was 'by the glory of Baal' or 'for the greatness of Ashur,' all while they were chopping up women and children, wholesale. The names of the gods have changed, but that's about all."

"What I want to know is who got me to kill people I've never met and never had anything against," Max said.

"Probably the same sumbitch that had me working my ass off for a pension that just got raided by a bunch of crooks. And then – after all that – they got *me* to pay for it all with *my* taxes. That's a hell of a thing to pull off, you know? Make you pay for your own hell."

"Yeah it is."

"Come to find out, that's old-school kingship, right there. We're talking feudal shit, with the surfs in the fields, making money for the king, so that he could afford soldiers to oppress the surfs in the fields. Oh, and to try and take over the next king's backyard too. It's tired. It's so god damned tired I could spit!"

"You notice that it wasn't until the middle class started turning into wage-slaves themselves that they stood up and protested about anything," Max said. "Before, it was OK to have wage-slaves, just as long as they weren't one of them."

Bud scoffed. "The middle class can worry about keeping up with the Joneses while the water rises up around their scrawny little necks as far as I'm concerned. The ones that weren't asleep at the wheel were running around worrying about getting theirs. And I'll admit it; that was my generation. The Baby-Boomers were raised during the '60s. There's no excuse for the way we sold out.

"But it's like back then, you didn't usually get too many people rising up against the gods, or against kingship. They were cool with replacing the king with another king, and gods with other gods, but real revolutions have been a long time coming.

"Democracy was a damn historic revolution and the moneygrubbers let the crooks they elected piss that revolution away every single day. They're throwing away the only chance we had at really breaking with kingship once and for all. I mean, I'm just an electrician with a GED that's read a few books and I can see it.

"Five thousand years of kings and asshole royalty. Then what? Communism? Dead. Socialism? Nobody knows what the hell that is anymore. Democracy has been the only real chance we've had to break the stranglehold on our necks."

Max took a look at the clay tablets on the cover of the history textbook, more enigmatic slabs of earth that had been peppered with cuneiform. "Considering how long ago it all started," he said. "You really think any of them can do a thing to stop it?"

"So, what, we don't have civilization without kingship?" Bud threw up his hands in frustration. "I mean, really? No civilization without fascism? No civilization without some rat-bastard pulling my chain? Bullshit! History may be saying it, but I ain't buying it. This garbage ain't in our natures, being a damn peon toiling in the fields ain't our destiny."

"No, going straight underwater is our destiny."

"Well, that book said the eggheads don't know what ended Sumeria. They said it could have been either war or climate change. It was probably both."

"That would be pretty pathetic if we go down the same way the first civilization on Earth went down," Max said. "We didn't learn a damn thing in six thousands years? There's no excuse for that."

Bud was back on his feet again, apparently unable to keep still from his righteous indignation. It was more than that. "And all those moneygrubbers out there, they're gonna have the nerve to be surprised when it happens too. I mean, even a dog knows better than to shit where he sleeps. You telling me the moneygrubbers are no smarter than a damn dog?"

He stopped in mid-rant after his keen eyes caught sight of something amiss. A homeless person he had noticed earlier suddenly spoke into his wrist in between swigs from the bottle. Though the man was quick and completely nonchalant, Bud still saw it.

"Damn, I can barely see the sky," Max said. "Why the hell do I live in a city where when I look up half the time all I see is clouds and buildings?"

Bud lightened up, becoming animated in his gestures, all the time keeping an eye on the suspect man across the street. "Because this is where the action is, soldier," he said. "Oh yeah, we're living the high-life up in here. Rome, Constantinople, Babylon, they were villages compared to Leper's Island. The Paper Aristocracy has to have their nightclubs and restaurants and Broadway shows, and five thousand dollar call girl services. Take it all in, son. You're at the center of the universe."

"Lucky me."

Bud's steely stare became locked on a grubby, tattered man walking up the stairs toward the pair.

"You kidding me?" he said. "I love New York. I'd never live anywhere else."

"Hey guy," the man said as he rubbed his greasy cheek. "Got any spare change for a vet?"

Bud winked at Max, inviting him to pay particular attention. "Nobody panhandles around here lately because of that damn mayor's new 'get tough on begging' crap. Don't want to hassle the tourists. The cops will lock you up and throw away the key. But then, you would know that if you were for real."

"I don't know what you're talking about. I'm just looking to score a bottle."

Bud erupted in a mordant laughter that ended in the classic head shake of pity. "You're gonna have to become a way better liar than that if you think you're going to make it in undercover ops."

The intelligence agent was momentarily confused about what to do next, continue the ruse or attack.

"Look, Max, he just got busted and now he's all embarrassed. That's 'cause calling them out gives you power over them. You tell their secrets out loud and they go from being the lions they wanna be..." Bud gave the undercover CIG agent an icy glare. "... to the sniveling little rodents they really are."

Realizing that further pretense was pointless, the agent folded over the lapel of his jacket and spoke into the tiny communicator on the back. "Move in, move in."

Bud was casual but lightning fast when he lifted his foot and brought it down on the right leg of the agent. The angle was awkward and the force was deft, causing the man's knee to let out a nauseating crack that everyone close enough could hear.

"Ah!" he screamed, falling back onto the cement, grabbing at his leg.

Max was wondering if Bud hadn't overreacted until he saw a small tranquilizer gun in the agent's hand. The agent was rolling down the stairs and firing wildly. The hollow sound of the air pistol went unnoticed as two of the darts hit bystanders also waiting for the library to open. They fell unconscious.

"Your tax dollars at work, Max. How you liking that?"

"What the hell's going on here? I know special ops when I see them."

Bud searched both sides of the street for the undercover agent's backup team. He knew what to look for. They would be nondescript people in their twenties who would appear as regular as your next door neighbor. He promptly spotted a man in a sports jersey and a baseball cap rushing toward them.

The agent running close behind in a t-shirt and jeans yelled into his wrist. "Agent down, agent down, seal the parameter, now!"

"We'd better get the hell out of here," Bud said.

Quickly but calmly they scooped up their books and descended the stairs, pushing through a ring of curious New Yorkers. They hurried in the opposite direction once they hit the sidewalk.

Max could tell Bud was genuinely afraid. "What the hell!"

"They're coming for your ass, soldier," Bud said.

"Oh yeah? Well all they're going to get is a crusty old first sergeant," Max said as he picked up his pace.

By then Bud was at a dead run. He and Max made a panicked dash down the rest of the block, through the next intersection, unaware of an old brown van that was shadowing them. It kept pace with the two men until it had to stop behind a long line of traffic.

Two CIG agents were in pursuit on foot barely half a block behind. "Targets are running!" one of them said. "Targets are running! 7th Street and 42nd!"

"Are they still back there?" Max yelled.

"What do you think?" Bud never looked over his shoulder.

They were too busy to react when a spine-shivering squeal of tires caught the attention of everybody else on the block. It was the brown van with Ben Spiritdancer behind the wheel. He had swung out of the stalled lines of cars into the open lane of oncoming traffic.

Taking advantage of the red light at the intersection, Ben gunned the powerful engine until he reached an alley in the middle of the block. After a sliding turn, he cut off several cars to get into the opening of the alley right in front of the two agents. The men were surprised by the van and the side door that slid open as Ben screeched to a halt.

"Go in peace, gentlemen," John said, presenting two police-issue tasers and firing them at the agents. The gun in his right hand shot two tiny darts attached to wires charged with up to 50,000 volts of electricity into the thigh of the second agent. The darts from the gun in his left hand hit the other pursuer directly in the chest. As soon as the second round of darts had brought the other agent down, John threw the spent weapons onto their subconscious bodies and slammed the side doors shut. Ben jammed the accelerator to the floorboard, sending the van careening down the cluttered alley.

While he was ramming dumpsters and scaring unsuspecting homeless men in the alley, on the street Max and Bud were reaching the intersection at the end of the block.

"Turn here, Bud!"

After rounding the corner, Max and Bud were sprinting down a sidewalk that was less densely packed with people. Max was about to quicken his pace but was waylaid by a man who was coming out of a shop, a man standing well over six feet tall and weighing more than three hundred pounds. Their collision rocked Max's slender, half-starved frame and sent him flying into a recently stocked fruit stand. Oranges, apples, and grapefruits were rolling around the feet of a stunned group of onlookers.

The man Max clobbered had fallen slowly across the remains of two demolished tables amid a mound of squashed fruit. His vision momentarily blurred by the nasty body check, Max instinctively began groping for the books hidden under his shirt. His pileup had knocked both of them under a car idling on the street in front of the fruit stand. He made a mad scramble for the Gilgamesh epic, then the history textbook, snatching them from under the tire before the car eased forward. He leapt back to his feet, unable to locate Bud until he was more than halfway down the block.

"Damn that old man can run."

He looked to the intersection behind him, at first finding nothing. But then, over all the cars and trucks speeding by, he located the rest of the CIG team in a black minivan pushing through the intersection with the horn honking the entire time.

Max spun back around to locate Bud; instead he saw the old brown van blocking his view. Ben was trying to enter traffic from the alley in the middle of the block, held up by a continuous line of cars.

Max was jumping up and down among the tumult he had caused, stretching for a glimpse of the driver of the van. The pedestrians on the sidewalk parted for a moment, long enough for Max to see the emotionless scowl Ben always donned when he was on an operation. Ben looked past Max, to the oncoming van full of CIG operatives, and knew he had to make a quick decision.

Without hesitating, he turned onto the sidewalk toward Bud. His horn honking continuously, sending frightened pedestrians running, he pushed the van down the tight walkway.

Max started running again.

Bud took a quick look back to find the front grill of the van bearing down on him. He rolled toward the front door of a restaurant, landing on his stomach in the archway. With the side door of the van sliding open, Ben rammed through the metal polls of the awning over the entrance to the eatery and came to a stop in front of Bud.

The old man growled like an animal at the inside of the van. He was about to jump to his feet and take flight but something about John's casual smile assured him it was safe. Bud flashed Max a wily grin, grabbed John's extended arms, and lifted himself into the back of the van.

John jumped out of the van and slammed the door shut. "Max, Max Stiner!" he yelled. "You have to come with us, they'll kill you!"

Ben bullied the van down the sidewalk to the cross street. In the clear, he swung around the corner and accelerated out of sight.

Max chose to run, feeling the CIG minivan close behind and presented with a threatening stranger ahead. He made a mad dash for the alley from which Ben had just emerged. He came around the corner of the building to find himself face to face with the chrome bumper of a two ton delivery truck. The driver stomped on the brakes, but Max was unable to avoid the slow moving behemoth. He was thrown back several feet from the collision, finally coming to rest in the mouth of the alley.

"Damn it!" John said. He moved toward Max, his hand on the automatic pistol under his jacket, as Max suddenly jumped back up, books still in hand.

"Max Stiner! You gotta come with us!" John yelled. He watched Max stagger around in front of the delivery truck for a moment, before disappearing through the space between the truck and the wall of the alley.

The driver of the truck jumped down from the cab to yell after Max, though by then he was running at full speed. Panicked, the driver got back into the driver's seat and lurched the rig forward.

The minivan stopped in front of the alley just as the truck was pulling away. The door flew open and six CIG agents in plain clothes piled out. John averted his gaze, turning toward the street.

He quickly scoured the block for a certain body type: average height, 165 pounds, brown eyes, and brown hair. He passed over several who fit the description before concentrating on one in particular. The man was on the sidewalk across the street, shadowing an elderly woman and concentrating on her purse.

John backed up to the storefront behind him until he was leaning against the cool brick wall. He closed his eyes; his breathing became shallow and rapid. He began humming an ancient Hopi chant, almost inaudibly at first. He slid his hands into his pockets and stamped his foot several times.

Just yards away, the CIG agents were about to enter the alley where Max had escaped, their tranquilizer guns ready, when one of them suddenly looked across the street. He located the shifty man John had singled out.

"That's him!" the agent yelled. He ran out of the alleyway into the street without looking. He dodged through the stalled traffic, undeterred. Four of his cohorts joined him in his pursuit. The guilty man sensed he was being chased once the first agent got close and took off like a shot.

"What the hell are you doing?!" the remaining agent said. "He's down here! You all saw him go down there with your own eyes, where are you going?!" The agent took out a laminated picture of Max to compare to the man the other agents were now chasing down the block at a dead run.

The agent threw up his arms as he searched the rest of the street for reinforcements. There were none. He opened his cell phone to report the situation just as the left side of his coat was shredded by the spontaneous detonation of two of the bullets in the clip of his automatic pistol. In the middle of recovering, he was met with a size eleven shoe in the face. The blow laid him out on the sidewalk.

"There's always one holdout," John said, rummaging through the agent's pockets. He came up with a pistol and the radio from his belt. He continued down the empty passage, hitting the redial on a cell phone on his hip.

"He's running, hard," he said into his earpiece.

"We can try him at his apartment," Ben said. "Otherwise Gina needs us in DC, we have to keep moving."

"What about his friend?"

"He says they just met this morning. He doesn't know anything about Stiner or how to find him."

"Well, the guy he hobbled got a real good look at him. Does he realize what kind of danger he's in?"

"He's starting to, Son. Pick up is at the alternate location in ten."

"Roger that."

Three streets over, Max stumbled out of the alley onto the sidewalk; his shoulder, the point of contact with the truck bumper, screaming in pain. He slowed his pace to a fast walk while he checked the ribs on his right side for breakage.

He had the translation of the epic and the history textbook tucked under his arm, weaving clumsily through the pedestrians. The faces of the people he rushed by were becoming a blur as he grew more and more disoriented. Through failing eyes he spotted another alley entrance and went deep into the deserted passage.

Powerful flashes of General Masterson's superior smirk ripped through his mind, bringing him to his knees. His body was aching and his head was throbbing, but Max knew he had to keep moving.

He raised his head again, his eyes drawn to a hastily scrawled line of graffiti on the wall across from him: "Faith is the refuge of the weak minded!"

He struggled to his feet toward the other end of the alley.

"This city is going to fucking kill me!" he roared.

Less than a half hour later, Max burst through the door of his tenement shouting curses at the top of his lungs. He threw the books down onto the top of a stack of newspapers on his tiny dining room table and stormed in to the kitchen sink.

After splashing water on his face, he picked up the receiver of his phone, paused, then slammed it back down.

Bud's rants, the look on the agent's face when Bud shattered his knee, Ben's stony expression, they all kept turning over in his Max's head. His close call, coupled with the very idea that somebody would try to abduct him, had him more panicked than he had been in years. It wasn't until his old battle composure began to return that he realized that he couldn't stay in his apartment.

He stomped into his bedroom, first to his dresser drawers. A quick stop in the bathroom and he emerged with a backpack full of his clothes and toiletries. He grabbed the Gilgamesh epic and the history textbook he had acquired from Bud on his way out the door, jamming them into the bag.

Mere minutes had elapsed before the two CIG agents from the street advanced cautiously on the door to Max's apartment, tranquilizer guns drawn. They entered the apartment and systematically searched each room one by one.

"Sonofabitch, I'm glad I'm not the one who has to report this to the General."

"Well I'm not telling him," the other agent insisted. "I'd like to live 'til the end of the day, thanks."

The second agent locked and closed Max's front door on the way out. "We'll send a text and tell the General that it doesn't look like the target has come back."

"And then what?"

"Then we set up surveillance and sit tight."

John allowed enough time for the agents to get to the stairs before he picked the lock on the door. He and Ben slipped into Max's ransacked living room.

"We better get off this island before Masterson has the entire town looking for us too," John said.

"We just need to get a good read on where his head is at," Ben said, drifting from the tiny front room to the even more cramped kitchen.

John leaned into the bedroom, noting the propped up pillows and cluttered nightstand on one side of Max's bed.

"Hey Pop, it looks like he spends most of his time in here."

Ben was careful to sit in the exact same spot Max had been just hours before.

"Bud's OK now with disappearing to Philadelphia for a few days until this all blows over," John said, searching through Max's closet. "I don't think he really believed he was in danger until he talked to his landlord."

"The CIG is moving fast if they got his address already." Ben closed his eyes, reclining on the propped up pillows. "Now let me concentrate, Son, maybe we can find Max Stiner before Masterson's thugs and get the hell out of this city."

4

Peter regained consciousness with his temples throbbing and his eyes burning out of their sockets. Graydin's voice rang in his aching head: "You're a walking cliché, a dinosaur..."

He threw his legs over the side of his bed, washing down some pills from an aspirin bottle on his nightstand with the last of a glass of water. He tried to calculate how long it had been since he was gripped by such self-abusive impulses. It had to be at least since he had traded in his addiction to alcohol for his much older addiction to the often perverse thrill of the "big scoop."

Peter had never imbibed before cancer took his wife, despite the stereotype of the hard drinking newspaper reporter. It had been in the years following her death that drink became the only thing that could dull his constant self-recrimination over what happened.

The possibility that he had allowed that older addiction to wrong a friend of Barbara's had Peter far more debilitated than the hangover. Although he had only the classified document and Simmons's message on the back to go from, he knew he had good reason to feel guilty over his story about Phil, even if he wasn't certain exactly why.

The phone rang for the third time. He was sure it was his editor with a carefully negotiated schedule of appearances on the usual cable news programs. No doubt capped off at the end of the week by the Sunday morning talk shows.

It was indeed what he had done the prior three times his anonymous source, Mr. Graydin, came to him with a juicy inside scoop. This time Peter had already decided to decline, regardless of the consequences.

An hour later, his face unshaven and wearing the same suit pants and shirt he slept in, Peter slipped into the Washington DC police station charged with handling Phil Simmons's suicide. He did his best to blend in with the beat cops and their prisoners buzzing around the main hall, but an observant officer noticed his ragged condition and immediately confronted him.

"Hey, what's your business here?"

"I'm Peter Anderson. I'm here to see... uh...uh... Detective Gianni."

When the officer didn't immediately react, Peter fished around in his pants pocket for his press credentials. "He'll want to see me."

The officer placed a call that summoned one of the few contacts Peter still maintained in the local police force. He had no doubt that the junior detective had been chosen by his superiors to feed Peter information when it was beneficial to an investigation.

"Marc," Peter said. "Can we talk?"

"I'm up to my neck in it right now, Peter. Damn, what happened to you?"

"I need to call in that favor. Off the record, I need a look at the autopsy report on Phil Simmons."

"Uh, look Peter, that's a seriously high-profile case."

"I know; I broke the story, Marc. I'm the one who started your investigation, I just want to follow-up on something. For me, not for the column."

"It's not my case. But from what I hear, the suicide looked pretty cut and dried."

"So they keep saying."

Soon the general clamor of the main hall was pierced by Billy's distinctive Southern drawl.

"He would never have touched a gun!" she said at the top of her voice. "I've known the man twenty-five years for Christ's sake! He would never even allow a gun in his house!"

"Please, ma'am," the officer escorting her said. "My captain told you that we will look into your concerns, but right now you need to go home."

They walked up to where Peter and Marc were talking.

"Ms. Billy—"

She quieted Peter with a slap to his face.

"You lying scum!" she said.

Marc prevented her from moving in for another blow by taking hold of her tiny frame, her anger and bulging backpack making it a more difficult task than it appeared.

"You people went too far when you went after Phil!" she said. "I'm going to destroy you for this! I'm going to make you wish you never put his name in print!"

"That's assault, Peter," Marc said. "You want to press charges?"

"Yeah, Peter, do you want to press charges?" Billy said through gritted teeth.

"Absolutely not."

Marc released her; Billy stormed past Peter, out of the building.

"I'll be in touch," Peter said before following her. "Help me out and I'll owe you more than one."

Peter rushed through the doors to find Billy on the sidewalk calling a taxi on her cell phone.

"Ms. Billy, please, if I could just have a moment of your time?"

"You better get away from me," she said. "You're gonna get clocked again."

"I don't believe he killed himself either."

She hung up her cell phone without reaching the cab company. "Yeah right," she said, hurrying down the sidewalk.

"No, really, that's why I'm here." Peter did his best to match her determined pace. "I hoped to get a look at the autopsy report."

"There wasn't even going to be an autopsy! But I raised hell, and threatened to go public if they didn't do at least that. I have the governmental authority of a three star general and I can't get anybody to listen to what I'm saying!"

"You have to understand, I have to ask this, did you have any reason to believe he did what I accused him of in my column?"

"Bit late for that, isn't it? I'm promising you right now that every single one of you hacks and sellouts down there at that rag you call a newspaper are going to regret the day you ever heard of Phil Simmons."

As furious as she was, once Billy acknowledged the despair hanging around Peter, the urge to smack his face abated. He looked at her with such an expression of sorrow and helplessness that it gave her a shiver.

"What happened to you?" she finally asked.

Peter opened his mouth in a vain attempt to explain except nothing intelligible came out. He could only dig a folded piece of paper out of his pocket and hand it to her. She skimmed it from top to bottom. Detecting the writing on the back, she flipped it over.

"What the hell is this?" She recognized Phil Simmons's handwriting immediately. "'Nobody deserves to be a guaranteed fatality'? I don't know what you're trying to pull, but if this is some kind of con–"

"Is that his handwriting?"

Billy looked Peter over. "If you're jerking me around on this, I swear to God..." She read the lines Phil wrote several time before turning the piece of paper over again to examine the document more closely.

"The Top Secret stamps look genuine," she said. "If it is real, the maniacs over at the Justice Department will drop you in a long dark hole."

The columns recording massive amounts of money going to what was obviously a top secret program caught her attention. "I don't know what the "WRC" or the "CIG" are, but I know an authentic departmental expense report when I see one." She took one more look at Phil's cryptic message. "It's his handwriting."

"And the CIG?"

"No, no, I've never heard of it."

Peter gazed up into the sky for inspiration, hazy headed and unsure as to how to proceed.

"You look like shit," she said.

"I don't know what to do now. My contact at the White House confirmed the CIG's existence by telling me that I'm not important enough to know about it."

"I'll bet I'm important enough. And now I want to know what the hell a 'guaranteed fatality' is."

"You get caught accessing information you're not supposed to and they'll try to implicate you."

"How can you be sure I wasn't in it with him?"

"Because you haven't been in the country longer than a few months since before Hurricane Katrina."

"So you did do *some* homework."

"Just not enough. If what I wrote contributed in any way to what happened, I want you to know how truly sorry I am."

"Phil Simmons did not shoot himself, period!" Tears were filling in her eyes. "Something is going on here and I'm going to find out what it is! If that means accessing the government database and getting the rundown on this CIG then that's what's going to happen!"

Billy went from blind rage to sorrowful crying once again, something she had done countless times since hearing of Phil's death. Peter waited quietly while she wept, the pangs of guilt bringing the taste of brandy to his lips.

Billy cried a moment more then proceeded to get angry once again. "Where'd you get that trash you printed the other day?"

"Anonymous source."

"Bullshit, who told you those lies about Phil?"

"I only know him as Graydin."

"Have you ever dealt with him before?"

Peter looked down at his scuffed shoes. "Three times."

"Who the hell is he? Is he government?"

"I don't know. I wrote the stories because they all checked out. They were all verifiable. I guess I was too desperate to care where they came from."

Momentarily surprised by Peter's candor, Billy looked him over, then she did the same to the surrounding street.

"C'mon," she said, searching the block for a place for them to talk.

Peter followed her half in a daze into a busy eatery around the corner from the police station. Uniformed officers occupied most of the tables in the main room up front, but Billy was able to find a free spot near the back. She dug out her laptop computer from her backpack.

"Can I get you something to drink to start?" a waitress asked.

Peter used a napkin from the dispenser on his waxy face. "Coffee, please."

"I'll take some OJ," Billy said. She set up her computer and it automatically located a wireless Internet signal.

"OK, Phil jumps off a building or pops some pills and kills himself, but he would never use a gun." She called up the FEMA database. "It's because of all the killing we saw when we were in Africa."

"More than half of men who commit suicide do it with a gun," Peter said.

"So what, I don't care about the stats. This is crap and I'm going to get to the bottom of it. And if you're involved, you will regret it."

"I'm involved alright. What did they say about the autopsy?"

"They said it proves he did it to himself. They're closing the case. Why do you think I was raising hell?"

She input the letters "CIG" under the search prompt. A page appeared containing a long list of results. She tabbed down to the heading that read: "Civil Integrated Group."

"'A small group of consultants specializing in urban and suburban emergency management scenarios for the purposes of planning and reaction assessment.'"

"What?" he asked.

She spun the computer around far enough for Peter to read the paragraph for himself.

"So it's a think tank?" he said.

Billy found a pencil and paper in her bag. "A think tank focusing on 'urban and suburban emergency management,' and I've never heard of it? Yeah, right. There's a Virginia address here."

"The only way I'm going to be able to get more than government doubletalk is—"

"By doing something ill-advised?" Peter said.

She called up a screen for classified inquiries and entered "WRC" as the waitress brought their drinks.

"You two ready to order?"

"I better, I get hypoglycemic," Billy said. "I'll take the avocado and Swiss with sprouts, please."

"I'll take more coffee," Peter said. "Just bring the pot."

The prompt was asking for her security code again, to confirm her intent to proceed. Without hesitating she typed her code in again and pressed the enter key. The Great Seal of the United States slowly appeared; a highly classified menu was to follow. That gave way to a column of headings of which "WRC, "ESC," and "OPERATION CLEANSWEEP" were only a few.

Simultaneously, in a computer-filled room in rural Virginia, a young CIG operative responded to a high-pitched computer alert and a computer screen flashing two words: "Unauthorized Access." He was typing wildly with one hand and picking up a phone to report the cyber-incursion with the other.

Billy's attempting to access the "CLEANSWEEP" menu item caused the screen on her monitor to go black and the laptop to go into its restart sequence.

"What happened?" Peter asked, nursing his cup.

She showed him the restarting computer.

"I don't know much about computers," he said. "But I would say that that isn't good."

"It means they have something to hide, and I'm going to find out what it is."

The waitress brought Billy's sandwich and a pot of coffee. Peter poured another cup, downing it as fast as the scalding temperature would allow.

"So what's the deal with you?" Billy asked between bites. "From what I hear you had a good reputation. Phil used to read your columns."

Peter shifted uncomfortably. He hadn't expected that morning to come face to face with one of the many people he had wronged.

"The evidence was airtight," he said. "He may not have killed himself, but the evidence says he did embezzle money."

"That's bull too," Billy said, at a higher volume than she intended. "I haven't seen all this 'airtight' evidence. But by the time I get done, you're going to write a retraction of all of it."

Peter's initial spurt of energy was fizzling out, allowing the hangover to return. "Whatever you want," he said.

"You know there's something seriously wrong here. And if there is something wrong here, then there might be something wrong with your other scoops too. That's a lot of devastated lives over your columns. I'm thinking you couldn't live with that in a million years."

"No, I couldn't. Let me do some checking on this."

Peter extended his shaking hand; Billy hesitated before giving him the address. Though he had managed to avoid eye contact up to that point, now there was no escaping her resolute stare.

"Are you a pawn or a player, Peter Anderson?"

"Who's more qualified to get something out of this?" he said. "You go poking around and you could get yourself hurt."

She finally handed it over. "You don't worry about me. You just need to worry about getting your act together, and keeping that document safe. I'm your confidential informant now. And you're going to be my source in the media, only this time you're going to print the truth."

"You have to assume that they're watching you," Peter said before he downed the last of his cup and stood awkwardly. "You have to assume your phones are bugged; mine too, for that matter."

"We need a way to leave messages without anybody knowing..." Billy thought a moment then snatched the piece of paper from his hand to jot something down. She ripped off a corner of the sheet of paper for him to do the same and handed the pieces back.

"First one is my cell," she said. "Second number is a friend but she doesn't know anything about all this so you better not use your name. And call from a payphone or public place. You can leave a message and I'll find a phone and call you back. Damn, she's probably taking the news about Phil pretty hard."

Peter was finally able to settle on a way for Billy to surreptitiously contact him. "This is the number to my bar. Ned doesn't hear too well but he'll put somebody on to take a message. Say it's for Jerry... Ned started calling me Jerry years ago when I first went in there and I never corrected him."

"Would you contact me after you follow up on the address? I haven't even been home yet. I came down here straight off the plane from South Carolina. Damn lot of good it did."

"You saw what Phil wrote. Did he know my wife? Did you know my wife?"

Billy stopped inhaling her sandwich long enough to give Peter an earnest answer. "I never met Barbara Anderson. I have heard of her, though. She got a lot done in this town to help people. So did Phil. It wouldn't surprise me a bit if they knew each other."

"I have to go. I'll be in touch."

Billy left the little café not long after Peter, gobbling down the rest of her sandwich during a short cab ride to a convenience store near her apartment. Her intention was to replenish the stock of edibles she kept in her backpack, before returning home for the first time in months.

What Billy found while wandering through the rows of snack foods and last-minute purchases only served to worsen her already dismal mental state. Before long she was standing in the middle of the aisle reading the label on a package of nuts, doing some computations in her head.

"Over four dollars for barely a half day's allowance of protein and omega 3," she muttered. "Highway robbery!"

Her fatigued brain flashed on an article she had read on the flight from Japan, about the millions of inner-city Americans who were now forced to feed their children out of a store just like the one in which she stood, simply because it was the only place to go in their neighborhood.

"You warned them, Phil," she whispered to herself. "We let you down... I let you down..."

Despite the fact that she was now certain Phil had been actively working to keep her away from him and the United States, there would be no separating the guilt she felt over abandoning her old friend, from the guilt she felt over abandoning the country they fought together to save.

Billy looked on in a virtual daze while the cashier was ringing up the pricy bill for the few things she finally decided to purchase. She got into her waiting cab experiencing more trepidation over her meeting with the president than she had since hearing about Phil's death.

She became fixated on how she would keep her mouth in check in the Oval Office, after Haiti and Japan and Phil. After so many promises of change made by a presidential candidate that even she voted for long distance. The question of whether her friend would still be alive if those promises had been kept would now plague her, she feared, until she said something far too honest.

The cab in which she rode rounded the corner, giving Billy her first view of the apartment building that she had paid rent on for almost ten years, but actually inhabited for far less. No matter how unfamiliar it may have become, at that point she was willing to take any refuge she could find.

She decided while getting out of the backseat that the building was nicer than she remembered, for some reason. Cleaner. Paying the driver she noticed that the front doors to the building were flapping open.

She paused for a better look at who might be flailing around in the entrance, although she already had a good idea. She threw her backpack over both her shoulders so she could get to the door as quickly as possible. It was her neighbor Mrs. Hawkins.

An elderly widow more than eighty years old, Mrs. Hawkins was wrestling a two-wheeled grocery cart through the heavy double doors. They kept closing on her, trapping the cart and preventing her from proceeding. Billy rushed to the woman's side. She took control of the cart while holding the door open.

"Billy, it's so good to see you my dear! Thank you!" Mrs. Hawkins leaned in for a quick hug.

"No problem. It's great to see you too, darlin'. What are you doing out alone? I thought the doc said that was a no, no."

"Nope, I saw him the other week and he said it would be good for me to get out."

Billy knew she was lying; she just didn't have the energy to call her on it. She dragged the cart past the mailboxes, triggering Mrs. Hawkins's spotty memory.

"I have some of your mail, dear. Phil left it the last time he dropped by."

Billy was unable to keep her eyes from watering up.

"What's wrong?"

"Oh God, you haven't heard." Billy helped her friend onto the elevator and selected the floor.

"Heard what?"

"It's Phil. He's... darlin' he's dead."

"What? No, I just saw him not two days ago. No, I don't believe it." Mrs. Hawkins started breathing heavily, fanning herself. Billy took her arm to steady her.

"I'm sorry for springing it on you like that darlin'."

They got off the elevator on Mrs. Hawkins's floor. "I don't understand," she said.

Mrs. Hawkins's arthritic hands struggled with her keys until Billy gently took them from her and opened the front door.

"It's a big sorry mess, Vivian," Billy said.

Vivian waddled into her living room, immediately taking off her sweater and collapsing into her favorite chair with a sigh of relief. Billy carried the groceries into the kitchen. She was careful to keep watch through the open bar area into the living room, to make sure her friend was calming down.

Studying the wrinkles on Vivian's elegantly aged face had Billy hoping she would look that good at eighty. In truth, she had been envious of Vivian Hawkins's life since the day they met.

"Let me put these groceries away for you, dear, it won't take a sec."

Her energy spent, the exhausted woman made a feeble attempt at rising. "What happened, Billy? What happened to poor Phil? He was here just the other day. He ended up leaving without your mail, though. I meant to call him but I figured he would be back."

"You just relax and I'll get you a cold drink."

After working for most of her life as a secretary for an insurance company, Vivian had outlived her husband and one son. Although her stubborn insistence on living in her own apartment made it seem as if she was an abandoned senior citizen, there were other sons, daughters, and grandchildren who all revered and loved her. If she died that day she could say that her life was complete. That was what always left Billy envious. It appeared she wasn't the only one.

Vivian's breathing was beginning to steady by the time Billy brought her a glass of lemonade. She drank deeply.

"Feeling better?"

"Tell me. What happened to Phil?"

"They say he committed suicide, Viv, with a gun, no less. It's just crazy."

"What? Phil was sad, but suicide?"

Billy sat in her usual place on the couch, across from a wall plastered with photographs of Vivian's long life and extended family. "What do you mean sad? I thought he was just picking up my mail, I didn't realize you two had talked."

"He would sit there for hours, right where you are on the divan, and look at my pictures," Vivian said between softening gasps. "We'd talk sometimes, about all kinds of things. Other times he would just sit. I got the feeling he was taking a rest, you know, getting away from the world out there. I didn't mind, I enjoyed his company. He was a very well-traveled and well-spoken man."

Billy was all too familiar with the collage of photographs that fascinated Phil so completely. They were snapshots of Vivian's life, from her time as a young working woman in the 1950s, all the way to birthday parties with her grandchildren that year. Billy quickly deduced why he couldn't take his eyes off of them, she usually couldn't. She went from anger to tears once again.

Vivian raised her arms. "Oh Billy, come here." Billy knelt in front of her friend and cried in her arms.

"It's going to be OK, my dear." Vivian looked up at the photos of her family, fully aware of how they impacted both Phil and Billy. "You know, people like you and Phil are heroes. In most of the stories he told me, you were the star, and you were sacrificing everything to help people. Now see, that's going to take its toll on your life. There's no way it couldn't. But I bet all those you've helped would thank you from the bottom of their hearts for that sacrifice."

Billy took several tissues from a nearby dispenser then sat back down on the couch. "They're trying to smear him, Viv. He's dead and they're calling him a criminal, after everything he's done. Are they going to do that to me when I'm gone? Is that going to be my legacy too?"

"That's nonsense, Billy. I know you'll make this right."

Billy used the tissue to clean herself up.

"I only knew him for a few months, but Phil was one of the most principled men I have ever met. And you know I've been around a while. If someone is accusing him of something bad then I'd be willing to bet it's a lie."

"I'm going to prove it. No matter what."

"You look beat, dear. Have you even been home yet?"

"Not in over six months. I don't even know why I bother keeping the place. If it wasn't for you, I'd probably give it up. I live in tents and hotels anyway."

"Well I'm glad you're back."

Billy gave Vivian another hug before throwing her backpack over her shoulder. Vivian looked as if she was trying to get up.

"You rest, darlin'. I'll let myself out. I'll be in town for a while. We'll get together for a meal. I'll cook."

"I need to go to the bathroom."

Billy moved quickly to help her when she tried to stand for the second time. Vivian hobbled toward the bathroom upon gaining her balance.

"Don't forget your mail there on the table."

Billy stopped by the table to gather the month's worth of mail.

"You know why everyone is so anxious for the future to come?" Vivian said. "...because they don't have the courage to handle the here and now. But you do, Billy, that's the strength you have. You go out in the world and face the 'here and now' so that the children will have a future. I can't think of anything more important than that."

As usual, Vivian found a way to make Billy feel better.

"Besides, there's no point in worrying about the future anyway," Vivian said as she neared the bathroom door. "It'll come whether we're all prepared for it or not, usually when we're not. But it shouldn't be something to be afraid of.

"I can remember when we still had to go outside to pee. I count my blessings when they come by. And thank God for them too." Vivian closed the bathroom door behind her.

Billy stepped onto the elevator haunted by the knowledge that the future Vivian was referring to wasn't going to be very kind, for anybody. She would never have gotten into all that with her, what would be the point? How could she explain how different the world would be when Vivian's grandchildren turned eighty?

Billy felt particularly out of place when she got off the elevator on her floor. The front door of the apartment she had kept for so long looked to her like any other in the hall. As if she was merely visiting a friend, not returning home after half a year.

Inside, the feeling of estrangement persisted. She put her backpack down on her desk and fell into her favorite chair. She glanced over the ceiling-high bookshelves packed with all her favorite volumes, the provincial white mantle, the hardwood floors and the tall windows, struggling to recall the days when she looked forward to coming back to it all.

The empty apartment she had at one time adored was compelling her to face the fact that although she had traveled the world several times, her life – like Phil's before he died – was going nowhere.

Lingering in the shower, Billy obsessed on the document Peter had received and the message written in a hand she had seen in field notes and reports for over twenty years, since she and Phil started in the international aid business.

"Guaranteed fatalities my ass!" she said.

A cup of tea in hand, she returned to her chair carrying her mail and her laptop. She ripped open envelopes and read bills for things she hadn't used in six months.

She wondered when she was in Japan why Phil had missed sending his regular package full of mail. She assumed it was because he knew she was coming home. Several letters into the pile she discovered the real reason.

She came to an envelope that was blank on the front with a small, solid object inside. She turned it over and a flash drive dropped into her hand.

She attached the drive to her computer to access it. A video file launched immediately. It began with a tight shot of Phil sitting at the desk in his house, his suit perfectly pressed, his face a wreck.

Billy was crushed when she saw her oldest friend staring helplessly at her from the computer screen. Then a muffled mess of words came blasting through the speakers of the laptop that almost sent her flying out of her chair.

She remembered that she had blown out the computer speakers in Thailand trying to keep a group of children occupied with some cartoons from the Internet. Though the volume was turned all the way up, she was still unable to understand what Phil was saying.

She paused the video to retrieve a pair of headphones from her backpack. Phil's guilty face watching her, she prepared herself a second time, plugged in the headphones, and pushed "resume."

"I'm sending you this, Billy, because I'm a coward," Phil began again. "I've worked for your respect for so long that I couldn't stand in the same room as you and admit what I am about to admit. I just couldn't do it. They're coming for me, I know it, and I wanted you to know a few things before they do.

"First, for the past seven years I have been lying to you. It's a fact that as long as we have known each other I could never keep a secret from you. But this wasn't just a secret; this was my worst nightmare come true.

"I've known about the Continuity in Government, I've known about General Masterson and his crusade to insure the survival of the United States of America, since not long after the Indonesian Tsunami, and I refused to speak.

"Whatever they're going to accuse me of, I didn't do it. You know me. But I had to confess to you what I am guilty of. I just couldn't do it to your face. I couldn't do it to the country, either. Like I said, Billy, I'm a coward.

"I did just about the worst thing I could have done in your eyes. I let them stop me. It's not important why, but you should know that I never wanted to give up. I had no choice."

Billy could see from his condition that he was terrified.

"I originally sent you this to tell you to leave this alone, walk away. To tell you that if you make them kill you, then they win. I wanted to tell you to go back overseas and forget about all this. But I know how you are.

"Right now you're not a threat to them, but you'll push this until you are a threat. So I want you to contact Hector. I don't think you two have talked in a while but he's the only one that can help you now.

"But you have to be careful. They'll be watching you to make sure you go away quietly. You'll have to be careful how you make contact. And stay away from the press, it's too dangerous.

"You're the best friend I've ever had and I let you down. I couldn't protect the thing I love the most in this world, and I couldn't tell you why. But now I can.

"A sociopath by the name of General Masterson controls an agency called the Continuity in Government. Technically it's a special access program, and it's funded directly by black budgets. Its mandate is to insure the orderly and continuous survival of the government of the United States. It is in no way concerned with the well-being of the citizens of the United States. In fact, population control is one of its missions.

"We've been around the government for a lot of years, Billy, and I think we've both seen some pretty sick things handed down by a faceless bureaucracy... This goes beyond all that.

"When impending climate change and the size of the population became national security issues, you can only imagine the kinds of depraved plans these people started coming up with to 'deal' with the 'problem.' The CIG is the result of one of those plans. What we've been seeing more and more, with people stranded on rooftops and dead bodies floating in the streets, is the future of our country.

"We've known it for years, that there is no law for the monsters that prowl this rotten city. There is definitely no law for a man that doesn't exist. But whether they know about General Masterson or not, they would endorse what he does and why he does it. He insures the future of the status quo. He protects the establishment from disaster.

"And I helped him do that by keeping my mouth shut all these years. It's just something you never would have done. You have too much integrity. You're too strong to let them break you like that. You would never let them win. Don't let them win, don't let them kill you.

"And please, Billy, don't hate me for letting this happen. I didn't deserve to be the leader of the Unity Council. I never did. Somehow you have to contact Hector and Maria. They've got resources now that you couldn't even imagine."

Phil paused to prepare himself for what he suspected would be his last words to Billy. "I'm sorry for so many things. I guess I don't know where to start. But mostly I'm sorry I lied to you. And I'm sorry I turned your life upside-down the last seven years, I really had no right. But the thought of you not living to be a very old woman was something I just couldn't bare.

"I guess I didn't want to believe it, not then and not now, but you can't protect the ones you love, not really. Not from man and not from nature. Goodbye Billy."

Billy threw the headphones off, bursting into tears. She didn't want to cry again and thought she had gotten it all out. Hearing Phil's confession and seeing his frozen look of shame on the computer screen broke her again. She wept until it felt as if she had no more tears. After another look at Phil's guilty countenance, she decided it was time to get angry again, and stay that way.

She closed the video file before calmly reaching for the television remote. She switched the channels in search of one running only weather. The sound was almost deafening by the time she stopped hitting the volume button.

Carefully she followed along the wall of the apartment, from the door to the bookshelves, peeking behind paintings and under lamps. If Phil and Peter were right, then she knew what she was looking for. It would be tiny and stashed in an unlikely but accessible spot.

She came to a small table of photographs of the trusted friends she made during her time in countries like Indonesia, and the Congo, and Somalia. Phil was in many of them. They only served to underscore how few allies she had left in the United States. She moved on to the bookshelves.

The collection of her favorite books reminded her that it had been years since she had had the time to read anything other than situation reports on the most recent disaster, or projections of future disasters.

A picture sitting on one of the shelves of her and Phil in Africa gave her pause. They went there in the early '80s to do battle with the ravages of AIDS, famine, and war. And whether she could bring herself to see it or not, the fruits of their alliance could be found there and on virtually every other continent on the planet.

Billy came to the last photo in the room, in the entire apartment. It was of Hector and his wife Maria among their three children. She knew it well. She had carried a copy of the snapshot in her backpack for years, at the adamant behest of Hector's daughter.

Billy reached out to pick up the picture, first noticing that the frame was off kilter from an outline of dust on the shelf. She was almost ready to pass it off as paranoia but more than one row of books had been moved and left out of alignment with the persistent layer of dust on all the selves.

She rushed to the mantle where it didn't take her long to discover that her prized Chinese vase had been wiped clean and placed slightly off-center from where it had obviously sat for a year.

Billy momentarily panicked. Although astute paranoia had told her to look for signs of surveillance after hearing Phil's confession, in truth she didn't really expect to find anything.

She couldn't look at the videotaped confession again; Phil's words kept running over and over in her head. They were words she would never forget.

She wanted so much to grab her backpack and walk out without looking back. And she would have, if not for the vow she made to herself to redeem Phil. All she could do was curl up in a ball on her couch and stare at her living room uneasily.

Down the block from Billy's apartment building, Gina was manning a carefully chosen surveillance position. The usually ravishing African-American woman in her early thirties was looking tired and disheveled, the result of days of living in her rented sedan.

She had an adequate view of Billy's apartment window from her parking space on the street, but she had a better view of a silver mini-van parked two blocks closer to Billy's building.

It didn't matter that the windows were too tinted to see inside the van; Gina knew exactly what was going on in the rear of the vehicle. Surrounded by banks of computers and surveillance equipment, a CIG agent was monitoring Billy's every move.

She answered the ringing phone with a button on her headset. "Gina."

"What's the status," Ben said. "Is she still alive?"

"Do you need to ask?"

"Does she have any room to breathe?"

"On that score I'll have to say barely an inch. Contact will be dangerous, but leaving her running is just as bad a proposition. She bumped into Peter Anderson. At the police station, of all places."

"They're both going to get themselves killed."

"They will without some serious intervention."

"What about Phil?"

"She screamed until they did an autopsy, but gunshot residue and forensics all checked out."

"As usual."

"I'm inclined to be looking for a less conventional answer, but–"

"You mean Carlyle?"

"I don't know," she said. "Billy is as convinced as Hector that Simmons wouldn't do this, not like he did."

"We're on our way to David's now. We need to drop this guy off and we'll get down there ASAP."

"If that psycho Carlyle is in this, Ben, then I'm definitely going to need some help."

On the other side of town from Billy's apartment, the man known only as Carlyle climbed out of a black town car in front of a luxurious Georgetown office building. His blonde hair perfectly coiffed, his suit impeccable, he strutted by the uniformed door man.

Considering that he was entering the offices of what many assumed was a very exclusive call girl service, Masterson's chief assassin could have easily been mistaken for a politician. In truth, The Scarlet Woman couldn't have been further from a brothel, common or exclusive, and Carlyle could have cared less about politics.

He walked down the blood red carpet that led from the elevator to the reception desk, through a lobby that was devoid of chairs and lit only by waist high candelabras.

"I have a three o'clock with Cameron," he said.

The darkly seductive woman behind the desk acknowledged Carlyle's presence with a nod. "She is expecting you. The information you requested has been laid out in conference room B."

Carlyle knew the way. He took the chair at the end of a long table, where three rows of scientific charts and technical documents had been laid out for his review. He sifted through the records on sunspot activity and the summations of geomagnetic readings without difficulty. He quickly reviewed data on the phases of the moon and the orbits of the planets. All was as he expected. He leaned back to let the information sink in.

Just then one of the candelabras in the corner of the conference room fell over on its side. Most of the candles were extinguished when they went flying, Carlyle had to move quickly to stomp out the remaining ones before they burned the carpet. He shuddered from a burst of cold air that overtook him.

"They're still following you around," Cameron said. "After all the measures you've taken to ward them off."

"Occupational hazard."

"They're so angry at you," she said.

The tall brunette who walked into the conference room wore a long black robe and red lipstick and was one of the most beautiful women Carlyle had ever seen in his extensive travels and adventures.

It wasn't merely Cameron's beauty that was renowned in the occult world, though. It was her magickal lineage that made her the most sought after Scarlet Woman in a hundred years.

"I believe you said your target will be at 44 degrees 21 minutes North; -71 degrees 24 minutes West."   "Somewhere over northern New Hampshire," Carlyle said.

"Geomagnetic activity in that area looks to be very high today, there's only a half moon, and you're an hour out of the optimal star time window. The signs are not favorable."

"That's why I'm here." he said.

"No, that's why I'm here. The room has been prepared."

Carlyle followed the woman down a hall lined with a series of doors.

She stopped at one and opened it for Carlyle to inspect. Inside the dark room, a black mat had been placed in a precise orientation in the center of four candle stands. The black candles that burned were the only source of light and the table at the edge of the mat was the only piece of furniture.

On the table, various items had been arranged for ritual significance and for Carlyle's use later in his "working." A ritual dagger, a brass bowl, a black tassel, and the book he carried would be all he needed.

He opened his grimoire on the table and took out the photograph inside. It was a manufacturer's publicity shot of a light passenger plane. He retrieved a small envelope from his jacket and emptied it onto the open book. A small lock of hair fell out, that he was careful not to touch.

"Everything looks good, as usual," he said.

"Then it's time," Cameron closed the door and headed toward the end of the hall.

Carlyle followed her into the expansive room, undressing immediately. He began to control his breathing as he loosened his tie, taking short breathes in rapid succession. He stretched his legs and arms once he was free of his suit coat.

Cameron stood by an antique four-poster bed in the center of the room. The sheets and pillows were all black satin. She closed her eyes, raising her hands over the bed to recite a string of incomprehensible words. She threw off her robe and got into bed while the incantations continued. Then Carlyle began his part.

The words they spoke during the ritual sex that followed were from grimoires that were as old as five hundred years, written by heretics and madmen when science and magick were, for all practical purposes, indistinguishable.

Their moves and positions were highly controlled, predetermined by the purpose of the "working" they were attempting. After almost an hour, Carlyle stopped abruptly and swung his legs over the side of the bed. The purpose of their encounter was not pleasure or orgasm, it was power.

He waited there with his eyes closed, chanting incantations until one of Cameron's people arrived with a robe. Another woman arrived to help her out of bed when Cameron sat up. The women threw the robes over the chanting couple and led them back down the hall, Carlyle to the room where he had left his book, Cameron to another room to work a spell of her own.

Carlyle opened his eyes to see the ritual table in front of him. He grasped the lock of hair in his fist and clenched it, the incantations rolling off his lips at lightning speed. He found the passage in his grimoire while taking hold of the photograph of the airplane.

The section of the grimoire he read out loud was in Latin and had to be pronounced in a very specific way. It was a good thing Carlyle had done it many times before. Enough times to know that it wasn't the book or the words that would make his intended "working" successful.

He closed his eyes again, this time to focus the psi abilities he had marshaled with his session of sex magick. It was time to concentrate on the map coordinates he had given Cameron.

After repeating the incantations several more times, Carlyle opened his eyes and was looking out the sunny front windscreen of a small airplane in mid-flight. Gradually he could feel the two engines running low and steady beneath him. He could feel the plane bob up and down over stray pockets of wind turbulence. He had made contact.

Carlyle looked down to the strange hands controlling the yoke of the airplane. He turned his head to the passenger seat, where a middle-aged blonde was sitting. She smiled at him, though she wasn't smiling at Carlyle. She was smiling at her husband, the man Carlyle had temporarily possessed.

He nodded then returned to the instrument panel. "Airspeed: 65 knots, altitude: 650 feet, " Carlyle said. "Great conditions for a flight."

Carlyle dropped the photograph so that he could hold his fists out in front of him, as if he were actually grasping the yoke of the airplane. "Altitude: 650 feet," he said.

Initially when Carlyle tried to push the yoke forward, the resistance was great. The link he was attempting to forge needed time to strengthen. He continued the incantations and concentrated even harder and eventually he was able to ease his hands forward.

"600 feet, 550, 500."

The windscreen of the airplane was no longer looking at clear blue sky, the scattered treetops of the New Hampshire forest now loomed in the distance.

"450 feet," Carlyle said. "400 feet."

He struggled to keep his concentration when a pair of panicked hands came into view, clawing at the wheel of the airplane, and at the body he controlled. He could only feel the woman screaming beside him. His working didn't require sound, so the spell didn't include it.

"300 feet," he said. "250 feet. 200."

The struggling from the woman stopped as hundred-year-old oak trees rushed toward the plane at accelerating speeds.

"100 feet."

The crash jarred Carlyle from his trance and to his knees. He rested there in front of the table for a moment, employing his rhythmic breathing exercises until he felt strong enough to stand. He had one last detail to attend to.

He threw the lock of his target's hair into the bowl, a lit match in after it. The piece of highly flammable flash paper inside insured that the hair caught on fire and burned to ash. The magickal working was done.

Carlyle found his clothes hanging on the door, perfectly pressed. Once he had put on his suit coat and tied his tie, he immediately went into his pocket for his cell phone. His thumbs working in tandem, he pecked out a message to his boss: "It's done, General."

To the world, General Masterson's Washington DC lair looked like much any other office building. Nestled in the woods of rural Virginia, the Eastern Shore Complex was five stories, covered in tinted glass, and surrounded by parking lots. Not an uncommon sight in the area, with such immediate access to the nation's capital.

What none of the daily commuters passing the front gates would have suspected was that the structure also extended ten stories deep into the ground. Nor could they have known that it was a fortress built specifically to keep them all at bay.

Masterson was walking the sterile halls of the ESC when Carlyle's text activated his phone. He barely reacted to the news before moving on to other texts, from other agents, on other operations.

Usually an extremely hands-on commanding officer, it had been weeks since Masterson had taken one of his authoritative tours of his domain on the East Coast, choosing instead to ride his private elevator from his public office on the fifth floor, down to his private office on sublevel ten without seeing anyone, without anyone but his elite bodyguards even knowing he was in the building.

His leadership instincts may have been admittedly impaired at the moment, but he hadn't lost sight of what the main source of his power was: personal intimidation. Without doubt, he was in the kind of particularly foul mood it took to properly terrify his disciples. He decided that he would begin with the public side of the Continuity in Government.

Another text lit up his cell phone: "Report pending: S. Billy attempted sign-on CIG main menu 8:30 A.M. - ETC of distorted audio from S. Billy: 30 hrs."

It was sooner than he had assumed. That didn't prevent him from putting on his most disapproving expression when he stepped off the elevator into a lobby crowded with uniformed military people and well-dressed civilians.

The stated mission of "specializing in urban and suburban emergency management scenarios for the purposes of planning and reaction assessment" meant that personnel from all branches of the military, and a vast array of power players from the Hill, would pass through the front doors of the ESC.

Those few who knew him by sight saluted or looked on with reverence when General Masterson passed. His title was honorary, as far as anybody knew he had never served in the military, and his political power was so insidious that his name would never appear in any news stories.

But to the select few of the CIG, and the less exclusive CIG light – the Intra-Guard – he was simultaneously a prophet of doom and a savior. He was a man who saw disaster coming and seemed to have all the answers for survival.

It was strange that such a paranoid misanthrope would be saddled with the task of insuring the continued existence of the government of the United States of America. Still, few questioned why so many politicians, soldiers, and intelligence agents served him.

Masterson inspected the lobby, then the main offices and meeting rooms of the think tank, until he was back at his private elevator. He input the correct code for the third sublevel, checking his cell phone for texts on the way. The elevator car zoomed past the first two sublevels of warehouse and storage space, down to the operations level.

Two soldiers on guard snapped to attention the moment Masterson came through the opening doors. The main operations room was hectic and thick with current and former intelligence operatives. Masterson's constant scheming required an endless array of secret intelligence ops and black projects. If any clandestine CIG activities were perpetrated on the East Coast or in Europe, they were coordinated out of the ESC operations center.

Masterson's people scattered upon realizing their boss was present and watching. His hands behind his back, he looked over the shoulder of every officer manning every computer in the room. He scrutinized each map and situation board. He moved on to the living quarters only after he was certain he had rattled enough cages.

There men and women abruptly broke from their particular recreational activities and jumped to attention when Masterson swaggered by, cutting through the gym, the cafeteria, and the common areas, rousing each CIG minion he passed.

One especially avid admirer began clapping at the sight of his commander; the rest of the CIG troops joined him. The applause erupted spontaneously on both sides of Masterson as he progressed down the hall. Before long he was walking through a barrage of adulation, sporting his most arrogant smirk.

He returned to his elevator, assuming that there was no need to continue his inspection. As much as his festering rage was prodding him to take it out on his lessers, the troops were obviously properly motivated, or terrified, or both. In his narrow estimation, one was as good as the other.

Masterson checked his text messages during the ride down to his office. There would be no meetings or briefings for at least an hour; it was time to deal with Erica.

Two of Masterson's elite bodyguards flanked the elevator doors on his private sublevel. Dimly lit and deserted, the corridor ended at a riveted blast door. A hand and retinal scanner came from the wall as he approached, something only his particular biometric readings could have triggered.

The wood-paneled walls and heavy oak desk in Masterson's private haven were accented by the deep pile carpet on the floor, appropriately luxurious but not extravagant. The impressive power players he would meet with fifteen floors up would never see his private office or any of the sublevels. Being an impressive power player wasn't qualification enough. Unfortunately for Erica, being a real psychic was.

Masterson approached a five drawer file cabinet in the corner, which caused the entire front to open in one piece. He was presented with an impenetrable safe door and a keypad. Punching in the code enable him to retrieve the ancient book he acquired from Thoth's Chamber during his trip to Iraq.

He placed the *Book of Thoth* on his desk as he consulted a tight cluster of instruments near his chair. Dr. Hasline's microwave device appeared to be working properly.

Masterson proceeded to the opposite corner. There he had but to wave his hand over a certain spot on the wall and a section of the paneling swung open. Bars blocked the entrance into the tiny white cell that was then revealed. Erica sat inside cross-legged and rocking slowly.

Despite the fact that her breathing was forced and labored, and that she was sweating profusely, the terrified young woman was maintaining her composure. The constant bombardment of low frequency energy waves had her weakened but not out.

"It's time for us to talk," Masterson said.

She opened her eyes and stood unsteadily. "I know who you are; I've seen what you did."

Masterson tensed up. "Through the micro-field? I doubt it." He stepped back from the cell door, drawing a vintage German Lugar pistol from a shoulder holster and training it on Erica. "Have a seat on the couch Sergeant Brown."

Erica stumbled to the couch in front of Masterson's desk. "I'm not the only one who knows."

"We'll get to that," he said. He kept the pistol on her while he stepped behind his desk to shut down the micro-field. "I need you focused."

Erica immediately sat straight up and her breathing calmed. Her defiance returned with her senses. She raised her head to give Masterson the judgmental look he abhorred.

"As usual you still think you're entitled to rule," she blurted out. "But you're not."

Masterson placed the *Book of Thoth* on the table in front of her. Erica tried to maintain her hateful stare at her captor, it was just that the book was too powerful to ignore. She resisted the temptation to swoop it up. Instead she settled for holding her open hands over the cover. The mere proximity of it imbued the exhausted women with wonder.

"You can touch it. It's not magick or dangerous or anything. That's all superstitious nonsense, of course. It just tells a story, a story of this planet that humans have no right to know."

The script on the wooden cover was undecipherable but Erica wouldn't let that stop her. "The fabled *Book of Thoth*," she said. "No, it's not magick, but it is powerful."

"Very good, Sergeant Brown. It's the author that I'm interested in."

Erica concentrated on the manuscript, and the history attached to it. "Why? Why would you bring all this down on us? You doomed yourselves. Then you doomed humanity. Why would you do that?"

"You wouldn't even exist if it wasn't for us," Masterson said. "Now I want you to concentrate. Use that 'anomalous cognition' of yours to tell me the exact location of the author of this book."

"What makes you think he's even on this planet?"

Masterson sneered. "He's here. I can feel it. But you'll never find him. He knows how to hide from you."

"Pick up the book! Now!"

"From what I hear, you've been stomping around your domain, terrifying your lackeys for weeks now. But I bet you don't even really know why, do you? You're still so hung up on the kingship! That's what will end up being your downfall!"

"Concentrate on the book, now!" Masterson pinned the end of the pistol to her head. "If you can't tell me where he is then you're of no use to me. And if you're of no use to me, then you're a threat."

Erica tried her best to laugh. "You still have no idea who the real threat is, do you? How have you been sleeping lately, Marduk?"

"What do you know about all that?!"

The mere sound of the ancient epithet enraged Masterson even more. He struck Erica's cheek with the back of his hand. She glared back up at him, as defiant as ever.

"He'll look into your black soul and see every one of your precious little secrets before it's all over!"

"What do you know about *him*?! Who is he?!" He smacked her again.

"Even if I knew, I'd never tell you!" Tears were streaming down Erica's hysterical face; the look in her eyes was manic. "It doesn't matter what you do to me! It's *your* time that's up! I've seen it! The clock started ticking the second the Unity Council was created!"

A veteran of interrogation, Masterson knew in an instant that it was pointless to question her any further. More than once he had seen the face of a condemned person who had made peace with their fate.

He raised his weapon again, his rabid paranoia insisting that if he let her live any longer, it would end up being her who would reveal all his "precious little secrets."

She closed her eyes to relish the thought of her husband. "I love you, Chris."

A single gunshot dropped her to the floor.

Chris Ritter was sitting behind the wheel of his sedan in the parking lot of Hasline's Washington DC laboratory, overcome by a palpable wave of grief. The normally vigorous and passionate State Department aid was staring at the front doors of the building in a daze after being rebuffed by a polite secretary and two not-so-polite security guards.

"I love you, too," he whispered.

A sense of foreboding joined the panic he had been experiencing since Erica disappeared into the Institute for Psychological Studies. It was at that moment he became convinced that his worst fears had been realized.

Tears poured from his blue eyes as if he were looking at the lifeless body of his wife, as if he knew for a fact that she was dead. He beat on the steering wheel of the car until his hands were bruised and bleeding, then he gripped the wheel and glared at the innocuous building where Hasline performed his "experiments."

"I swear to God, I will kill you all."

5

The room to which Mary was compelled by law to return once a month looked very much like any other government agency in the country, even though it was populated by criminals of every type.

Murderers, rapists, and the most petty of thieves, they all waited in that bland office to fulfill their post-incarceration obligations, staring at the same dingy whitewashed walls and unambiguous public service placards about abortion and drug abuse.

Wearing headphones attached to a laptop that was propped open on her knees, Mary's one hundred and thirty pound frame was squeezed between a hefty biker, his flowing beard almost covering the motorcycle logo on his t-shirt, and a frail crack addict whose body was shaking furiously.

Mary had to admit to being extremely intimidated the day she walked through the doors of the Los Angeles County probation office for the first time, and never in her life could she have been called a shrinking violet.

It had taken a good portion of seven years for her to grow accustomed to the depression that hung low in the waiting room from open to close. That particular day, however, that ever present gloom couldn't even touch her. Not on the very last day of her parole.

The little man to her left smiled through uncontrollable tremors at Mary with a strangely contented expression. She always made a point of smiling back at poor Stuart. By her estimation, he needed all the positive reinforcement he could get.

And when they were both in the waiting room together, she always sat beside Gary, the behemoth ex-gang member to her right. Literally beauty and the beast, the wiry Italian-American woman and her bearish admirer would talk and watch TV while they waited for their turn.

Mary felt Gary poke her thigh. "Hey, sweet thing, check this out."

He directed her attention to a news program on a television mounted high in the corner. She brushed back her headphones but it didn't matter, the sound button on the TV had been turned all the way down and then broken off long ago, to avoid disputes.

After a flash of Hector Madrano at the podium, the story led into coverage of the Unity Council's publicity stunt in front of the United Nations Building in New York City. The Unity Council's most recent bid to get the attention of the country and the world. A few second clip of the Council's efforts during the hurricane in South Carolina preceded a quick cut to another story in the news cycle.

"That was my new boss," Mary said. "They've been running that all morning."

"What was he talking about?"

"This." Mary gave Gary a look at what was on the screen of her laptop computer.

"That more of your climate change shit?"

"They're simulations from the website," she said. "They show sea level rise and drought over the North American continent for the next fifty years."

"What the hell is all that?" Gary asked.

"Just wait."

Set on a ten second loop, the simulations all restarted at the same time, giving Gary a better idea of what was happening.

In every scenario the ocean would encroach on the East, West, and Gulf Coasts of a black silhouette of the North American continent, slowly pushing the established shoreline back with a creeping blue tide. The third simulation went the furthest into the future and, thus, was the most extreme.

Mary drew Gary's attention to that scenario. "I'm going with the worst-case because really they can't be sure about anything, only that it's gonna get a lot hotter. This is Sara's future, dude, as far as they can tell, anyway. This is your little Jeanette's future. You and I will both be dead, but this is the world they get to deal with."

In the simulation, the Pacific Ocean would creep over the edges of the Western Coast at multiple points, flooding lower Los Angeles and even reaching portions of the southern San Fernando Valley.

Simultaneously, the southern tip of Florida would turn blue, as would much of the area on both sides of the Mississippi delta.

"You see?" she said. "All the most well-known places on the coasts, not just New Orleans, are toast. Miami, DC, New York, you name it."

Also in all three scenarios, to varying degrees, a swath of bright red-orange would spread across the Southwest region of the blacked out maps. It ran from just east of the California coast, across Arizona, to the higher elevations of New Mexico, and north, through the western slope of Colorado, southern and middle Nevada, to Salt Lake City, Utah.

"All this orange means heat," she said. "Like summer temperatures averaging 110 to 130 degrees. That means cities like Phoenix and Vegas will be basically unlivable."

Mary pointed to the San Fernando Valley, with the sea encroaching from one direction and the heat encroaching from another.

"That's where we are right now," she said.

"So it's drown or fry?" Gary said. "That ain't much of a choice."

"Screw that choice. After today, I'm free."

"That's why I don't watch that shit. Nothing we can do about it anyway. I never did ask, as long as I've known you. But what's a sweet little thing like you doing worrying about all that all the time?"

"You kidding me, Gary? How can you ask that? Your daughter is what, ten?"

Mary minimized the simulations and launched the video of Hector's address from the streets of New York. She had heard the speech plenty of times before but it comforted her to put it on.

"How's that rig working out?" Gary asked.

"I don't know yet, haven't been driving it. But I'm getting ready to though. This time next week I'll be in Colorado. After there, we'll see."

"That was a thing of beauty, right there. Full two man camper set on a jacked up four-wheel drive frame with off-road suspension, a deluxe lift-kit and six-cylinder with turbo charge, plenty of power but pretty good on gas. That sucker will go anywhere, over anything. It'll take you and your daughter to hell and back, I swear it."

Mary patted his husky shoulder. "I know it will, Gar. And that expanded bathroom was just great. You know a girl's got to have her bathroom."

"Yeah, you lost a little space making it bigger but not too bad after all."

"There's no doubt you're an artist. Thanks for working so hard on it and giving me such a deal."

"That was no problem. So why are you still here?"

"I'm not, after today Sara and I are out of here!"

"Your turn, Mary," the secretary said.

"See you around, Gary," Mary said with a wave.

"Hang tough, sweet thing."

Mary charged through a maze of cubicles thrilled by the prospect that it would be the last time. After close to seven years of paying for her mistake, and of being watched constantly, her sentence was finally over.

"How have you been Mary? It's good to see you," the stocky little man said.

"I'm doing a lot better today, now that it's over. Thank God."

To her mother, Mary described Steve as a young and idealistic public servant. She had to admit that she was lucky to get him for a parole officer. She knew he was firmly on her side, even though procuring the transfer out of California that Mary had sought for years turned out to be beyond his power. In actuality, he stopped trying to help her leave the state not long after he fell for her.

Steve squirmed in his chair and rifled through the piles of paperwork on his desk. Seeing each other month after month for so long allowed them to learn each other's moods. Mary could feel Steve's trepidation.

"There seems to be a hitch," he finally said.

"When isn't there?"

"Well, it seems the administrative offices have lost all record of your community service."

Mary was instantly incensed. "They've what?!" She regained her composure quickly, leaving Steve somewhat surprised by her anger. "I don't understand, they're gonna find them right? I mean, I was there. I painted, I picked up trash and gladly, damn it. And now I can't even get credit for it?"

"I know, Mary. I'm running this down now, but–"

"But what?"

"I can't say how it will affect your current disposition."

"Steve, I want out of here, damn it! Out of this town, out of this state! When will this insane system let me go? I know that damn ADA has always had it in for me every since he couldn't make me roll over, but–"

"You never gave the money back, Mary. That ADA is the district attorney now and he's held a grudge all these years. You were one of the few black marks on his record and he hasn't forgotten it. He's blocked all your petitions to move out of the state because he wants to keep an eye on you.

"That's probably why the parole board finally gave in and let you work in computer programming again. I think they were hoping you would go after the money so they could bust you. Your sentence would have been cut in half, and you never would have seen any jail time, if you had just given it back."

"You know why I couldn't do that. So, how long does this crap take now, huh? A week, two, four? I have a job offer."

"That was denied, you know that." Steve struggled to hide his feelings, as Mary stared at the floor, brooding. "Why, Mary, why are you so determined to leave?"

"You can ask me that after Haiti, after Chile, after Japan? Steve, you know why I have to get out of here. You remember Northridge just like I do. My child could wake up under a pile of two-by-fours tomorrow; I'm not going to let that happen."

It took almost seven years for Steve to convince himself that he was worthy of the unrequited love he harbored for Mary. Due to her status as a parolee, pursuing her would have been unethical, even if he could have mustered the courage. Now all he could have were mixed feelings about her nearing the end of their association. Part of him wanted her unencumbered, the other part knew that the moment she wasn't required to come visit him she would pack up her daughter and drive out of his life.

"I'm gonna do whatever it takes to get this straightened out. You just have to be cool a little longer. Just stay put." Mary crossed her arms. "I mean it, Mary, just until I can get this worked out. You've been doing great at your job. Everything has been going perfectly. You'll be through this before you know it."

Steve knew that with Mary bad news took some time to sink in. When it did, though, she could always cope.

"If all else fails we'll get you going on community service again, just until they get this mess straightened out. If we don't, they might want to try to say that you are in violation of your parole."

"You have got to be kidding me."

His earnest and loving expression prevented Mary from browbeating him any further. She knew the system well enough to know that Steve wasn't behind what was happening to her, he didn't wield that kind of power. With nothing left to say, she reached out to shake Steve's hand, except when he took it she lifted him to his feet. She wrapped her arms around him and gave him a friendly hug that took his breath away.

"Thank you, Steve. I know you've always done what you could for me, even when maybe I wasn't making it easy for you."

He did his best to act casual. "You've never been a bit of trouble for me, Mary."

"I'll be waiting to hear from you." She sulked out of his cubicle leaving him speechless.

Mary wasn't dense, she had been aware of Steve's feelings for her for some time, but the clock was ticking in her head and it wasn't counting down to an opportunity to go on a date with her probation officer. She was marking the days until her departure.

As he watched her leave, Steve resolved to do whatever it took to give her the freedom she so longed for. Even if it meant he would lose her forever.

After some time on her second home, California's Interstate 5, Mary trudged into the vast office where she worked, more defeated than she had been in years. She cringed at the sound of fingers striking keys coming from the cubicles around her. It was a reminder of every mind-numbing day she had worked at that software company. Saying goodbye to that dead-end job had been a big part of her now thwarted plan to leave California.

She cleared her desk of her workload in less than two hours. She took to tapping her pen on her keyboard in an effort to maintain her sanity until five o'clock. The feelings of persecution and outrage that had become her fast friends over the previous seven years were now about to make her implode.

Eventually, her supervisor snuck up from behind, jarring her from her pout. "Did you finish debugging that program?" he asked.

Mary handed the squirrelly young computer nerd a stack of printouts. "I finished that one and the next four jobs on the schedule. Oh, and I found that backdoor in that accounting program. Jesus, it was big enough to drive a truck through."

"I'll have to follow up on that one," he said. "I don't know how that could have happened."

"Damn Donald, you'd think you were writing software for electronic voting machines or something. If you want me to check your code before you turn it in just say so. You don't have to pretend it's from the guys in development. "

"I don't need you to check my programs," he said.

"I'd know your code anywhere," she said. "It's limp and unimaginative."

"Now listen here, Mary—"

"I've gotta get out of this office," she suddenly said. "Before I strangle somebody, probably you!" She gathered her things and left her boss irritated but relieved she was gone.

Mary was back on I-5 again, heading north toward her parents' home, and the apartment she shared with Sara.

She knew it had become unhealthy, but the only time she felt at ease was when she was with her daughter. Even then the constant anxiety that the ground was going to open up and swallow them both would creep into her mind.

It would happen at the strangest times; during a visit to the park or a trip to the mall, invariably Mary would be overcome by panic. Previously she had been prepared to chalk it up to memories of the Northridge earthquake. That explanation was now wearing thin.

Until she had a child of her own, for Mary living in sunny Southern California was comparable to living anywhere in the country. Even with the specter of another quake haunting her dreams, she never thought about moving away from the only home she had ever known.

Then by the time her daughter, Sara, was born, she got mixed up in felony grand larceny and embezzlement and her fate was sealed for seven years. No travel outside the county without permission and definitely no moving out of state.

So Mary did what most people do when they're trapped on the verge of destruction. She kept herself constantly distracted. Living in constant denial was easy to do when the requirements of day-to-day survival kept her too busy to reflect.

Her daughter would get sick, or her car would break down, and her anxiety over living on a fault line would be pushed to the back of her mind. There it would fester until something small would bring it back out. A rude driver would cut her off on the freeway or an impolite shopper would jump in front of her at a cash register and she would be reminded once again of how trapped she felt.

Mary took her usual off ramp into the neighborhood where she was raised. The streets she had driven since she was a teenager had become a prison to her now, a prison that could come crashing down around her at any moment. The shopping malls and the hospital, the library and the office park, they barely showed signs all those years later of the most powerful earthquake ever recorded in the continental United States.

With scenes of ruin from Haiti, Chile, and Japan fresh in her mind, the devastation after Northridge was all Mary could see when she looked out the windows of her car. Every time she came home it gripped her with the same indignant rage that had caused her to commit ill-advised – if noble – acts of civil disobedience in her youth.

She had decided years ago that she could no longer allow that rage to derail her, or her daughter's, future. Even so, the undeniable urge to do something reckless nagged endlessly.

Mary recognized what street she was on and veered impulsively into a strip mall. She parked and turned off the engine. She was pleased to find that The Metaphysical Bookstore was still in operation, although a

"Business Closing" sign was posted near the entrance.

She opened the door to the shop and was greeted by smoldering aromatherapy candles and wind chimes. She wandered through the eclectic selection of new age crystals, glass knick-knacks, and candles. Reproductions of ancient Egyptian art hung high on the opposite wall beside dreamy prints of Native American warriors and elaborate Middle Eastern tapestries.

Initially she thought she had the place to herself, then she noticed that most of the patrons had gathered in the rear of the store around an alcove. Their backs were turned to her, blocking her view, yet it was apparent that most of the assembly was engrossed by what they were witnessing.

Natural curiosity pushed Mary toward the back wall, reviewing the extensive rows of books and pamphlets along the way. She stopped for a look over the tables to find the date "2012" repeated over and over again on books and magazines and DVDs.

"It's gotten a little creepy," a young blonde woman said from the next row. She popped open a can of soda and took a drink.

"It's been a few years since I've been in," Mary said. "But it sure seems like this 'Mayan End of Time' thing has taken over."

"That's sounding familiar, right?" Like many popular twenty-something women, she compulsively paged through the text messages on her cell phone.

"What do you mean?"

"Well, I was only what, eleven, in 1999? But I remember it, they were all freaking out. It was the end of the world then, too."

"It looks like it's the end of the world all over again," Mary said. "Sure feels like it sometimes."

"Yeah, that sucks." The woman flipped her long hair from one side to the other then took out a small mirror. "So you're here for the show?"

Mary looked to the crowded alcove. "No. I mean, I don't know. What show?"

The young woman touched up her meticulously applied makeup in the mirror before taking another big swig of soda. "Oh, he's channeling Geb in there."

"He's doing what?"

"Go check it out."

Mary was hesitant at first.

"It's OK, he doesn't bite." The young woman gathered her things and headed down a short hall out of sight.

Mary inched up to the wall of people, straining for a look into the alcove. She had to squeeze by a rotund man before she was finally able to see what had everyone so engaged.

The man seated in front of the crowd reminded Mary of the hick farmers she used to see on trips north through the San Joaquin Valley. The sleeves of his flannel shirt were rolled up, his work boots were off and sitting beside his chair. His eyes were closed but his eyeballs were darting around behind the lids, as if he were in deep REM sleep.

It was all a strange enough sight to Mary. However, the trance the man was in, that he was gripped by, was chilling to her. The tiny alcove was charged with a palpable energy that washed over Mary once she got close. Her involuntary reaction, after fascination, was to recoil.

The man's speech was abrupt and monotone. "Your Native Americans call it 'The Great Cleansing'. And unfortunately that is what it will be. There is a great upheaval coming to all the peoples of Earth."

"When?" a silver haired woman eagerly asked. "People here need to know when, so that we can prepare." She was on the edge of a chair in front of the man, searching through the pages of questions that had been prepared for Geb.

"Your Mayans knew," was his cryptic response.

A satisfied murmur went through the crowd and the questioner got even more animated. "You mean 2012?" she asked.

"Of course," the man droned.

Mary was simultaneously impressed and incredulous. While the others were abuzz with confirmations of the supposed Mayan date for the end of the world, Mary took a moment to examine the man in the trance.

She dared not draw closer, as something very disconcerting surrounded him. That should have been proof enough of his veracity. But she couldn't help feeling skeptical, if not of the messenger, than of the message.

"Shh, shh," the questioner said to those gathered. "What can we do to prevent this?" she asked. "Why have you told us this if we can't do anything to stop it?"

"Because those who have heeded our words and been mindful of what is coming will have a chance," the man said. "When it is time, we will return from our galaxy to assist those who have been vigilant."

"And what happens to the rest of us?" Mary blurted out.

Many in the crowd joined the questioner in scolding Mary for her outburst. "I'm the only one who asks the questions," she said.

"How nice for you," Mary said before turning and squeezing her way out of the alcove. The oppressive feeling eased as she got away from the crowd. Shaking the affects completely would take time.

She paced around trying to calm herself as the voice of the woman she met earlier drew her down the short hallway. She followed the frenetic chatter to a spacious reading area that was lined with brimming bookshelves and adorned with art and ancient relics from several different cultures. Plush couches had been placed in front of the shelves for people to lounge on and read. The young woman was reclined on one of them talking on her cell phone.

"OK girl, I'll ring your ass later, hear?" she said when she saw Mary come in. "So, what did you think?"

Mary was still breathing heavily. "What the hell is going on in there?"

"I don't know. But that guy Byron, he's got something. He ain't no con, that's for sure. He used to grow alfalfa up in Chula Vista. Just as happy as you please. Until the voices started."

"The voices, huh?" Mary said, sitting on the couch near the woman.

"It's supposed to be some old Egyptian god, I guess."

"The guy said that? Or the god said that?"

"Got me." Unable to sit still for even a moment, the woman jumped off the couch to run her finger along the books on the shelves. "So, you want a reading?"

"Oh, I didn't really bring any money for anything like that."

"It's free. My mom owns the shop, gives me a few bucks to do readings, keep people coming back in."

Mary had to squint to pick out titles among the hodgepodge of book spines. They were all about UFOs or ghosts or government conspiracies.

"So you were raised around all this?" she asked.

"Yeah, that's my moms. She's out there pretty good, but I love her."

"And you do readings?"

"Yeah, looks like I do." Half-embarrassed, she got over it by checking her cell phone.

"So what are you getting from me?"

The woman abruptly turned off her cell and plopped back down beside Mary. "Then you want me to read you, right?"

"Sure, why not."

"My name is Denise. And you are?"

"I'm Mary."

"Nice to meet you, girl." Denise reached over the back of the couch for her purse. She produced a balled up piece of black velvet and opened it, careful not to touch the smooth, pill-shaped rock inside. "Grab a hold of that," she said.

Mary picked up the rock.

"Just hold on to it a minute."

"OK." Mary held onto the hefty piece of granite, moving it from one hand to the other. "So how does this work?"

"Now we just shoot the shit a minute," Denise said. "What made you come into a store like this? I mean, a lot of people think this is all just a bunch of bunk."

"I don't know, I was in years ago and remembered you were still here."

"Do you believe at least some of the weird stuff these books talk about is possible?"

Mary circled the room, the rock in hand. "I don't know. I've always felt like I've had a special connection to my computer, that's for sure. Maybe it could be psychic. I mean, how many times have you been listening to a supposedly random mix on your MP3 player and heard the song you were just thinking about?

"And not one of the favorite songs you listen to over and over either, the program remembers that. But a song you hadn't played or heard in years and up it pops right after it crosses your mind? Depending on the algorithms used in the 'shuffle' code, and the size of your music library, the odds can get pretty long that you could see one particular song coming like that."

"Everyone's psychic," Denise said, reaching for the rock. "OK, that should be enough." She cradled the stone with both hands. "Let's see now." She closed her eyes for a few moments then opened them, inspired and wagging her finger. "You're trouble, aren't you? I see a light around you and it's powerful, but it can also be trouble."

"Maybe."

"You're always on the right side, though, aren't you? And it kicks your ass on a pretty regular basis. You're a single parent."

"Yes."

"You're freaking out right now."

"Yes, I am."

"You had a pretty crappy decision to make, a bunch of years ago, and you're still paying for it to this day."

"Yes, I am."

"Now you don't know what to do, to make sure your kid will be safe."

"No, I don't."

Denise's face grew solemn; she avoided eye contact by busying herself with wrapping the stone back up in the velvet cloth and slipping it back into her purse.

"What? Did you get the 'death card' or what?"

"You didn't say you worked for the Unity Council," Denise said.

"You're good. All the other stuff you could have guessed but that. What do you know about the Council?"

"Why did you come here? I mean, how much do you know?"

"Apparently not enough." Mary agonized a moment longer. "I've been through every report. I've looked at every forecast I could find..." She plunged her face into her hands. "They don't know. With all their computer models and simulations, they still don't know, not really. There're just too many variables."

"What are you getting at girl, what's got you all racked up?"

"Where can I take my daughter that will be safe? Do you know? Can you see? The coasts are no good. The plains, well, when Yellowstone blows they'll be buried in ash up to their waists. North will be too cold during the winter, even with global warming. The south: drought and storms. There's no place to go, to be safe."

"You need to get with Hector. Hell, I need to get with Hector."

"Hector? How do you know Hector? What the hell is going on here?"

Denise took out her cell phone and was about to check her messages. Then she remembered her mother's insistence that such dodges were rude. The young psychic stammered as she fished for the right response.

"Not cool, Denise, and you know it. You know how it works. If you see something then you have to say it. It's up to me to believe you or not."

"If I tell you, you may not go, OK?" Denise finally said. "And you have to go, so..."

"Tell me what?"

"You're going to get beside some real evil, OK?" she said. "True darkness, alright?"

Mary crossed her arms and pursed her lips. "Is that it?"

"I think I saw enough."

"Well, what the hell?" Mary said. She stood; her purse in hand. "Damn it, Denise."

"I'm sorry, OK? I see you there, in Colorado, but it doesn't come anywhere near to solving your problems."

"Are you talking about some kind of danger? I mean for real?"

"Would it matter anyway? You're an Aquarius, aren't you?"

"How did you know that?"

"You're stubborn, huh? Got a hard head? Nobody can tell you nothin', can they Miss Hardhead. That's why you've been so pissed. For like years. Oh, and because you just know that you can change the world, don't you? But it ain't changing, is it?"

Mary couldn't deny that little would have stopped her from taking a job with the Unity Council at that point. Nor could she refute the accusation that she was stubborn to the end.

"I'm late," she said on her way toward the hall. "And I will be talking to Hector about this. You can count on that."

Denise sprang from the couch. "Hey."

"What?"

"See you there, Miss Hardhead."

"I'm going, Denise, thanks anyway."

When Mary turned to leave, Denise moved quickly to snatch a stray strand of hair from the shoulder of her blouse. The young woman got comfortable on one of the couches and closed her eyes in meditation, wrapping the single thread of hair around her finger.

One state over, in Arizona, Hector stood on the bustling Third Mesa, his cell phone in hand. He dodged the workmen who were tearing down the stage while he waited for his new recruit to answer. She finally picked up after several rings.

"Mary, this is Hector, will you be leaving like we arranged? Can we expect you in Kingman?"

Mary was talking into the headset of her cell phone, sitting in deadlocked freeway traffic. "I don't know, Hector. Things have gotten kind of messed up. Who's Denise?"

"Denise? What are talking about? What's gotten all messed up?"

"Now they're saying that they can't find any record of the three years of community service I did. It's that damn DA; he's doing whatever he can to punish me now that it's all over."

"So how was it left?"

"My probation officer says I have to stay here. At least until they figure it all out. But honestly, I'm more inclined to take my daughter and drive straight the hell out of this city right now."

"You've fulfilled your obligations out there, and pretty soon you'll be able to move on. But right now you've got to keep your head. Don't do anything that might get you arrested. It wouldn't look good for the Unity Council's new IT manager to get thrown in jail. Let me make some calls and I'll get back with you."

Her silence concerned Hector. He waited for Mary to assure him that she would do as he suggested. That assurance was not forthcoming.

"Have you been watching the news, Mary? This is going to happen, the Unity Council is happening, and we want you to be a part of it, if you're still willing?"

"I'm willing but–"

"Then sit tight until I get back to you, OK?"

"OK, Hector."

Hector hung up from the call and his cell phone rang. "This is Hector."

"Hey, man, this is Curtis."

"Where are you?"

"Outside Columbus."

Hector's phone lit up, notifying him that a photo had been sent. The grainy snapshot was of Max asleep in the last seat of a cross country bus.

"It's the guy you had in the bulletin."

"Are you sure?" Hector asked, looking at the photo a second time.

"It's him. So is he a bad guy or should I be looking out for bad guys, or what?"

"I'm not going to lie to you, Curtis. He's hot as hell. The CIG is looking for him; they've already killed over him and likely will kill again. How did you find him?"

"We got on the same connection to Denver. He was coming from New York. So why is he so important?"

"We don't know."

"You weren't shitting about that CIG were you?"

"Why do you think we need people like you? I told you this job was going to be more than just organizing co-ops, but this may be too much."

"So what do you want me to do?"

"We're spread pretty thin. At least as far as trained operatives are concerned. Honestly, Curtis, I don't feel comfortable asking you to do anything. It's too dangerous. We have people in Denver; I'll try to send them your way."

"It's too far. There's no time. Look, I'll keep an eye on him and call if he gets off the bus. Or if anything goes down. How's that?"

"I don't know. There's something going on with him. We haven't figured out what it is yet, but it isn't good."

"It's cool. I told you that I'm here to help. If this will help, then you've got it."

"Be careful, Curtis, the people after him are professionals."

"The only thing worse than the crazy ones are the pros. Cold as ice. But that's OK. I've seen my share of cold-blooded killers."

"I'll have a rental car waiting for you in St. Louis. If you can get him off that bus without putting yourself in danger, do it. He's a sitting target on that thing. And so are you if you get close to him."

"I'll call you in the morning."

Curtis flipped off the light of the cramped restroom and opened the narrow door. The twenty-five year old African-American scrutinized the brightly lit bus suspiciously. As of then, any one of the previously harmless passengers could have been a possible threat.

He returned to his seat, careful to ignore Max when he passed. He decided, after the third time of trying unsuccessfully to sneak a peek at his quarry, that when he got the opportunity he would gather his bags and move closer.

The bus driver's subdued voice came over the loudspeaker. "Turning off the lights 'til the next stop. Reading lights are available above all seats."

The intense fluorescent lights of the bus cabin finally relented, leaving the interior of the bus in virtual darkness. Two reading lamps shining on their individual seats were the only sources of light left in the cabin.

While everyone's eyes were adjusting, Curtis dared a glance back at Max, who was sleeping restlessly with the seat next to him still vacant. The young man decided it was time to make his move, hustling silently down the aisle of the bus. He slid his bag under the seat and reclined beside Max, careful to keep perfectly still until he was certain he wouldn't stir.

Curtis was enveloped by a suffocating heat when he opened his eyes again. Laying flat on his back, all he could see was a red and brown canopy that flapped in the wind overhead. It shaded him from what was obviously a burning sun.

He leaned up, in search of some clue as to where he was. At first he saw only the wooden legs of a long table. He used it to lift himself out of the sand, unable to make any sense of what he was seeing once he was on his feet.

Clay tablets littered the table, along with ancient vases and bowls full of foods that Curtis was unable to identify. He looked out of the shade of the canopy into the horizon. The surrounding plain was flat and abundant, despite the waves of heat that wafted from the distant terrain like a desert highway.

Curtis was carefully searching each direction for something he might recognize when, despite the blinding glare of the afternoon sun, he located a man in the distance that he was certain was Max. He was at a loss as to who the dazzling figure standing beside him could have been.

The young man was disoriented and unsure, his initial instinct was to stay put until the bad dream had ended. It was only Curtis's intense curiosity that compelled him to join Max. He needed to know just exactly what Hector had gotten him into.

He left the shelter of the canopy and approached cautiously. Drawing closer it became clear that they were at the edge of a steep escarpment. And that the man standing beside Max wore the gold-lined robes and the horned headdress of an ancient Mesopotamian king.

"Who are you?" Max asked, surprising Curtis.

"What? I–"

"You're not a part of this," Max said. "Why are you here?"

A leather-clad taskmaster ran up to the king before Curtis could answer. The hulking, sweating character reminded them both of something out of a movie, and brought their attention back to the wonders all around. They observed quietly while the king laid down instructions that his foreman rushed to carry out.

Curtis couldn't get over the fact that he understood the two strange men when they spoke. He looked over the edge of the plateau onto a sprawling construction project: a partially completed step-pyramid standing in the center of two square miles of artificially leveled ground.

"This doesn't look like Mexico," he said.

Workman hauling bundles of timbers and barrels of earth scurried around two gargantuan levels of stone – granite quarried miles away in the Zagros Mountains – which had been cut and placed with exacting precision. The platform that had been created was over a hundred feet off the ground, the size of several football fields, and level to within inches.

"Look at that," Curtis muttered.

Unlike most Mesopotamian step-pyramids, instead of telescoping up five more levels, a chiseled stone column had been erected in the center of the second course. Ascending ten stories into the air, a complex system of scaffolding made from heavy timbers had been attached to the column. Daring workmen swung from one section of the mighty trellis to the other.

"What the hell is it?" Curtis asked.

"It's a launch pad," Max said, pointing to the gleaming but ancient city beyond the construction site. "And that's Babylon, the 'Gateway of the Gods.'"

A solitary figure dressed all in black hurried up to the king. The exhilarated oracle-priest did his best to maintain his holy barring.

"He comes, Lord! The Great God Marduk comes to council his son here on Earth!"

The king and his priest scoured the sky, for what Max and Curtis could only imagine.

"My father will be pleased," the king said. "We have fulfilled the wishes of Marduk, Lord of all Anunnaki. All blessings will be upon us."

Max and Curtis had involuntarily joined the others in the search of the cloudless expanse overhead. A low, distant rumbling caught their attention just as they were about to question what they were doing.

The quaking toppled several stacks of clay tablets on the table under the canopy, signaling to the king and priest that it was time. They moved to an open area away from the escarpment and fell to their knees. With palms held to the sky they began reciting prayers of adoration to the Great God Marduk.

Max and Curtis were stunned when, one by one, men all across the construction site dropped what they were doing to prostrate themselves. Men everywhere were falling to their knees and covering their heads on the ground.

"What's happening?" Curtis asked.

"Look." Max pointed out a long white exhaust trail in the distance that was barreling toward the escarpment at breakneck speed.

"Behold," the king said to his oracle-priest. "Marduk, King of the Gods, the Ruler of Heaven and Earth."

The normally stoic priest gushed. "This is a supreme omen, Lord!"

It wasn't long and the very ground beneath Max and Curtis shook. The deafening roar that gradually dominated the entire area had them slightly panicked. Meanwhile, the thousands of workmen on the valley floor were not. They stayed perfectly still when a gold and silver aircraft the size of a fighter jet buzzed the plateau at low altitude, its two booster rockets emitting solid blue flames during the high speed maneuver.

"Sonofabitch," Max said.

The cockpit of the craft sat atop the oversized engines and was open, allowing all to see the man wearing fine robes and a gleaming gold helmet inside. He took two more triumphant passes over the construction site before bringing the craft in for a vertical landing in front of the king and priest.

The whine of disengaging turbine engines cut through the air and a billowing dust cloud engulfed the entire area upon its landing. Marduk dismounted the smoking vehicle, prompting the king and priest to hasten to his side, both throwing themselves to the ground.

The middle-aged man lorded over the pair, drinking in their praise and admiration. Marduk eventually ordered the king to rise, but only after the appropriate amount of worship. He imparted a short list of commands, then handed him a single clay tablet.

Max tried in vain to make out the man they were treating like a god, the distance was too great, the dust too thick. He was just making his way toward the landing site by the time Marduk was returning to his vehicle.

The king took his place beside the still bowing priest as the roar became deafening once again. Max was at a dead run as the craft lifted off above. He tried to chase after it but it gained altitude and sped away, all he could see was blazing engines and choking smoke.

The king and priest waited until the sound of Marduk's chariot was trailing off in the distance to return to the table under the canopy. They began eagerly pouring over the tablet the king had just received, oblivious to an astonished Curtis pacing outside.

"So, what? They can't see us?" he yelled to Max, who was walking back from where he had chased Marduk's chariot.

A distinctive sonic boom drew Max's attention back to the horizon before he could answer. The resounding noise sent the king and priest back out from under the canopy and had them searching the sky again as well.

"My father returns?" the king asked. They continued to search the heavens, except Marduk's chariot did not appear.

Max started looking around frantically for some kind of cover. He knew incoming fire when he heard it. He dragged Curtis down by the collar with him. He covered his head, encouraging Curtis to do the same. Mere seconds elapsed before the explosions began in mid-air above the plateau and the valley like flack from anti-aircraft canons.

The king, the priest, and thousands of their Mesopotamian followers immediately panicked. Once Max and Curtis could see nothing was hitting the ground, they chanced a look upwards. Immediately following each explosion, dark and ominous storm clouds would form. Max identified multiple high altitude projectiles incoming and finally exploding overhead.

The clouds increased rapidly from the bombardment, and as they drew ever closer to the ground, they began to obscure the midday sun. High speed winds blew across the construction site, battering the trellis and fueling the already uncontrollable chaos among the workers.

"That's high velocity ordinance!" Max shouted to Curtis, the winds swirling all around them.

After the canopy was torn out of the ground and the table overturned, the king and priest rushed to the edge of the escarpment. Max and Curtis joined them. That was when a piercing sound cut through the air, the unmistakable whine of a missile in flight.

"Incoming!" Max shouted to Curtis.

They barely had time to dive for cover before a large section of the trellis on the platform was spontaneously obliterated. The second and third mysterious concussions sent pieces of the colossal granite column hurdling to the ground. Below, the workmen were scattering in all directions, abandoning the construction site and the city nearby.

Max poked his head up long enough to search for projectiles, there were none that could be seen. The piercing sound occurred again, followed by a booming detonation that virtually atomized the top of the column.

"Why?" the king yelled to the sky. "Why have you forsaken me, Great Marduk? Why have you forsaken the task you have set for me?"

"It is the Seven Anunnaki who Judge!" the oracle-priest said. "They would deprive Great Marduk of his right to rule the bond between Heaven and Earth!"

"This is the time of Aries!" the king said. "It is Marduk's time to rule!"

The radius of the explosions began to expand once the platform had been reduced to crumbled sections of rock. The escarpment was hit twice before a hypersonic shell detonated directly over where the table and canopy had been. The force of the blast blew the king and the priest over the edge of the plateau.

The explosion also woke Max and Curtis from their dream. They both opened their eyes at the same time and were startled to see each other.

Curtis jumped out of the seat, falling back into the door of the bathroom. "What did you do?!"

An elderly woman under one of the reading lights looked back with disapproval at Curtis before returning to her novel. He made sure his outburst didn't disturb anyone else.

"What the hell was that?" he whispered.

"Who the hell are you?" Max asked, rubbing his face, careful not to take his eyes off of Curtis.

"That was some crazy shit, man. That was insane. Did that really happen?"

"I said who are you?" Max clutched the *Epic of Gilgamesh* and the history textbook Bud had given him in New York to his chest.

"Hey man, I just sat down, OK? I must have crashed out."

Max didn't allow his suspicion of his fellow traveler keep him from getting down the details of his dream while they were still fresh in his mind. He turned on the overhead light so that he could jot some notes in the margins of the Gilgamesh epic. Curtis saw out of the corner of his eye that he had done the same to the opposite page.

"Just tell me," Curtis said. "I mean, I love the sci-fi, but you got *Stargate* in your head."

"It wasn't a TV show," Max said, without looking up from his notes.

"Then what was it? And how the hell was I able to see it?"

"It's not just about the Flood," Max mumbled to himself. "It's about them, it's about *him*."

"Who? The dude riding that pimped out jump-jet? Why did they call him Marduk?"

Max abruptly stopped writing in the Epic translation. He paged through the history textbook, to one of the many sections he had read many times during the previous days. "In the original Sumerian version of the Tower of Babel incident, Marduk was the bad guy."

"The original?"

"This book talks about how there are Sumerian versions of a ton of Bible stories. The Creation, Cain and Able... The Garden of Eden and Noah and the Great Flood are in the *Epic of Gilgamesh*. They even have a Sumerian king that was sent down a river in a reed basket as a baby."

"You read all those stories? No wonder it's stuck up in your dreams."

"I didn't read all of them," he said. "This book talks about how those Sumerian stories came as much as a thousand years before the Old Testament was written. It was the pagan gods, the Anunnaki. They were the gods in all of those old Sumerian stories. And Marduk was an Anunnaki."

"My Grams in South Carolina liked to go on about the pagans. She was always all head up about those heathen pagans, boy."

"If it really happened, the Tower of Babel incident was well before Gilgamesh," Max said. "Check it out." He lifted the textbook toward the light and began reading. "En's envoy tells of a golden age when 'there were no snakes, there were no scorpions... humankind had no opponents.' In those days the people could talk to their god Enlil in a single tongue. But Enki, god of magic and civilization, was unimpressed by the doings of humankind and chose to 'estrange the tongues in their mouths.'"

"I'll be damned," Curtis said. "That kind of shit happen to you a lot?"

"No, not that. So I'm asking you again. Who are you?"

"I'm Curtis, man. I'm just on my way to Denver. Who are *you*? That wasn't my dream. And no one has ever looked into my head, that's a promise. I mean, that shit only goes on in the movies, right?"

Max returned to his notes in the Gilgamesh epic, scribbling another detail that crossed his mind. "That wasn't my dream," he said.

Curtis hadn't intended on saying another word to Max, but it was clear that Hector had only scratched the surface when he said that there was 'something going on' with him. Their shared experience was simply too compelling to allow Curtis to remain a detached observer. He was only able to keep quiet for a few moments more.

"What are you writing?" he asked.

"I've been trying to record what I've been seeing."

"It was just a dream, right?"

"Right."

"But it was so real." Curtis jumped to his feet, paced a few times, then sat back down.

"Too real."

"Did you smell it? The smell, that was way too real."

"But it was just a dream."

"What are you, some kind of psychic or something?" Curtis asked.

"No, not quite."

Curtis was on his feet again. "Then how?" He plopped back down.

"That's what I'm going to find out."

The photo of the clay tablets were staring Max in the face once again when he closed the book cover. Running his hands over the photos on both books, it registered that now those ancient slabs of earth meant something different. They signified pieces in a puzzle that was much larger than he previously assumed. A puzzle he was assembling not so much in the conscious world, as in the subconscious.

"It's those mud slabs that that guy gave to that king," Curtis said. "Was that Gilgamesh?"

"No, he was another king that was supposed to have ruled in Iraq almost two thousand years before the Bible was written, somewhere around 2900 BC. This version was written in like 1800 BC."

"So what's it about?"

Max thought about how to answer Curtis's question and it occurred to him how much he had learned about the adventures of Gilgamesh, knowledge augmented by the history textbook he had acquired from Bud. Max also noted that, with the exception of Bud, he had never discussed the subject with anyone.

"Well, the first few tablets are about how Gilgamesh went on this quest, and traveled to the home of the Anunnaki with this buddy of his. This hairy, Bigfoot-type guy.

"The second part is about how he tracked down the Hero of the Deluge, basically Noah. And then Noah tells him about what happened during the Flood. It was that part that became the Bible story."

"Damn, it had to piss some people off when they found that out."

"I guess they've been fighting about it for over a hundred years, whether the hero in this one, Utnapishtim, was the real Noah. But there's no doubt about who came first."

"Don't tell my mom that," Curtis said. "She seriously believes that the Bible is the 'Word.' Period."

"Abraham was from the same Mesopotamia as Gilgamesh, just a lot later. And his dad was a priest, no reason to believe he wouldn't know the story of the Flood."

"Of all the stories my Grams used to read to us out of the Bible. That's the one I never forgot."

"You're not the only one. But most of this story is about this jackass king, they don't get to Noah until close to the end."

"The hero is a jackass and it's been around for how long?"

"According to the guys that translated it, the *Epic of Gilgamesh* was like the first hero legend ever."

"And he was a jackass."

"Well, it starts out with Gilgamesh getting all liquored up and running around his city dropping in on brides on their wedding nights and making them have sex with him before their husbands."

"A rapist, nice."

"He had turned into such a jerk by the time it was all done that the people of the city went to his mother, this Anunnaki goddess, and asked her for someone or something to calm him down."

Listening to Max, Curtis began to unwind. He took a long stretch while Max recounted by heart the story he had read hundreds of times.

"That was when the god Enki created this kind of half-human, half-Bigfoot dude named Enkidu. The gods said Gilgamesh would foresee the guy in two prophetic dream-omens. After he had the dreams, his mother listened to both of them and decided they meant Enkidu was on the way.

"Well, Gilgamesh was out drinking and whoring around in the city one night when Enkidu jumped him. They started wrestling through the streets. They wrestled all night until finally Gilgamesh tapped out."

"So did it settle his ass down?"

"Kinda, they became friends and between Gilgamesh thinking the gods were calling him from one of his dream-omens, and him wanting to get the women of his city all hot and bothered with some heroics, he decided they needed to go on some quests together."

"It said that?"

"Pretty much."

"Hot and bothered, huh?"

"So Enkidu said he knew how to get to the home of the gods – they say that it had to be in Lebanon because of the trees – but that it was guarded by this pretty nasty monster..." Max stopped and went into the history textbook. "Hey, I think it said something in here about..." He turned over several pages. "Yeah, it says that Gilgamesh went to this place they called Baalbek. It's this huge platform, it says the stones they used to build it are some of the biggest in the world, over a thousand tons... They even called it the 'Landing Place' on the Gilgamesh epic..."

"Well, hell, we saw something like that in your dream," Curtis said. "The Gateway of the Gods?"

"Yeah we did..." Max made several notes in the margins of the Gilgamesh epic then returned to the text. "Anyway, Gilgamesh is like screw it, if I live I'll be a god. I'll live forever. And if I die, then I'll be famous forever. My name will go down in history."

"Can't argue with that."

"Gilgamesh's mom and Enkidu sure couldn't. So the guys got all set up with the best weapons and left on their quest. They started walking, for days, weeks. When they got to the entrance to the forest around the mountain of the gods they waited for another dream-omen. After that, they were convinced they had reached the mountain of the gods. They looked around and found this gate. But when Enkidu touched it, he was paralyzed."

"The sidekick is already down, they always do that shit."

"Yeah, but he was able to heal himself, and by the time Gilgamesh found a way into the forest, Enkidu was ready to go. They went in and the guardian attacked them right off. Check it out." Max showed Curtis a Mesopotamian representation of the legendary scene, and the robot-like guardian Humbaba."

"So that's like some pre-*Lord of the Rings* shit," Curtis said with a giggle. "Mr. Frodo!"

"It was the first fantasy quest, action adventure, buddy flick. And really the first disaster story too."

"Damn," Curtis said. He leaned even farther back in the seat and closed his eyes, suddenly thinking better of it. Not wanting to risk falling back asleep, he perked back up. "So what happened next?"

"Oh, well, they did battle with the guardian. They were into it pretty good when Gilgamesh kind of pussed out and Enkidu had to pick up the slack. He chopped off the creature's head."

"Bet I know who got the credit though."

"Hey, it ain't called the *Epic of Enkidu*."

"See, they always screw over the sidekick."

"Yeah and he didn't even get the girl either. On their way back to

Mesopotamia, Gilgamesh was washing up by a river when the goddess Ishtar flew over in her 'sky chamber.' She decided that big, strong hero Gilgamesh deserved a little something for being such a stud."

"Oh yeah?"

"He said no. It was harsh too." Max found the quote he had in mind. "'Which of your many lovers lasted forever, which still serve you? None.'"

"He shut her down. That's funny."

"Yeah, but it pissed her off. So she went to the father of all the Anunnaki and had him sick the Bull of Heaven on them. It chased them all the way back to the gates of Gilgamesh's city. You'll love this. Enkidu and a bunch of soldiers stood up in front of the gates while Gilgamesh hid inside."

"What a punk."

"Of course the grunts got wiped out right off. But Enkidu was able to jump up on the back of the Bull of Heaven and grab a hold of its horns. Then he set it up so Gilgamesh could come down with the kill shot."

"And then they both got seriously laid by the women in the city."

"Nope, they pissed off the gods, again. So the Anunnaki called a council together – they liked to call those councils together – and they decided that someone had to pay. It was supposed to be both of them, but since this god Shamash spoke up for Gilgamesh, of course he was going to get off. Enkidu got sick all of a sudden, and after a few days he died."

"Meanwhile, the jackass is getting all the credit for being this big hero, right?"

"Yup, but Gilgamesh isn't happy. He starts bawling and crying about how if his buddy could die, what about him. He wasn't worried about getting his friend killed, he was worried about himself.

"See, he was like Alexander the Great; he was half-man and half-god. So I guess there was a chance that he could have been immortal. That, like the gods, he could live forever. That's why after Enkidu dies he decides to go looking for The Hero of the Deluge, Utnapishtim. Guess it was common knowledge that Utnapishtim and his wife were taken to live with the gods in a beautiful garden after the Great Flood."

"Damn, man, that's straight-up fantasy/sci-fi from thousands of years ago."

"That's the way it was with a lot of this old mythology. They had some seriously active imaginations."

"I love the fantasy/sci-fi," Curtis said.

"Then there's the Noah part. It's not everyday you get to meet a character from the Bible and have him tell you all about the Great Flood. It's like talking to an eye witness to apocalypse."

"Those are my favorite movies," Curtis said.

Max buried his head in the book. "At first I thought all this... the dreams... I thought it was all about the Flood, about the End. But there's more, there's more about the beginning too. That bastard just won't show me what it is."

"I don't know about all that, but I bet the End is why you picked up that book, isn't it? I'm telling you, somewhere inside all of us, we have a hard-on for the end of the world."

"Well they didn't tack that Flood story on the end of the Gilgamesh's Epic for nothing."

"Right?" Curtis said. "They even have a post-apocalyptic reality show now. And when you're talking the biggest movies of the last say forty years, a whole shitload of them are post-apocalyptic hero flicks."

"I guess that's true."

"I remember *Mad Max – Beyond Thunderdome* first," Curtis said. "That was some 'the Bomb went off then the gas all ran out' apocalypse right there. Talk about before its time, damn."

"There was *Terminator*," Max said.

"The 'machines kick our asses' apocalypse, nice. That trilogy was strong all the way through to the last movie."

"*The Matrix.*"

"More 'the machines takeover' chaos. Sci-fi ain't never been the same since that flick."

"There was *Waterworld.*"

Curtis took pause, shaking his head. "Man, that one stuck with me... That boat Costner had was freaking sweet and I don't even like the ocean. Good thing I was born at sea level, on an island."

"The *Planet of the Apes*. The old movies and the new one."

"Yeah, you know your sci-fi. The 'monkeys take over because we blew it all up!' apocalypse. Wasn't that one a bitch?"

"*The Day after Tomorrow* was pretty bleak.

"Straight 'global warming kicked our asses,'" Curtis said. "I got a feeling that kind of apocalypse ain't going away any time soon."

"No, it ain't. But it's only been around since about two thousand BC."

"So what happened when Gilgamesh went to find Noah?" Curtis asked.

"Well–"

Once the driver had successfully veered the bus off the interstate and onto a frontage road, he rang a bell three times, awakening several of the passengers.

"Transfer station," he announced.

The bus emerged from the darkness into a large parking lot in front of a combination diner and bus stop. "From here, you can catch connections to Topeka, Des Moines, and Oklahoma City. This bus will continue through St. Louis to Denver in twenty minutes. Thank you."

The cabin lights came on, stirring the rest of the passengers. Max and Curtis joined them in preparing to disembark.

"Which way are you heading?" Max asked.

"I'm on my way to Denver. Max, I have to tell you something..."

A blue neon light radiating from the sign reading "Monk's Mound Diner" was flashing steadily through the window. A series of highway lamps illuminated the parking area in front of the small white house. Just beyond the glow was a wall of black until the beginning of one of the many rural neighborhoods that bordered the area. Interstate 70 lay beyond there to the north.

The driver engaged the air brakes and crawled out of his seat to wait near the open doors. He nodded to each one of the travelers as they got off. The bus emptied except for an elderly woman who was still struggling with her bags.

"May we help you, ma'am?" Curtis asked.

"That's very kind of you," the woman said, still wrestling with her suitcase. The two men loaded up her luggage and waited patiently for her to waddle off the bus.

The restless passengers dispersed through the parking lot to various parts of the way station, most going inside the front restaurant area, with others stopping in an information kiosk to read about connecting bus routes.

Max and Curtis elected to visit the bathroom at the side of the building. They were joined by several of the men who were on the bus, and a few who weren't.

The stalls and urinals filled up quickly then emptied almost as fast. Knowing they needed to get back to the bus, all the passengers who had ridden in with Max and Curtis were heading back out of the bathroom without delay. Curtis couldn't avoid doing the same after he had finished in one of the stalls and washed his hands twice. Max was nowhere in sight, so he decided to wait outside.

Max came out of another stall blowing his nose and coughing from the fresh air. The last man at the urinals finished and left, leaving only Max and another at the faucets.

"You'll need to come quietly," the man said, his hands still under the running water.

Max was able to size him up in the mirror over the sink that separated them. His initial impression was that it wasn't good. The man's dark hair was cut in a military crew and the bulge under his jacket was obviously a pistol. He has a full two inches on Max and at least fifty pounds.

"Just don't hurt anyone," Max said, ripping several paper towels from the dispenser to dry his hands.

The agent was shaking off his hands as he faced Max. It was almost time for the cuffs. Max turned toward the agent and flung the wet ball of paper towels toward his head. The agent reacted quickly enough to bat the diversion away, but not quick enough to avoid the right cross that followed. Max's rough and scarred fist connected with the agent's nose at an upward angle that was momentarily devastating. He turned and ran out of the bathroom without looking back.

Fortunately the luggage compartments on the side of the bus were still open for the departing transfers to retrieve their bags. Max ran straight up to where the driver had tossed in his rucksack and snatched it out. He was on his way down the dark frontage road before anyone saw.

Max considered hitchhiking for a moment, then he thought that maybe he shouldn't even be on the road at all. He drifted away quickly into the shadows of the soft shoulder, confused as to what to do. He paused there, seriously considering going back and leaving quietly with the agents.

It certainly would have solved a lot of problems, particularly since he had vowed to find the cause of his subconscious torment, one way or the other. It occurred to his panicked mind that maybe running wasn't what he needed to do.

He stumbled past a sign that was lit from below. "'Monk's Mound'" he read. "'With the same base as the Great Pyramid on the Giza Plateau, and larger than the Pyramid of the Sun in Mexico, Monk's Mound is the largest pyramid in the New World.'

"'At one time, Cahokia had a population of 20,000. It was one of the largest cities in the world both before and after 1250 BC.'"

Only the parking lot in front of the enormous earthwork was illuminated by street lights, the mound itself took some effort to spot from the road on that particularly dark night. Max was drawn toward the darkness. For some reason he had to see it.

As he got closer, a flight of cement steps came into view. He ran up the first level of the mound to where a short landing was connected to another upward span that ended at a pancake-flat top level.

He got moving up the stairs as fast as he could. He wasn't even at the first landing and he was getting a strategic view of the area. He pressed on, his heart beating frantically. It took considerable effort to haul his trembling body up to the very top of the 100 foot man-made mountain.

He found that it was worth it, however, as the 360 degree panorama allowed him to see all the way across the Mississippi River to the lights of St. Louis. He decided he could walk it and possibly disappear into the city for a while.

He turned toward the steps that ran down the north side of the mound and was tackled from out of nowhere by the agent from the bathroom.

The grass they landed in was deep green and wet from the sprinklers that had turned off only an hour before. They slid around some as they grappled, but the agent used his training to quickly get the upper hand with an arm lock that Max couldn't break.

He lifted Max up by the hold, guiding him back onto the cement sidewalk. Even the slightest deviation from the agent's lead caused Max excruciating pain. The stun gun was suddenly in his hand, Max never saw him draw it.

The agent had it inches from Max's neck before Curtis came out of his blind spot to tackle him to the ground. The powerful young man had lowered his shoulder and picked up considerable speed by the time of impact. The collision threw the agent off balance, then tumbling down the flight of cement stairs.

"What the hell are you doing?" Max yelled. "That man's a killer!"

"Then we probably better get the hell out of here!" Curtis said, making for the north stairs.

Max didn't bother checking on the downed agent.

"Hey, Max, ever heard of something called the Unity Council?!" Curtis asked, jumping down three steps at a time.

Back at a wooded rest stop near the diner, the injured agent appeared alongside a semi-tractor trailer rig, limping and holding a bloody handkerchief to his forehead. He took a remote control from his pocket, pointing it at the cab area of the semi. Activating the button caused a narrow access door to open behind the driver's side seat and a small stairway to automatically extend down to the ground.

The man broke through a dark curtain into the middle of an extensive surveillance and operations center. The older woman Max and Curtis helped off the bus earlier was working at one bank of computers, wearing a black tactical suit, headset, and microphone. The veteran agent of the Continuity of Government looked twenty years younger. Her haggard colleague fell into a chair beside her.

"Where is he?"

"What the hell does it look like? He got away!"

"You tell him then," she said.

The shaky agent initiated a text on his cell phone then immediately canceled it. "We have until tomorrow to report in... He's going to be furious if he finds out we had him and let him get away. Everyone is saying that he's obsessed with this Stiner guy."

"Three agents who missed him in New York haven't been heard from since. But that's the General now, nobody ever sees him anymore unless he's popping up to have someone disappeared. When I heard who the target was on this operation, I wanted to call in sick."

The man threw the bloody rag onto the console. "Yeah, because that's an option."

"Well, I know we better get a plan together right now," she said. "Because we're running out of time, and if we miss the next report window, we'll have even bigger problems than Max Stiner has."

6

The muffled sound of celebration coming from the next room was the first thing Bud heard when he regained consciousness. His surroundings were strange to him – as he had arrived in the middle of the night – and they were made even stranger by the lingering affects of the whiskey he had downed to get to sleep.

He lifted himself out of bed, still in his clothes, now regretting his adamant demand for a liquor store upon their arrival in Philadelphia. Ben and John had complied before they dropped him off at the doorstep of David Shaw and headed on to assist Gina in the nation's capital.

They had arranged to have one of David's assistants let Bud into the intercity storefront, the home of David's "Interfaith Center." Bud came to rest in an unused bedroom on the second floor.

The cheering and clapping from the other room exacerbated Bud's headache and generally worsened his mood. He coughed and hacked his way around the bedroom until he located his jacket, wallet, and keys. Those familiar items reminded him of his responsibilities back in New York City, and that he needed to call in to work.

He was hit by another wave of cheers and applause upon throwing the door open. He followed the sound through a small kitchen past a bathroom, where he stopped off to relieve himself and wash up.

Inside the bathroom, the old man splashed water on his face, grasping for some feasible reason for the bizarre situation in which he had found himself. He decided while wiping his salt and pepper beard dry with a hand full of paper towels that he had no regrets over his actions in New York. He emerged refreshed from the bathroom with significant questions about why it happened.

On the other side of the wall several elated men and women were standing around a big screen television at the end of a spacious office area. Bud made his way through the rows of desks toward the person in the crowd he thought was in charge. He was met by a middle-aged African-American man who had stepped away from the group to introduce himself.

"I'm David," he said. "How are you feeling this morning?"

"Pretty fair, but I need to call in to my job. I've got sick time, I just have to call in or they'll dock me."

David directed Bud to a phone on one of the desks. "Hit nine to get out," he said.

Bud reached his boss and begged out of work for the rest of the week, still wasn't sure what had happened to make it necessary. After hanging up, he couldn't resist joining the exuberant people in front of the television.

A sequence of images flashed across the TV screen, a tightly edited montage of morning rush hour traffic at a standstill on freeways across the West Coast.

"The press conference on the tip of the virtually inaccessible Third Mesa was supposed to be on behalf of a coalition of Native American tribes which had fallen pray to an infamous Washington lobbyist," the news anchor said. "After losing almost fifty million dollars between them in the process, the coalition was supposed to be announcing a civil lawsuit against the lobbyist's high-powered lobbying firm in Washington DC. A firm stocked with a headline-grabbing amount of former senators and congress people.

"It quickly became obvious that that wasn't the purpose of the conference at all. This was the scene in Arizona, while the morning rush hour drives of possibly thousands of people in five major cities on the West Coast were disrupted."

The leaders of the Unity Council crowded the stage: men and women wearing everything from business attire to jeans and t-shirts, their ages ranging from the teens to the nineties. Eventually a diverse collection of political, civil, and environmental activists from all over the world were standing behind Hector and several Native American elders. He hurried to the podium before the reporters had a chance to rebel at the sight of him.

"Thank you," he said. "I'll get right to the point. Most of you came here for the announcement of a multi-million dollar lawsuit. Well, representatives from several Native American tribes are here for an announcement, just not the one you expected."

The correspondents and their camera crews quickly became impatient. After his stunt in New York City, Hector had become quite unpopular with the East Coast news establishment, both liberal and conservative. That meant that he was also unpopular with the lowly affiliate reporters who got the duty of driving out to Hopi country to cover the lobbyist graft story for their network bosses.

"So here's the real scoop," Hector said. "The Unity Council is directly responsible for the traffic jams on the I-90 out of Seattle, on I-84 out of Portland, I-5 out of Oakland, I-10 out of Los Angeles, and the I-8 out of San Diego."

The screen behind Hector came to life with footage shot by Unity Council cameras earlier that morning in inner-city neighborhoods along the West Coast. In each frame, rows of school buses and old tour buses were being boarded by people carrying bags and luggage.

The video moved on to live coverage of the bus convoys on the open highways in each state as they made their way toward southern Colorado. By then they had all unfurled banners on the sides of the buses announcing the Unity Council, the website, and the eight-hundred phone number. Hovering news helicopters were following several of the convoys, broadcasting multiple scenes of traffic backups, some stretching for miles.

The reporters' collective skepticism immediately turned to rabid curiosity, tantalized by the possibility that the Unity Council could have been responsible for what their studios in Phoenix were saying had become the biggest story of the morning and probably the entire week.

"What we're seeing here is footage from West Long Beach, California," Hector said. "From the Lower Bottoms neighborhood in Oakland, from Barrio Logan in San Diego, from the St. Johns neighborhood of Portland and from Yesler Terrace in Seattle, from St. Louis Place in St. Louis, and from locations all around Memphis, Tennessee.

"Like the 9th Ward in New Orleans, many of these neighborhoods are poor and impoverished, particularly since the economic collapse. And like most of the low income areas of New Orleans before and after Hurricane Katrina hit, many of these neighborhoods are in danger from floods, earthquakes, tornadoes, or rising sea levels. In some cases, like Memphis, it's from a combination of catastrophes: earthquakes and floods.

"The fact is there are neighborhoods just like the 9th Ward all over this country. Those neighborhoods have already been forgotten, basically because they're already in economic ruins – some for decades – they'll bear far more of the burden when a flood or tornado or hurricane hits.

"We've been seeing for years the poorest people on this planet being victimized by terrible natural disaster. Now it's happening right here in this country, over and over again.

"But there was one tough lesson Hurricane Katrina – in particular – taught us all. That was thinking that since the modern era, there are no more natural disasters. It's already become a cliché.

"Neglect, greed, even bigotry played a large part in the terrible aftermath of Hurricane Katrina. Neglect, greed, and bigotry all played a large part in what happened during the recent Mississippi floods, with low income areas in St. Louis and Nashville swallowed up by the Big Muddy, never to be reclaimed.

"And let's not fool ourselves; neglect, greed, and bigotry will play a large part in how the United States government will react to the next big disaster, as well. If the last decade hasn't made that plainly obvious, nothing will.

"That's the reason why these caravans of buses have set out from Long Beach and Oakland and the other cities I've mentioned, clogging freeways from Washington to California, to Missouri and Tennessee.

"Some of the men, women, and families boarding those buses were unemployed, some have been foreclosed on, some have already been devastated by natural disaster. But now they're all taking steps to make sure that they won't become victims of the future disasters we all know will happen. They've made sure that we won't have to pull them from the rubble of a building in five years, or two years, or one month.

"And in the process, they've gone a long way to secure some level of stability in this increasingly chaotic world. So, the question becomes: what have they left behind now that they've made the decision to move?"

The looming screen behind Hector transitioned to the computer simulations of future climate change and sea level rise for the North American continent that Mary had helped create.

"Well, the historic floods that have drowned so much of Missouri and Tennessee, and other states, will continue to do so in any given year from now on. And will only get worse, long before they get better.

"But what most people aren't aware of is that New Madrid fault runs beneath the Mississippi River and is threatening St. Louis and Memphis with utter destruction from earthquakes that could last literally months.

"Upwards of ten million people could be affected by seismic events unlike anything we have ever seen. What's more, they will be taking place in areas that have already been devastated by flooding and by economic recession.

"Not to mention the fact that the region has done next to nothing to prepare in terms of building codes and retrofitting, any more than they've spent the money needed for flood mitigation like levees and protection walls.

"As far as what's happening on the West Coast... Well, two-thirds of the population of the U.S. lives on the coasts, something that up until recently wasn't necessarily fatal. Now things have changed. Like it or not, for more than one reason, we need to seriously reexamine where we live when it comes to the coastal regions of this and many other continents around the world.

"The Cascadia Fault, for example – off the coast of Washington and Oregon – is threatening to wash large sections of the Pacific Northwest shoreline away with an earthquake-generated tsunami, as it has periodically for thousands of years. And to make matters worse, research has shown that quakes on the Cascadia can actually cause quakes on the San Andreas.

"And of course, the idea of a massive earthquake in Southern California on the order of the San Francisco quake of 1906 has been predicted, forecasted, and joked about for years. And still the number of people moving into the state has actually risen steadily for decades.

"Personally, I was born in San Diego, a beautiful city. I was raised not far from where those buses were leaving from earlier this morning. It's a poor to lower middle-class neighborhood that sits on top of the Rose Canyon fault. A fault line with as much destructive power as the San Andreas.

"Today over twenty million people live in danger on the West Coast alone. And that doesn't count those who will inevitably be displaced by rising sea levels or inland drought, the victims of the coming disruption of the region's entire climate system.

"The overall effects of climate change have been varying from continent to continent, ocean to ocean. And honestly, due to the complex factors involved, even the simulations of future climate change we're working from are inadequate. There are just too many wild cards.

"But what is certain is that the impact on innocent men, women, and children everywhere has already been overwhelming, and the impact on the poor has already been catastrophic. What is also just as certain is that it's just the beginning.

"Since the Unity Council was formed, many critics have tried to use the recent economic meltdown as an excuse not to attempt what we're attempting. 'There are no jobs,' they say. 'The housing market is crashing. We need to be focusing on labor and social justice issues right now.'

"While the people and organizations of the Unity Council coalition certainly agree with all of that, we also believe that the increasingly destructive consequences of climate change and natural disaster stand as the most critical social justice issue we face as a society, as a whole civilization. It's clear that there will be no social justice in a world rocked by natural disaster, not unless we all join together now to make sure it happens.

"Beyond that, we had our analysts look into the consequences of an ideal unemployment rate of 4 percent nationally, for example. And under the current systems of manufacturing and transportation, it would have catastrophic consequences for the planet. 'Bringing those manufacturing jobs back home,' as so many people say, would actually spell doom for America, just like they have spelled doom for China and other nations, with their environments destroyed and their people demoralized.

"We believe that the recent financial collapse and the fallout since are really the perfect opportunities for long-term, systemic change. The past few years have shown the public that our current system of pure, unrestrained capitalism just isn't working. And that the people driving this economic and political freight train into oblivion don't care about us or even themselves. They're too deluded by greed and vanity to stop.

"If there is going to be a real reform of our financial and political system, which now seems inevitable, it's going to have to be designed for a future of near catastrophic climate disruption. If we're not seriously considering the worst case scenarios, then we're not seriously looking out for our children's futures.

"Are there alternatives to moving? Of course, but most of them rely on the government. And since not just Katrina, but a long line of other indignities, we would be fools to sit around thinking the United States government is going to help us in any way.

"Since we can't come up with the trillions of dollars needed for sea walls and effective levees – we're too busy paying taxes – and since phenomena like earthquake faults and 'tornado alleys' can't be defended against, moving out of harm's way is the only chance the people who live in these areas have to survive."

The display on the screen came full circle back to scenes of the different bus caravans leaving earlier that morning.

"Anyone who would like to learn exactly what the Unity Council is doing to help these people relocate, you're welcome to contact us at our eight-hundred number displayed here, or access our website. We will be happy to talk to you personally or send you information about how we may be able to help you, and about our conditions for aid.

"Over the last few days, we've been meeting with the newly formed Council of Southwest Native American Tribes, here in one of the oldest continuously inhabited settlements in North America, to ask some serious questions about the future of not only Native Americans, but everyone living on the West Coast and in the Desert Southwest.

"We would like to thank the Hopi people for their hospitality; our time here on the Third Mesa has been inspiring. And our talks with the Southwest Native American coalition have been extremely productive – , more on that this Sunday, when it will be the Unity Council's turn to host.

"Our convoys coming from Southern California are looking forward to joining up on the road with tribes from across the Southwest, including the Hopi, Navajo, and Pueblo, on their pilgrimage to the largest high-alpine valley in the world, the San Luis Valley in Southern Colorado.

"The Unity Council – along with many of those leaving the West Coast and the Midwest this morning – will be coming together with the people of the CSNAT on our property a few miles north of Alamosa.

"We will all be meeting for a huge Pow Wow and to continue our talks about the turbulent future of the West Coast and the Desert Southwest. On Sunday we will report on the results of our talks with a contingent from the CSNAT.

"Again, if you're curious about the Unity Council, just call or visit our website. If you're on the street or in a shelter, call our eight-hundred number from a payphone. Obviously, it's free. But we will not be making any more public statements until the press conference in Colorado on Sunday. Thank you all for coming, and we hope to see you again very soon."

Hector walked away from a barrage of questions without looking back. All of the Unity Council personnel assembled on the stage for their photo-op marched off without acknowledging the agitated reporters.

The people around Bud delighted in Hector's accomplishment. Though most already knew the text of Hector's speech, they were thrilled that the entire address had made it onto the news network they were watching.

One of the people changed the channel to another station and then another, they were all parroting the same commentary on Hector and the Unity Council. The extent of the negative attention only increased the collective glee of those present. Back slapping and hand shaking ensued.

"What's going on here?" Bud asked.

"Well, it's a pretty big day for the Unity Council," David said. "Hector there pulled a fast one that got us some attention."

"Yeah, looks like they'll be sniping about it for days," Bud said.

David eagerly shook the hand of one of his colleagues. "That means people will call or go to the website, if only to see what it's all about."

"Who are you people anyway?"

"We're the Unity Council!" one of the men said between high-fives.

"And?"

David led Bud away from the noise of the crowd and the television toward the front of the building. He opened the door to his office wide enough for Bud to squeeze by.

Inside, the office was spacious, at more than twenty feet by twenty feet, but it was cluttered by two uniformed rows of tables and chairs. The perfect stacks of books on all the tables made it seem like a small library. It was curious, but not as surprising as the walls.

The ceiling of the 1940s era building rose well above the windows and provided ample space for several rows of large white placards made of rigid construction paper. Taller than they were wide, they had been plastered in perfect rows over virtually every inch of the walls.

On the placards, written in black marker and large, easy to read script, were detailed outlines and subheadings of various arcane and paranormal subjects.

"What the hell is this?"

David had implemented the standard outline structure, with a subject heading, then a subheading indented below that, and then details of those subjects indented under that. Many entries consisted of books and their page numbers referencing more information. Most of the placards were covered with script top to bottom and all were carefully written.

"I'm going to go out on a limb here and say that you got something on your mind?" Bud said.

David closed the door before taking his place behind his desk. He rummaged through a small box on his desk.

"I'm terrible at keeping things organized," he said. "My eyes have never been great for reading either." He propped his reading glasses on his nose, looking very much like a college professor.

The walls were a haze of black lettering.

"You can see these I'll bet."

"It was the only way I could get a handle on the big picture."

Bud began circling the room. "The big picture, no shit. I'm all about the big picture. So how is that going anyway?"

"Well, all this started out as a hobby, then it turned into an obsession, and now it's pretty much my job."

"The big picture is your job, is it?" Bud tried to take in as many of the subject headings as he could. "Conspiracies, aliens, secret bases, looks like a pretty wild picture to me."

"I'm trying to compile a database, from my perspective. Then the plan is to compare it with the databases of others. Information compiled from their perspective. And hopefully then we'll get a look at the—"

"The big picture."

"Yeah. I have to leave tomorrow and I haven't entered nearly enough into my laptop yet. I got distracted by this." He pointed to the box.

"What's that?"

"Ben and John grabbed some things from Max's place, to try and get a line on him. So, what do you think happened to your friend?"

"He's not my friend. I just met the guy yesterday." Bud continued his bewildered inspection of David's research efforts. "I can't believe I've spent all this time living off the radar and now I got half the special ops guys on the East Coast after me."

"The Continuity in Government. Did Ben and John give you some background on the ride down?"

"I think I got the gist: a bunch of psychos and bureaucrats planning to screw us over when the shit hits the fan."

"Really, considering the Cold War – and the idea of 'acceptable losses' – the CIG was inevitable." David pointed to the far corner of the room, to the "government conspiracy" area.

"How the hell did you put all this together?" Bud closed in on the section.

"I've had occasion to meet a pretty wide range of conspiracy researchers and paranormal enthusiasts over the years. It's allowed me to uncover more about the Continuity in Government than just about anyone, though it still isn't much."

Words like "population control" and "strategic losses" stood out to an already-agitated Bud. "Why do they want Max?" he asked.

"All we know is that the head of the CIG, General Masterson, put out the word on his informant network for information on the whereabouts of one Maxwell J. Stiner."

"The arrogant sonofabitch thought that would work?"

"The Intra-Guard, what we call 'CIG Light,' is a network of a couple hundred thousand mostly business and professional people who, for special and exclusive 'War on Terror' bulletins, will inform on you or just about anybody else."

"Yeah right, and I thought I was paranoid."

"This is a matter of public record," David said. "They'll get contacted first when something bad happens. You know, like that big terrorist attack that's always right around the corner. They've even been provided with the provisional right to shoot to kill after the given disaster hits. Looters, of course."

"What the hell are we talking about here?"

"We're talking about a top-down quasi-governmental organization that has been preparing for disaster for sixty plus years. We're talking about a man that rules that organization with absolute ruthlessness, holding and exercising the power of life and death over not only his own minions but everyone else as well."

"Sounds like just another wannabe king," Bud said. "And the peons in the CIG and the Intra-Guard are his ass-kissing royalty." He scowled. "We're never getting away from it, are we?"

"Away from what?"

"Kingship."

David looked up from the box. "What do you know about that?"

"You kidding me? I know it's been the only way to live for about six thousand years."

"The history of kingship from Mesopotamia to now." David directed Bud to another section of outlines near his desk.

Bud marveled at David's detailed account of the social, religious, and political phenomena known as kingship.

"Max and I were just talking about all this. Seemed like he was kinda hung up on it. Well, on Mesopotamia anyway. He's a Gulf War vet, did you guys know that?"

"Hung up, was he?"

Bud was able to get through the summation quickly as much of it had been in the various books he had checked out of the library.

"So it's your job to make peace between the Big Three Cults?" he asked. "Into lost causes, are ya?"

David laughed. "It's not as tough as it sounds. Most of the churches, synagogues, mosques, and temples in the area all participate in the interfaith program we run here, the food drives, the clothing drives, the carnivals and fairs. I didn't have to twist any arms. The real problem has always been the money."

"If only it were that easy; the Middle East wouldn't be on fire right now."

"It is true that fundamentalism has had a stranglehold on world affairs. But truly spiritual people of all religions have a lot of common ground. And the democratic revolutions taking place all over the region have shown that politically they have common ground as well."

"You don't get any more fundamentalist than kingship," Bud said. "And kingship is everywhere in religion. You got the hierarchy of angels in Heaven, for starters. Hell, one of Jesus' titles in the Bible was the Prince of Princes. Oh, and the King of Kings.

"And what's the deal with the whole *Da Vinci Code* thing? Jesus' ancestors become this lost line of kings? Really? Because I'm seriously doubting he would have been cool with that. Chapped my ass the first time I heard of it." Bud read on down the outline. "'My own mind is my own church.'"

"Indeed," David said.

"That's Paine," Bud said. "He saw it two hundred years ago when he slammed the Israelites for screaming for a king, after all those generations without one. Basically, he compares hereditary rule to original sin."

"My job at the Unity Council will be to convince the 'Big Three,' as you call them, to come together and address climate change action as a religious and moral imperative essential to all humanity."

"OK...."

"The movement has already been growing for years now. Hopefully we can help them take it further."

"So it's that kind of stuff that got this Masterson all pissed off at you guys?"

"Oh, he's fairly pissed at you too right now, I'd imagine."

Bud stopped in front of one of the outlines. "That bastard can get glad in the same shoes he got mad in. They come after me again and I'll plant them in the ground."

"You can't kill them all, there's too many. But we are fighting them, and we won't stop."

"Clogging up a couple of morning commutes, is that how you're fighting them?"

"Hector has put together an amazing thing. Empowering people, helping them avoid becoming future victims, it will save lives."

"And that's what has Masterson sending thugs after people?"

"Masterson plans on exploiting the disastrous future we have ahead of us. It's not a new strategy, but it is definitely effective."

"So you needed all this other shit to figure that out? What's this: 'Alternative theories of the origins of humanity,' huh?" He looked across the room. "'Atlantis and Cayce,'" he read. He moved on to yet another placard. "'Ancient astronauts and mythology,' that's a good one. Oh, and the whole sorry kingship story."

"What do military men like to say: know your enemy?"

"What does all this have to do with that bastard?"

"That bastard is surrounded by other bastards who are up to their necks in all this."

"Yeah, that would look good on the morning news," Bud said. "'Environmentalist ghost hunters fight sinister government agency.' That'd play in the Heartland."

David confirmed the time. "There're some in the Council that are dubious of what Ben and John and I are doing, but they know that we aren't just dealing with some rogue government agency. It's not as simple as that."

"Yeah, I guess not."

Bud quickly read through the subheadings of several of David's outlines then went back to review the details.

"'History is essentially a war of secret societies,'" he read out loud. "I thought it was a war between inbred kings."

"Depends on which part of history you're talking about... Ishmael Reed."

"'The thriving mercenary business in the 1500s,'" Bud read. "Sounds familiar."

"Yes, there have always been mercenaries. But it was around then that the lucrative business of war joined up with the inflatable money system. That was when war became even more profitable than it had always been. Especially the debt on the war."

Bud's critical eye darted from one heading and subheading to another of the various outlines.

"'The rise of the Paper Aristocracy,'" Bud read. "Nice."

"It's an interesting phenomenon, what madmen and despots do with a little truth. Hitler and the cult of madmen around him were right, there were conspiracies all around them to start wars and destroy countries.

"There were secret societies, wannabe royalty and real royalty, Aryans, Jews, and anti-Semites, Masons, and Communists. And they were all funded by English, American, and German bankers: the Paper Aristocracies of America and Europe.

"Bankers in America, Germany, and England funded the supposedly Jewish-led Bolshevik Revolution in Russia. Then bankers in America, Germany, and England funded Hitler in Germany, while he was raving about the Jewish-led Bolshevik conspiracy.

"Throw in the petty schemes of aristocrats and bankers from just about every other European country and you have the makings of a couple world wars and about two hundred and fifty years of Western history right there."

Bud was actually impressed. "The Paper Aristocracy."

"And what those early Nazis neglected to mention during their hate-filled rants seventy, eighty years ago was that most all of the war profiteers of their time, and ours, learned their business from 16th century *Austrian* aristocracy. German, Austrian, Bavarian royalty made huge fortunes conscripting the men of their kingdoms to die in foreign countries for profit. Sound familiar?"

Without looking up, David pointed to an outline near the one Bud was reading.

"You have the Baron von Thurn und Taxis, a proto-Nazi and member of the Thule – you know, the secret society of aristocrats that created Hitler – you have him dying at the hands of the communists in 1919 in Austria. It turned out to be a pivotal event in the development of the anti-communist/anti-Jewish movement that would become the Nazis.

"But two hundred years before, you have his ancestors, the Thurn und Taxis family working with the Rothschilds, Jewish bankers. And you have those same Jewish bankers working with the royal German Hess family – from the famous Hessian mercenaries – to make money off wars in Europe and the American Revolution."

"Money-grubbing has no race, religion, or creed," Bud said. "Could have told ya that."

"Then Machiavelli takes it all back to the late 1400s, anyway." David gestured to the appropriate outline. "He talked about playing both ends against the middle to make wars for profit. All the time warning about what could happen if both sides find out what you're up to. Then he talks about how the 'ancestors' knew the tactic well."

Bud became momentarily paralyzed in front of the meticulous collage of arcane facts and subjects, his eyes constantly scanning.

"What are people up to out here?"

"We're a relocation service, technically. We help people get out of harm's way."

"Alright."

"That's essentially it. I'll admit it; we have ended up making some pretty nasty enemies. You've seen that firsthand. It's made it necessary for us to adopt some, let's say, unconventional tactics."

"'Wars, so far as possible, should not result in territorial gains,'" Bud read. "*The Protocols of the Elders of Zion.* I heard about this, but I always thought it was a hoax."

"The infamous *Protocols*," David said. "The original title was: *Dialogue in Hell between Machiavelli and Montesquieu.*"

Bud picked out another protocol. "'The need for daily bread forces the masses to keep silent and be our humble servants.'"

"It's really is tragic," David said. "'...that something written to shine a light on oppression would end up being used to inflict so much oppression and anti-Semitism."

"'In order that the masses themselves may not guess what they are about,'" Bud read. "'We further distract them with amusements, games, pastimes, passions, people's palace. Soon we shall begin through the press to propose competitions in art, in sport of all kinds.'"

"You know the *Protocols* were originally written as a joke," David said. "Didn't have anything to do with Jews. It was a piece of scathing political satire aimed at the aristocracy of Europe, primarily Napoleon the Third's scheming. Whether the author was exaggerating or not, he hit a nerve for sure. It probably wasn't so funny when he ended up in prison for a while."

"Looks to me like he laid it straight out for everyone to see two hundred years ago," Bud said. "This is how you keep the slaves in check, 101. '*Dialogues in Hell*' is right! Machiavelli, that prick!"

"The czar was terrified of the communists doing exactly what they did: taking him out and shooting him. So he twisted the Brotherhoods' blueprint for domination until it all got blamed on the Jews."

"The Brotherhoods?"

"It's what some researchers call the vast array of predominately male secret societies and organizations that seem to control things on this planet. You know, you have financial brotherhoods and political brotherhoods and mystical brotherhoods and religious brotherhoods. And they often overlap."

Bud was sporting a rare expression of admiration at the sight of so much effort. He stood back with his hands propped on his waist. "Where did you people come from?"

David smiled proudly. "Honestly, this all started as a personal investigation into the history of religion and war."

"But then you got onto kingship, huh? You saw it, didn't you? There's been a few of them on the idiot box that have seen it. They're calling it all kinds of other names; the kids yelling in the streets got their own names for it too. But you saw it, huh?"

"Certainly with the attack on the Constitution, and then the economic debacle, it's all finally become much harder for the world to ignore. Oligarchy, plutocracy, even the more exclusive hyper-mystical fascism we've been seeing since 2000, it's all just–"

"Kingship with elections? But you don't need any of this freaky shit to explain it, or the cluster fuck it's turned into nowadays, either. It's just what happens when a bunch of swinging dicks get together and start scheming for more food and a better hut.

"Isn't that what the books say? People were greedy, evil sonsofbitches back then, 6,000 years ago, and they're greedy, evil sonsofbitches now. And kingship is what we have to show for it."

David gave his guest a tolerant smile.

"Hey, I don't like it any better than you do, believe me. But you've seen the shit the Brotherhoods have been up to, better than anybody. They're the new 'royalty' and they've still got us all by the shorthairs. Still? After 6,000 years?

"When you turn on the idiot box and see the shit everywhere, you gotta start thinking that maybe it's true, maybe we are all just a bunch of bloodthirsty maniacs. Maybe we deserve kingship because that's all we can do."

"It's certainly true, Bud, philosophers and theologians have speculated for millennia on whether there really is some kind of original sin that has tainted us since our creation. And strangely enough, the Church joins modern psychoanalysis in being fairly convinced that we're all ruled by our animal sides. And that that animal side is essentially bad.

"But others insist that there is no original sin, *per se*. That it's our willingness to blindly follow a monarch, or a despot, or an ideology, or even a religion that leads to death and destruction. It's our willingness to give ourselves up to a system that is corrupt and evil that has led us all astray."

"What did Paine say about how vicious patriots can be? Yeah, maybe, but somebody had to come up with that system, didn't they?"

"Well that is the question, then, isn't it?"

"It looks like you've had a little time to think about that question."

"Like I said, it started out as a hobby. Now it's a job."

"Because of Masterson? I mean, why the hell does he want Max anyway?"

"Honestly, I don't know; we don't know. But I am going to find out, that's for certain."

Bud was drawn back to the outlines. "Always hated bullies, especially when I was acting like one. Kingship runs on them, wouldn't survive without them. And for all the crying Americans do about the underdog, we're the biggest bullies on the block now."

"Masterson is that and so much more," David said. "Using the fear of something unknown that has become near inevitable is particularly effective." He opened the office door. "That's what this meeting downstairs is about, the fear of the 'inevitable unknown,' so to speak."

"And that makes some kind of sense to you?"

"Join me, please."

David ushered Bud out of the office. The old man could barely tear himself away from the dazzling array of information on the walls, but couldn't resist following either.

"Basically, many of the clergy I work with from all the different faiths have had an influx of people who have been haunted, obsessed, really."

"Obsessed with what?"

"Disaster, with the 'end of the world.' They're searching for some reason why they would be so overcome by such irrational fixations."

"Yeah, that's no mystery. Besides being clobbered with the idea 24/7, look around, it really is all going to hell."

"That's the challenge of living in this time in history, isn't it? How do we find happiness living in an empire in decline?"

"I think you're a little obsessed yourself."

"A little, maybe. I have to go join them. You're welcome to sit in."

"Hey, if you don't have time to copy it all," Bud said. "You should have someone take pictures."

"Excellent idea, I hadn't considered that."

They slipped through the office area where David's people had returned to their desks, on their phones or busy at their computers. The muted television ran coverage of stalled traffic, to remind them of their temporary victory.

Bud held back at the top of the stairs and watched as David descended into a large crowd of people milling around the meeting area on the first floor of the storefront.

"You know who was preoccupied with apocalypse?" David said before reaching the bottom. "Leonardo da Vinci. He wrote a lot about the end of civilization. And it wasn't in code either. For him it was floods."

People streamed in from the front door, into the long open space reserved for just such gatherings. A sign in front of the assembly read: "Disaster Support Group Today."

"What the hell did I get myself into here?" Bud said. He slipped away quietly to return to David's office and the outlines.

General Masterson's limousine sped through the middle of acres of verdant Maryland ranch property. The sound of the engine scattered the horses that grazed behind the white fences on both sides of the road. There wouldn't be any other traffic, Masterson owned everything in sight.

He sat inside the bulletproof glass and armored chassis, his twitchy hand on a keyboard that controlled the flow of emails streaming into the computer console to his left. He trolled the reports from his media watchers and agents in the field for the one he had been waiting for, while keeping one bloodshot eye on the big-screen television mounted behind the driver. Four news channels played simultaneously in individual quarters of the massive screen, all reporting on the Unity Council.

A priority report came in that he clicked on immediately. He topped off his cup with the last of a spent pot of coffee while the message loaded.

"The safe deposit box has been confirmed," it read.

It wasn't the text he needed. He stabbed angrily at the keyboard as he typed his reply.

"I want that document on my desk in an hour! And tell Team Two to send me their report, now!"

He initiated an email to his technical department demanding an update.

"Analysis of audio from S. Billy progressing but not complete," was the reply.

"Your 30 hours are almost up!" he wrote back.

He couldn't wait any longer. He initiated an email to the agents chasing Max on Interstate 70. "Your report is twelve minutes overdue!" He sent it with another stab of the "Return" key.

The mere fact that the team had missed their report window meant that they had either failed to acquire Max Stiner, were apprehended by local authorities, or they were dead. None of those prospects pleased the already frayed power player.

A blinking symbol appeared in one of the four sections on the big screen television, indicating that his resident mad scientist was requesting a video conference. Masterson authorized it and Hasline's face appeared on the screen.

"Report, Doctor."

"Well, I was skeptical at first, sir. But the frequencies I have now been able to isolate definitely disrupt the orchestrated collapse of subatomic particles in the microstructures of the synapses."

"And?"

"Well, General, they interfere with the brain's ability to interact with the quantum world. As I said, I was skeptical, but they actually inhibit psi abilities. I have years of testing to do on this process, of course. But initial results are very promising."

"So you're telling me that you believe your experiments were successful?"

"They were, very. I've ordered my system deployed immediately and I will be traveling to the WRC to oversee installation personally. Is there something wrong, sir?"

"Just do the meeting in Dulce and then get up to the WRC. The system better be up and running before Sunday night."

"Yes s–" Masterson disconnected the video link.

The limousine came to a stop in front of a vine-covered astronomical observatory that had been built in the mid-1800s, along with a small home for the resident astronomer.

The place was quaint and rustic, except for the state-of-the-art radio telescope visible at the top of the building. Masterson got out of the back of the car as soon as it came to rest. His bodyguard in the front seat tried to follow but was waved off.

Inside, the telescope dominated the room, with its gigantic nose jutting out of the opening in the domed roof. Segment by segment it shrank down to an eyepiece that was suspended over a platform. All was as Masterson had arranged.

He tugged on one cuff of his fine silk shirt until it was even with his suit sleeve, then the other. He went straight toward the astronomer's cluttered workspace at the base of the telescope, breaking into a labored applause that made the high-strung young man flinch.

Masterson's anticipation even resulted in a rare smile. He had always been a fan of science and technology but astronomy was something else altogether. To him, surveying the heavens was as critical as seeing the future.

"Mr. Masterson, you're Johnny-on-the-spot, as usual! Whoa, are you OK? You look beat."

"You have good news for me, Dr. Evans?"

"This is big, sir, I found it! Your approach worked! And that translation! Where did you get that translation?"

Masterson focused on the dense array of stars on the smaller video monitor, too captivated to speak. A flashing arrow was singling out one obscure white dot among thousands near the far right corner.

"Well, the guys at the Society aren't going to like it, but it worked! I mean, we've been looking for the Tenth Planet for over thirty years now! When they found Tyche, I thought that was it for my research. But Tyche isn't Planet X. Actually, come to think of it, I found the Ninth Planet, now that they downgraded Pluto."

The young man looked for some recognition from Masterson but all his patron could do was stare at the faint white blob.

"I personally sifted through a couple of years of Hubble data to calculate its orbit," Evans said. "It's in a part of the sky where nobody would think to look for it, but it's definitely orbiting our sun. Too bad the infrared indicates such high quantities of carbon dioxide and sulfur particulates."

"Speak English boy!"

"Don't you see? The atmosphere on the surface may have actually been breathable at one time. Very recently, in fact. But not now... Awe, man, this is big!"

The young scientist flitted around his desk enthusiastically while Masterson stood unmoved.

"Using Sitchin's translations of the Sumerian creation myth as a guide to find Planet X was genius, Mr. Masterson. Velikovsky tried something like this over fifty years ago with the Bible. Everyone but Einstein laughed at him.

"It was that translation, all these verses are clues to a cosmological event most astronomers would have said was impossible a generation ago."

Masterson's vision blurred.

The young man consulted his notes. "'...then an invader appeared, from the deep,'" he read. "'Marduk, the Planet of Millions of Years.'"

"Invader," Masterson said. "That's a very interesting word."

"Yes! Yes, it is! You see, we're just starting to realize that maverick planets are pretty common in the galaxy, floating around between solar systems, basically free agents, until one gets snagged by a strong enough source of gravity. That's why Planet X's orbit is retrograde like a comet, about 3,600 years give or take, because it invaded this solar system and got caught."

"'In the beginning there was only an infant star, the Sun,'" Masterson recited from memory. "'...the brilliant red Mercury, and the primordial Tiamat, she who bore them all, with her moon Kingu.'"

"That's in the story! You sure know your mythology."

"Yes, mythology, indeed."

With the press of a few keys, the display Masterson had been ogling was transferred to a widescreen TV behind Evans's desk. Masterson drew close to the display.

"Earth was merely a statistical improbability in a universe of infinite possibilities then. And if it hadn't been for the–"

"'Seven winds did the great god bring to bear,'" Masterson quoted. "'The West, East, North, South. And, to seal the watery giant's fate, Marduk created the Evil winds, the Whirlwinds and the Hurricane.'"

"That was word for word! Hmmm, you sure seem to know a lot about this story... Should I ask?"

Masterson didn't respond.

"I can tell you one thing, sir; it sure is going to burn them all up when they read the conclusion of my paper on all this. The peer reviews should be insane. It turns out that humanity owes its very existence to that 'invader.'"

"In more ways than one."

"And ancient peoples knew it thousands of years ago!" Evans was by then frantically trying to gather together the many scattered pieces of his research. "In Babylon they called it Marduk, after their chief god. Sometimes it was Nibiru, the Planet of Crossing.

"It's coming closer to Earth, too. It's still a thousand years away, but it's heading toward perihelion, it is coming this way. I would need to get the scope exclusively for more details, for sure, but at least I've got enough data to confirm beyond a doubt that it exists.

"Man, this is too much. I used to dream of shit like this when I was riding a desk at NASA. I knew I had to get out of there, no money for anything but military projects. But now. You realize the implications of another planet in the solar system, another planet that may have supported life? That may have spawned life on this planet?"

Masterson's jaw locked as all trace of emotion disappeared from his face.

"Do you realize that if a life form from that planet were to come here," the young man mused. "It would live approximately three thousand six hundred times longer than a human?"

"A thousand years is but a day," Masterson whispered. "In Heaven..."

"Screw finding planets around other stars! I found one right here! Do you realize how long they have been looking for this? I'll be famous. You'll be famous for bankrolling my research!"

Masterson sidestepped behind Evans, retrieving a slim black cylinder resembling a fountain pen from his coat. He twisted the top of the device, to adjust the voltage.

"Nobody's going see this coming, Mr. Masterson. I want a supermodel. No, two supermodels, who just can't wait to lay the man responsible for the greatest discovery of the century. You might even be able to get some residual action there, big guy."

"Impressive work," Masterson said. "Truly."

Evans could barely contain his excitement. "This is bigger than finding Pluto in the '30s! I need to download the telemetry onto a disk so you can get–"

A touch on the young man's neck with the tip of the device instantly pumped a lethal jolt of electricity through his body. The force of the current slammed his face into the computer monitor, sending sparks flying and smoke erupting from the screen.

Masterson retrieved a tiny black box from his coat pocket, detached a miniature remote control, and placed the larger device on the bank of computers. After spinning on his heels, he engaged the remote. It caused all the electronics in the entire room to short out, ejecting Evans's lifeless body out of the chair in the process.

"Wet clean up at these coordinates," Masterson said into his cell phone.

Barely an hour later, Masterson was preening behind a heavy wooden podium on a stage that ran the width of a grand meeting hall. The smell of soap and aftershave hung heavily in the air over a tightly packed assembly of smiling Caucasian faces in black silk robes. The room full of men was applauding and cheering their beloved "Unknown Superior."

Masterson perused the elaborately framed oil paintings that covered every inch of the Colonial meeting hall, taking in the adulation from his devout followers. It seemed to invigorate his tired brain.

George Washington, John Quincy Adams, Benjamin Franklin, and several other Founding Fathers were represented on the walls around him. Some wore aprons and held trowels in paintings that had never seen the light of day. Others posed proudly under the drafting compass, trowel, and "All-Seeing Eye" that were the centuries-old symbols of their secret affiliation.

Masterson stood unimpressed among the architects of the United States of America, the men clapping furiously at his feet revered him more than any former president or political figure. And the secret society that had formed around him rivaled in scope and reach any Masonic group that had ever existed in the past. Eventually, the crowd saw that he was ready to speak and quieted.

"We stand on the verge of an important and incredible time," Masterson said. "I don't have to remind any of you of that. And as it has always been throughout history, the select few will be called on to save the many. The best humanity has to offer will be needed once again. Your sacred knowledge and deliberate intent will shepherd the masses through yet another calamity."

The crowd erupted in applause that lasted for a few seconds then died down.

"It is a weighty responsibility to uphold the traditions of this society. Traditions that are thousands of years old, traditions that have ensured, time and time again, the orderly survival of humanity. As this new millennium advances, those ancient traditions will become even more essential.

"We all know what happens when the masses are given even the slightest amount of autonomy. The chaos of real autonomy would destroy this Republic. Their naïve fantasy of freedom may sustain them and give them hope. But you know the truth of history. You understand how the world works and you have refused to be a part of the ninety-nine percent of commoners that walk the Earth today.

"You have chosen to be great, and your appetites for acquisition have shown to be equally as great. As the primitives of the past craved the guidance of their priests and hero-kings, the commoners of today crave your leadership. They would be lost without it."

Besides Masterson's resounding voice, an occasional cough was the only sound that could be heard in the hallowed hall. His disciples, the heads of lodges from all over America, were exhilarated by his mere presence.

The men there had passed through the degrees and dedicated their lives to learn the inner secrets, the ones not even the low ranking members of their own organization would learn. That their mythic leader was personally gracing them with his words at such an important time in history sent them beyond religious fervor, beyond hero or idol worship. For their Unknown Superior, rumor persisted, was immortal. He guarded the secrets of the ages and held the key to the future.

As far as the finely manicured group of business and government elite were concerned, Masterson ruled the real world. Legend stated that he always had. He was the lord of the only world that mattered anyway. The world only a miniscule fraction of humanity would ever know existed.

"Since the first lodge was founded in Scotland over five hundred years ago, the destiny of this society was cast. The masters of the Old World, the men portrayed around us, had a singular vision for this country. Who would have thought that the New World would become the bastion of such an ancient and sacred association?

"It is for America that we sacrifice, that we work so hard. We must preserve this country through a time when far more than just a rogue terrorist or renegade dictator threatens its survival. This time it's nature itself that threatens America's sovereignty, and your sovereignty as well.

"Disaster will jeopardize your right to rule over the rabble. Chaos is always lurking! On the edge of civilization, on the edge of constant vigilance! That's why what we must be now is ever vigilant!"

Applause echoed throughout the hall, the pink faces of the crowd were all beaming. Again it subsided.

"Be mindful of the fact that the people will never be able to govern themselves. They've shown time and again that they are incapable of handling the realities of the world that we all live with everyday. They're too weak. So as it has always been, their betters will watch out for them.

"And when the long-anticipated Armageddon begins, this society will protect the future by protecting the traditions of the past. You will maintain order by maintaining the creed."

General Masterson's limousine waited in front of a compact stone building that appeared completely untouched by time. Though the lodge dated back to the rebuilding of Washington DC in the 1800s, its tightly fitted blocks and Roman columns demonstrated the kind of architectural precision that would last for centuries to come.

Like Mason temples reproduced in cities and towns all over the country, the meeting hall exhibited the kind of superior knowledge the builders of the still unparalleled ancient wonders like the Great Pyramid flaunted with everything they constructed.

Only "The Royal Temple Knights of the Strict Observance" was a quasi-Masonic brotherhood that few Masons had ever even heard of, an ultra-secret society operating clandestinely at the top of a semi-secret society.

The doors burst open with a steady flood of satisfied men; they soon clogged the steps leading to the parking lot. They ranged in age from forty to eighty, all wearing business suits and the self-satisfied smiles that came from sitting in on one of the most well-kept secrets in the world.

A man near the entrance began applauding and others joined him, the crowd parted so that their Grand Master could pass.

Pascal was 50ish with intense, European features and a penetrating stare. Looking regal in his red robe and tall black hat, he took in the praise that he knew wasn't all for him.

General Masterson trailed behind, somewhat less irritated than usual. Keeping his troops in line was one thing, but appeasing his loyal worshipers was a necessary and often satisfying chore. He would have been the last one to admit that as his very existence had become more of a secret, and he slipped deeper into the shadows, his need for open and unabashed reverence had grown.

"Pascal, I'll be in touch."

The bodyguard opened the door for Masterson to climb back into his rolling nerve center. He sped away to the sound of fevered applause.

Masterson was nearing the end of his agenda for the day, only one more stop to make. His driver headed back into Washington DC, eventually turning onto Pennsylvania Avenue.

Masterson made a call upon seeing the White House and an extended backup of limousines at the security checkpoints.

"Nina, this is the General. Tell the President I will be able to make his meeting after all, would you please? We're approaching security now and it looks like quite a bother. Could you take care of it?" He hung up.

A report from his media monitoring department caught Masterson's attention. News of the Unity Council's activities on the West Coast was spreading across the country. He changed the channels in the sections on the television to coverage of traffic backups from San Diego to Seattle.

"Why in the *hell* wasn't I told about this?!"

Another email came in; the one Masterson had been waiting for all morning.

"This is completely unacceptable!" he yelled after reading it.

The excuses the agents offered for missing Max at the Cahokia site never had a chance of placating their superior officer, he had been waiting too long to hear that his torment was over.

He almost broke the "Return" button calling up Max's military photo on his computer. Taken when he was still fresh faced and clean-shaven, Max looked almost hopeful in the mug shot. His slight grin and youthful eyes only served to mock Masterson. He initiated a text to his department of special operations.

"Dispatch Theta Team to Team Twelve's last location!" he typed. "I want those failures dealt with and Stiner found! Now!"

"Understood sir!"

Masterson got Hasline back on video conferencing.

"Did you gather the information I requested, Doctor?!"

"Yes, sir, I did. Everything I have on lucid dreaming is in my latest status report. Is there anything you would like to talk about, General?"

Masterson disconnected without a word.

Dressed in a smart black pantsuit, with her ragged backpack by her side, Billy brooded in the backseat of a government sedan that was idling several cars behind Masterson's.

"Looks like they're going to hold us up, Ms. Billy," the driver said. "They have to unload some VIPs. Oh, no offense."

"None taken, darlin'."

They waited for another half an hour before they were allowed to pass the cement barricades that lined the majestic front lawn of the White House. Billy would have had the driver turn around long before then if not for the report on the South Carolina hurricane she had spent the previous 12 hours preparing.

Approaching the White House's security checkpoints, the heavily fortified palace reminded her of the palaces she had visited – inhabited and abandoned – of banana republic dictators in South America.

The opulence of the presidential mansion was intended to overwhelm and intimidate the foreign dignitaries who visited, while inspiring the Americans who saw it. The same went for the city of Washington DC as a whole. As a person who considered herself an employee of the American public, Billy couldn't imagine the arrogance it took to revel so unapologetically in the taxpayers' largess.

Armed with just two file folders and her righteous indignation after security forced her to relinquish her backpack, Billy met Phil's temporary replacement, McCrea, in the antechamber to the meeting room of the presidential cabinet.

The slick newcomer to FEMA was someone that Billy had done her level best to avoid when their paths crossed overseas. He embodied all of the bureaucratic narcissism and casual indifference Billy loathed.

"Director," she said in an almost drawl free tone.

"Billy, is this your report?" Billy handed him the first folder, inspecting him with a particularly critical eye.

McCrea was younger than her and sported an arrogance that made her want to refer to him as a "Glory White Boy." That was before he was in charge of the entire agency.

"Tokyo is still dragging their feet on getting the first shipment of seed accepted," he said.

"That's because the farmers in Japan won't touch it," Billy said. "And you know very well why, too. They've lost thousands of acres of farmland; they're not going to be blackmailed into ruining what they have left. They knew better in Haiti and they know better in Japan."

McCrea dropped it quickly, not really expecting Billy to be of much help in the matter. Billy took the opportunity to hand him the other file folder.

"What's this now?"

"This is a comprehensive assessment of where they were in South Carolina as of this morning," she said.

McCrea didn't even glance at the report. "The president will take this under advisement," he said.

"You guys are dragging your feet up here, Joan needs your help. They all need your help."

"The president has a lot going on right now. There was talk of me getting a few minutes later today. I will brief him on your report if I get a chance."

"These people are in serious need down there and they're looking to see if FEMA is going to live up to its promises. Tell him to do it because it's an election year. We're not going to try to take away their vote now too now are you?"

"I'm supposed to go to the President and tell him that millions, possibly tens of millions, more dollars will have to be spent on nothing but damage control. I'm supposed to tell the Presi–"

"Yes sir," Billy interrupted, her thick accent returning quickly. "You're supposed to look him straight in the eye and remind him that lives are devastated and that real help isn't cheap. That is your job."

"Don't tell me my job."

"OK, the United States government is too cynical and opportunistic to help just anyone abroad. Unless of course they have something we want! But at least we can help our own people! After Katrina, this is our chance to redeem ourselves!"

"Lower your voice, remember where you are! I realize the situation, but we're doing what we can with the money available. The war–"

"Don't say that word to me! Don't say it's because of September 11th and don't say it's because of Iraq or Afghanistan, because I don't want to hear it anymore!"

"Lower you voice!" he said again. "Or you won't be asked back here again, Ms. Billy."

"Thank God for that."

"You're the one that keeps pushing about relieving the Haiti debt, aren't you?"

"I'm the one."

"Well they got all they're going to get down there. And if that isn't enough, well that's too damn bad. This country has more important priorities right now than pouring money into a black hole."

His flippant tone and casual racism incensed Billy. "If the geniuses of *realpolitik* in the administration weren't spending billions of dollars killing innocents in foreign countries for oil and political gain, there would be plenty of money to go around! Or is it all going to those detention camps that are being built in every state right now? Yeah, I read that report. What's going on here? New Orleans was just the beginning, wasn't it? You people don't intend on doing a damn thing while this entire country crumbles around us."

The door to the meeting chamber opened. "You're lucky you're a GS or you would be gone. The agents will escort you out."

"Oh, I'm lucky alright. We all just keep getting luckier and luckier."

"I'm going to recommend limited future expenditures on the hurricane. The insurance companies and state agencies will have to kick in."

"And my report?"

"It will be taken into consideration."

"I'm so glad I rushed down with it," she said, turning toward the door. "You'll have my resignation by the end of the day." She didn't look back.

Billy's head was spinning and she thought she would choke as she made her escape. If she could only reach the security station, she could get outside for some fresh air. Maybe then she could think about how she had just quit her job.

The metal detectors and the doors to the outside were in sight when she heard an eerily familiar voice from behind.

"I knew you'd be back," the voice said.

She didn't stop, hoping the man was speaking to someone else.

"Sylvia Billy, how quickly they forget."

She stopped to face the man. It was Victor Duncan, an old flame she hadn't seen in years. By then she was on the verge of tears; seeing him tightened her back up. They hadn't exactly parted on good terms.

"What the hell do you want?" she said.

"What's going on here?"

"I just quit."

"Why would you do that? What's happening here?"

"You know, you work for them. We're all being hung out to dry, Victor. And I, for one, will not stand for it!" She stomped off before Victor could respond. "And if you and your President are in on it, you're going down too. That's a promise!"

Victor knew Billy and he knew that following her at that point in time could have been dangerous. It appeared he was going to have to make a pass at his ex-girlfriend when she wasn't mad enough to knock him out cold.

7

The front of the extended caravan that had left California so spectacularly during the morning commute had, by later that day, finally stretched into western Arizona. Hundreds of cars, trucks, and buses now clogged the eastbound lanes of I-40 into Kingman. It was an uncommon sight for such a remote spot in the desert.

The sudden influx of people was temporarily swamping the services and accommodations of the quaint tourist town. It was fortunate the Unity Council had planned ahead.

Large areas of the desert around the city had been cordoned off and equipped with water and mobile toilets. With the help of Unity Council employees, the areas were filling up with tents, RVs, and campers.

Meanwhile, Kingman itself boomed with travelers browsing through the shops and eating at the few restaurants still in business in the old town.

Sara, Mary's daughter, was a bright 10year-old with long black hair and a pixie's smile. She pressed her nose against the glass of the passenger side window of her mother's pickup for a better look at the people slowly parading by.

The curious young girl had been far too distracted by the sights and sounds of the Council's massive publicity stunt to notice that her mother had been fretting since they left Los Angeles. The intensity of the traffic and the backup was only serving to heighten Mary's apprehension.

Her cell phone rang and the caller identification confirmed it was her mother, yet again. She took a deep breath.

"Hey, Mom. How's it going?"

"How's it going? How are *you* doing?"

Mary inched forward a few feet until she was forced to stop again. "We're doing great," she said. "You should see it out here. It's so beautiful."

"My God, Mary Margaret, it's all over the TV. You should hear the things they're saying. And you're going to work for these people?"

"What do you mean 'these people,' Mom? We're helping homeless people and poor families, in a time when our own government won't, so of course the news is going to try to tear us down. I told you that you can't believe everything you hear on TV. Just because they said it, doesn't make it so."

"You uprooted your whole life, Sara's life, for this?"

"Everyone's got to leave home sometime."

"How is Sara?"

"She's great. A fault line is no place to raise a child, you know that."

"Oh, I know you're right, dear. We're just so worried about you two. We love you both so much."

"I know you do. I'm worried about you and Dad in that city. Something bad is coming, Mom. I can feel it. You should get out of there."

"Now you know your father. This is our home. He works hard to keep it. You know we couldn't just up and leave. He's very angry with you, Mary Margaret. Your probation officer will be calling. What should we tell him?"

"I don't care anymore. I'm never going back there again and neither is my daughter. I did what I was supposed to do. Now I'm going on with my life."

"The news says this will end up turning into a national mess, all this moving around. They say this Unity Council is trying some kind of a scam."

"That's what they say, is it? Well, they don't know what the hell they're talking about."

"But they—"

"I'm not worried about what they say about anything, Mom. You should know better. Listen, I have to get some stuff done so I'll call you tonight maybe OK?"

"OK dear."

Mary hung up before her mother could go on any further. She didn't want to be questioned just then. She had parted with her parents on bad terms and that didn't help the gnawing doubt in her stomach. Her phone rang again.

"Mary, we're down!" said the man on the other end of the line. "Looks like a DoS attack."

"Keith? What?" She slowly turned onto the shoulder and came to a stop. "Just switch over to one of the mirror sites. We're prepared for this."

"Every time we try to bring up one of our mirror sites, it gets hit as well."

"Damn it! There's only one way something like could happen. Alright, I have a clone of the site on one of my hard drives. We're close to Kingman; we'll be back online within the hour. I'll call Hector and tell him."

An SUV came to a stop behind her as she was calling Hector.

"This is Hector."

"Hector, this is Mary Jenkins, I—"

She was interrupted by an extremely tall, middle-aged white man, with thinning brown hair and broad shoulders.

"Mary Jenkins?" the man asked.

She covered the lower half of her cell phone with her palm. "Yes, I am, I'm on with Hector Madrano right now."

"I'm Leonard. We need to get you into the camp." He looked over the bumper to bumper traffic leading into the town, in search of the best way around the backup.

"I was hoping for a little special treatment," she said. "Is everything OK?"

"Everything is fine Mary," he said over his shoulder. "We just need to get you into the camp as soon as possible."

Mary remembered Hector on the phone. "Yeah, Hector? Sorry about that, we're outside Kingman. I know what you said. I mean... I left the Los Angeles county limits, so..."

"It's OK–"

"I had to leave, Hector, that's it. If you want to fire me, I understand, but I had to leave."

"Of course I'm not going to fire you. We have important work for you to do, work that you won't be able to do with anything hanging over your head."

"I just had to leave."

"I know... I guess it's a good thing because we have a problem; more than one, in fact."

"I just talked to Keith; we'll be back up ASAP. But you need to get me close to the high-speed Internet connection, quick."

"You're just outside Kingman?"

"Yes."

"And you haven't seen one of our people yet?"

"Actually, yes, one just showed up a second ago."

"They'll get you in here. I'll make some arrangements; the specifics will be waiting for you at the information booth. Just give them your name."

"Man, Hector, thanks for that."

"We need to talk, Mary. The situation has changed and there are things you need to know."

"OK, is everything alright?"

"It will be once we get you and your daughter in here."

With the approval of the Unity Council personnel stationed along the road, Mary carefully followed Leonard as he sped along the soft shoulder toward the makeshift Unity Camp outside Kingman.

"Just give them your name when you get here. So you aren't waiting around."

"Hector, I'm sorry if I've messed things up. I guess I'm still kind of impulsive sometimes."

"I'm glad you're here, for more than one reason. But right now we need that site back up as quickly as possible. A couple of our phone banks have also gone down."

"That can't be a coincidence. We're under attack."

"In more ways than one. We'll talk when you get here. Leonard is an ex-cop, he'll look after you."

"I'll call Denver when we get there. We'll get that site back up within the hour, I promise."

The ride to where the weary Unity Council motorists were stopping for lunch was only a few minutes away from where Mary pulled out of traffic. It probably would have been more like an hour had she stayed in line.

Restrained by her seat belt, Sara squirmed in the front seat for a better view of the activity. Her mother was doing her best to keep up with Leonard, until they slowed in front of one of the Unity Council's many information booths. Rows of campers, RVs, and tent sites spread out for acres behind the hastily constructed shelter.

"I've got Mary Jenkins here," Leonard said through the window. "Hector Madrano said we were supposed to check in when we got here."

A busy young coed behind the counter sprang into action. "Mary Jenkins, they've been waiting for you. An escort is coming to take you back. Could you park over here a sec?"

Leonard found a space out of the flow of traffic and people that was large enough for both he and Mary to wait.

Sara continued to squirm until Mary let her out of her seat belt and they all marveled at what was transpiring around them. The amount of people pouring into the temporary rest stop was slowly becoming overwhelming.

Mary couldn't help but be inspired by the chaos. She leaned out her window to talk to Leonard, who was doing the same. "Was there supposed to be this many people?" she yelled.

"I'm only in security, but as far as I know this was not in the plan."

Two SUVs pushed their way through the foot traffic to where Leonard had been standing watch over Mary's pickup. Following a quick conversation between him and the men in the trucks, Mary was in the middle of a caravan with Leonard at the lead, winding slowly into the Unity Council campground.

The endless rows of RVs, station wagons, and minivans were reminiscent of weekends tailgating with her father at football games to Mary. Most of the genial campers were buzzing around barbeques and coolers, taking advantage of the lunch stop before continuing on to the overnight campgrounds in Flagstaff.

Rolling slowly but steadily, the caravan didn't stop until they were on the far side of the camp, in front of a tight grouping of old school buses and recreational vehicles of all types and sizes. Most had their hoods up with mechanics working under them.

The two other SUVs broke and left Leonard to lead Mary around the huddle of vehicles, through an opening between the buses that had been left specifically for her arrival. Mary came to a stop under a tarp covered courtyard that had been created by the buses and RV's all around.

Two picnic tables had been set up in the center of the space beside a swing set that was being used by two enthusiastic siblings. The sight of kids playing excited Sara. Unable to open her door, she climbed through the opening to the camper then skipped to the back door.

"Sara, I need to put the steps down."

Jumping down onto the sandy ground imbued Sara with a sense of well-being so powerful that she had to giggle. Mary grabbed a bag and her laptop and joined her.

"Stay close!"

"It'll be cooler in Flagstaff," Leonard said, getting out of his truck. "It even gets chilly up there at night."

Mary stepped away from Sara to assess the situation. The men who had accompanied them from the gate had parked and taken up guard positions near the corners of the courtyard, she noticed. And with a little effort she was able to locate three more people, two men and a woman, looking rather vigilant. Not armed, that Mary could see, but alert.

"What going on here, Leonard?"

"Hector's coming, you should talk to him. We'll get power and water to your camper so you can get to work."

"Hector shows up and I get the whole story, OK?"

"Fair enough."

Mary led Sara around to the rear of her pickup, to the door into the camper. She lowered the stairs and helped Sara in. The exuberant child climbed into the sleep area over the cab of the pickup for a look out the tiny windows at the swing set.

"It's just like camping, huh, Mom?"

"Yes ma'am, but we'll be in Colorado tomorrow."

Mary carefully placed her state-of-the-art, graffiti- and bumper sticker-covered laptop onto the miniature table in the camper. She took a quick look around her escape vehicle, her means of freedom that would make it impossible for anyone to ever keep her tied down again. She couldn't help thinking how much smaller it seemed now than when it was sitting in her parents' driveway.

"Can I go play, Mom?"

"Yes, but first we need to check out the area, OK hon?"

Sliding in front of her computer, Mary remembered her father's face when she and Sara left.

"Too clever for your own good," was what he said. It was what he always said when Mary got into trouble.

She fired up the laptop, refusing to regret her decision, even though she knew his disappointment was made complete by the news that his daughter was running away.

Sara made a dash for the door.

"And where do you think you're going, young lady?"

"I wanna go outside. We were in the car all morning."

"We're in a new place, Sara. We have to stay close for a while."

"Mom, I'll stay right here. I promise."

"In front of this window, OK?"

Sara pushed open the screen door and carefully climbed down the stairs. "OK."

She was met by a group of young boys and girls that had drifted over from the other RVs in the repair line. Mary was observing them with motherly skepticism through the window and noticed that a topless four-wheel drive was approaching with a van trailing behind.

She recognized a familiar face from the Unity Council website behind the wheel of the lead vehicle. She and Hector had spoken long distance several times since her phone interview, but had yet to meet in person.

Hector stopped at a small gap in the buses, where an imposing man in plain clothes was on guard. Leonard was already through the opening and heading toward the van before it could stop.

Hector jumped out of the four-wheel drive, two box lunches in hand. "Everything OK?" he asked Leonard as he passed on his way to the opening van door. "Any sign of trouble?"

"Not so far, but we're ready either way,"

It had been over a week since Leonard left his wife, Sheila, and their two children in Los Angeles to help the Unity Council prepare for their big day. Sheila leapt from the passenger seat into her husband's arms the moment the van came to a stop. Their children joined them for a heartfelt reunion.

"Looks like you have the rest of your passengers," Hector said.

"Looks like we're just about ready," Leonard said. "You just have to talk to Mary."

"What did you tell her?" Hector asked.

"Not much and she's getting antsy."

"We'll only be exposed out here for one more night, in Flagstaff," Hector said. "Then we'll be on home ground."

"Sounds like a plan."

Hector climbed the stairs to Mary's camper and knocked on the door.

"Come on in!" Mary called.

He entered to find the Unity Council's new information technology manager busy at her laptop.

"The site is back up?" he asked.

"It is, the clone I had is handling the traffic and we're setting more. If they try that again, we'll be ready."

"It's nice to finally meet you face to face." Hector placed the lunches on the table and extended his hand for a shake. "I've been on the East Coast basically since we contacted you about the job."

Mary took his hand. "It's really nice to finally meet you too, Hector. Look, I'm sorry to cause problems. But I wasn't going to wait around anymore."

"We understand, Mary. It's better you did. So what was the cause for the site going down? I've been getting reports from Denver that the hits since this morning have been high, way high. Wouldn't that crash a website?"

"Yes, but with the set up we designed, it shouldn't have mattered."

"So you're saying that the website was brought down on purpose?"

"Yeah, I just hadn't had a chance to call you yet. I wanted to do some hunting around and get some more info on what exactly they did, but all I can say right now is that it was more than just a denial of service attack. They did bombard the website with enough fake hits to bring it down. But they knew about our mirrors. That's an issue."

"Then we can't trust the hit rates we've been seeing, can we?"

"My people have been able to determine the real hits from the fake and, yes, traffic on the clone is still way higher than projected."

Hector scratched his head, contemplating a hundred different details. Mary took the opportunity to assess her new boss: his dark Latin features, his clean-shaven face and coal black hair, his solid frame and perfectly white dress shirt. She could virtually hear the man thinking.

"I would fly you to Denver," he said. "But considering...We've had phone banks in Denver and Arizona go down today, someone will be investigating that too. But we have to pursue this hacking thing on our own. If they're successful at keeping our word from getting out, then this whole weekend will have been for nothing."

"It won't be for nothing," Mary said. "As long as I have the Net, I can do anything I need to do from my laptop. Everything we have in Denver, we have in the San Luis Valley. It wouldn't be a bad idea to get another dedicated server up and running in the valley as well. Go for double redundancy."

Hector was still computing the next move.

"I know I've caused problems by leaving, Hector, I'm sorry again. I just want to say that."

"No, it's not that. There's something you need to know, Mary."

"Is it why you've had us in lockdown since we drove in?"

"So you obviously remember Denise? I believe you two met in L.A.?" Hector placed a jewelry box onto the table. "She sent you this. And we're... *I* am recommending that you wear it."

"What is it?" She opened the box to find a dice-sized glass cube that enclosed a tiny piece of black crystal.

"Knock, knock," a voice said from the door to the camper.

"Oh, Sheila, great," Hector said.

A voluptuous, middle-aged dishwater blonde woman climbed into the camper.

"Mary this is Sheila. You two will be working very closely together in Colorado, so we thought you could use this time to get to know each other. Mary is our IT person," he told Sheila. "...and Sheila is accounting," he said to Mary. "We better get Leonard in here for a talk."

Max woke curled up in a cramped backseat with his bladder burning to be emptied. He nursed the bruises on his face and head as he unfolded his legs and sat up. He was shocked by the flood of activity all around the car. Curtis woke in the front seat with an uncomfortable groan.

"Curtis?"

"Yeah."

After their punishing clash at the top of Monk's Mound with Masterson's recovery team, and their early morning walk into St. Louis to pick up the car Hector arranged for them, Curtis drove west until he was too exhausted to see the road. Somewhere in the middle of Missouri, he parked the rented compact in a secluded section of a densely wooded rest stop and fell asleep.

In the light of day, all the spaces of the formerly empty rest stop were now occupied, and the lanes between the rows of cars were clogged with Unity Council migrants walking in the morning sun.

"What the hell is all this?" Curtis said.

"I think it's your Unity Council."

"What? Oh shit, they were all leaving this morning! I was too busy getting shot to remember! These must be the people from St. Louis. Damn, Hector's been tearing it up."

"Where are they all going?"

"Straight the hell out of St. Louis, that's all I know. I think they said at least a hundred miles off that nasty-ass fault line they have down there, runs right under the Mississippi. But these people are probably going down to the San Luis Valley for this big show Hector cooked up."

"I need to piss," Max said.

"Yep!"

Max unlocked the door at his feet and crawled out. Headed toward the bathrooms, they waded into a thick flow of people meandering around the rest stop and the adjoining campsite. As in Arizona, the migrants were taking a break from the road before carrying on to points closer to Colorado.

"The Unity Council, huh?" Max said.

"Yeah, I knew Hector had skills, but damn. This is a shitload of people."

"So what are you supposed to be doing for them?"

"Whooping secret agent ass!"

"Yeah, right," Max said. His sustained stare indicated that he would require an honest answer from his new traveling companion.

"Straight up, I worked in a homeless shelter for a while," he said. "Then I got this program going to get people living on the streets into apartments of their own. Did you know that it costs more to put someone up in a shelter than it does to have them in their own apartment? It's all messed up."

They weaved through people who looked like tourists, then people who looked like they were one step from Curtis's homeless shelter. The vast array of class and race represented – as well as the trailers full of personal belongings – made it clear they weren't vacationers.

The men emerged from the facilities, refreshed and much more alert. Walking back through the people, feelings of alarm began to consume them both. They reached the car weary and suspicious of those same travelers they were so fascinated by earlier.

"So you think those punks after you will give up?"

"Well Curtis, you whooped his ass good but I doubt it."

Their eyes began to search the passing people for threats, for the undoubtedly bruised face of the agent they evaded at Cahokia. Curtis went for his cell phone. He hit redial and waited for Hector to answer. The phone acted as if it was about to connect before static interrupted the call.

"No service?"

"It doesn't sound like it does when you're out of the calling area. It almost went through."

The men took a closer look at the crowds in the parking lot, at the many people holding cell phones unable to complete calls.

"You see that shit?" Curtis asked.

"I see it. They're close; I bet they're jamming up the phones. We better get up out of here double quick."

"I'm not arguing with that. Maybe we can drive into some cell service."

Curtis steered the car through the crowds of people and out of the parking lot. They were both gratified to find at least one lane moving on Interstate 70.

As it was in Arizona, the right lane of the highway was crawling, thanks to the RVs and semi trucks and overloaded trailers. Seeing that time could be made in the left lane, Curtis cautiously merged with the faster traffic and accelerated. A mile down the road they got past the slow movers and were able to cruise in the right lane once again.

"We probably should stay ahead of them, if we can," Curtis said.

"Yeah but we still got most of Missouri, all of Kansas, and half of Colorado to get through. We're going to have to stop."

"Then they'll be able to come at us with no one around," Curtis said as he let off the gas pedal.

"But we might make it to a cell area and get a call out to Denver, get some help coming our way."

"Hector said they're running low on trained ass whoopers. I'm not thinking they can get anybody out here in time."

"Hey, man, slow down," Max said. "Maybe we should be blending in, instead of sticking out. That mess back there will be here before too long."

"We can ride it all the way into Colorado without getting noticed." Curtis let off the accelerator completely and allowed the car to coast.

"Here, take this exit and we'll hold back a second."

Curtis veered up the ramp, to a road that went over the highway. They looked each way at the crossroads, the rural route cut through dense Missouri woods north and south. Curtis found an open area near the ramp back down to the I-70 and parked. The same static interrupted the call when he tried Hector's phone number again.

"No go."

"So either the cell towers are down in this entire area, or somebody is jamming us."

"That's heavy shit, right there. What did you do to have 'the Man' jamming your cell phone?"

"I don't have a cell, don't like them, but all of a sudden you can't make a call since we left St. Louis? We jammed phones and communications in the Gulf during an operation, it was SOP."

"So what did you do to have somebody running an operation on you? Somebody that ain't the cops."

"How do you know it isn't the cops?"

"Because Hector would have said. Ben would have known."

"Who's Ben?"

"I've never met the dude, but I hear he's the head security dude for the Unity Council. And he's an ex-cop. If this was official, he'd be hip to it."

There was little traffic on the road that crossed over I-70 so Max and Curtis got out of the car and walked to the overpass. They looked to the east for signs of the oncoming migration. The traffic racing beneath them was dense but moving too fast to be the main body of the convoy.

"What's the deal with this Unity Council anyway?" Max asked.

"How long has it been since you seen the news?"

"It's been a few days. I've been avoiding that stuff at all cost."

"No doubt, don't blame you."

"Why do they care what happens to me?"

"I don't know. Why does the Unity Council care about what happens to any of us? The way Hector put it to me was that it's our job. Look at it this way, somebody gives a shit whether you survive or not. I don't think you can say that about that dude back there in St. Louis."

"Just surviving isn't enough anymore," Max said.

"In some places, surviving is all you got. With what I was into when I was a kid, I should have been dead or in Ossining. The fact that I survived all that shit meant that I got a second chance. And we all deserve a second chance."

"Yeah we do. And for you that's the Unity Council?"

"My second chance was the Upper East Side Homeless Shelter. The punks at City Hall made sure that got closed down. And they screwed us on the program to get people in their own places too. No money, they said."

"Right when everybody is being thrown out on the street."

"That's America, baby, love it or leave it."

"Check it out." Max pointed down the interstate to the oncoming mass of traffic. "That's cool you were working for a homeless shelter. At least you were doing something. All I've ever done is pollute the environment – and my own body – in a machine shop."

"It just happened. After my dad died, we had to go to this homeless shelter for a while. We were down. We were way down. And they helped us. My mom was able to get assistance and we got a shitty little place up in the Bronx. She got into school for office admin. and we were able to get it back together. I was just a kid but I remembered that. How they helped us out when we were down.

"So later on, after I got tired of watching dudes I knew since kindergarten get cut down in the streets, I went into the shelter one day and asked if they needed any help. I figured I couldn't get in trouble if I was working there. And they paid a little better than fast food, anyway."

The caravan of vehicles inched closer to the overpass where Max and Curtis stood. They watched a news helicopter trace the line of cars as it wound around a distant curve and extended out of sight back toward St. Louis.

"I sure hope Hector knows what he's doing," Curtis said. "It can be an unholy bitch just getting twenty people organized to do something, I know. This right here is crazy."

"I think right now I'm a little more interested in what Ben can do for me than Hector."

"You're not going to tell me why, are you?"

"You saw him, in the dream."

"Some fat-assed power player is all over you because of your dreams?"

"It wasn't my dream."

"Like I said, you're a psychic."

"Not quite."

A flurry of faster cars and RVs accelerated past the leader of the procession: a late-model pickup towing a trailer full of furniture. Max and Curtis watched the old truck chug under the bridge ahead of a seemingly endless line of equally over burdened vehicles.

"You probably better get out of sight," Curtis said.

"Yeah, no shit."

They pulled themselves away from the oncoming spectacle. On their way back to their car a pickup truck broke from the pack and limped up the ramp towards them. They heard the tell-tale sound of a flat tire echoing through the area around the overpass.

"See, that shit sucks," Curtis said.

A top-heavy camper in the bed of the truck was causing the entire vehicle to list to one side while the shredded rear tire flapped on the pavement. Max and Curtis started back toward the car with their eyes glued on the pickup. They watched a frustrated middle aged man jump out of the cab and stomp back to the rear wheel well. He quickly assessed the situation then he began opening panels on the side of the camper. He lifted out a jack and other tire changing equipment.

"That lift kit is going to make changing that tire a bitch," Max said.

"It will if he doesn't have the right gear."

A woman joined the man in helping him get the jack under the axle of the pickup.

"He looks good to go," Curtis said, turning over the engine. He put the car in gear, but while adjusted the rearview mirror before backing up he caught the reflection of the man wrestling with the jack handle. The man leaned into the handle and it gave way, throwing him to the ground. He came back up with a bloodied forearm.

"Damn, did you see that?" Curtis asked.

"No, what?"

"I think he just messed up his arm pretty good."

Max rubbed his bandaged hand. "Think we should help?"

"That's the job," Curtis said. He turned off the engine and opened the car door. "Hang out a minute, keep your head down."

"You wanna take this?" Max asked, pointing at the pistol on the seat.

"Naw." Curtis saw that the woman was now tending to her husband's wounds. "No sense in scaring the straights."

"Your call."

Curtis dodged a passing truck on his way to the couple. "Hey, you guys need some help?"

"I'm alright," the man said, after he momentarily looked Curtis over. "Just cracked my arm." The woman did the same, quickly returning to her first aid job.

"So what happened?"

"Looks like there was a leak in the hydraulics in the jack," the man said.

"It's had it," Curtis said, trying the handle. "I think we have a jack, it's a rental car, but they always have something. Let me check it out. We'll see if we can't get you back out on the road."

"We appreciate that," the woman said.

Max met Curtis at the trunk of the car with the keys. He opened the hatch and dug out a jack and tire iron. "You're gonna need a hand," he said. "But I don't think this little thing is going to work."

They returned to where the woman was picking gravel out of the man's knuckles. "I'm Curtis, this is Max."

"I'm Ted and this is Connie."

Curtis crawled under the rear of the pickup to position the miniature jack under the axle, while Max got the broken one out of the way.

"Yeah, you were right, Max. There's too much clearance here."

"We'll have to lift up the jack."

"Here, I've got some cinder blocks for camping in the other side." Ted attempted to rise until Connie prevented him.

"Stay there, tough guy. We'll get them."

Curtis followed her around to the other side of the camper, to another series of panels.

"You guys heading to Colorado?" Curtis asked.

"That's the plan. You too?"

"Yeah, Denver. It's something else down there on the road, huh?" He took hold of one cinder block and adjusted his grip before going after the other.

"We were surprised this morning, that's for sure."

They circled around to the front of the vehicle, to where Max was using the tire iron to remove the spare from a rack on the grill. He bounced the tire once to confirm that it was viable.

"Let's slap this baby on here and get rolling." Curtis said.

"Man, thanks for the help," Connie said.

"Just tape me up, Connie, I can get it."

"I need to clean that gravel out, Ted, or it will get infected."

"You guys just leave it, I can get it done after she fixes me up," Ted said.

"It's cool, man. You're wounded in action," Curtis said. "We got it."

"It'll only take a minute," Max said.

Curtis positioned the cinder block directly under the axle as Max placed the jack between the two. Max inserted the handle, pumping it several times until it was snug under the axle.

"How's it look?" Max asked.

Curtis inspected the situation and turned to Ted. "What do you think?"

"That looks good and stable to me," Ted said. "Ouch!"

Connie removed another pebble from his hand. "That was a big one."

"Bump it up a shot and I'll loosen the lugs," Curtis said.

"You got it."

"So where are you guys relocating to?" Curtis asked, slipping the tire iron over one of the lug nuts on the shredded tired.

"Wish we knew," Connie said.

Curtis bore down on the lug nut until it finally gave. He repeated the procedure on the rest. "You don't know yet? Hector said that everyone coming this weekend had been relocated."

"We've seen him on the news," Ted said.

"I'm gonna lift her up," Max said, pumping the jack handle several times before the truck began to rise.

"That should do it," Curtis said. He went back through the lugs, spinning each one off with the tire iron. "So have you talked to anybody at the Unity Council?"

"Not yet," Connie said.

Curtis gave Max a curious look. "But you guys hit the road anyway?"

"I got laid-off from the office where I worked," Connie said. "And when the electrical work dried up because the housing market went south, he got laid-off too."

"They foreclosed on us and we ended up living in this," Ted said. "We had it parked in my brother's backyard."

"In St. Louis?" Curtis asked.

"Lived there all our lives," Connie said.

"Then you guys qualify for a bunch of the programs the Unity Council is offering," Curtis said.

"We've been seeing the blips about them for the last week now," Ted said. "We tried to call but the phones have been down. The website says they have work for electricians, to help fix up old foreclosures. So Connie and I decided that since we didn't have any kids in school or anything, what the hell."

Curtis struggled with the tire, distracted by what the couple was saying.

"Let me get in there," Max said, taking one side of the blown tire while Curtis took the other. They worked the rim from the axle and threw it clear. Together they lifted the spare into place and screwed on the lugs.

"That's it," Max said.

Curtis tightened down each lug nut in turn. "You said you guys were going to Denver?"

"That's the Unity Council headquarters, isn't it?" Connie said, applying bandages to the last of Ted's injured fingers then packing up the first aide kit.

"One of them," Curtis said. "But the overnight thing was happening down in the southern area of Colorado. They call it the San Luis Valley. There's camping and a big HQ. You might want think about going on down there. I don't think they'll have much room for you in the city. At least Hector never mentioned anything like that to me."

"You work for the Unity Council?" Ted asked.

"Yeah, for about four years now."

"What do you do for them?" Connie asked.

"Co-ops, my thing now is co-ops. I help people get their own businesses going. Cut out the middle managers and the corporate scammers. So the workers can keep the money they bust their butts to make."

Ted carefully squeezed his wounded hand. "So can they help us get into those programs down in the San Luis Valley?"

"Sure enough, that's their backup down there. They have everything Denver does. Plus camping, and from what I heard, there's this Native American Pow Wow going on before the big thing on Sunday. That's really where everyone was supposed to go."

"I guess we're going to have to discuss it," Connie said.

"You know, we met this couple back at the rest stop," Ted said. "They had a few kids. But they hadn't actually talked to anybody at the Unity Council either."

"Really? Damn, I need to call Hector."

"Connie tried to call her sister right after we blew the tire, wouldn't go through."

"You used to jam communications during an operation, huh?" Curtis said to Max.

"It was standard operating procedure."

Down below, on I-70, the first third of the ragtag convoy had cleared the bridge and were well on their way toward the border with Kansas. Cars and trucks towing trailers, RVs, and reworked school buses stretched for miles, all the way back beyond the rest stop where Max and Curtis had slept.

Stuck behind all the traffic was the nondescript tractor-trailer carrying the CIG search and retrieval team. Inside, the agent that Max and Curtis grappled with back at Cahokia was manning the surveillance bay, a headset resting gingerly over the bruises on his face and head.

"Did you email the General his status report?" the driver asked over the radio.

"If all I can tell him is what car they rented in St. Louis then no. I was hoping we would hear from Jean. Maybe she's spotted them."

"He gets just as pissed when status reports are late, than when they suck," the driver said.

"I know, I know."

8

"Where are you, Ben?" Gina asked.

"At the house. We'll do a little recon. Maybe we can figure out what happened."

"You know damn well who did this."

"I know. We just want to be sure."

"Whatever you find, we better be taking steps to make sure we're protected or he's going to slip in under the wire."

"We have to figure that he's already done that. That's why we need to know exactly how he works. As far as John can tell, nobody has ever been this close."

"Right where it's the most dangerous."

"What about Sylvia Billy? Hector has been calling about her. He wants to fly out and talk to her personally."

"She had the White House meeting today," Gina said. "They'll be keeping their distance until she gets clear of all that. You should be able to pick up her tail at her place. Anderson's on the move and they're all over him; I don't know where I'll be."

"Copy that." Ben hung up his cell phone then touched the miniature communicator in his ear. "That's quite a partner you got there, Son."

"She'd drop you like a bad habit, Pop."

"Actually, I don't doubt it."

"We have maybe a day before the estate people come and clear the place out."

"Plenty of time." Ben climbed out of the car. "Sweep the perimeter and I'll see you inside."

Looking quite official, the distinguished Hopi wore a black suit and carried a notepad on the way to the front door of Phil's provincial two-story manor house. He knocked while he stealthily made use of the lock-picking tools he carried. He soon stood in the foyer of Phil's home, surrounded by stacks of boxes.

"They didn't start packing early, did they?" he whispered into the communicator.

A pan dropping in the kitchen at the rear of the house alerted Ben that he was not alone. He stuck close to the stairs leading up to the second floor as he proceeded cautiously down the hall.

He kept one hand on his old badge, knowing full well it had no authority – even in Phoenix where it was issued – and the other hand on the semi-automatic weapon in the small of his back.

"We have movement in the kitchen." He stepped through the doorway into Phil's sunny country kitchen, immediately dropping to one knee. The air from a broom handle whipped just over his head.

"You sonofabitch, I'll kill you all!" Billy screamed.

John appeared out of nowhere, wearing the uniform of the local gas company. He took Billy by the arms. He prevented her from swinging the broom but not from using her knee. She tried for his crotch; only his quick reaction prevented a direct, incapacitating blow.

"Hector!" Ben said. "Hector sent us!"

The sound of her old friend's name distracted her long enough for John to regain control of her trembling frame. It was the last thing she expected to hear.

"Hector!" Ben said again. "We work with Hector and Maria!"

"I thought... I thought you were here to kill me."

Billy's hair was frayed and the dress shirt she wore to the White House was filthy from packing Phil's personal effects. Her hands were throbbing from gripping the broom handle and she couldn't stop shivering.

She was unable to protest when John led her gently by the arm through the dining area and onto the couch in the living room. Ben met her there with a glass of water.

"We have two teams watching, one up close, and a support team a block over," John said. "They must have picked up their bugs before the FBI showed up because the place is clean of audio surveillance."

"We didn't mean to scare you, Billy," Ben said. "I feel like I know you a little bit. Hector and Maria both speak very highly of you."

Billy's breathing calmed, and with a few sips of water her throat cleared enough to speak. "How can I believe you?" she said. "I don't know who to trust anymore."

She snuck a good look at Ben in his suit, and John in his utility worker's disguise, while she nursed the glass of water. She couldn't help feeling comforted. However much she wanted to stay on guard, her alarm and mistrust slowly melted away. John handed her his cell phone.

"Billy?" Hector said. "Are you there?"

"It's really you. Hector, where the hell are you?"

"*Mi hermana*, haven't you been watching the news?"

"Phil's dead, Hector, they killed him!" Tears flowed down her freckled cheeks. "And I don't know who to trust out here!"

"Do you trust me?"

"Always. Where are you? Where're Maria and the kids?"

"You really haven't been watching the news. You're in danger out there. Whether he killed himself or not, Phil was in way over his head. But he was trying, Billy, at the end he was really trying."

"I know. I quit today. This morning, I resigned."

"It won't protect you from them. They've been watching you. They know how close you were with Phil."

"Who are they? Who is this god damn CIG?"

156

"They're the ones standing in our way, Billy. Just like always. As long as we've done what we do there have been power hungry men in our way. But we've got good people, and two of them are with you right now. You better stay with them, at least until we can get this whole mess exposed. We'll be telling a national audience all about it on Sunday."

"Really? You're serious?"

"I wouldn't lie to you, *mi hermana*. We need to talk. Maria and the kids want to see you."

"OK, Hector." Calm washed over her, the likes of which she hadn't experienced since returning home.

"Listen to Ben and John. We've worked in the real world helping people for most of our lives, but Ben and his team work in another world. And believe me; it's chock-full of weirdos and killers. Let them do their jobs and keep you safe."

"I will...."

She handed the phone back to John, who stepped out of earshot to talk to Hector. Ben sat in front of her patiently, as he had countless victims of crime, his caring expression only serving to reinforce Hector's words.

"You didn't pack up Phil's office yet, did you?"

"No, I couldn't go in there."

"Show me?"

Billy led Ben through the foyer to a door on the other side of a small den. She tried her best to clean up along the way.

"Why? Why did he have to die?" she asked.

"When it comes to the CIG, there's no room for a crisis of conscience."

She stepped into the office hesitantly. "Is that what he had?"

"There was talk of him running our relocation efforts. Yes, I would say he had a change of heart."

"Then what kept him quiet for so long?"

Ben answered her with a kind smile. He avoided eye contact by moving into the office. His evasiveness was her answer.

"No," she said. "It can't be." She sank into a leather chair near Phil's desk.

"It's not your fault, Billy. They regularly use family and loved ones against their targets. It's extortion, pure and simple."

John appeared at the door, finished with his report to Hector. "It's standard operation procedure is what it is."

Ben closed his eyes and stretched his arms out wide, drifting around the room, eventually taking Phil's chair behind the desk.

"What are you doing?" she asked.

"A little recon," John said.

Suspicion temporarily overwhelmed her grief as she watched Ben cinch the chair closer to the antique oak desk, picking up the pen he was certain Phil used everyday. He doodled on the corner of a piece of paper with it. He operated the computer mouse, the tower missing, confiscated by authorities. He picked up the receiver on the phone, put it to his ear, then returned it.

"He sat here night after night, writing memos that he knew no one would read."

"Get the hell out of his desk. What are you doing?"

"He thought about Africa, a lot. He considered it the last time he ever did any real good."

"What did you say?"

"And he thanked you for that, Billy. His memories of you and of that time, they were all mixed up with his regret. They were inseparable."

"Don't...," she said, burying her face in her hands. "Please don't."

"It started with a knock on the door, just after he got home." Ben kept Phil's pen in one hand, resting his other on the computer keyboard. "He was terrified, he thought for sure that it was them, coming to kill him, but it wasn't. It was just a delivery guy from one of those overnight services."

Billy didn't want to listen, she didn't want to hear him, but Ben's voice was so engrossing that before long a vision of Phil on the day he died began to form in her mind's eye.

"What's happening?" she said, her eyes still sealed shut.

All at once, the trepidation Phil had felt while he signed for the package and took it into his office washed over her.

"He sat it down right here, on his desk," Ben said. "He stared at it for almost an hour. Was it a bomb? Was it the infamous 'white powder' that terrified DC after 9-11? He went through all the possibilities."

"He was completely confused," Billy said. "He had no intention of touching the gun again. For the few seconds after it hit his desk, he was thinking about who to call: the police or the FBI. Then–"

"He finally just decided it was time and he opened it," Ben said. "He ripped off the top of the box and a gun fell out."

Billy could see Phil's worried face so clearly that it gave her chills. She found herself gripping the armrests of the chair with trembling fists, her eyeballs darting around behind her lids.

Ben's body bucked abruptly, as if he were taken over by something. He slammed both hands down on the desk, spontaneously reciting haunting verses in a language John immediately recognized as arcane in the extreme.

Billy curled up in the chair, her whole body now trembling. "No... no... this isn't good."

"It's going to be OK, Billy," John said, rushing to her side.

"No!" she insisted, still in a trance. "This is wrong... it's evil!"

Ben continued to spew incantations, the intensity of his speech and the look on his face began to concern his son. Billy involuntarily gripped John's hand when Ben acted as if he were able to pick up the imaginary pistol. He put it to his head and fired. Then he dropped to the desk, lifeless.

"Pop, Pop, are you OK?"

John shook his father's shoulders and lightly slapped his cheek until he regained consciousness. He splashed a few drops of a liquid from a vial he kept in his pocket into a glass he took from Phil's bar set. He added a shot of whisky before serving it to Ben.

"I'm OK. I'm OK," he said after taking a deep drink.

"All Carlyle had to do was look online to confirm that the package had been delivered," John said. "It even shows who signed for it."

"No wonder the gun couldn't be traced," Ben said, gradually shaking off the effects of the trance.

Billy roused and began to unclench. "What did you do to me? How in the world?"

"He's found the perfect way to commit murder," Ben said. "And the forensics will always check out, because he makes the victim do it to themselves."

"Probably got a hold of some hair or skin cells," John said. "Even a fingernail would work. He never has to be in the room at the time of death. Theoretically, he could be a million miles away."

"That's crazy," Billy said, rubbing her eyes. "You're both crazy."

John picked through the wastebasket until he found a torn overnight envelope. "It's quantum physics," he said. "It's very old quantum physics."

"He's tapping into the phenomena known as non-locality," Ben said.

John went to the window and performed another sweep of the block through the part in the curtains. "Basically, when two particles are what they call 'entangled', the spins of their electrons become synchronized."

"What the hell are you talking about?"

"In theory, you can take one of those particles billions of miles away from the other and if you reversed its spin, the spin of the other particle would also reverse. They don't know how they're connected, only that they are, and at a level that is beyond subatomic."

"And beyond our current understanding," Ben said.

Billy's confused and distraught expression moved Ben to do something more to convince her. He leaned into the desk, taking hold of Phil's computer mouse for the last time. He closed his eyes.

"I see him," Ben said. "He was so full of guilt that it hangs here like a fog."

"I said stop!"

Ben was obviously growing tired, but he took a deep breath and continued. "He sat right here and confessed. But only to Billy, though, only Billy."

"Damn you," she said.

"There's a video, Son. He left it with someone he knew he could trust."

"OK, OK," Billy said. "Just please stop." She held her head in her hands once again. "Jesus, I wanted to know for sure that he didn't kill himself but that..."

"Gina is already talking about how to defend against him," Ben said.

"Conventional countermeasures won't work with this guy," John said. "We're going to have to come up with something special."

"I've been to Indonesia and Haiti and parts of Africa," Billy said. "I've seen some pretty strange things. I know a little bit about what's possible, but does Hector know about what you people are doing out here in the name of the Unity Council?"

"He knows," Ben said. "I'm retired from the Phoenix PD, Billy. I put in twenty five years. All I can say is that I've dealt with some pretty strange stuff myself during my time on the job: Matamoras and the Company. You know, criminal enterprises steeped in the occult. But they have nothing on the CIG."

"My God, he was so scared when he saw that gun."

"Statistically it would raise fewer red flags," Ben said. "Most people commit suicide with a gun."

"This is pretty damn advanced, Pop. I knew Carlyle would get the spell right eventually, but he's gone way beyond experimenting now. Each success just makes him more powerful."

"Phil's confession, Billy, would it help us?"

"He doesn't give any kind of sworn deposition or anything, but he does admit that he was involved with the CIG. I swore I would do whatever it took to clear his name, if what he left me will help, then Hector is welcome to it."

"Did you tell anybody?" Ben asked.

"Not a soul."

"They'll be running the plates on the car by now," John said. "There're only so many scenarios that work for you being in here this long, Pop."

"We have to get you out of town for a while. After Sunday, they won't have any need for you. Where is Phil's confession?"

"I left it with a friend in my building."

"Then we need to pick that up and get out of here. We have air transport standing by. Hector should be in Denver by the time we get there."

"I have to go to Phil's funeral."

"Billy, you realize that if they even suspect that you know what Phil knew, or that he left that confession, they will kill you."

Billy collected her self and stood stubbornly in front of Ben and John. "I'm just fine with you taking me to see Hector and Maria, wherever they are, but I'm not going anywhere until after Phil's funeral."

Ben had to get out of Phil's chair and away from his desk. A tactical plan was forming as he regained his senses. He was beaten to the punch by an equally astute strategist.

"I have to go," she said. "They'll follow me. I have to load up some stuff and go back to my apartment, just like I was going to do."

"Not a good idea," John said.

"No, she's right. I'll drive to the Federal Building; see an old FBI buddy of mine. If they tail me, they'll think I'm just another Fed following up on Phil's case. Follow me to the door; we'll make a good show of it."

"Here, take this." John handed Billy a cell phone. "It's clean, just hit redial. But you can only use it once, and not from your apartment. I'm pretty sure you're also being bugged."

"I am; I'm sure of it."

Billy shook Ben's hand in the open doorway and they parted without a second look.

"Oh, what about Peter Anderson?" Billy said to John.

"We have someone keeping an eye on him."

"He had a document; Phil gave him an internal document that had to be straight out of the CIG files. The last time I talked to him he was going to check out this address I got off the government database."

"For what?"

"The CIG office in Virginia."

"Then he's in bigger trouble than we thought." John dialed his cell phone.

"What?" Gina answered.

"Your guy has more than we thought. He got hold of an address, looks like the Virginia installation."

"Then he's a dead man."

"Not with a gorgeous kick-ass professional like yourself looking out for him."

"Yeah, yeah, you can stow the flattery. I'll see you at the rendezvous."

Gina was pushing her rented sedan to its limits to keep up with the elusive silver minivan in traffic ahead of her. She had donned an inconspicuous pantsuit with a government ID around her neck. She could have been an FBI agent, a staffer on the Hill, or any number of Washington DC vocations.

Like a rolling chess game, she was countering each move the van made, correctly anticipating two somewhat abrupt turns. She knew it wouldn't last, traffic was swelling. The silver minivan took a final turn onto a major thoroughfare out of Washington DC.

"This idiot is going to get himself killed," she said.

She punched up their location on a GPS unit sitting on the seat beside her. With one hand on the wheel and one finger on the GPS screen, she plotted an intercept course. It necessitated a right turn that she took, without hesitation, across two lanes.

Gina kept watch for police while she used her horn to bully her way through intersections, and when she would accelerate through the open patches in traffic. Now that she was running parallel to the minivan, it was imperative she make up some ground.

She watched the blinking red dot that represented her car on the GPS screen. It neared the cross street she needed, a left against the traffic was going to be necessary. She moved into the left lane before taking the green light through the intersection. She turned the wheel over with both hands while standing on the brakes. Before the sedan had a chance to spin all the way around, she stomped on the gas pedal. It propelled the car down the open street.

The traffic was stopped at the red light, leaving the two lanes wide open. Gina was accelerating to top speed when she saw the flashing red and blue lights of a patrol car appear in her rearview mirror. She made another left at the intersection, and while she was accelerating she found the switch to the driver's seat. As it began to lower back, she clung to the steering wheel so that she could stay upright while the seat belt unreeled behind her. Once the seat had gone all the way back as far as it could, she hit redial on her cell phone.

"John, I'm in the shit!"

"You can't stay out of trouble for one minute, can you?"

"I'm gonna need transport!"

"Don't you already have a car?"

Gina steered the sedan across the solid yellow line in the middle of the roadway. She dodged an oncoming compact and made it into the far lane in time to see the minivan coming straight toward her.

"Not for long!" she said.

In the CIG minivan, the two agents riding up front were helpless to avoid the imminent head-on collision. Airbags deployed with violent force upon impact, knocking them both unconscious.

The operations agent in the back of the minivan fell out of the side door almost immediately, closing it behind him. Fighting to free his identification from his pocket, he realized that both his arm and head had deep lacerations.

He would stop the incoming police before they got curious about the surveillance bay inside the vehicle or he would be in bigger trouble than he already was. But first he needed a look at the driver of the car that ended their pursuit of Peter Anderson.

He stumbled to the driver's side window of the smoking heap that was Gina's rental. He forced open the crumpled door to find nothing but shattered glass and a spent airbag.

Thanks to Gina's reckless – albeit effective – maneuver, Peter was allowed to go on to his destination undetected: a five-story office building on the outskirts of Washington DC.

His third pass by the address Billy gave him for the Continuity in Government, he realized that it would be pointless to approach the guard tower. It blocked the only open space in the impenetrable grove of Virginia oak trees that ringed the building. He needed a vantage point.

An hour of casing the Eastern Shore Complex from a dense stand of trees and bushes across the road hadn't yielded anything of interest, besides men and women in business suits and military uniforms coming and going. Peter had been on enough stakeouts of cheating politicians when he was a cub reporter to know that they took time and patience.

His notes for his next article were among the many crumpled sheets of paper strewn across the passenger seat next to him. Some of the aborted attempts contained several paragraphs, others only the opening sentence. Every time he tried to write a summary and analysis of what he was certain had happened to that point, it stuck in his throat. Fortunately, he brought something to wash it down – a fifth of brandy for his coffee.

The phone interrupted him as he was spiking his thermos. He didn't immediately reach for it until he realized it could be Billy. Checking the caller ID confirmed his less-favorable suspicion. His boss would be put off no longer.

"There you are!" Ed fumed. "I rescheduled all the interviews you blew off this morning but they're all going to want you tonight. Get your ass over to Rockefeller Center by five."

"I'm not doing it."

"Yeah, right. You'll do it because you love to hear yourself talk, just like everybody else in this town."

"I can't do it. I can't lie to millions of people anymore."

"Well, Pete, if you won't do TV then what the hell good are you to this organization?"

"Don't waste your time trying to intimidate me, Ed. You don't have anything I want or need anymore. But I have something you need."

"What?"

"How about an exclusive with Sylvia Billy, Simmons's longtime assistant?"

"There's no way you're getting anywhere near her right now. No way, you're bluffing, Peter."

"Believe it or not, I'm long past arguing or bluffing. I just told you what I can deliver, now you can hassle me about the television appearances, or you can stay off my back for a few days while I get the interview of the year."

"Just get it done," Ed said before hanging up.

Peter threw the phone into the seat, taking the binoculars in hand when he noticed that another car was snaking toward the guard station through one of the parking lots that fanned out around the building. He monitored the blue SUV as it passed through the security gate onto an adjacent road.

"I'll be damned!" he yelled at the sight of his informant, Mr. Graydin.

Peter promptly dumped the entire cup of coffee and booze into his lap. He fought the searing pain to get the engine started, too shaken to let it delay him from throwing the car into gear and speeding in pursuit.

He had to complete several harrowing maneuvers to get back on the main road and on Graydin's tail. His mind still reeling, Peter followed his anonymous source at a distance out of the wooded area, through increasingly plush neighborhoods.

Eventually they turned onto a tree-lined street populated with very large homes. Peter veered his car to the curb and ducked behind his steering wheel when it became obvious Graydin had reached his driveway. Graydin hurried to his front door and Peter took the opportunity to look over the rest of the street.

Well groomed two-story mansions ran every half block in both directions out of sight. The houses were vine covered and the yards were all expensively landscaped.

It was what every upwardly mobile intelligence officer below Graydin worked for: to live like royalty in a failing world with the assurance from a secret government agency that when the 'End' did arrive, they would live on to rule all the other hapless survivors.

Graydin came back out of the front door accompanied by his wife and their young son and daughter. The cynical old spy kissed his wife passionately then helped his children into the car.

In between the anger induced eye twitches Peter had been experiencing since the CIG headquarters, he detected a genuine tenderness in Graydin and it gave him momentary pause.

Surprised but undaunted, Peter recorded it all on a palm-sized notebook as information he might be able to use later. He followed the man again, careful to keep his distance.

The surrounding homes gradually began to shrink in size and stature as they passed through several middleclass neighborhoods, to a lively shopping center where Peter waited at the edge of the parking lot. He watched Graydin through his binoculars stop in front of a crowded movie theater to drop off his children. They hopped out after kisses from their father and trailed inside.

Peter wondered while he followed Graydin back into the city whether Phil meant to help him or damn him by sending him that top secret document. He didn't know what he would do when he confronted Graydin, but he was itching to unload some of the guilt he was carrying around over the destruction of several careers and possibly even one life.

Before long Graydin was parking in front of a boutique toy store in the downtown Washington DC area. Peter grew more and more agitated watching him through the front window after Graydin went in.

Initially, Peter had planned on following him around for the entire day, logging everyone he met with so he could pursue every lead later. It was the caring father of two however, not the shadowy agent out to manipulate the front page of a major newspaper, that was making Peter grind his teeth. That was who Peter was enraged at. It was the hypocrite browsing through five-hundred-dollar teddy bears. He could stand by no longer. He entered the store intent on cornering Graydin in an aisle.

"Always another birthday popping up, huh?" he said.

"Yeah, my son's birthday is—" Graydin was interrupted by Peter's furious embrace. He threw Graydin up against a toy rack by the lapels.

"You killed him!" Peter screamed. "You bastard, you helped me kill him!"

Graydin calmly balled up his fist for a lightning fast jab into Peter's solar plexus. The expertly placed shot dropped Peter to his knees, hacking and coughing.

"You better stay the hell away from me!" Graydin warned, sweat already dripping from his flushed forehead. He cased the aisle in an instant and was almost to the front door before Peter had a chance to look up. Peter staggered in pursuit, still choking from the blow. Graydin got all the way onto the street before he could reach him.

"Get away from me, Anderson!"

Peter should have taken heed of how serious Graydin was and how dangerous he had become on being discovered, but the old reporter was down to his last and dazed by the blow. It prevented him from recognizing that his life was in mortal danger.

"We had a relationship before, hell, we should be fast friends now," Peter said. "...after killing a man together. Were we supposed to drive him to suicide or was that one of your 'operations' as well?"

"I told you...!"

"Oh yeah, you told me a lot of things, didn't you Mr. *Graydin*?"

"You don't know what you're doing! Get the hell away from me!"

"Oh, OK, that's fine. I'll just go out to Virginia and ask your wife a few questions. Then I'll run one hell of a story!"

Graydin was trying not to cause a scene on the busy street, despite the fact that it seemed to be exactly what Peter wanted. He searched for and found the entrance to the closest alley. He drew Peter toward the end of the block – still raving – and motioned for him to follow him to the back of the alley.

Graydin spun around at the dead end with a hard right to Peter's jaw that knocked him to the ground. Then the lightning fast agent took Peter by the lapels and ran him face first into a brick wall. He was violently frisking him from behind by the time Peter regained his senses.

"Where is it? I know how you geniuses work," Graydin said, digging through Peter's pockets until he found a small tape recorder. "Ah, there it is. You know, until today, I would have said all you reporters were pathetically predictable."

He allowed Peter to fall back against the opposite wall. The reporter's adrenaline was surging, Graydin was just barely in control.

"How the hell did you find me?" he asked.

Peter leaned back against the wall, resting his hands on his knees. "Is it true?"

"The stories? They were as true as they needed to be."

"You bastard, a man is dead. How many others?"

"Don't you understand, you idiot! You've killed us both! Do you realize what he would do if he knew you were talking to me?"

"All those careers, all those lives, destroyed! Over what? Why?"

"We all do as we're told. My reasons, I left back in Virginia. Three of them." Graydin reached into his suit jacket for his shoulder holster. He took hold of his pistol and cocked it. Before he drew the weapon, he paused to consider the implications of murdering Peter.

"Damn it, do you know how long I've survived this shit! I just knew it; I knew something stupid was going to fuck it all up! And here you come!" Normally resolved in every deliberate move he made, Graydin was actually confused as to what to do.

"Why me?" Peter asked. "There're plenty of journalists in this town."

Graydin released the hammer on his automatic pistol then went into his pocket for a handkerchief to use on his face and head.

"Tell me something, Anderson. After I gave you that disk and you verified it, did you even once try to look into the reason an upstanding government employee of twenty plus years would steal from the very people he swore to help?"

Peter flopped down on an old crate, swabbing blood from his nose. "The Justice Department jumped all over the records. They were authentic, as you well know."

"Yeah, yeah, I know. In a time when most of the mainstream media has abandoned even the pretense of trying to find the real truth on anything, here you are serving the public interest, reporting the 'news,' getting those fat cats in Washington and bringing them down to size for the little guy, huh? That's an impressive body of work, Mr. Anderson."

Peter cupped his throbbing face in his shaking hands. Graydin smelled Peter's vulnerability and dug deeper.

"I know a lot about you, Ace. About your wife and how she died... about how she was a better person than you, and about how you couldn't handle the guilt of her dying instead of you, so you fell into a bottle. Everyone knows that one talented, ambitious reporter is worth ten trained assassins."

Peter launched to his feet.

"Oh, don't bother getting all pissed off now. Like most of the rest of the press, you gave up any claim to righteous indignation years ago. Journalistic valor is just embarrassing when it comes so late. It's useless, too. That's one of the essentials of information and media management. A truth delayed can very easily become a truth denied."

"I have something... a piece of real evidence."

"Something stamped 'Top Secret'? Something really incriminating? Not for long."

"You know?"

"I don't know anything for sure. But *he* knows everything, always. Drop this or you will die."

Peter sat down again. "Who are these people?"

"They can be anybody. There are too many loyal members, in all walks of life, ready to kill for their own survival. That's why you can't hide and you're never safe. You have evidence? I'd be willing to bet you don't know what the hell you have. Besides, it won't matter a damn bit if you're dead."

"I could go to the FBI. I'm going to go and scream my head off. I know where your little base is, out in Virginia. I could make your life miserable. Unless you're on the right side."

Graydin got into Peter's face. "You sorry sonofabitch. You're going to end up getting me and my family killed, aren't you? Jesus, look at you, you're pathetic."

Peter rose again, this time full of false courage. "You're correct about that, but I can still write an article: a small collection of words that the 'lowly masses' may actually read. The free press works, sometimes, you know? I'll paste it all over the Net. 'What is the CIG?' and more importantly 'What is its purpose?'"

Graydin laughed at first. "The Internet is where a story like that belongs."

When Peter headed toward the alley entrance, Graydin drew his pistol and took aim.

"Stop! If you think your editors will print anything other than what we say, then you really are a fool! Do you think your ultra-paranoid ramblings are going to matter to a society that's been conditioned to believe that there are no conspiracies? And that their government is a government of the people, for the people? That's a kind of faith you'll never shake. Not with *any* evidence to the contrary!"

Peter faced Graydin, raising his hands in the air. "I may not have a damn thing to live for but you're going to have to kill me to stop me."

Graydin's right eye was still aiming down the barrel of his pistol. He could end all his troubles with a shot, but would it really settle things? He was stuck.

"I'm going to tell you something above top secret," he said. "I'm going to confirm your story, but when I'm done, if you ever contact me again or try to blow my command at CIG, I'll put two bullets in the back of your head, personally. Whether I have the OK or not, understand?"

Peter didn't believe Graydin was serious about telling the truth but never doubted his threat.

"Two years ago there was a story in *The Independent* newspaper out of London about a Pentagon study on climate change. Look it up, you can download the PDF of the report from the Internet.

"Some scientists took a one hundred year period of extreme climate change that happened some eight thousand years ago and speculated on the effects on the world if the same kind of change were to happen today. What they found wasn't pretty.

"That report is just the latest example of proof. The U.S military and select intelligence agencies have been conducting studies on the ramifications of severe climate disruption on national security for well over twenty years."

Peter was paying full attention by then. He was even tempted to believe the crafty intelligence agent.

"They've been suppressing scientists' research and findings since before the '70s. They wanted to control how and when the ugly truth would be released."

"What ugly truth?"

"That we've already passed the point of no return to stop ecological disaster. The Greenland ice sheet is going to melt and nothing is going to stop it. They may act stupid but the smart ones in the government know that it's time to start cutting losses. We already missed our chance to prevent what's coming. The mega storms, the hurricanes, the tsunamis. Now it's time for damage control.

"Let me see if I remember... oh yeah, the report said something along the lines of the U.S. and Australia are likely to build defensive fortresses around their countries because they have the resources and reserves to achieve self-sufficiency."

"I don't suppose with the whole globalization scheme they considered how hopelessly interdependent America has become on the rest of the world?" Peter said.

"How many terrorists from Afghanistan and Pakistan and Iran will be launching jihads when their homelands have been rocked by earthquakes, famine, and floods? They may try to blame it on the "Great Satan" but it won't matter. They'll have their own problems to deal with. That is until they all start coming here for food and protection. And that's what the Pentagon report was all about, protecting our own." Graydin searched the alley for eavesdroppers. "They fully expect that the transition to a more manageable society will be nasty, but they think that in the long run the United States will be stronger for it."

"You mean after you get rid of all those hungry, complaining mouths?"

No longer afraid of being killed execution-style, Peter listened to Graydin, thinking that maybe a bullet in the head would have been a far more merciful end than the one his own government had planned for him.

"They've also been studying major climate events over the last two hundred years and–"

"What major climate events?"

"The ones you didn't learn about in school. Ecological disasters like the year with no summer in 1884. A dust veil event from a volcano that almost killed the world's crops for one entire season. In some cities in Europe people were rioting for food and hundreds of thousands died before it was over. There was actually talk that the governments at the time would collapse.

"Shit, if we have the New Madrid fault slip like it did back 1876, with the ground shaking almost constantly for a damn month, this country will tear itself apart. Besides the disruption of two of the main distribution points for goods on the North American continent, the panic will be uncontrollable. And that's just one of many scenarios they've been working over.

"Everybody is waiting – hell, expecting – California to blow, but they don't talk too much about how the electrical grid for virtually all the western states depends on facilities in California not falling into a crack in the earth.

"The climate is going to change, and drastically. Whoever doesn't adapt to those changes will die. Now do you think, realistically, America will be able to adapt to anything more discomforting than higher prices on milk and gas? Do you really think this country won't slowly come apart? The government has known that it will for years."

Peter stumbled unsteadily around the alley while he spoke.

"I'll bet you didn't catch the latest Quadrennial Defense Review: 'Humanity will revert to its norm of constant battle for resources... Once again warfare would define human life.' And those are just the cheery highlights.

"They've spent tens of millions of dollars on scientists and computers trying to calculate all the possibilities. They think they know exactly how Americans will react and for the most part the scientists aren't wrong."

"Of course," Peter said. "They've always assumed the people are just waiting for a chance to start rioting. That's what the 'lowly masses' do. Nobody says anything about whether they have reason to rise up. But you're not talking about people rioting. You're talking about governments warring, aren't you?"

Graydin was getting impatient. He checked his watch for what had to be the tenth time. "The bastard I work for is obsessed with the preparations necessary to survive the disasters and with finding out when they will happen. There are some who have even deluded themselves into thinking they can predict the future. They lord over thousands of people in every area of government with the guarantee of notice and assistance in the coming disasters.

"They looked at the total destruction of the 2004 tsunami. They saw the devastation in New Orleans. They saw Haiti, Chile, and Japan, and they knew that those events are only the beginning, and that the natural disasters that are coming will be as nasty or worse.

"It was decided a long time ago that there was no sense in trying to save a city after a natural disaster destroys it. Especially when there was a high probability that the same kind of disaster would happen again the next storm season, or the next time the fault line gave. Just close it off and let it die. Save the resources for places that can be saved. Places where the survivors end up."

"The survivors, huh?"

"The coasts are screwed, other areas as well."

"All those people in the cities?"

"Expendable."

"But they could be evacuated! Something!"

"Impossible."

Peter paced the alley in confusion.

"So there's your headline. You can tell everyone that it's only a matter of time before a disaster like New Orleans, or the earthquakes, or the flooding in China and Pakistan, will happen to them. Oh, and don't forget to mention that they're on their own when it happens too. Because their government has no intention of doing a damn thing to help. Then be sure to mention how many of them believe that most of the country will be getting what they deserve."

"What do you mean?"

"Wake up. It's the god damned 'End of the world'! Judgment Day has arrived and Jesus is on the way. Now the 'sinners' will get theirs."

"You're joking, right?"

"It's no joke to them. And it could be seriously debated that it is the end of the world. It will be for most of the people on this planet, whether they die or not."

"If you agreed to a statement," Peter said. "I could write a story that would blow the lid off this whole thing."

"Who the hell do you think you're dealing with here? Their mission, not to mention their life's work, is to ensure the survival of the United States government at any and all costs. Do you think getting rid of an old spy and an even older reporter is anything for them?"

"And the WRC?"

"The Western Range Complex. They looked at Colorado for NORAD because it's in the center of the country, harder to hit with a nuke. It's also nice and far from the coasts."

"My paper is waiting right now for a story from me. If you would record a statement, I know I could—"

"Your editor would laugh you out of his office. Even if he did make his own decisions, which he doesn't, he would probably say there wasn't enough proof in the world to get him to print this little bit of bad news. You know how many ways the administration has to crucify somebody trying to sell a story like this. What do you think an officially non-existent special access program like the CIG could do? That's why I told you the truth. Now you know all about it. Feel better?"

"I know very well respected people who blog," Peter said. "I know journalists who run alternative news websites. They'll spread this all over the world in a day."

Graydin brushed a small patch of dust from his sleeve. "It's crank news," he said. "All they'll say is that the Pentagon study has been out for years. And that it's all a bunch of conspiracy theories. Nothing new. That's a favorite in information management.

"And you can say what you want about the blogs and those sites, but the established ones, the ones people actually read, they're constantly checking each other and actually demanding proof of the allegations that fly around. I know; one of my jobs is to monitor them. They won't push anything you don't at least have half-decent proof of. The last thing they want is to be branded conspiracy theorists. That's one of the most effective tools a propagandist has, slapping a 'conspiracy theorist' tag on anyone talking about conspiracies. That's your life if you come anywhere near this."

Peter slammed a trash can lid.

"I was pissed off. Now I'm just making sure my family stays alive. If you want to continue breathing, drop it. The truth is overrated when there is nothing you can do about it. Especially when it's a truth no one will ever believe. All it will do is make you more miserable than you already are. Then it will make you dead."

"I still have a top secret document. And now I know what it means."

Graydin chuckled under his breath. "You do, do you? What are you? A wall safe man? No, I'm thinking safe-deposit box. That's it, safe-deposit. Too bad."

Peter bolted toward the street.

"Good riddance!" Graydin yelled.

Peter did his best to subdue his panic when he hit the doors to his local bank, jerky movements in such a place could draw attention. He wisely took a moment to pull it together before he approached the attendant in charge of the safe-deposit boxes. The woman working there recorded his identification and accompanied him back to the vault.

"What if it isn't there?" he fretted out loud.

"Excuse me?"

"Just mumbling, sorry."

He examined her carefully as they simultaneously unlocked the small metal door protecting Peter's safe-deposit box. He found a private cubicle outside the vault and made certain the attendant was well away before attempting to open it.

Leaning over the slim steel container, his heart was beating furiously. If the top secret document was gone, he had to consider himself in as much danger of disappearing. He flung the top open to find the box empty.

"Impossible!" He stomped around the cubicle, eventually swiping the box off the table, sending it crashing to the floor. "What about Billy!" he said.

He went back out of the vault area, back to a customer service desk. "My cell phone died," he told the attendant. "Any chance I could use a phone?"

Dr. Hasline's Institute for Psychological Studies was located in an aging office district not far from Peter's bank, in a building that looked like any other office building. The nondescript appearance belied the nature of the activities that went on there.

Chris Ritter lurked around a room full of industrial sized trash bins wearing a pair of green overalls and long rubber gloves. It was only his second day and he knew he needed to look busy, so he grabbed a mop and rolling bucket and began swabbing the tile floor.

Chris had called in every favor he had accrued during his promising career at the State Department to be where he was at that moment. And when that wasn't enough, he resorted to more unsavory methods.

The badge that hung from his pocket would give him access to almost every room in the facility, except for Hasline's office, of course. He reviewed his plan to overcome that obstacle while he worked the mop around the utility room.

Chris hadn't been shown anything critical or even interesting by the veteran janitor charged with his training, and his patience was waning. He needed that to change now that his new, if temporary, boss had arrived for the afternoon shift.

"Damn Chris, you can't be coming in early and showing us up." The man slipped his jacket over his thick forearms and put it in his locker. He immediately went for a tiny comb and mirror inside the locker, to groom his finely trimmed black beard.

"So, we doing the rounds today?"

"That's the plan. If I'm going to go to dayshift before my wife takes the kids and bails, then I'm going to have to get you up to speed quick."

"Well, I'm ready, Russell."

"I don't think anybody is ever ready for this."

"Oh, it hasn't been too bad so far. I'm hanging in there."

Russell rummaged through the rolling cart full of janitorial equipment near the lockers. "You've just been in the offices," he said. "Usually we keep newbies on the first floor for the first week or so, let them get nice and used to the killer money before..."

"Before what?"

"Second shift cleans the third and fourth floors; those are Dr. Hasline's floors."

"So?"

"So you wouldn't be here if you didn't pass the security checks, but what they do up there is top secret. That means you keep your mouth shut about what you see, got it?"

"Like you said, the money is killer. That tends to make me shut right up."

"Then you might just stick around, and I might be able to dodge a divorce."

"Well, we'll see what we can do about that."

Although he had been in the diplomatic corps, Chris was no stranger to espionage work. That didn't make him any kind of professional, but with little to lose he was finding it easier and easier to be duplicitous. Becoming Jeff Newton – experienced floorman – for a few days to get a lead on his missing wife now seemed not only sane but logical.

He dutifully followed Russell around the lower floors of Hasline's putative research institute. He kept his head down and his eyes open while he and Russell emptied wastebaskets and vacuumed emptying offices. Still, to that point, he had seen nothing out of the ordinary. He was getting impatient once again when Russell started pushing his cart toward the elevators.

"It's time," he said.

Chris made a few more swipes with the mop then joined Russell before the doors closed. "So do we have a lot of hours up here?"

"Two or three, to get everything done. They have orderlies that do the medical waste in the rooms and nurses stations. Good thing, too, because there are bedpans. That's nasty. We don't do the blood or the shit or the hypodermic needles. That's in the contract."

"So we've got the common areas?"

"That's it. Halls, floors, staff bathrooms. There are three offices, but we only clean two. No one is allowed in Dr. Hasline's office. He's gone right now."

"Got it." Chris wrung out the mop during the short ride, in an effort to hide his confusion and anger.

How could he choke the life out of Hasline with his bare hands if the man wasn't there? How could he find his wife if he couldn't beat the information out of him? And worst of all, how could he find out where Hasline went without being discovered himself?

The only piece of advice Chris could remember, of all the advice he elicited from his friends in the intelligence world, was to maintain. Keep looking them in the eye and maintain.

"So the Big Cheese is gone, huh? That's cool for my first week."

"Yeah, he took an unscheduled trip; they just told me when I came in. Doesn't matter much anyway, chances are you'll never see him."

They stepped off the elevator on the top floor, where Hasline's office was located, along with the most extreme of his experiments. Chris felt the air of gloom immediately. And it wasn't just that the lights over the halls that ran to the left and right had been dimmed, to promote catatonia.

"Get on that mop, Jeff. Start at the end of the hall and work your way down. I'll start at the other end and meet you back here. When you're on your own you'll have to do it all yourself."

Chris abstained from trying to look into the individual cells that lined the hall. He suspected Russell would be keeping an eye on him. But after he got set up and was working the floor with the mop, he was able to steal glances through the porthole-like windows on each door.

He took broad strokes, from one side of the hall to the other. Then he acted as if he needed to clean in front of each door, where he would sneak a peak. All he could see was unconscious people, in each bed, in each cell.

He met back up with Russell at the offices across from the elevator, certain his wife wasn't in any of the rooms he was able to glimpse. He was also certain that each person he saw was not sleeping, they were in comas.

"What are they doing to them?"

"All I know is that they keep those people drugged for days, weeks. They only wake them up for a little while and then they put them out again. They play shit into their ears, you know, like subliminal shit. I heard a nurse one time, she called it 'psychic driving.' They're messed up in the head, you know, schizos. And this is supposed to be some kind of project to cure them."

"If they weren't crazy before, I'll bet they are now."

"Just go through your checklist and get the work done, everyday. And then go pick up your check every other Friday. It's not a bad job. I've been here twelve years and we ain't going nowhere, recession proof, you know?"

"That's comforting."

"We'll hit these two offices and go on down to three. They do the outpatient stuff down there. People coming and going, that means nurses."

Russell used his key card on the office closest to him. Chris had only to confirm the nameplates on the other two doors and he knew what had to happen next. He didn't want to do it, he liked Russell, but there was no turning back.

"Get the trash cans, would ya?" Russell asked.

"No problem."

Chris waited until Russell was vacuuming to make his move. Russell started in the far corner, the screaming of the machine drowning out everything in the small space. It allowed Chris to creep up behind him and reach his arm around the man's neck before he could react.

The move he attempted had been shown to him by a chatty bodyguard one day at an embassy in Europe. Being young and athletic made up for the fact that Chris had no idea what he was doing. He grappled the man's head with his other arm and clinched as hard as he could.

Russell's massive frame began to buck. "Get off of me! What are you doing?"

He was swinging Chris around the office unable to shake him off. The bodyguard told Chris that he would know that he had applied the hold properly when he could feel his forearm on the side of the man's throat. That was when he was interrupting blood flow through the carotid artery and robbing Russell of consciousness.

"Just relax, Russell, it'll be OK! I don't want to hurt you!"

Russell's thrashing and struggling lessened as he slowly lost control of his faculties. His arms went from swinging wildly to hanging limp; Russell finally relented. The man keeled over face-first onto one of the desks, Chris still attached to his back.

"God damn it!" Chris yelled, loosening his grip and falling to the floor crying.

Since he felt her die, a singular vision of his wife had been etched into Chris's brain. She was sitting cross-legged on her Yoga mat, as usual, smiling at him with such acceptance and love that it was overwhelming. That was why he was so certain she was dead, he no longer felt that all-embracing light.

And with that gone, so went reality as he knew it. Now he lived in a world where he could assault innocent people, and murder the guilty in cold blood.

Chris's despair ebbed with the recognition of how close he was to Hasline's secrets. It motivated him to get off the floor and regroup. He leaned around the desk in search of Russell's pulse. It was beating strong, to Chris's relief. He lifted Russell off the desk and dragged him carefully to a small couch near the door. A pair of plastic ties went over his wrists and ankles.

Russell's master key card in hand, Chris turned out the light and closed the office door. He paused in front of Hasline's door, unsure if the card would work, or set off alarms. Since it no longer mattered either way, he swiped it through the reader. The green light engaged and the doorknob gave. He got inside as quickly as he could. He didn't want to attract attention so he kept the lights off.

The first thing Chris noticed about the darkened room was the smell: like incense had been burning sometime in the recent past. What his flashlight showed him were messy, chest-high bookshelves, an even messier desk, and finally a desktop computer. Maybe he hadn't done what he had for nothing.

He went for the file cabinet; a small aerosol can at the ready. He put the nozzle of the can flush with the lock on the cabinet and sprayed. A white foam immediately flowed from the keyhole.

He searched the haphazard shelves of books while he waited for the acid to take effect. He wasn't expecting to find anything out of the ordinary, thus the presence of well used candles everywhere came as a surprise.

He followed a continuous line of red candles that had been arranged along the top of the book shelves with his flashlight. They went all the way around the office, breaking only at the door to the hall and at a ceiling high cabinet behind Hasline's desk. He sprayed the lock on the larger cabinet before engaging the power button on Hasline's computer.

The lock on the file drawers stopped hissing, an indication that there was nothing left to dissolve. He jerked the top drawer open and began searching for his wife's name, to no avail. Halfway through the second drawer he came across the name "Erica Brown."

Chris sat at Hasline's desk, by the light of the computer screen, hoping that somehow the file he held was on a different Erica Brown. The first lines of the report summary immediately dispelled that hope: "Subject displayed impressive accuracy and endurance during the entire battery of tests."

He solemnly turned to what should have been a page in the report that would log her disposition. All it read was: "Forward to ESC." Chris knew what that meant, because he knew that Hasline's "institute" was funded by Masterson's CIG. Thanks to his connections, and Erica herself, Chris knew a lot of things about Hasline and Masterson. Like how hard it was to gain entry to Masterson's Eastern Shore Complex.

Thinking he had a better chance of finding Hasline, Chris tried to access his calendar on the computer. Fortunately, it launched and he was able to plot Hasline's movements for the next several days.

He rifled through the drawers of the desk, none of which contained any patient files. He tried to open what he assumed were computerized files on the experiments, a prompt for a password stopped him so he turned to the cabinet behind the desk.

The acid had eaten away the lock on the doors and allowed him to swing them open with ease. He lowered the flashlight to come face to face with a very old human skull resting on a red velvet pedestal.

At first Chris was unsure of what he was looking at. He had to step back to allow the flashlight to illuminate as much of the inside of the cabinet as possible. It was some kind of alter, he realized, though judging from the paraphernalia, he doubted Hasline prayed to it.

Everything seemed to emanate from the skull on the center shelf. Brass bells, golden goblets, and assorted daggers littered the other three shelves above and below. Sacred beads from various cultures hung from hooks on the inside of both doors, along with a cross, a Star of David, pentagrams, and swastikas.

Chris had discovered a decidedly different array of magickal items than those Carlyle utilized in his rituals, but then the doctor's intent was far different. Carlyle sought to impose his will on the universe by using age-old methods to trigger certain mechanisms in his own mind. Hasline sought to make contact. By any means possible, with anything or anyone that would listen. Be it the Nine, Spectra, God, or the Devil.

Chris wasn't surprised by what he found, the woman he loved was immersed in that "world of weirdos and killers" Hector warned Billy about. The only question he had was if she was killed because she discovered the doctor's proclivities.

He used his can of acid one more time on two drawers at the bottom of the cabinet. He stepped away from the alter while the corrosive foam went to work on the inside of the locks. He didn't feel comfortable standing near the ominous mixture of the sacred and the profane. Indeed it was an image few laymen could reconcile.

He tried one of the drawers when it appeared the lock had been disabled. He cautiously peeked inside to find stacks of digital video tapes, all meticulously labeled with the date and the name "Set."

Chris scanned the room with the flashlight, speculating on what atrocities would be revealed by the tape he held. Since it appeared it would be the only evidence he could safely smuggle out of the building, he decided he better make use of the television and tape player he found in the corner to see what he had. He put the tape in and pressed play.

The flat screen came alive with a wide angle view of Hasline's office, his desk at the center of the screen. Chris turned off the flashlight and drew closer as Hasline appeared in the shot.

Hasline got comfortable in his desk chair then he repositioned a flat screen computer monitor directly in front of him. He adjusted his chair, mouse, and the monitor until he had things just right. He set a metronome in motion, leaned back into the chair, and activated his computer mouse.

Chris could hear the rhythmic ticking of the metronome as it swayed back and forth. He heard Hasline's slow and steady voice. Only it wasn't coming from the Hasline Chris was watching on screen. He was confused for a moment until he recognized that Hasline was watching a video of himself on the monitor in front of him. Chris was unable to see what was on the computer monitor from the angle of the tape but the audio was loud and clear.

"You are feeling very relaxed," the voice from the computer said. "You can feel your breathing, you can feel your lungs taking in the air and letting it back out."

"He's hypnotizing himself?" Chris said, much louder than he had intended.

"You can feel yourself slipping into a very peaceful sleep," the recording said. "You can feel your mind open to the universe. All you can hear is your own voice, the questions that will be asked, and then the voice of Set, One of Nine."

Chris watched Hasline succumb to his own words and fall into a deep trance. He scrutinized the image of Hasline's rigid and seemingly unresponsive face, searching for any sign of deception or delusion.

Little time passed before Hasline spoke. "I am One of Nine," he droned. "I am one of *the* Nine."

The voice-activated program on the monitor waited for Hasline to stop talking before it engaged and asked another question, the metronome beating away in the background.

"Do you speak for the Nine?" the recording asked.

"Yes," Hasline said.

"Are you Set?"

"Yes."

"Oh, Great Set, what does the rise of the Unity Council mean for the future you have foretold?"

"What has been prophesied will come to pass. The old gods are gone; it is time for the new gods to reign. The imposter fears the new gods. He fears the return of The Nine."

"What would you have us do?" the recording asked.

"Keep the faith you hold that though this coming transformation may be painful, it will be necessary. The planet will not be the only thing altered as this future unfolds. The people will be as well. The root races will fall away and all that will be left will be the rightful stewards of this planet. They will nourish and maintain Earth until we return."

"Are there any other messages you wish to impart?" the recording asked.

"Not at this time."

Upon receipt of the negative response the computer program launched into another sequence. "Listen to the sound of my voice. Follow the sound of my voice back."

Chris observed closely as Hasline finally began to stir.

"Follow your voice back to consciousness. When you hear the sound of the bell ring three times you will awaken feeling refreshed and very rested."

The computer monitor emitted three short rings that woke Hasline completely. He sat up in his chair, rubbing his face and yawing as if he had slept for hours. He looked directly into the lens when he pointed a remote control at the camera, startling Chris. The screen went black.

Chris brooded in the dark that descended after the tape ended. He may have been fueled by grief and wrath, but he was still lucid enough to recognize when his mission was in jeopardy.

He switched on the flashlight, shining it on the candles and over the bizarre alter and dozens of videotapes in the drawer. He decided it was time to contact the only person Erica ever trusted in that weird world of psychics and the occult. He would try the last phone number he had for John Spiritdancer.

9

Evening was descending on the high desert of northern Arizona, and with it a bracing chill. Leonard monitored the gauges of Mary's pickup as it surmounted the steady rise in elevation leading up to Flagstaff, a prelude to the mountainous ascent to the San Luis Valley ahead of them.

Sheila climbed through the opening from the camper into the cab wrapping her arm around his shoulder. "How goes it driver?"

"We're making good time. This thing runs like a top."

"Good deal. We need to get the kids settled in the hotel before it gets too late."

"Yes, ma'am. We'll have to hit it early tomorrow morning to get into the San Luis on time."

Just above them, the couple's two children, Heather and Michael, had been sequestered with Sara to the loft area over the cab of the pickup.

Mary was working in the miniature booth in the camper kitchen, the table covered with Unity Council financial data and her laptop. She took another worried look out the side window.

The Unity Council caravan stretched for miles in front and behind, reminding her of the haunting coverage of freeways out of New Orleans and Houston years before: four lane interstates clogged with long lines of panicked storm refugees, the ones fortunate enough to be able to evacuate before the deluge struck.

Mary hadn't forgotten those scenes of evacuation which had shocked the country's consciousness to the core and then were promptly forgotten by all but the victims directly affected.

Stories of vehicles running out of gas while sitting in gridlock, scuffles over water and food, they were events unseen in America since the creation of television. Mary had lived with those images of imminent disaster for years.

She had waited restlessly the whole of Sara's life for it all to happen again, in her neighborhood and all over California. She had paced and cursed and cried for ten years, all in anticipation of that day.

Now that she was taking the action she had convinced herself the entire state of California had been preventing her from taking, she wasn't sure how to feel. That she was leaving her home state for the first time in a convoy of people who were never returning made the whole thing that much more surreal. And stranger still was that they were evacuating a place that was still standing.

The Internet blackout between Kingman and Flagstaff lasted less than an hour. Motivated by word that more Unity Council phone banks had mysteriously gone down, Mary was back patrolling cyberspace as soon as possible.

Sheila was passing through the miniature kitchen just as a bump in the road sent a loose saltshaker rolling off the counter. She stopped it before it got too far.

"I better sit my butt down before I go flying too," she said.

She caught her son sticking his tongue out at the faster moving vehicles zipping by in the left lane. "Michael, no one wants to see that," she said.

Sara and Heather were jumping from one narrow window to another in the overhead sleeper area, fascinated by their bird's eye view of the scenery and the traffic.

"The troops are getting restless," Sheila said, sitting in front of the laptop Mary set up for her. "Are we there yet?" she yelled to Leonard.

"We get over this hill and it's smooth sailing. Less than a half an hour until we get to the hotel."

"The desert just melted away and now it's mountains," Mary said.

"Yeah, Flagstaff is up there pretty high. We're going to cut through the Four Corners area, so it'll be anything from high desert to mountains from now on to the valley."

"I don't know, Sheila. I'm getting that itch."

"What itch is that?"

"The itch to jeopardize my entire future... again."

"I wouldn't blame you for taking all this personally, Mary, but you can't let it make you do something you'll regret."

Mary couldn't help brooding, staring at the computer screen. Sheila could see that her new friend was conflicted.

"Would hacking be absolutely necessary?"

"If we really want to get to the bottom of who's sabotaging our websites, yep. There's more going on here than it appears. Either someone in my department is blabbing or the government is involved."

"I hate the idea of some fascist pinheads out there jerking around with what we're trying to do just as much as you do. And we can't go to the cops, not if the government is behind it. But you shouldn't do anything that could land you back in trouble."

"It looks like I never really got out of trouble. I don't know; all I keep thinking is that this time it's not just my life I'm playing with."

"It's always different when there are people relying on you. There's no doubt it changes everything," Sheila said. "But you're already doing the best you could ever do for Sara. I know in my heart it's the right thing."

"I thought I was doing the right thing ten years ago, too. And I got screwed for it."

"I heard about that."

Mary finally looked up from her computer screen. "If we're going to be working together, I guess they would have told you."

Sheila laughed a hard, hoarse laugh, as she often did when she was deeply amused. "I thought I was idealistic but what you did has to take the cake."

"I was so stupid; I actually thought it would make a difference."

"It did... for you. What did Hector tell you about us?"

"Not much, but I'm guessing there aren't any heavy stories involving felonies and children born out of wedlock?"

"No, I'm afraid not. We met just out of college and we've been together ever since." She laughed again. "I wouldn't say it's been easy but the things that tried to pull us apart always came from outside our relationship. This move will change a lot of that, I hope. Not immediately... but eventually."

"My mother and father are pissed at me for leaving. I think that whole 'technically breaking parole' thing might have had something to do with why my dad is so mad."

Sheila rolled her eyes. "If major earthquakes weren't enough of a reason to high-tail it out of that state, then I don't know what the hell would be."

"Yeah, well the district attorney of L.A. County has a different opinion on that."

"Yikes, that is a bad enemy to have."

"That was my life," Mary said. "Sitting around trapped, waiting for my future to start."

"We've been so worried about the future for so long... me and Len. I tell you, by now we're tired. We're just flat exhausted from worrying and it's just now starting to really hit the fan."

"But it's been coming since 2000," Mary said.

"It's been coming since after Reagan, really, since the early '90s. By then we were fairly convinced that the world wasn't making it out of the year 2000 alive. I'll admit it, we were millennium freaks. Between the millennium bug and all the prophecies about war and natural disaster, so were a lot of people.

"But we had already been worrying about it for almost ten years leading up to the turn of the millennium. That's twenty years now, since we were in our twenties, that we've been waiting for it to get so bad that someone would recognize."

"I was on the Net before there even was a World Wide Web," Mary said. "I go online one day and suddenly there are all these sites screaming about how the end of the world is coming."

"God, do you remember? Even people who didn't believe in the conspiracy stuff were scared."

"Sometimes I think it would have been better if there had been some big disaster," Mary said. "Because it's all happening, all the shit they bitched about back then is coming true, just not on one day."

Sheila's ruddy, wrinkled face contorted into a wince. "Yeah, it's been more like a slow motion car wreck," she said.

"And it does seem like it all started in 2000 too. It didn't really, but it sure feels that way."

"Then we keep our heads down for eight years waiting for some sanity to come back," Sheila said. "And some smooth-talking sonofabitch comes along with a spiel about how he's going to make it all better. Of course, like a bunch of shmucks we buy it hook, line, and sinker. He ends up totally betraying us all and still millions of people love him for it."

"That's my parents; they live their life in degrees. As long as the next guy is even marginally better than the last, then somehow that's the best progress we can hope for. I try to tell them that Sara doesn't have time for that."

"My grandfather was just like that. Being able to endure adversity was a matter of pride for his generation, it showed character, toughness. Asking about the cause of the adversity wasn't something they did much of. And expecting everything to change for the better was just plain foolish."

"It probably is foolish, but that doesn't mean we should stop."

"Absolutely," Sheila said. "The Internet still up?"

"Signal strength is good."

"I'm going to hit a few websites, see what they're saying about the Council."

"According to my mom, it is not good."

"'Local reporter has a meltdown at Unity Council camp in Kingman, Arizona,'" Sheila read. She activated a short video clip.

"Hey Mary, check this out. Apparently this happened this morning, right in the middle of the camp back in Kingman. It says that a local reporter they sent from Phoenix to cover the migration got into it with one of the campers."

Sheila spun the laptop computer to give Mary a better view as the video launched. Captured from a live satellite feed, the clip began toward the end of the interview in question. The irritated voice of the man being questioned came through the speakers that Mary had positioned around the alcove.

"Who the hell said anything about a fraudulent organization?" he said.

"The Justice Department and the Congress," the correspondent said.

"Maybe if someone with a little more credibility was talking, then I'd be worried. Tell you what, you go ask any one of those New Orleans refugees the Council helped move out of those poisonous trailers. You go ask them about who the frauds are: the Unity Council or the politicians!"

"Cut! Cut! What is it with these people?" The correspondent waved off her camera crew and had already spotted another person to interview.

"What's with you? I wasn't finished," the man said. "You ask a damn question, then when I try to answer it, you cut me off? Do you want to hear the truth or not?"

"I don't have time for this! I've got better things to do than deal with these weirdos."

"You're kind of a dumb bitch, aren't you?" the man said before closing the door to his RV behind him.

Mary was moving to turn the volume down on the speakers as the correspondent's shrill voice delivered the line that had quickly made the video clip the hottest download on the Internet.

"Hey, fuck you buddy!" she yelled.

Mary and Sheila strained to see if the children had overheard the obscenities but they were too preoccupied with the action outside to pay attention to what the adults were doing.

"That's too funny," Mary said between giggles. "Those people embarrass themselves every day."

"Now that will get played over and over again," Sheila said.

"While the story about how the Unity Council has been helping won't get mentioned. Watch, I'll ask my mom what she's heard about the Council after another two days of news. I'll bet she'll know everything there is to know about that reporter's little meltdown, but she won't know a thing more about what we're trying to do out here."

"You have to tell her. Explain it to her."

"She won't listen to me. Didn't you know? It isn't real unless it's on TV. My mom said there was supposed to be some ex-members of the Unity Council who had left and were making the rounds on the talk shows now saying the Council ripped them off and took their houses. Funny thing, the Unity Council hasn't ever heard of any of them."

"Just barely provable stories of fraud and financial malfeasance from disgruntled ex-employees," Sheila said. "The only thing left is allegations of sexual harassment, something like that. Guaranteed to get some ratings."

"I guess reporting that the Unity Council is just a glorified relocation service, a nonprofit one, at that, isn't nearly as exciting."

Sheila skimmed through another homepage full of headlines, each one dealing with a pressing issue of the day. "Why do you think Hector has had to resort to some of the stunts he's been pulling? How much attention is a not-for-profit effort to help low income people relocate out of disaster zones going to get outside the alternative press, without some drama to keep the public interested? It's a damn shame, but it's true."

"The damn shame is that not everyone has a computer," Mary said, glancing at several of the headlines on the webpage Sheila had called up. The Unity Council's name appeared in the titles of many of the stories being presented. "I may be biased, but you get everyone online and you get a seriously better-informed country."

"Yeah, but how realistic is that? Even the poorest people have a television, even if they can't afford cable, but a computer with access to the Internet? They'll own and control the entire Net before it's allowed to reach that many people."

"'They' huh?"

"Oh I'm good and paranoid, you better believe it. And every minute out here is making me think that maybe I'm not paranoid enough."

Unaccustomed to wearing necklaces, Mary fidgeted nervously with the pendant Hector gave her in Arizona.

Sheila leaned in to whisper. "I have to admit I was surprised by how seriously they took what Denise saw. Hector was playing it cagey, but he was obviously concerned. Len too, he knows stuff that he isn't talking about and that ain't like him. When he was on the job he usually told me everything."

"Honestly, Sheila, I don't know what to think, but if any of it really is possible, then there's no way I couldn't take all this personally. If they really are targeting me and my work, then I'm definitely going to fight back any way I can."

Leonard slid the pickup into its lowest gear in preparation for the final hill up to Flagstaff. The resulting jolt sent Mary's cell phone sliding into Sheila's lap. It rang in her hand as she was returning it to the table; she gave it to Mary.

"This is Mary," she said. Her face went blank and turned pale upon hearing the voice on the other end of the line. "Hello, Steve. How have you been?"

"I'm doing fine. Surprised to hear from your parole officer? Excuse me, former parole officer?"

"I knew we would have to talk sooner or later. So, have they issued a warrant for my arrest yet?"

"No and that's why I'm calling," Steve said with a chuckle. "I have to ask, though, do you have some kind of guardian angel?"

"Besides you, Steve, I can't think of one. Just say it. Did that sonofabitch Aronson call the cops on me?"

"Normally your favorite district attorney wouldn't have needed a parole violation like you leaving the county to have you picked up, but this time nothing happened."

"Nothing happened?"

"And all of a sudden they found those records of your community service. You know, the ones that were supposedly lost? I still think Aronson had somebody 'lose' them to try to keep you in L.A."

"That's one sorry little man," Mary said. "He's held a grudge for ten years now, that's a long time to just suddenly let it go. Trust me on that."

"Ever heard the name Ben Spiritdancer?" Steve asked.

The camper jogged one more time as it finally conquered the slope, Flagstaff spread out among the pines ahead. The line of slow-moving vehicles in the right lane began to stretch out and pick up speed on the descent. Sheila felt her way up to the front seat to give Mary some privacy.

"No, I think I would remember a name like that," Mary said.

"Spiritdancer is a retired police lieutenant from Phoenix, and I don't know what he had on Aronson, but now its hands off Mary Jenkins out here. As far as L.A. County is concerned, your parole requirements have been fulfilled and Aronson can't do a thing about it. Damn, Mary, you have some serious new friends, bigger friends than me."

"That's not possible, Steve. I know you were looking out for me all along and I'm grateful. You've been one of the few who really cared."

It took a moment for Steve to gather the courage to speak intimately with his long time parolee. "Why did you leave, Mary? I guess I always thought when I was no longer your parole officer, maybe I could be your friend."

"I know. I thought that, too. I really did. But I had a chance to get out and I took it. I would have been stupid not to."

"Well, thanks to someone you apparently don't know, you have a clean start."

"How can you do it? How can you stay? You better get the hell out of there before they strip away every shred of humanity you have left."

"You're probably right. But somebody has to stay behind. We can't all just up and leave."

"Why the hell not? What? Are you going to fight your heart out in a losing battle until the ground opens up and swallows you whole?"

"Well thanks for the cheery assessment of my future."

"You deserve more than that, Steve. You deserve to be happy. And I know for a fact that living there and doing what you're doing doesn't make you happy."

"There was one thing about my job that I looked forward to... I can't imagine not seeing you every month."

Mary was flattered by Steve's obvious show of love, and would have worried more about reciprocating, if she hadn't already moved on. "Go to www.unitycouncil.com and read. A bunch of the communities the Council is relocating people to are in serious need of dedicated people. People like you. Check out the website and then call me. Promise you will call me?"

Steve was merely relieved that he and Mary hadn't had their last conversation. That she wasn't completely disappearing from his life. "I promise I will check it out, and I promise I will call."

Mary hung up pondering whether his desire to avoid an earthquake, the constant hell of working in that parole office, and lastly his feelings for her, would finally be enough to shake him from his life in Los Angeles. If all those things weren't enough to convince him to leave California, she thought, then there was no point in even considering a relationship with him.

Mary looked with new eyes out the window at the tall pines that lined the western approach to Flagstaff. She felt as if a crippling weight had been lifted from her back and now she could walk again.

She joined Leonard and Sheila at the front of the camper as Flagstaff was peeking through the dense stand of evergreens that lined the four lane highway.

"Everything OK?" Leonard asked.

"Well, no one will be looking to extradite me back to California, so we have that going for us."

"Nice, no criminal proceedings," Sheila said.

"That's probably the best way to get started in a new state," Leonard said. "Without all those pesky extradition warrants bombing in from the place you just left. Let me guess: Ben Spiritdancer?"

"How did you know?" Mary said.

"Len, what did you do? I know Spiritdancer works for the Council. Beautiful name, huh?"

"With everything else that's going on now, you didn't need to be dealing with all that back there. And besides, Hector's plan doesn't allow for it. So it needed to be settled, once and for all."

"My God guys, I just can't believe you did this."

"Get ready kids, we're almost there!" Leonard yelled to the ruckus above his head. "We'll get something to eat and some sleep so we can leave early in the morning! Then we'll be there before this time tomorrow!"

Sheila gave Mary a friendly smile. "Sounds like this Spiritdancer guy just put things right."

"Yep," Leonard said without taking his eyes from the road.

Mary would have said more, had she known the couple better. At a loss for words, she struggled back to her laptop. She placed her hands on both sides of the keyboard, her conversation with Steve sinking in slowly.

The kids were chattering about the snack they wanted after dinner. Leonard and Sheila were laughing at the front of the cab. The engine revved beneath her. All those things were coming in loud and clear and still Mary couldn't hear them.

All she could do was try to hold back the tears by staring at the screensaver on her computer, a photo of her and Sara on Sara's last birthday. She allowed her eyes to water but her feelings of vindication prevented her from crying.

To her surprise, the resentment she had been harboring for a decade wasn't just melting away, as she hoped it would. It was turning into a rabid impulse to protect what had become, in Mary's mind, her daughter's only hope for the future: the Unity Council.

She grasped her laptop with both hands as a strategy formed in her head. She began typing so loud and hard that it attracted Sheila's attention.

"You've got a wild look in your eye, girl."

"It's time to get to work."

Night had fallen on the lone Kansas rest stop where Max, Curtis, and much of the Unity Council caravan had camped for the night. Pitch dark prairie encircled the oasis of cement restrooms and adolescent trees, with parking lots large enough to accommodate semi-tractor trailers.

Much to the chagrin of the truckers that frequented that section of I-70, every inch of every parking lot had been covered by the vehicles in the convoy, and every fire pit and picnic table had been occupied by amiable campers. Lanterns that had been placed all around the area were augmenting the lights from the parking lot and providing a cozy atmosphere.

After a long and relatively slow day on the road, Max and Curtis decided to accept an offer of dinner from Connie and Ted. Both exhausted, their nerves frayed, they hoped to get lost in the mass of overnight campers and catch up on some sleep. They ended up staring at each other over a spent barbeque pit near the edge of the overflowing rest stop.

The dinner hour had passed and gradually the people who had been hanging around the individual camps began to disappear into their tents or RVs in anticipation of an early morning. The area was settling down considerably, but it wasn't the activity that was keeping Max and Curtis awake.

They may have come from very different places, but both men had endured their share of sleepless nights wondering whether they would survive the next day. Max was thousands of miles from his home when that happened, Curtis was in his home. Those individual recurring memories of fear were affecting them more than either would admit.

Curtis stuffed his phone into his jacket. "Still no go."

"Ted was talking to a sheriff's deputy. They launched a big investigation to find out why cell service has gone out over two states, but only along I-70."

"Anybody happen to tell them that you're the reason?" Curtis said.

"It would be cool if you could just keep that one to yourself."

"It don't matter, since we can't get through on the regular lines either. Everyone is saying that the Unity Council phones are whacked out too. I'm telling you, man, 'It's sabotage.'"

"We could just make a run for it," Max said. "We've probably got six, maybe seven, hours until Denver."

"That's a long way on our own. We don't have any more ammo, and we probably won't have any phones. There's no telling how many agents are around. We could take down another, maybe two, but if we're outnumbered, we're dead. At least I am; Hector said they want your ass alive and kicking."

"Lucky me."

"Ted and Connie decided to go on down to the San Luis Valley. I think I shook them up a minute. I talked to as many people as I could about doing the same. Connie and Ted said they would too."

"Good job, what about the people at the rest stops we passed before we stopped? What about the people at the rest stops down the road?"

"There're supposed to be a few Unity Council info booths along here somewhere. But like I said, I'm just glad I'm not the one in charge of all this."

"I don't know, you'd probably do a hell of a job, Curtis. I can't remember drill sergeants that could get people organized like you did earlier."

"That's my biz. And it got my mom and brother out of New York too. Thanks to the Unity Council."

"So how did that work? The Unity Council just found you and offered you a job?"

"Shit man, after they shut down my homeless shelter, I was out of work. They didn't pay much but I got by on it. But around that time, this painting co-op started up in my neighborhood, me and my little brother went down to check it out.

"He was cruising down a bad road, same road that almost killed my ass. But we started working in this painting crew and it helped to get him out of it. You know how it works: we were part owners in the business from the start. We got medical coverage and a piece of the profits.

"We just took jobs around the neighborhood, so we weren't rolling in it or anything, but we got some good work from some of the 'Beautify the Hood' projects painting buildings in parks and public areas. Stuff like that. Then a lot of the money ran out for those programs, too. Now they're using it to not build roads and schools in Iraq and Afghanistan.

"But after a while these people wanted to set up a farm co-op with the stuff they had been growing in all these little patch gardens that had been springing up everywhere in the neighborhood. You know the people in the neighborhood didn't even have a way to get fresh vegetables for the kids. No grocery stores were willing to set up shop in the area. It was messed up.

"After we helped with that, Maria called about putting together this manufacturing co-op in this little town outside Cincinnati. The Cleveland Foundation had been working this co-op setup called the 'Cleveland Model' in that town for years, and that part of the country doesn't look to be in too bad a shape in the future. So it sounded like a good way to go.

"Ours is in alternative energy. Building these sweet-assed hot water heater units. They can go into like 90 percent of the houses in the country, retrofit, you know? They say that a huge part of people's energy costs comes from heating water.

"My brother is in the co-op, working on the line, and we were able to move my mom too. So, yeah, I'm cool with the Unity Council. Especially since all they want to do is more of the same around the country. Where people aren't going to get snuffed out by a bunch of climate change."

"That's why you left New York City?"

"It had been coming for a long time anyway, but yeah." Curtis downed the last of the beer Ted had given him. "Ohio ain't bad, I'll probably be traveling around the country for a while, but I loved New York. The action of the city, you know? It's not always pretty, but it's never boring.

"I think some people are mountain people, some dig the ocean, and some are all about the city. Guess I'm just the type that will always be a sucker for the Big Apple."

"One city is the same as another as far as I'm concerned," Max said. "And I've never been too partial to the ocean, or the mountains, for that matter. I guess I don't know where I belong."

The conversation diminished and the men took to staring into the smoldering coals of the barbeque pit. Some time passed before Curtis was moved to speak again.

"You remember about in the middle of *Waterworld* when Costner took that fine chick down in that air bubble? He took her down under the ocean that covered almost the whole planet, and he showed her the cities down there."

"Yeah, I remember that."

"Well, it wasn't too long after I saw that flick that I had a dream, about my neighborhood. I was walking on my block, like always, but there was water everywhere, so deep that it covered even the tallest buildings. It was *Waterworld*, man.

"I could still breathe somehow, like Costner with his gills, but it wasn't any kind of fun or anything. All I did was trip around my 'hood, watching the fish swim in and out of the busted up windows.

"The bodega where we used to steal candy bars, the newsstand where this old brother used to yell at us all the time, the corner where we used to hang... all of it at the bottom of the ocean. That's when I decided: not me, not my mom, and not my little brother, we aren't going down like that."

Max moved a nearby lantern to the ground beside him. "I did start worrying a little when all those specials kept popping up about hurricanes in New York City." He drew his bag close and had the Epic in hand once again, fighting the urge to open it.

"That doesn't even include the rising sea levels," Curtis said. "In 2050, me and my mom may be dead, but my little brother will still be around. At least he will if he stays the hell out of the way of hurricanes... You know you want to read it."

"I've read it a hundred times. I could recite it by heart by now."

"Why?"

"I really wish I knew. If it was *Catcher in the Rye*, I'd think I was turning into a serial killer."

"Great, how the hell am I supposed to sleep now?"

Max stared at the cover of the translation of the Gilgamesh epic as if in a trance.

"So the rest of the story is just like in the Bible? With the Flood and all that?"

"Kind of, in some places, but not really."

"Well, I ain't sleeping, you?" Curtis propped himself up against a rock and stretched out. "Read me some."

Max yawned, knowing full well that sleep would be impossible. He finally ceded to the reality that he would end up reading from the translation before the night was through and opened the book.

"My bookmark is at where Gilgamesh's friend Enkidu had been killed by the gods for something both him and Gilgamesh did. Well, watching his friend die started Gilgamesh thinking, but about himself, of course. He got all freaked out about kicking the bucket."

Max turned the lantern and tilted the book for better reading light. "'Enkidu, my friend, my younger brother, who chased the wild ass of the open country and the panther of the steppe. We who conquered all difficulties, who ascended the mountains; who seized and killed the Bull of Heaven; who overthrew Huwawa (Humbaba) that dwelt in the cedar forest! Now what sleep is this that has taken hold of thee? Thou hast become dark and canst hear me.'

"He just didn't want to believe that this great king, who was two-thirds god, could actually die. He was holding out hope that his blood would give him immortality.

"And he knew because of the knowledge from before and after the Flood that the 'Hero of the Deluge' didn't die. For following the orders of his god, he was blessed by Enlil and taken along with his wife to live forever with the gods.

"'When I die, shall I not be like unto Enkidu?'" Max read. "'Sorrow has entered my heart. I am afraid of death and roam the desert. To Utnapishtim, son of Ubara-Tutu, I have therefore taken the road and shall speedily go there.'

"So it made sense to Gilgamesh to go on a second trip to the abode of the gods to talk to the only immortal human he knew of: Noah. But in the original story, the 'Hero of the Deluge' wasn't named Noah, it was Utnapishtim."

"Damn, that's a mouthful."

"It means 'He saw life.' Like, 'He found immortality.' But 'Hero of the Deluge' says it all."

"According to my moms, Noah's one of the ten main Bible Patriarchs that you do not mess with, brother."

"Gilgamesh was all about messing with him. He left his city and wandered a vast desert. He was thirsty and starving and already down to his last when he was attacked by a pair of lions. Gilgamesh took on the two lions and eventually killed them both, using the animals' skins to wear on the rest of his journey.

"So Enkidu didn't pop up to save his ass?"

"No, according to the legend he did that one all on his own. The book said that that event became one of the most reproduced in ancient history. They say that the image of a great warrior flanked by two cats has been found as far as Iraq, Africa, and maybe even South America."

"Alright, I guess he did that one legit."

"Fresh from the only victory Gilgamesh could claim as his own to that point in the story, he found his way out of the desert and ended up at the base of some legendary mountains. Some say it was in the Sinai where Moses got the commandments.

"It was there that he met 'the scorpion people,' one version called them. In another version, they were called the 'eagle men.' Either way, they were the people whose 'radiance is terrifying and whose look is death.' Gilgamesh got pretty spooked when he saw them, but his royal blood would smooth things over.

"'He who has come to us, his body is the flesh of gods! The Scorpion-man's wife replied, Two-thirds of him is god, one-third of him is man.'

"'Why hast thou come all the way to me?' the Scorpion-man asked Gilgamesh. 'The purpose of thy coming I should like to learn.'

"'For the sake of Utnapishtim, my father, have I come,' Gilgamesh answered. 'Concerning life and death I would ask him.'

"'The Scorpion-man opened his mouth and said, speaking to Gilgamesh. There has not yet been anyone, Gilgamesh, who has been able to do that. No one has yet traveled the path of the mountains.'

"'Though it be in sorrow and pain, in cold and heat, in sighing and weeping, I will go!' Gilgamesh said. 'Open now the gate of the mountains.'"

Max looked up from the book to find Curtis not only still awake but paying close attention.

"Looks like the scorpion men were guarding some kind of mountain pass or tunnel because Gilgamesh started walking in the dark for all these hours until he came out on the other side.

"That's when he travels for a while until he comes to an inn. An inn on the shore of the Waters of Death."

"Nice," Curtis said. "The 'Waters of Death,' you gotta love that."

"Well Gilgamesh starts bawling about Enkidu to the barmaid. Really he's just crying because he has to die.

'Gilgamesh, whither runnest thou?' the barmaid asked. 'The life which thou seekest thou wilt not find. For when the gods created mankind, they allotted death to mankind, but life they retained in their keeping.'"

"That's cold."

"Then the barmaid gave Gilgamesh some good advice that he didn't follow: 'Thou, O Gilgamesh, let thy belly be full; day and night be thou merry; make every day a day of rejoicing... Cherish the little one holding thy hand, and let thy wife rejoice in thy bosom. This is the lot of mankind."

"That wasn't bad advice. But he was havin' none of it, was he?"

"Nope," Max said, locating the next verse. "'Now, barmaid, which is the way to Utnapishtim? What are the directions? If it is possible, even the sea I will cross!'

"'Gilgamesh, there has never been a crossing,' the barmaid said. 'And whoever from the days of old has come thus far has not been able to cross the sea. Valiant Shamash does cross the sea, but who besides Shamash crosses it?' But it turned out that she knew of a boatman."

"The boatman on the Waters of Death. Wonder what that gig's like?"

"The book says that one of the legends said the boatman was the actual pilot that steered the ark during the Flood."

Curtis erupted in a toothy grin. "You gotta love the legends about the legends."

"No doubt, like the one that says the ark landed on a mountain in Turkey, but it never says that in the original Sumerian flood story. The one before the one in Gilgamesh."

"Aw man, I loved that search for Noah's ark shit."

"It may be there, but the original says the ark just came to rest when the waters went down. But my favorite is the one where the body of Adam was supposed to have been taken in an alabaster coffin aboard the ark before the Flood, for safe keeping."

"That's two biblical patriarchs in one legend," Curtis said. "That's working it."

"But anyway, Gilgamesh makes a deal with the boatman and they set out across the Waters of Death." Max adjusted the lantern for a better look at the verses. "They sailed along until Utnapishtim could see Gilgamesh from the opposite shore. 'The man who is coming there is none of mine,' Utna said.

"'Should not my heart be sad and my features distorted?' Gilgamesh said. 'Should there not be woe in my heart? And I, shall I not like unto him lie down and not rise forever? Gilgamesh furthermore said to him, to Utnapishtim: That now I might come and see Utnapishtim, whom they call the Distant.'

"So finally, after all the shit he went through, he was standing in front of the Hero of the Deluge, Utnapishtim the Distant.

"Gilgamesh starts whining and bragging about the mountains he had to cross and the wild animals he killed, trying to justify his right to something no human besides Utnapishtim and his wife had ever scored. But Utnapishtim couldn't help him.

"'Do we build a house to stand forever?' Utnapishtim asked. 'Do brothers divide their inheritance to last forever? Does evil remain in the land forever? Does the river rise and carry the flood forever? From the days of old there is no permanence. The sleeping and the dead, how alike they are! Do they not both draw the picture of death?'

"'The Anunnaki, the great gods, gather together; Mammetum, the creatress of destiny, decrees with them the destinies. Life and death they allot; the days of death they do not reveal.'"

"The 'days of death,' oh baby. The boy got screwed."

"It looked like it, but then Utnapishtim started to tell Gilgamesh how the gods gave him immortality. He started to tell Gilgamesh about everything that happened when the Flood hit."

"And that's the story that went into the Bible?"

"That's it; they know that there were way older versions of just the Flood story, and that one of them was added to the Gilgamesh legend later."

"My moms can never hear this," Curtis said. "So we learned about the Flood because some king wanted to live forever? That's jacked up."

"There were other versions, but the one in Gilgamesh was the most complete, and the most well-known, at least later, when it was time to write the Bible story."

"They're always talking about how the Bible is so old."

"They do, but it wasn't first put together until around 900 BC. But the oldest flood stories go into the 3000s BC."

"And when was Abraham?"

"Like 2000 BC. And they put Gilgamesh, if he really existed, at around 2900 BC."

"What about Moses?"

"They're not as sure on that one. But they say 1200, 1300, 1400 BC?"

"And the Tower of Babel?"

"They're not sure on that one either, any time between after the Flood and before Abraham."

"Damn, you've gotten way up into this, haven't you?"

"That's what being obsessed will do," Max said, all too happy to be able to talk about the object of his obsession. And being able to say the words out loud, that he had read in his head so many times, was giving him a fresh perspective.

"OK, let's see here." He skimmed through the verses. "So, Utnapishtim started telling Gilgamesh about what went down leading up to the Flood.

"'Gilgamesh, I will reveal unto thee a hidden thing, namely, a secret of the gods will I tell thee.'

"'Shurippak – a city which thou knowest, and which is situated on the bank of the Euphrates – that was already old, and the gods were in its midst. Now their heart prompted the great gods to bring the deluge.'

"Shurippak was one of the golden cities of the gods that was supposed to have existed in Iraq before the Flood," Max said. "The city where Abraham would be born later was supposed to have been one of those too."

"What about the Holy Land?"

"It didn't exist yet. People knew about Baalbek, the Landing Place, that's supposed to be where Gilgamesh and Enkidu went, but Abraham was Mesopotamian. He was born in a city in Iraq."

"Alright, see, you're never meeting my moms now. She'd sit your ass down and give you a good talking to over that kind of blaspheming."

"Hey, I didn't write it," Max said before he went back to reading. "'Enlil opened his mouth to speak and addressed the assembly of all the gods. Come, all of us, and take an oath regarding the killing Flood!'

"Enlil was the king shit god on earth, and he was pissed at the humans. There were too many of them, they were everywhere and he was over it."

"Damn, in the Bible, God was pissed off because the sons of God were laying up the daughters of man."

"Yeah, and creating little demi-gods."

"Like Gilgamesh."

"Yep, but Enlil had an older brother by the name of Enki. He created humans, and he couldn't see us wiped out. So he stands up in the assembly of gods and he's like, 'Why will you bind me with an oath? Am I to raise my hand against my own humans?'

"But he was overruled: 'The gods commanded total destruction. Enlil imposed an evil deed on the humans.'"

"Fire and damnation," Curtis said. "That shit's the same in any religion."

"Yeah, but this other book, it's a history book, it talks about how there was a little more going on with the Sumerian story. It's not in Gilgamesh, but it's laid out in the Mesopotamian creation myth, the original to the one in the Bible too.

"Enki was the oldest and he came to earth first, but Enlil was next in line according to kingship rules. So their daddy came down from Heaven and told Enki that Enlil was the one in charge, after Enki basically discovered Earth and created humans.

"After that, they go at it pretty good in a bunch of different Mesopotamian stories. They're the first brotherly rivalry, long before Cain and Able."

"Everyone knows that you don't get in between brothers," Curtis said. "They'll mess you up, while they're busy messing each other up."

"That's it. So Enki decided, for whatever reason, vanity or to piss off his brother, that he was going to warn one guy, one lowly human. But he couldn't do it out in the open because of the oath that Enlil made him take.

"It was right about then that good old Utnapishtim had a dream that he couldn't understand. So he called to his god, Enki, to come and interpret it. Enki popped up at Utnapishtim's reed hut and straightened out the dream he said he sent to his follower in the first place.

"It turned out the dream meant that since he was a true believer, Utnapishtim was going to get a heads up about Enlil's plan not to warn the rest of the humans that a flood was coming. But he couldn't tell anyone else. It had to be a secret.

"'Man of Shurippak, son of Ubara-Tutu! Tear down thy house, build a ship!'" Max read. "'Abandon thy possessions, seek to save life! Discard thy goods, and save thy life!'

"Utnapishtim got the message, but what was he supposed to say when the townspeople asked what he was up to building this huge boat? Enki had an answer for that. Telling the truth wasn't an option, apparently, so Utnapishtim and Enki cooked up a nice little cover story.

"'Thus shalt thou say to them,' Enki said. 'I have learned that Enlil hates me, that I may no longer dwell in your city, nor turn my face to the land of Enlil. I will therefore go down to the apsu and dwell with Ea, my lord.' Ea is another name for Enki.

"Utnapishtim told the elders what his god instructed him to say. And then he went a little further to grease them up real good. 'On you he will rain down plenty...' Utnapishtim said. 'In the evening the leader of the storm will cause a wheat-rain to rain down upon you.'

"'Bullocks I slaughtered for the people,' Utnapishtim said. 'Sheep I killed every day. Must, red wine, oil, and white wine, I gave the workmen to drink as if it were river water, so that they feast as on New Year's Day."

"He was punking them," Curtis said. "He's punking them into building the ark. That's some shit, right there."

"The townspeople were going to be fat and happy when this Flood hit, like on 'New Year's Day,'" Max said. "They were going to be in for a big surprise, but Utnapishtim would be long gone by then."

"Gilgamesh was a bitch-ass glory boy," Curtis said. "But good old Utna ain't coming off so cool either."

"At least in this story, Utnapishtim never tried to get the people together and tell them shit," Max said. "Even if they did all worship Enlil instead of Enki; even if they were all sinners; even if it wouldn't have made a difference, at least he could have tried to warn someone. After all, Enlil was out to destroy all the humans, the followers of Enki and the followers of Enlil alike. No one was going to be spared anyway."

"That's the thing I always thought was wrong about the Noah story," Curtis said. "You know, in the Bible. If Noah and his crew were floating on top of the water after the Flood, all the people who didn't believe, or who didn't get the heads up from Noah or God, were at the bottom of that bitch, drowned like rats. And it was one thing if Noah was screaming his head off telling people to load up on the ark, but he was more about the animals, coming in two by two."

"In this story, he does go out of his way to make sure everybody besides some craftsmen, the boat pilot, and his own family, are left in the dark. It works too, they get the townspeople to build the ark for them and when the Flood hits, Utna and his crew are safe inside.

"'Like a battle it came over the people,'" Max read. "'No man could see his fellow. The people could not be recognized from Heaven.'

"But the Flood was so awesome that it even scared the gods: 'Even the gods were terror-stricken at the deluge. They fled and ascended to the heaven of Anu; the gods cowered like dogs and crouched in distress.' Ishtar, the one who propositioned Gilgamesh in the first part of the story, she: '...cried out like a woman in travail. The lovely-voiced Lady of the Gods lamented: In truth, the olden time has turned to clay... The Anunnaki-gods wept with her; the gods sat bowed and weeping.'"

Max skipped ahead several pages without even thinking. "The next section is just like the biblical story. They floated around and Utnapishtim sent out birds until they finally got hooked on this mountain. Then when the waters went down enough, everybody went ashore.

"'I poured out a libation on the peak of the mountain,' Utnapishtim said."

Curtis chuckled. "What? He did not 'spill one on the curb?'"

"Oh they were all in the making-up mood by then," Max said with a laugh. "'The gods smelled the savor, the gods gathered like flies over the sacrifice.' The gods were hungry and pretty happy over Utnapishtim's barbeque, particularly Ishtar.

"'I shall remember these days and shall not forget them ever! Let the gods come near to the offering; but Enlil shall not come near to the offering, because without reflection he brought on the deluge and consigned my people to destruction!'

"But then Enlil came down, and he was hot when he saw that the humans had survived. 'As soon as Enlil arrived and saw the ship Enlil was wroth,'" Max read. "'He was filled with anger against the gods... Has any of the mortals escaped? No man was to live through the destruction!'

"It was obvious to all the gods that Enki was the only one who could have warned the mortals. He fessed right up. 'How O how couldst thou without reflection, bring on this deluge?' he said. 'On the sinner lay his sin; on the transgressor lay his transgression.'

"Enki played it off by saying that Utnapishtim had a dream and figured it all out, so Enlil needed to shut up and thank Utnapishtim for surviving. So Enlil went into the ark with Utnapishtim and his wife and blessed him.

"'He took my hand and caused me to go aboard,' Utnapishtim said. 'He caused my wife to go aboard and kneel down at my side. Standing between us, he touched our foreheads and blessed us: Hitherto Utnapishtim has been but a man; but now Utnapishtim and his wife shall be like unto us gods. So they took me and caused me to dwell in the distance, at the mouth of the rivers.

'But now as for thee,' Utnapishtim told Gilgamesh. '...who will assemble the gods unto thee, that thou mayest find the life which thou seekest?'

"Gilgamesh heard all this, about how he had pretty much no chance of living forever and he fell out, passed out for days."

Curtis stretched his arms yawning. "Damn. So instead of trying to get some info on if there was going to be another flood, I mean, he had the perfect chance to quiz a dude that went through the 'Big One,' instead he throws a fit and passes out?"

"When Gilgamesh finally woke up, Utnapishtim told his boatman to take Gilgamesh to get cleaned up and put him on the boat for the trip home.

"'Gilgamesh and Urshanabi boarded the ship; they launched the ship on the billows and glided along.'

"They had cast off and were sailing away when Utnapishtim's wife spoke up for Gilgamesh. 'His wife said to him, to Utnapishtim the Distant: Gilgamesh has come hither, he has become weary, he has exerted himself. What wilt thou give him wherewith he may return to his land?

"'Then he, Gilgamesh, took a pole and brought the ship near to the shore. Utnapishtim said to him, to Gilgamesh: Gilgamesh, thou hast come hither, thou hast become weary, thou hast exerted thyself; what shall I give thee wherewith thou mayest return to thy land?

"'Gilgamesh, I will reveal unto thee a hidden thing, namely a secret of the gods will I tell thee: There is a plant like a thorn...If thy hand will obtain that plant, thou wilt find new life.'

"Without thinking twice Gilgamesh tied stones to his waist and dived into the pool, all the way to the bottom. He snagged the magical plant, cut his weights, and surfaced.

"'Gilgamesh said to him, to Urshanabi, the boatman: Urshanabi, this plant is a wondrous plant, whereby a man may obtain his former strength, I will take it to Uruk, the enclosure, I will give it to eat... Its name is: The old man becomes young as the man in his prime.'

"Then when he grew to be an old man," Max said. "After a life of cruelty and drunken whoring, he could eat the plant and become young all over again. Not immortality, but a handy little do-over, without a doubt."

"Like he even deserved it."

"Banished for taking Gilgamesh across the Waters of Death and leading him to Utnapishtim, Urshanabi went along with Gilgamesh on his trip back home. That's when it happened.

"'Gilgamesh saw a pool with cool water; he descended into it and bathed in the water. A serpent perceived the fragrance of the plant; it came up from the water and snatched the plant, sloughing its skin on its return.'

"'Then Gilgamesh sat down and wept, his tears flowing over his cheeks... For whom, Urshanabi, have my hands become weary? For whom is the blood of my heart being spent? For myself I have not obtained any boon.'

"Gilgamesh made his way back home empty-handed. When they got to Uruk, Gilgamesh told the boatman to examine the monuments of his great city, bragging to him about the fine workmanship.

"'Urshanabi, climb upon the wall of Uruk and walk about; inspect the foundation terrace and examine the brickwork, if its brickwork be not of burnt bricks, and if the seven wise men did not lay its foundation!'

"The book says the ending means that Gilgamesh learned his lesson and decided that the only way he would find immortality would be through building monuments to himself and his gods."

Curtis smirked. "Guess the slaves better get to work on that then."

"Enkidu and the soldiers who followed Gilgamesh to their deaths probably wished he could have learned all that before he went off on the missions that got them all killed. But, oh well."

"That's the way it's always been, ain't it?" Curtis said as he sat up. "The 'Big Bad Man' that's got everyone down all the time. He's always been around, hasn't he?"

"It's called 'kingship,' my friend. When people say that the system is against them, they aren't talking about democracy. I don't think we've ever really had a democracy." Max reached into his bag and presented the textbook he had gotten from Bud. "Damn I hope he got away alright..."

"Who?"

"His name was Bud... He gave me this book in New York. It lays it out: kingship gives guys like Gilgamesh the right to do the shit they do. There is the king, the priests, the royalty, and then all of the rest of us. That's the way it was before George Washington, and it looks like that's the way it is after him too."

"Damn," Curtis said.

"Oh and by the way, 'Kingship came down from Heaven.'"

"It doesn't say that."

"It does. Not in Gilgamesh, but it does in the Mesopotamian creation story. According to the Sumerians, like the first whole civilization ever, we were created as slaves to toil for the gods."

"Damn, that's cold. It don't surprise me, but it is cold."

"The story goes that after they came here, to Earth, a bunch of Anunnaki started complaining about how hard the work was in the mines. So Enki got the idea to create a slave they could use instead."

"This is in their religion?"

"It's part of the original creation story. That part didn't make it into the Bible but... well, Adam and Eve were supposed to tend the garden in the Bible story."

"What kind of people write stories about how they were created as slaves?" Curtis asked. "I mean, they could have said anything, and they picked that depressing shit?"

"And then they said that the system *they* created, that oppressed most of them except for just a few, that that system came from Heaven."

"I bet the kings and the royalty figured it did, they had it so damn good."

"Yeah and I guess if the scholars had any idea how the Sumerian civilization became a civilization, or how it came up with kingship, then maybe we could bust the stranglehold it has on us."

"No wonder we're so fucked up. Kingship, I never heard that one in school."

"Bud..." Max said. "Man, I wonder what happened to him. But he's fairly convinced that kingship is the reason for all the world's problems."

"And we ain't never lost it. You can see it now, everyday."

"They watch every move we make, but they really don't give a shit about us. And we all know it."

"They cut every program the government ever had that helped the slaves," Curtis said.

"They take the food out of our children's mouths to bomb the children in other countries. We get mad and they call out the cops to start swinging clubs."

"Metal detectors in schools... Still any fool can get a Mac 10 for a few hundred bucks. Ever seen one of them suckers spit lead, Max? Kids running everywhere, it's like Baghdad. I mean, how many people have you known been shot by a gun?"

"I was in the Gulf, so it's more than most, nine, ten guys maybe. They didn't die though."

"I've known twenty-two dudes been shot with a gun, eight of them dead as hell. I counted it up one day. We live in a Third World country; it's just that most people don't know it.

"You think some old natural disaster is gonna scare a generation of kids that have been dodging bullets since they popped out of their mommas? Shit, our whole lives have been a disaster. For a lot of people all climate change is going to do is even things up.

"Because whether those kingship mothers know it or not, it's going to get them too. It may take a little longer, but it'll get them just like it'll get the rest of us."

"They don't care about the future," Max said with a shrug. "That's for their firstborn sons to inherit. Then that jackass will do just like his jackass daddy did, and the whole thing starts all over again."

"It doesn't help to know it goes all the way back to the beginning, does it?"

"All the way back to *before* the Flood," Max said. "In most of the versions of the story, Utnapishtim was a king. He's in the Sumerian King List. Here he is a schemer in the gods' plan to get rid of the humans, and he goes down in history as the Hero of the Deluge."

"There aren't any heroes, not then and not now," Curtis said. "What kind of people would have their own gods scheme behind their backs to wipe them out?"

"What the hell kind of people would make prayers, and spells, and incantations out of verses from that story?"

"Slaves."

The red and blue lights of a police car lit up the sleepy camp grounds, parting the few people still loitering around the parking lot. The officer that got out of the vehicle shined his powerful flashlight over the camping area until he located Max and Curtis lying around the distant barbeque pit. He headed directly for them.

"Are you Max Stiner?"

"What's the problem officer?"

The officer produced a set of handcuffs from his belt. "I have a warrant for your arrest. You're coming with me."

"How the hell did you find him all the way out here?" Curtis asked.

"You keep your mouth shut, or you can come too," the officer said as he led Max away.

"What's the charge?" Max asked.

"All points bulletin," the officer said.

Curtis dared to follow. "Are you taking him to Salina or–"

"You can call the district office for that information."

"Do you have the phone number, officer?" Curtis asked.

"Look it up."

"But the phones are down."

"It's OK, Curtis." Max's expression was eerily peaceful. "Just let it go. Tell them to let it go."

Max was being loaded into the backseat of the squad car as Curtis tried the phone number he had for Hector, to no avail.

"This is some shady shit right here," he said, watching the squad car peel out.

Max was slumped down in the rear of the vehicle, his hands cuffed behind his back. "You're not a cop, are you?"

"Shut up." The man accelerated along the shoulder until he could merge with the sporadic traffic.

"Who do you work for?"

"I said shut up, or I will drug you."

Max surprised himself when he involuntarily breathed a long sigh of relief. It was clear that the man behind the wheel was no police officer. And Max knew that if the orders had been for his death, it would have already happened. That meant there was a good chance he was being delivered to the man who had haunted his dreams for weeks. As frightening as it sounded, Max found himself looking forward to such a meeting.

He got comfortable for what he assumed would be a long ride but the inside of the car lit up. He was then thrown violently into the passenger side door by a powerful collision. His bound hands clutched the stray seat belt he had been sitting on while the car spun off the road into the darkness.

"Bastard!" the agent yelled, doing his best to muscle back control of the wheel and avoid an imminent collision. Max was able to duck before the impact with the telephone poll, the agent was not. His head and shoulder were thrust into the driver's side window.

Penetrating beams of light illuminated the inside of the battered squad car again when another vehicle drew close and parked. Through glazed eyes and blinding smoke, Max watched Curtis circle around to the driver's side of the wreck to confirm the agent was unconscious. Max could see from his vantage point that the man was out cold with blood dripping from his head.

Curtis tried the rear door, it was still locked. He used the butt of Max's pistol to break the window with one blow. He found Max curled up into a ball in the backseat, blood seeping from the bridge of his nose.

"Yo, Max, you OK?"

When he didn't respond, Curtis reached and pulled him out of the car, leading him away from the wreckage.

"Oh shit, need the keys." He went back to the police car leaving Max to wobble around on the side of the road, trying to keep his balance. Curtis fished through the agent's pockets for the keys to the handcuffs, then he grabbed the unconscious man's 9 mm pistol before returning to Max.

"Come on, man. We gotta get outta here before the cops show up!"

The distant sound of sirens followed their escape.

Inside the damaged rental car, Max was too exhausted from his ordeal to move. He reclined in the passenger seat trying not to watch as Curtis weaved in and out of traffic, desperately trying to put some distance between them and the wreck.

"It's more dangerous out here than it was in New York City!" Curtis said, squirming around behind the wheel, too excited to sit still. "And here I thought it would be boring out in the country!"

They both noticed a trickle of blood fall onto Max's hand. Curtis punched open the glove compartment. "Check in there for a napkin."

"Where the hell did you come from?" Max used a piece of tissue to wipe his nose.

"He wasn't a cop was he?"

"Not even remotely."

"Good thing! Don't tell me I came all the way out here into the sticks just to commit a major felony! I could have done that all day long back home!"

"You should have just let them take me."

"You're not thinking straight, Max." Curtis floored the accelerator. "Did you see that PIT maneuver? That's P-I-T, fool. Spun that car around just like on *COPS*. Never even done it before either!"

"We get away clean? No witnesses?"

"Couldn't say, I was at the movies at the time, officer."

Beaten and bloodied, Curtis's wild grin and mocking laugh still made Max smile.

"That's twice we beat down those bastards!" Curtis yelled. "The CIG can kiss my ass!"

10

"Ignorant primitives!" Masterson yelled, throwing his coffee cup across his Virginia office. It shattered just below one of the televisions.

The report detailing Max's escape in Kansas had just arrived. As Masterson had ordered, it did end with the statement that those responsible for the failure had been "taken care of," but that did little to assuage his frustration.

He lumbered to his feet in pursuit of a fresh pot of coffee, snatching up a bottle of designer amphetamine along the way. He popped several into his mouth, followed by two big swigs from his topped off cup.

He went to his safe, incorrectly punching in the numbers to the combination several times before he finally got it opened. Taking out a silver flask, he poured a small amount of the contents into the coffee cup. He returned it to its hiding place, stirring the coffee carefully before taking another long drink.

The bank of televisions opposite his desk was alive with on-the-scene coverage from multiple channels in multiple states. Unity Council convoys dominated the overnight news cycle, as did the reports of sabotage perpetrated against the Council's website and telephones.

Instead of going back to skulking behind his desk, monitoring the progress of the Unity Council and the reports pouring into his computer, Masterson went for one of the books Hasline had given him. He opened *Advanced Techniques in Lucid Dreaming* to the first page.

"'It does not take a particularly psychic person to experience lucid dreaming,'" he read. "'Anyone can do it, but it does require a certain level of self-awareness and mental discipline.'"

That Masterson had little of the former and too much of the latter may have been the very reason he hadn't already perfected the techniques desperation was finally forcing him to try.

Now that success had become critical, he was relying on his enduring conceit to make it happen quickly. And it might have, if he had been able to concentrate on one thing for longer than five minutes at a time. He jumped to his feet to pace some more.

"Father, I bow to your wisdom," he said, his eyes to the ceiling. "But why, why did you burden this planet with a species that is too ignorant to complete the simplest of tasks, yet has the ability and inclination to destroy that same planet several times over? When? When will the flood come and wipe them all out?"

An email from his tech department brought him back to his desk. He launched the enclosed audio clip causing Phil's voice to come through the computer speakers, tinny and harsh from hours of digital processing.

"I'm sending you this, Billy, because I'm a coward," he said. "I've worked for your respect for so long that I couldn't stand in the same room as you and admit what I am about to admit. I just couldn't do it. They're coming for me, I know it, and I want you to know a few things before they do. First, for the past five years—"

The recording ended abruptly, denoting where Billy had plugged in her headphones.

Masterson crushed the button on his phone. "Where is Sylvia Billy?"

"After she left Phil Simmons's house, she returned home. No record of her leaving, sir."

"No record? I want all audio from her apartment since she got back. What about that damn reporter?"

"We can confirm that he hasn't contacted his editor, sir. He hasn't submitted any copy for editorial or legal review either. Internet monitoring has no reports of blogs or online articles. So far there has been no indication that he is about to release anything."

Masterson disconnected the call then placed another. "Report!"

"We've reacquired the target, sir. He's drinking in a bar near The Hill. What are your orders when they apprehend him?"

"Terminate!" Masterson said before hanging up.

Peter had occupied his usual stool in Ned's Pub for far longer than his usual time. Last call fast approached and he wasn't giving any indication that he was about to leave, nor were his fellow holdouts.

A man in a business suit was drinking at the opposite end of the long oak bar, his tie loosened and his suit jacket lying over the stool next to him. He downed another shot to wash away the stresses of the day.

Beside him – in stark contrast – sat a pair of homeless men nursing dollar draws of beer. They were talking so intently to each other, as if they were solving all of the world's problems. In reality they were merely rambling about what had happened on the street corner earlier that day.

Disheveled and wobbly, Peter sat two bar stools down from them with a stomach full of liquor and a head full of desperate rage. Shaving seemed pointless to him, so did answering his cell phone. He wasn't even really hiding at that point. Ed could have easily found him. He was wearing his new favorite outfit: a wrinkled white dress shirt and slacks, and staring into his snifter of brandy. The mocking image of the empty safe-deposit box stared back at him.

"Democracy, hell! It's a damned capitalist republic, a fascist regime, an imperialist empire. You can even say a kakistocracy: the rule by the most mentally infirmed of society. You can call it whatever you want, but don't say democracy because it would be a lie! And we don't tell lies, we don't write lies, because, my good fellows, we are the *Fourth Estate!*"

Ned was dunking dirty draw glasses into one sink, and then another, watching the patron he knew as Jerry grow more belligerent by the drink.

"Free press? That's a damn joke! All they want is scandal, Ned. Nice and juicy and easily explained, if you please."

Ned nodded in agreement, though his hearing impairment prevented him from understanding much of what Peter was saying.

"Did you know something, Ned? Did you know that Washington DC was burned, almost to the ground, during the war of 1812?"

Ned shrugged.

"Well, you may have learned that in history class. But you know something I'll bet you didn't learn? That this city, the Capitol building, the White House, they were all rebuilt by slaves.

"Yes sir, they were shipped up from the South to break their backs and recreate the capital of this free and fair country. I don't know how my ancestors got to this city, but I have to figure it was in the cattle car of a train!"

Ned was called away by a thirsty patron, leaving Peter to address the room instead. "This country is based on a lie!" he lectured. "Do you think when you throw that switch in November that your vote counts? You think it matters a damn bit? Maybe if America was a real democracy. But the Electoral College and audit-free electronic voting machines took care of all that! Now we just go through the motions like unsuspecting little sheep!

"We insist on laboring under the delusion that we're all equal. That we're free! That naïve delusion is going to get us all killed one day! It has allowed them to sit back and write us all off like so much human refuse!"

Ned came back to Peter and gave him "the look." When the slick and cynical reporter started pontificating about the role of the press in a democracy, it was time to call it a night.

"Sure the government has been secretly tapping phones and Internet traffic and banking transactions without warrants for years. We all know it, but raiding a safe-deposit box without due process or notice?!

"And OK, sure, the White House has been trying to prosecute reporters, entire newspapers for that matter, for uncovering any kind of covert program. But you can be sure, fair citizens, that it was just that kind of program that just violated my civil rights. Bold as you please. Robbed me blind is what they did! No wonder just about every real journalist I know has laid down and given up in the last ten years!"

Peter's trusty source made sure that he continued to get the scoops through much of that time of attrition, only as Peter thought back through each story he got from Graydin, he realized how small and inconsequential the so-called exclusives really were.

Considering the story Graydin had just burdened him with, Peter had to admit that for all his columns and investigations throughout his career; he never came anywhere near reporting a really essential truth.

Graydin's taunt echoed in his ears. "You're a cliché."

Ned had turned down the sound on the TVs at the request of more than one patron, like much of the rest of the country the dial was parked on the cable news channels and what was becoming relentless coverage of the Unity Council's mass exodus from the West Coast. Each update, each montage of scenes from Oregon and Washington and California of migrating people, reminded Peter of how big, how horrific, the CIG conspiracy was.

The bartender moved closer to his longtime patron. "Damn, Peter, I've never seen you so plowed. You need to go on home. Can I call you a cab?"

"Cab, hell, this is *my* town! I can get myself home just fine."

Peter stumbled out of the bar into the middle of the harsh Washington DC nightlife. The pollution and the noise from the traffic enveloped him with a heartrending familiarity.

He staggered through the same garish collection of pimps, hookers, bums, and street people that he had living as a child in America's capital city. He looked upon the same hopeless victims and vicious predators and had to question why, in all the years since he was a boy, things had not changed.

One of the many regrets that had plagued Peter was that he hadn't turned his high-powered journalistic skills onto a local issue or two, like the homeless or the skyrocketing murder rate. Whether it would have helped or not, he would have felt better about himself if he had.

Peter feared lucidity, depression couldn't be far behind, but the endless city blocks he roamed prevented him from staying drunk. Before long his head was pounding and his empty stomach was gnawing at him.

Nevertheless, Peter probably would have wandered and obsessed over his sorrows for the rest of the night if it hadn't been for the two young men who stepped out of the darkness behind him.

The blonde one was tall and as wide as a football player. He wore a crew cut and two earrings with tattoos covering both of his forearms. The other was dark and unshaven, his dirty jeans and t-shirt coming off as decidedly heroine chic. Though they were very convincing, the way they took positions on both sides of Peter indicated tactical training.

"You look like you're holding, bitch," the blonde said reaching behind his back.

Peter wasn't too drunk to recognize the distinct feeling of gun barrels on both sides of his body. The two men prodded their silenced pistols into his ribs while whisking him into a long alley before he was able to utter a word of protest.

Near the end of the deep, brick-lined corridor, the men cornered Peter under a solitary lamp, his back to a metal door. He reached behind him for the doorknob to find there was none.

"OK, guys, OK. Just take my wallet. It's right here."

Peter reached for his wallet; the fair-haired assailant answered with a lightning fast front kick to the face.

"Oh, there'll be plenty of time for that," the other attacker said.

Peter was hurled back into a pile of garbage by the deft blow, where he landed spread-eagle and half-unconscious. It was only the realization that they weren't after his money that brought him back enough to be able to see the agents surrounding him.

"We better make it look good," the blonde said.

Peter wiped the blood from his mouth and laughed. "OK, boys, if that's how we're going to play it. I guess it's time for me to get what I deserve."

The blonde attacker threw another front kick that caught Peter square on the chin and drove him back into a row of smaller trashcans. They both kicked him a few times more while he was down.

"Better get his wallet and watch," the dark haired agent said, priming his pistol.

His partner fished through Peter's pockets for the wallet. He ripped Peter's watch from his wrist.

Peter squinted through the blood in his eyes at a "No Admittance" sign faintly illuminated by the single light bulb overhead. He assumed they would be the last things he would ever see, the blinding bulb, the sign, and the door with no doorknob. Calmed by the knowledge that very soon, after all the lonely years, he would finally join his beloved Barbara again, Peter relented.

"Look at him, smiling like a fool," the dark-haired agent said.

At that moment, the door under the sign flew open, followed by a blast of dance music from the club inside.

The heavy steel slab connected with the dark-haired agent's shoulder and sent him flying off Peter, into the wall opposite the door. An apparently inebriated Gina fell backward through the entrance, a drink in one hand, her cell phone in the other.

"Look, girl, I gotta go outside because I can't hear a damn thing you're saying!" she shouted into the receiver.

She wore her Capitol Hill pantsuit and appeared genuinely surprised by the blonde attacker standing over Peter.

Staring down the barrel of the pistol, Peter knew he was dead. Initially he was at peace with it. But then that feeling of resignation passed and to his surprise he was overcome with the will to live. That was when the hammer on the pistol dropped.

"No!" he heard Gina shout.

Instead of a gunshot, a dull thud shocked everyone, including the agent. He quickly ejected the dud and took aim at Peter again.

Gina saw that the dark-haired agent was trying to stand so she threw a spinning back kick that knocked him back into the trash cans.

Peter waited for his death shot once again as the other agent squeezed the trigger.

"No!" Gina yelled again. She pointed at the weapon that time. Again the gunpowder in the bullet failed to ignite.

A reassessment of the situation prompted the agent to turn the weapon on Gina. With her pistol in her belt, and the distance between them too great for her to cover in time, the situation looked grim.

"Stop!" was her final command. The weapon misfired a third time.

Peter was stunned to see Gina still standing and the agent's attention on the malfunctioning gun, not him. The last misfire frustrated the professional killer long enough for both Peter and Gina to move.

Instinct told Peter to head toward the traffic flying by at the end of the alley. Gina went into action as he was in the process of climbing out of the pile of trashcans. The blonde agent wasn't fast enough in ejecting the third bullet to beat a powerful kick that snapped his head back, the weapon flying out of his hand.

"Hey, wait!" Gina shouted after Peter.

The dark-haired agent sprung up with his silenced pistol pointed down the alley at Peter's back. He was able to fire twice before Gina kicked the weapon out of his hand. The bullets ricocheted off the alley wall beside Peter just as he rounded the corner out of sight.

His right hand broken, the agent drew a knife with his left and came at Gina. She sidestepped him while delivering a nasty chop to his throat that made him fling the knife and gasp for air.

"Hey, asshole, come back!" Gina said to the empty alley entrance. "I'm trying to save you, goddamn it!"

The blonde agent made a feeble attempt at grabbing Gina's leg, his other hand holding his bleeding nose. She vented her frustration with a heel kick to the side of his head that knocked him out cold.

Outside the alley, Peter hobbled down the street, his condition so gruesome that he was scaring the people he passed. His right eye was swollen shut and gashes on his chin and lip were dripping inordinate amounts of blood all over his formally white shirt. His head was on fire and spinning to the point of nausea. Through it all he was able to spot a cab stopping at the curb to pick up a fare. He slid up to the man who hailed the cab and body blocked him out of the way.

"Go, Go!" he screamed while diving into the backseat.

Peter closed the door and kept his head down, waiting for the squeal of tires. The taxi never moved. Instead, the shabby young man behind the wheel maneuvered for a better look at Peter.

"I need a destination or I need to see some money, dude."

"Just get me out of here!"

"Money or a destination, or get out."

Peter threw a small wad of bills from his pocket over the seat; they landed in the driver's lap.

"Now go, please!"

Finally the driver got the cab moving.

"Where to, dude?"

"I can't go back to my apartment..." Peter mumbled.

The driver caught a glimpse of his passenger through the rearview mirror. "Jesus, what happened to you? Shit, I don't need any static. My boss is already on my ass."

"It's OK. I'm OK. I need to go to, um..." Peter fumbled through his pockets, to realize that his wallet and his cell phone were somewhere among the garbage in the alley. There was only one option left.

"Hey, I recognize you," the cabdriver said after looking him over. "You're that writer. Yeah, Peter something. I'm sure of it. Man, what happened to you?"

"I tripped over one of my big exclusives."

"You sure have nailed some Washington big boys in your time."

Peter let out an uncontrolled moan that further split his lip and caused him to cup his throbbing lower jaw in pain.

"You're looking pretty bad, dude. You're going to need a hospital."

"A phone, I need a payphone," Peter insisted after finally coming to the pocket containing Billy's phone number.

"Gotcha. You sure I shouldn't take you to the emergency room?"

"Just a phone, please."

The cabdriver stopped alongside a curb near a rundown old payphone. Peter dialed the number on the piece of paper and it rang several times before Billy answered.

"Can you go to the address I gave you, now?" he asked.

"You don't sound too good. Are you OK?"

"Well I'm still alive anyway, can you get out now? I'm sorry for calling you at this number but I couldn't wait for you to get back to me... I left you the address."

"I will."

Peter hung up and fell back into the cab. "Gaithersburg," he told the driver.

Billy was perched on the side of the bathtub in her apartment, the shower running full-bore, her tactical brain working overtime. The encrypted phone Ben and John gave her vibrated in her hand and she answered under cover of the racket.

"How are we getting you out of there without me having to hurt someone?" Ben asked. "And maybe without drawing the attention of every local cop in the area?"

"I just talked to Peter Anderson."

"On *your* cell?"

"Yes, I know...I didn't say anything and neither did he, but apparently he left the address with my neighbor downstairs, Vivian."

"And now we have to assume that they know that."

"They have no way of knowing where. I'm not trying to give you any problems, Ben, I know you have your hands full, but I have to meet him."

The momentary silence marked Ben's own tactical brain in full operation. "You know, for a while there, there was serious talk about approaching you to run the relocation division."

"What? I... I don't know what to say. What happened?" The moment she asked, she knew the answer. "Let me guess, Phil?"

"He wanted to keep you safe, and so do Hector and Maria. So you know why–"

"I'm going, Ben. Whatever Peter did, he's stuck his neck out. Phil wanted him to have a chance to make things right. We all deserve that.

And besides, if he is in trouble then he might have found something we can use."

"And you're not going to tell me the address so I can just send one of my people over there, are you?"

"Nope."

"Well you're stubborn enough to run the Council, that's for sure."

"The 84L bus line, it passes right in front of my building going east," she said. "Meet me four stops down."

"You sure you can get out without them seeing you? They have a unit on the front and the back."

"I think I've got it figured out, and I can get Phil's confession, too."

"Better make it five stops down. Be careful, please. If anything happens to you, Hector – hell Maria – will kill me dead."

Not knowing when it might be safe to return, Billy hustled from one room of her apartment to another gathering what she thought she might need in the coming days. Her laptop computer, a first aid kit, some towels, a wig, bags of dried fruit, and the standard cans of beans, they all went into her trusty backpack.

Her talent for last minute improvisation had made Billy exceptional at the job of saving people in jeopardy. That talent was now going to be vital for her own survival. As she gathered her backpack and two other bags full of clothes together, her passion for the details demanded she check and double-check each element of her hastily laid plan.

All loaded up, she located the television remote control and dialed the volume to its maximum. She got her front door open without making a sound, carefully easing it closed behind her.

Several levels below the CIG office building in Virginia, an eager young control agent was listening to a headset at a bank of computers.

"She's moving," he said into a microphone. "Stations two and three get ready. She should be at the front door in under a minute."

Down the lively city block from Billy's apartment, an agent waited in a sharp new taxicab, the "Out of Service" sign illuminated.

"Copy that. Ready here."

Another operative of the Continuity in Government waited in a squad car at the back of her building, in the uniform of a Washington DC police officer.

"That's a roger, Control."

Despite the fact that she was weighted down by the bags and her backpack, Billy flew by the elevator and down the one flight of steps to Vivian's floor. She knocked and waited nervously.

Vivian greeted her with her usual warm smile. Billy heard the sound of women laughing and talking inside; her plan was still viable.

"Well hello, dear," Vivian said.

"Hey there darlin'. How you doing tonight?"

"Oh, just fine. My bridge club is just wrapping up now. Come on in and meet the girls before they leave."

She squeezed past Vivian.

"You've got quite a handful there," Vivian said. "Everybody meet Sylvia Billy. She's my neighbor upstairs. Oh Billy, I almost forgot, a very distinguished-sounding gentleman called earlier and left a message for you…"

"No sign of her at the front," said the undercover agent in the cab at the front of the building. "Is she still in the apartment, Control?"

"This is Control. Bird is loose, bird is loose. Station three, report."

"No activity. Out," the agent said from the police car in the empty alley behind the building.

The control agent nervously called up the audio file from the microphone in Billy's apartment on his computer. He heard only the blaring television and the faint sound of a door closing.

"It's almost time to report to the General," the control agent said. "We better find her and now."

"She's still in her apartment," the agent in the cab said. "Just report that."

"I'm certain I heard the door close. I'd run friends in the building, but by all accounts she's rarely at home."

The agent in the cab pointed a small set of binoculars at the front of Billy's building in time to catch the lobby doors opening and several of Vivian's guests coming out. Before long a significant group of elderly ladies had gathered around the front door, saying their goodbyes for the evening.

"We've got action. Hold on."

The agent in the cab searched through the crowd with the binoculars, all he could make out was a muddle of short, round bodies. A few of the ladies walked in opposite directions down the street, the rest remained in a tight group, talking and laughing. A city bus came to a stop in front of them and they lined up to board.

"It's just a coffee clutch breaking up. No sign of target."

The control agent dialed Billy's home phone number. He listened to the headset as the phone rang in her empty apartment. Her answering service picked up. The agent immediately disconnected the call.

"She's loose, she's got to be. You probably better get in there and search the building, the General is not going to like this."

The agent in the cab threw down his communicator and scrambled toward the front of Billy's building, barely acknowledging the city bus that was accelerating away in front of him. Vivian's friends were gone as well. With each successive stop the city bus rolled farther away from danger.

Inside, Vivian's friends huddled toward the back, giggling at Billy. She wore an old coat, silver wig, and black scarf, her eyes darting over the riders on the bus in search of possible pursuers.

Except for a faint light escaping from behind the shades of the front window, Barbara Anderson's family home remained, by all appearances, as abandoned as it had been for the past three years. Peter let himself in with the key he fished out from under a nearby rock.

An antique stained glass lamp shone on thick mahogany molding and ceiling-high shelves of books inside the cluttered living room. An intricately carved mantle covered with photographs dominated the wall opposite the entry way. A baby grand piano waited in the bay window facing the street, untouched for considerably longer than three years.

The cozy room was overflowing with photos of family, along with the personal mementos of Barbara's mother and father, and Barbara herself. A life's worth of memories carefully assembled over the decades, then neglected for years.

Normally Peter would have been unable to tolerate even looking at the place that had become a monument to Barbara's life. Now, at his lowest point, he was holed up in that monument, nursing his many wounds and having somewhat of an epiphany.

His brush with death had electrified his exhausted body and sent him stumbling aimlessly around the living room. He mumbled curses to himself, when he thought of Graydin. Then he shouted declarations of love to Barbara, more certain than ever that she could hear him.

His vision was blurred, indicating a possible concussion. Dried blood on his eyelids prevented him from seeing where he was going half the time; still, he was physically unable to sit still.

His trembling hands fumbled with a bulky television remote until the old television came to life. The familiar voice of a particular news anchor immediately filled the room, reminding him of his former life. He began skipping through the main news channels. All of which he had been a guest on at one time or another.

Eventually he caught a glimpse of his own tired, heavily pancaked face as it flew by. He backtracked to a rerun of an interview he sat for before his story on Phil Simmons was published.

It was the 24 hour news channel with supposedly the least bias and most integrity, yet somehow he and his interviewer were still engaged in what Peter knew – then and now – was inane chatter.

A hard knock sent him to the front door. All he could make out through the parted curtain was a short, heavily dressed figure with a scarf obscuring the face.

"Is that you Billy?"

"Open up, Peter," she whispered.

He fell back into the foyer, allowing the heavy oak door to swing open. He swayed in front of Billy while she closed the door, barely able to keep his balance, a stupid smile on his pummeled face.

"I didn't know who else to call. I mean... I didn't have anybody I could trust."

"What the hell happened to you?"

She led Peter back to the couch, quickly assessing the extent of damage to his face. The first aid kit was the first thing to come out of her backpack.

"You should be in a hospital," she said, noting his swollen eyes and his lip ballooned to the size of a marble.

"Out of the question."

"Oh I know. Where's the bathroom in this place? We're going to need some towels for this."

"Down the hall and to the left. Are you sure you weren't followed?"

"Are you seeing this getup?" she said over her shoulder, ripping the wig from her head and tossing it onto her opened backpack. "I'm positive I wasn't followed." She headed in the direction of the hall. "Besides, I had help."

A thick coating of dust covered the tastefully decorated bathroom where Billy found a stack of towels. By the smell of them they had obviously been laundered and folded years before.

"What do you mean you had help?" he asked.

Billy returned and went to work on Peter's mangled face with speed and confidence.

"They'll be here in a bit," she said.

"You know what you're doing?"

"Relax, darlin'. I've patched up more than one person, in more than one war zone."

"They tried to make it look like a mugging," he said. "I got lucky and somehow got away."

"Lucky, huh? They kicked the living shit out of you."

She dabbed his forehead with the medicine soaked towel.

"Ouch!"

Once she had removed the dried blood and brought down the swelling, Billy was able to determine that Peter was badly beaten but not in any mortal danger. She applied a bandage to a deep cut in his cheek, then one to his chin, and began collecting the bloodied gauze she used to clean his wounds. That done she cleared a spot on the couch to sit down.

Peter looked up in time to catch Billy as she loosened the bun at the top of her head, her crimson hair falling down around her shoulders. He appreciated for the first time since their meeting how attractive she was. It was the first of many things he was seeing anew. He jumped back up again.

"You need to rest," Billy said. "You could have a concussion."

"I just can't... You'll never believe what happened tonight. It was a miracle. I mean, they took the document Phil sent me. Right out of my safe-deposit box, but that's not what—"

"And that was a miracle? I haven't known you long, Peter, but I'd say you're raving. You need to sit down."

"Don't you see? I don't know why he chose to send me that document, after what I did to him. I mean, I do know why he did it now. It was Barbara...

"I followed up on the address you gave me," he said. "It was the

Virginia headquarters of the Continuity in Government. I staked it out and I saw Graydin.

"He's been playing me for months now, feeding me stories. Every one of them checked out, too. Nothing like ironclad corroboration when you're decimating someone's personal and professional reputations."

"I know, Peter, just calm down, it's going to be OK. I promise. Ben—"

"She saved me," he said. "I couldn't believe it. Hell, she couldn't believe it. Three misfires in a row? From the gun of a government trained killer? It was either a batch of bad ammunition, or she really did it. For the first time in about six years, I actually wanted to live. It was quite a thing."

"Yeah, almost dying will tend to do that to you," Billy said. "I don't understand, what did she do?"

"Don't freak out," Gina said from the hallway, her drawn pistol scanning the room. Not worried about appearances, she now wore a black tactical suit, body armor, and a radio headset.

Peter involuntarily reacted, backing into the middle of the living room. "It's you! How the hell did you get in here?!"

"I said don't freak out! Sit the hell down, right now! If I wanted you dead, you'd be a memory."

Peter was jarred enough by her forceful voice to comply. He returned to the couch.

"Are you kidding me?" he said. "You saved me! It was incredible. I mean... Did it happen? I mean..."

"You probably have a concussion," Gina said. "You don't know what happened."

"Are you Gina?" Billy asked.

"Yep, is he going to make it, because we have to move. Ben's bringing transport around back."

"He'll live."

"We need to get to our safehouse across town until the funeral tomorrow, when we use you two as bait. Come on, I can't get you out the way I came in."

Billy slung her backpack over one of her shoulders before throwing Peter's arm over the other. They hobbled down the hall toward the kitchen at the rear of the house.

"We'll have to—" Gina's instincts were suddenly piqued. "Hold on a sec..."

A momentary sniff of the air prompted her to charge toward Billy and Peter, shoving them into the kitchen. She opened the refrigerator door for shelter just before a tiny rocket propelled explosive pierced the living room window. The shoulder fired projectile detonated upon contact with the brick fireplace, demolishing the entire front of the house.

"Go! Go!" she yelled.

With fire and smoke erupting from the front of the property, Gina pushed Billy and Peter through the backdoor into the wooded backyard.

They scrambled toward the fence that lined the alley, where Ben was screeching the van to a stop. He opened the side door and climbed up on top, his pistol ready.

"Duck!" he shouted.

Gina threw Billy and Peter to the ground, diving over them as a volley of bullets lit up the area around them. She barely reacted when two of the shots impacted the back of her vest.

Ben closed his eyes; it was too dark to see his targets in the trees anyway. He took aim at an area midway up an overarching oak tree and fired twice. The CIG agent hiding there fell from his perch, mortally wounded.

The agent in the tree on the other side of the property was turning for a shot at Ben but Ben winged him with the third of four more shots. Fumbling with his rifle, as well as his wounded arm, caused the agent to lose his grip on the branch he was draped over. The twenty foot fall that followed knocked him unconscious.

"Let's go!" Ben yelled over the fence.

Gina was slow to move at first. Billy had to crawl out from under the pile to help her to her feet.

"My God, Gina!" she drawled.

The adrenaline kicked in for Peter and he was up in a flash. In one fit, he lifted the stunned Gina off Billy's shoulders, carrying her to the back fence almost faster than Billy could follow.

There he opened the gate with a blunt kick and slung Gina into the van. He did the same to Billy once she reached the gate, throwing himself in after. Ben was in the driver's seat and peeling away in an instant.

The fire reached the ruptured gas lines in the kitchen of the old house as they were turning out of the alley and onto a clear street. The resulting explosion reverberated for blocks.

"You guys alright?" Ben said over his shoulder.

After checking herself, Billy went about examining Peter then Gina for gunshots. Gina was coughing and choking for breath on the floor of the van.

"Looks like we're good! Gina's got two in her vest, may have had the wind knocked out of her but they didn't get through! Damn, girl, you saved us!"

"That's the job, right boss?" Gina said to Ben through hacks, giving him an approving nod.

"Yes, ma'am!" He wheeled the van around another corner then accelerated to top speed. "Now I know what my son sees in you, you're just as crazy as he is."

Gina's cell phone rang but she was too incapacitated to get it out of her vest pocket. Billy dug it out and answered.

"Hello?"

"Who is this?" John asked.

"John?"

Gina was still too winded to speak so Billy climbed to the driver's seat and handed it to Ben.

"John! We've got them, we're heading back!" He wheeled the van around another corner with one arm.

"I'm just getting ready to meet Ritter. I can see him now."

John was concealed in the shadows of the parking lot of the Washing DC city morgue, observing Chris get out of his car.

"He already knows she's dead," John said.

"How?"

"I don't know, but he's burning with hate. I can see it from here. And I don't blame him. Erica deserved way better."

"Revenge makes people sloppy and operations unnecessarily messy. You're not going to get all emotional like you do, Son, and start looking for some payback, are you? We don't need that kind of exposure right now."

"No, I know it's usually the people around the one settling the grudge that get hurt. But unless we're ready to take this man clean out of the action for a few days, he's not going to stop. I'll talk to him and see if we can work something out."

"Anderson is cooperating," Ben said. "We need to tell Hector."

"Sunday may end up being a real party after all. I better go, if this guy really breached Hasline's clinic looking for Erica, maybe he'll help us. It might bring up the odds on the plan."

"We're not going to find Graydin," Ben said. "He's too smart. The man is gone in the wind. If not, Masterson has already taken care of him."

"Maybe, we'll see soon enough."

John closed the phone and waited for Chris to get into the front doors of the morgue to make his move. It took no time, and he caused little notice in his black tactical suit, slipping into the backseat of Chris's sedan.

Inside the building, Chris was emotionless during the check-in and perfunctory questioning about his relationship to the deceased. He followed the coroner through the sterile halls, through the sickening smell of death, to where his beloved Erica had been laid out on an examination table.

"Good thing you caught us," the coroner said. "For some reason she didn't come up on any missing persons' databases. She would have been buried tomorrow as a 'Jane Doe' if you hadn't come down."

Chris wasn't surprised to see his wife lying there under the harsh light. He had intended to confirm her identity so he could bury her and quickly return to his plan for vengeance. He didn't want to get sidetracked by mourning for the woman he loved so deeply.

Nevertheless, her perfect face — though pale and lifeless — was a piercing reminder that his life had been utterly destroyed. He fell to his knees at her side, sobbing like a child.

The coroner gave Chris a few moments of privacy but knew not to leave him there wallowing too long. "I'm sorry for your loss, sir. We will make arrangements with a funeral home of your choice, so that she is laid to rest properly."

Chris tore away from the bed out of the room.

"Sir, we have to make arrangements."

"I'll call. You better not bury her!"

Chris raged and wept all the way to his car. He dented the side panel of the vehicle with a kick before opening the door and climbing in. He put the key in the ignition then a powerful hand took hold of his mouth.

Panic caused his legs and arms to swing wildly, although only for a moment. Once he stopped struggling he looked into the rearview mirror at John, who was applying pressure to a spot on his neck. The resulting release of endorphins made it virtually impossible for Chris to feel threatened.

"I'm John Spiritdancer, I knew your wife."

Chris went limp, his mistrusting stare into the mirror remained. John removed his hand and stopped employing the pressure point. He sunk back down in the backseat.

"Where have you been? I've been calling."

"Drive."

Chris negotiated the parking lot before melding into traffic.

"Are you being followed?"

"No, nobody at the CIG knew we were even married."

"I mean now, they could have been watching the morgue."

Chris made several erratic moves in traffic to confirm in the rearview mirror that their tail was clear.

"I'm sorry about Erica."

"She would have been buried tomorrow in an unmarked grave if I hadn't found her."

"She was something special. She was that rare combination of talent and compassion. I wouldn't be surprised if you saw her, or heard her speaking to you. Her spirit was just that strong. Her memory won't fade that easy."

"I have been hearing her... whispering in my ear."

"What's she been saying?"

Chris smashed his bruised fist against the wheel. "She's telling me to stop! OK? She's telling me to walk away."

"You should listen to her, Chris. There probably isn't much she doesn't know right now, about this world or the next. Nobody is going to give you better advice."

Still crying, his voice trembled. "I'll walk away when he's dead!"

"I've known Erica since right after she joined the army; I'll bet longer than you. She would never have allowed you to do something like this to yourself. You know that."

"Erica cared about what was right. And it isn't right that he'll get away with this. It just isn't right. But I'm going to make it right, somehow."

"How did you get into Hasline's office, anyway?"

"I can't even believe I'm saying this, but I blackmailed a guy that I used to have beers with. I assaulted a guy who never did anything to me, and I'm going to kill a man I've never met."

"Did the guy you blackmailed work at the clinic?" John asked.

"No, he's in the CIG."

"Do you know his clearance level? Turn right up here."

"He's in security or something."

"He's what? And you're blackmailing him? And you're still alive?"

"I met him when he did security for the embassy in Jordan. I only planned to hit him up once, for clearances and a new name to use with the janitorial contractor that did Hasline's little shop of horrors." Chris turned the corner at the light. "Where now?"

"Keep going straight for a few miles. I'll tell you when to make a left."

"Erica said that you could be trusted. Do you really work for the Unity Council?"

"I tried to track her down, to recruit her. But she was already reassigned. She had disappeared."

"We were only able to see each other in person maybe three times in the last month. I should have known something was wrong, that she was in danger. It's just that Erica was so incredible, it made her seem invincible. But she wasn't omniscient."

"Nobody is. Get on the George Washington going north. We have a safehouse where we can talk."

"Unless it's to talk about how Masterson is going to die–"

"First let's talk about why you called."

"I already know for sure that she was transferred to Masterson personally out in Virginia before she disappeared."

"So what do you think you're going to do now?"

"I'm going to get into his precious Eastern Shore Complex and I'm going to kill him. And you're going to help me."

"You'll be dead before you make it to the elevators. But then, that's the point, isn't it?"

"What do you know about anything?"

"And just why would we help you destroy yourself?"

"Because I learned a little something about that mad scientist of his." Chris hoisted a black leather bag up onto the passenger seat, fishing out one of the many tapes and dropping it over the back of the car seat. John caught it.

"I took a bunch of his digital video tapes. I'm not sure what the hell he was doing but he had put up this video camera and went into this trance."

"Set," John read on the label. "A trance, of course."

"He mentions the Unity Council and then he talks about predicting

Masterson's downfall. At least I believe he's talking about Masterson."

"He said what?" John took out his cell phone and dialed.

"This is the 'spirit' talking or whatever he was channeling. From what I had been hearing, I was thinking Hasline was just a run of the mill sadist, but this... this is the kind of thing Erica always warned me about. It was the only thing she was ever really afraid of when it came to this psi crap."

"Yeah, Pops, I think we have something here."

"What's happened? Did you find him?" Ben was easing the van to a stop in front of a warehouse door. A remote control opened it high enough for him to quickly drive through.

"He claims to have a tape of Hasline channeling Set."

"Oh yeah? David's gonna love that."

"You sure he's talking about Masterson going down?" John asked Chris.

Chris moved the bag back down to the floor of the passenger side; he made eye contact with John through the rearview mirror. "I'm sure."

John pressed the speaker function on the cell phone.

"I don't care what you do with them," Chris said to them both. "Just put me in the same room as Masterson. I'll take care of the rest."

Ben's voice came through on the tiny microphone of the cell. "Mr. Ritter, I'm Ben Spiritdancer, I'm in charge of security for the Unity Council. I can't stress enough how important this is. You're saying that the video John has in his possession shows Hasline channeling information about Masterson, specifically?"

"It's Masterson. I'm sure of it. And you can have that one for free. If you want the rest, I want at least a chance at the murdering sonofabitch."

"What if I told you that this right here," John said. "...if it's what we think it is, will help bring Masterson down? Would you at least consider not going and getting yourself killed?"

"Like I said, I don't care how you want to use them–"

"We know where Stiner is," Ben said.

"What?" Chris inadvertently cut someone off when he changed lanes. "You mean from all the bulletins?"

"One of our people is with him right now. We need a chance to debrief the guy and find out why Masterson wants him so bad. He's been the only crack in Masterson's defenses we've been able to find in two years of reconnaissance."

John nodded in agreement. "Look, Chris, we don't expect you to be overjoyed but he's been looking for this guy for weeks now. We've been hearing the reports, and the rumors, that Masterson is obsessed.

"Obsession can lead to distraction, and distraction can lead to a mistake. I don't think I have to tell you that. We're going to make him make a mistake. Then we're going to expose him to the world."

Chris got quiet.

John took the cell phone off speaker. "Looks like we're only a few miles out," he told Ben. "Did you tell Hector what you were thinking for Graydin?"

"He said it was too dangerous. And he's right."

"But he didn't tell you not to do it, did he?"

"No, he just said that if we get caught, he doesn't know us and he's never heard of us."

"Wasn't it you who made that rule, Pops?"

"The very first day. We're at the safehouse, come on in."

Ben parked the van in a line of inconspicuous cars and trucks in the corner of the vast, unused warehouse. The battered group fell out of the opening doors one by one. With Ben's help, they limped through a hall and up a flight of stairs to the empty office space adjacent to the warehouse.

He led them into a large conference room that was lined by several couches. An opaque tarp hung over the windows, preserving the appearance that the place was still vacant.

A big-screen television was broadcasting coverage of the Unity Council in one corner, in the other a series of card tables had been arrayed with laptops and monitors, cameras and surveillance equipment. Various blueprints and schedules were stuck to the wall in front of Ben's command center.

"We have food," Ben said, assisting Gina onto one of the couches. He undid the straps securing her riddled body armor.

Muddy and harried, Billy sat Peter down on one of the couches, only to collapse beside him.

"Thank you, Billy," he said.

Ben pointed down another hall. "There're bathrooms and individual offices with cots back there. You guys can get cleaned up and we'll get you something to eat."

"Are you going to be OK?" Peter asked Gina, who was still getting out of her gear and testing her bruised back ribs.

"I'm OK. That body armor is state-of-the-art. I never leave home without it."

Ben produced a large first aid kit that Billy opened beside Gina.

"I should probably check for breaks and get those wrapped up," she said.

"No argument here," Gina said.

"I thought a safehouse was a house," Billy said.

"This works better," Ben said. "We rented the space through about five different shell companies, so no connection with the Council. And since the recession, nobody has been coming anywhere near this kind of industrial park. Most of these units have been sitting vacant since this place was built.

"We have cameras all around the perimeter so we can see threats coming from literally a mile away. And there are multiple ambush and escape points, not to mention access to the freeway."

"Sounds like you've thought of everything."

The multiple bathrooms allowed the group to recover quickly. Ben's time in the kitchen produced a meal that satisfied everyone's gnawing hunger, which they ate in stunned silence.

Peter had showered and settled in on one of the couches closest to the television, near where Gina was nursing her bruised torso.

They were going back and forth between the coverage of the many convoys on the television, and a monitor on Ben's table that was broadcasting a live video feed from the front of the Unity Council headquarters in Denver.

It appeared as if at least one caravan had already arrived, with cars, trucks, and motorhomes occupying most of the parking spaces of the Colorado office building.

Ben was working at his command center while Billy was talking to Hector on the phone in front of a couch that was covered by her bags and her 'old woman' disguise.

"How many phones went down, for how long?" she asked.

"They overwhelmed our two main banks here in Colorado for at least three hours off and on this morning. I can't get a straight answer from the phone company, and our lawyers are saying that an investigation will take too long for the results to even matter."

"Damn, Hector, and I thought I pissed people off."

"It's too late to change the phone numbers, the website either. The tech people are telling me it wouldn't matter anyway."

"Yeah, the best you have now is to play the victim in the press, big time."

"I'm getting reports about the people on the road," Hector said. "When they all reach us, here in Denver and the valley, we won't look like the victims anymore. They'll say we planned it all."

"Hey, maybe you should get someone on running down all the national campgrounds there around the San Luis Valley, for the overflow of people. If it's close enough, they can still drive into the valley for the show on Sunday night."

"Good idea, we have the option for another hundred acres next to us, the owner will lease it if we need it. But if they keep coming to Denver, we won't be able to get them all redirected."

"You may be looking at a real mess. Any idea of the numbers?"

"We have staff coming from both coasts. They're all reporting talking to at least one person who isn't enrolled in our program."

"Did you get people calling your people and having them redirect people on the road?"

"Over the years we've relocated almost twenty thousand people, Billy, it would be impossible in the time we have here. But we're telling everyone we can."

"You moved how many people? But that's a whole damn town, Hector."

"That's been over the last four years, but that's about right."

"Wow, I can't believe it. You and Maria, you did it. You made a dream happen that you two had how long ago?"

"Twenty years? But it didn't come together until after Katrina. It was like no one believed it was possible, that a whole city could be destroyed."

"At least not one as popular as New Orleans."

"Now at least some people are finally getting around the idea that we're going to have to move whole cities to save the people in them."

"Did you send some staff out to the rest stops outside of Denver?"

"I have staff coordinating in Kingman and Salina, but I didn't even think Salina would be necessary. St Louis and Memphis have been our toughest areas to convince people to move."

"I'd concentrate on heading them off at the pass, if I were you."

"I'm worried that it's too late."

"It probably is." Billy admired the persistent coverage of the Unity Council. "You always knew how to motivate people, whether they hated your guts or swore their undying loyalty, you always got them motivated."

"That's what we do. But right now I'm doing what you do, and not nearly as well. When are you taking off tomorrow?"

"I don't know; I've got Phil's funeral first thing."

"Awe mi *hermana*, Phil was just stuck in an impossible position. That's what that *cabrone* that runs the CIG does; he puts people in impossible situations to control them."

"I just feel like I don't know him now, like maybe I never knew him. If he was hiding all this, what else was he hiding?"

"That he loved you."

"I know, I loved him too but—"

"That's all that matters, Billy."

"I guess I'll see you guys in Denver tomorrow," she said. "Are Maria and the kids there?"

"They will be by Sunday; they're still out in Oregon. Let me talk to Ben a sec and we'll see you tomorrow."

"You got it, darlin'."

She handed the phone to Ben. He was about to take it privately but thought that maybe Billy would benefit from listening in, so he turned on the speaker function. Peter lowered the volume on the television, enabling him and Gina to hear as well.

"We've got Billy, Gina, and Peter on speaker. How's it going out there, Hector?"

"We're getting ready to have a security nightmare in Denver and down in the valley. Your people have it under control so far, but we're going to have to work with the police here pretty soon if it keeps going like this. "

"We've got a shot at as high an inside source as we will ever have," Ben said. "You said you wanted me to build a criminal case against these people. I just need one more day. Then I'll be there to deal with the cops.

"But I'll tell you one thing, you better keep the cameras rolling and around at all times, because those cops will start knocking heads. And they'll do it in the name of national security, too."

"This isn't a national security issue," Hector said.

"It is if they need it to be, to break heads and do it with the public's approval. And we better make sure we don't have anybody running around smashing windows or anything. That's all they'll need to bring in the riot control. I went over all this with Gary."

"Yeah, he's not much for reporting in, Ben, at least not to me."

"I'll talk to him. These are real 'chain of command' type people. They'll have to get used to you being at the top of that chain."

"How would they feel about taking orders from a woman?" Hector asked.

"You haven't met Gina yet, have you?"

"No, not yet."

"No word about Curtis or Max?" Ben asked.

"Not on this end."

"Well, the fact that the cell phone blackout is still moving indicates to me that they're staying ahead of the retrieval team. David seems to think that Max is the key to getting close to Masterson. He just doesn't know how yet. He wants me to drop everything and go out there and find him."

"Last I heard the blackout was in the middle of Kansas," Hector said. "If they can keep moving, they'll be here sooner than you will. Unless this Max Stiner has worked directly for Masterson, then you're right, you should stay and try for Graydin. Anderson can corroborate his statement and that'll make for a hell of sound byte."

"Work that sound byte, Hector!" Billy said.

"They do it to us enough. It's about time we do it, too."

"We'll get you an update after we talk to this Ritter guy," Ben said.

"Good enough, Ben. We'll see you, Billy. I'm glad you're safe."

"You have a problem with that?" Gina asked Peter.

"You're serious, you're going after Graydin? Hell no, I don't have a problem with that."

Billy put her hand on his shoulder. "I'm sorry about the house. About her house."

"Thank God she wasn't alive to see it," he said. "I found him. You know? Graydin, I cornered him downtown."

"And he didn't kill you?" Ben said. "What did he say?"

"Would you be surprised to hear that the Continuity in Government was created exclusively to formulate and implement plans that guarantee the survival of the United States government, but not its citizens?"

"No, I wouldn't, darlin'. That kind of planning has been going on since the beginning of the Cold War. It's no surprise that the rich white men in DC and New York were going to make sure they survived the nuclear holocaust they, themselves, were going to cause."

"Well, according to Graydin, the CIG's mandate is a bit more long-term than that."

"More long-term than a sixty year threat of nuclear winter?" Ben said.

Peter dabbed his forehead with a wet rag. "They took the damn allotment document."

"Right out of your safe-deposit box, we know." Gina said.

"How do you know that?'

"I'm your guardian angel."

"Is there anything I've done in the last week that you don't know about?"

"Not much," she said. "I've been keeping my eye on the CIG team that has been following you."

"I know our civil liberties are about gone by now, but who has that kind of power?" Peter asked.

"You know what an S-A-P is?" Ben said.

"Special access programs," Peter mumbled through his throbbing lip. "They say there are SAP programs that not even the presidents are briefed on."

"Well, if that's what they say," Gina said.

"Is that what you are?"

"That's what the CIG is," Ben said. "They sent a team for you. Consider yourself lucky that the house was the only thing destroyed."

"Then Graydin was right, I did put him in danger."

"Yep."

"And his family?"

"Possibly."

"He told me so many lies that I don't know what to believe from him anymore."

"If he told you that the CIG is a special access program with a deep black budget and no regard for the Constitution, then he was telling the truth."

"How do you feel about confessing your sins on national television?" Gina asked.

"Do what?"

Ben checked the monitors displaying the feeds from the perimeter cameras. "You're going to fly out to Colorado and on Sunday you're going to help us expose them to the whole world. How do you feel about that?"

"Exposure of the entire CIG operation?" Peter said.

"That's the plan," Gina said.

Peter leaned forward on the couch, tears forming in his eyes. "It had to be some kind of miracle, right?"

Gina tried to act like she didn't know what he was talking about.

"I was ready to die, I really was. Then you–"

"What did she do?" Ben asked, noting Gina's discomfort.

"She... the gun, it wouldn't fire. He had me dead to rights and the gun just wouldn't fire. It was either a miracle that happened three times in a row, or it was her."

"John's rubbing off on me, OK?" Gina said. "But you seriously can't tell him that. You either, Ben."

"I don't know what that means," Billy said.

"It means that Gina is coming along nicely," Ben said, returning to a stack of blueprints on the table.

"How did you do that back at Phil's, for that matter?" Billy asked.

"What? I didn't do anything."

"Don't give me that. You figured out how Phil died, and you made me feel it. You figured out that he confessed to me, nobody could have known any of that... Hector would want you to tell me."

Ben turned the chair around to face her and Peter, his worn out face stretched with an engaging smile.

"I mean, I'm just trying to understand here," she said. "I've known Hector and Maria my whole professional life... I've worked with the army or police in plenty of countries. But I've never seen anything like you people."

"It's not a cliché, or a stereotype," Ben said. "Native people's connection to our ancestors is one of the most import things in our culture.

"My father, he was something, he went way beyond that. He used to say that our greatest power here on earth is not just our deep connection to this planet but our connection to other people as well, whether they're family or not.

"When I was a kid and we were in council meetings with the elders, he always pushed for more contact with the world outside the reservation. It was one of the only reasons I left and went to Phoenix.

"My father was convinced all his life that our ability to understand where another person is coming from and to put ourselves in other people's shoes – basic empathy – was not only the key to peace, but a source of very real power.

"When we can feel what our ancestors went through. Hell, when we can feel what the people around us go through everyday, then any future becomes possible. All I had to do was put myself in Phil's shoes. That made it easy to empathize with what he was going through."

"How did you make it as a cop?" Billy said. "...being a bleeding heart and all."

"How have you made it as an aid worker? From what Hector tells me, you actually want to help people. If that's the case, then you know you're in the wrong business."

"Not anymore, I'm not going back there."

"You're not if it's up to Hector."

Billy looked to the monitor again. "How did he do it, the man who killed Phil?"

"You sure you want to know?" Ben looked to Peter, then Billy.

"Of course," Peter said.

"Love," Ben said. "The Laws of Attraction."

"What?" Billy shifted in her seat.

"From what my son has been able to put together, Carlyle is old school, that's Bruno and Crowley, and for some practitioners, it's sex magick. Those old white men had their own understanding of 'connection' and their own approach. They understood that love is the most powerful emotion humans can experience. Nowadays it's called *Eros*."

"I don't know," Billy said. "Hate can be a pretty powerful motivator."

"Well yeah, but love can also be just as selfish, destructive, and twisted. Hate is powerful, but for magick, it can be dangerous, and it's about pushing things away. By its nature, love is about making a connection; it's about bringing something or someone close. So the magician has to fall in love with his target, in a sense."

"So he can destroy them," Peter said.

Billy shivered. "I think that has to be one of the most disturbed things I have ever heard in my life."

A perimeter alarm brought Ben back to the electronics table. The multiple display monitor tracked Chris's car the moment it turned off the main road into the extensive industrial park.

"That's John," Gina said, slowly climbing out of the couch.

Ben waited until she had gone down stairs. "John and Gina were both trained by the United States Government to..."

"Stop bullets?" Peter said.

"To do what you did at Phil's?" Billy said.

"Armies have used psychics to gather intelligence for thousands of years," Ben said. "The Germans and the British both used the pendulum technique to locate warships during World War II.

"There's a good story about how they used psychics to locate Mussolini after Allied Forces captured him. German commandos used the information, found him, and broke him out, too.

"During the Cold War, they were worried that Russian psychics could use their minds to set off American nukes in their silos, all the time sitting in Moscow. That was one of the reasons for the creation of the first psychic soldier programs: counterespionage."

"Damn, how long have they been playing around with this crap?" Billy said.

"Generations."

"So it wasn't a miracle." Peter asked.

"A miracle? No, don't say that. They'll start yelling for raises over that. Uh, let's see, how do the scientists put it: 'the remote influencing of biological systems over non-biological systems.'"

Billy's little pixy nose crinkled up. "The what, over the what, now?"

"Retarding chemical reactions with the mind, as well as causing chemical reactions with the mind. Making electronics malfunction at a distance."

"You mean chemical reactions like in gunpowder?" Peter said.

"That's what I mean."

Peter's shaking head was saying he didn't believe him. His silence said that he did.

"Gina as well?" Billy asked.

"She's been John's handler since she was in the CIA and he was in Army Intelligence. Basically we're running around trying not to get crucified for doing something the government has been doing in secret for over forty years."

"That sounds about right," Peter said.

"I don't doubt it's possible," Billy said. "I've seen a thirteen year old girl in a trance stick a six inch needle through her cheek and not bleed or feel pain. I've seen an African shaman literally walk through fire and not get burned. I'm not surprised to hear that the government has been trying to exploit that kind of freaky stuff. It's just that for the Council, it's all a PR nightmare."

"She isn't wrong about that," Peter said.

Ben just grinned. "The man my son is bringing in; we'll talk to him and take a look at what he has. I've got a feeling that afterwards, you'll have a little better idea of who we're dealing with here."

High over the Appalachians, on the red-eye flight from Philadelphia to Denver, David called up a video file on his laptop, noting that it had been prepared by Ben barely a half an hour before. The text that accompanied the video teased David with the mention of channeling.

He put on his headphones, so as not to disturb Bud, who was snoozing restlessly in the aisle seat. File folders and books were stacked on the empty seat between the men, as well as on the tray tables.

David was thrown at first by the footage of Hasline's channeling ceremony. The sight of Masterson's right-hand man hypnotizing himself was solid confirmation of a previously improbable theory. A theory few in the Council were prepared to believe without proof.

David quickly settled down to take notes. He was on his fourth time through the video when Bud stirred. The old man struggled with the narrow airplane seat until he was awake enough to catch sight of what was playing on Peter's laptop.

"What are you watching?" he asked. He bumped his arm when David didn't answer.

"This is amazing, Bud," David said, removing his headphones. "This guy has got at least two PhDs, some biographies say three. He's been on the board of the American Psychiatric Association for over twenty years now, been the president of the whole board, in fact. The Canadian Board as well. He's published in medical journals. Oh, and let's not forget that he's a twisted sociopath."

"What's he doing there?"

"He's hypnotizing himself."

"You can do that?"

"Oh, yes, you most certainly can."

Though neither man could hear the audio, somehow they both still recognized the exact moment when Hasline ceased to be Hasline.

"Now he's channeling Set: one of the nine great gods of Egypt."

"The what?" Bud said, perking up. "It looks like he's lost his damn mind."

"Here, listen."

Bud put one of the headphones up to his ear. Peter played the section of the tape where Set mentions Masterson's downfall.

He isn't the only channeled entity to try and predict the future during a séance."

Ever wary, Bud listened to the rambling phrases and incoherent diatribe that followed and was immediately inclined to dismiss it. The problem was that he simply couldn't. Hasline's vacant stare and monotone voice were chilling, even to a man like Bud who didn't rattle easily.

"There's no way Hasline's that good an actor," David said. "If he is, he's Academy Award material."

Bud handed the headphones back to David. "I don't know but he sure comes off like a true believer."

"Their message has been presented and to a certain extent received like a religion," David said. "And they usually always identified themselves as the same group of gods of Egyptian mythology. Set was one of them."

"Set, huh?"

"The past hundred and fifty years of occult brotherhood history have been dominated by the idea of contacting one of those old Egyptian gods. I believe it's one of their most closely held secrets."

"You're serious about this?"

"Look at him. Whether he's really communing with an incarnate alien or not, he believes that he is. And that's all that matters."

"To who? There's people like him running all over New York."

"You have to admit, he's convinced that he really is a conduit for The Nine."

"The what?" Bud made eye contact with David for the first time in the flight. "What did you call them?"

"The Nine. They were worshiped for thousands of years as the nine mystical aspects of the One: Atum. Kind of like the trinity, only with nine. Ancient Egypt had this seriously hyper-mystical cult phenomena going on for thousands of years. Nowadays they're known as The Nine."

The smart comments stopped coming from Bud's direction and soon it became obvious to David that he was taken aback. Something David had yet to see in the two days he had known the man.

"What's going on?" he asked Bud.

Bud scoffed before proceeding to go through several contortions, mostly out of revulsion. David waited patiently, confident that after Bud had thrown back the last of his vodka shooter, he would fess up.

"What's going on, Bud?"

There was more scowling before the old man spoke up. "It was back in '70," he finally said. "We had this green assed lieutenant. He was some Ivy League puke, you know, ROTC, officer's training. But when he got into the bush, he got scared. He got real scared.

"Well, one morning before it was time to go out on patrol, I caught him in his tent hunched over this metal bowl and speaking in tongues.

"I got him drunk one time on leave after that and asked him what that shit was all about. He said that he was convinced that he had made contact with something from the 'Other Side' and that it told him he wouldn't die in combat.

"He said he asked the spirit guide for protection, and the spirit said yes. He said his dad and uncle showed him how to do it. I guess they were loaded and it was some kind of big family secret that they passed down... that he blabbed to me about after only a few beers. But he said he was told to call them The Nine."

"Did it work? Did he survive his tour?"

"He stuck his head up one day in a firefight and got it blown off by a sniper."

"So that's a no. Well, the occult significance of nine and especially 3-3-3 is pretty serious. Three groups of three knocks are important in certain occult rituals.

"Plus, 3-3-3 is considered to be the numerical representation not of the 'Beast of the Apocalypse,' which is 6-6-6, but the 'Beast of the *Abyss*.'"

"Satanic freaks, all of them."

"But then you have the three knocks showing up in UFO abduction experiences, too. That's like the cold metallic voice that channelers of The Nine and others have heard. There's lore about the 'cold metallic voice' stretching all the way back to before electricity, to Andrew Jackson's time even."

"So what does all this have to do with Max?"

"I've been trying to figure out his connection to Masterson. We have reason to believe that they have never actually met, not in this world anyway. The reading Ben did at Max's apartment revealed that much.

"But the threat to Masterson must be very real for him to risk exposure with such a comparatively public search for Max."

"Those black-ops dudes sneaking around the library. That was public alright."

"That's what I mean." David opened a photograph on his laptop. "Desperate."

"That him?"

"The best picture anyone has snapped of him in twenty-five years. A public man he is not."

The long range photo was of an obviously white man who was getting into a limousine under a bright noon sun. Masterson's frown was just visible under the harsh light. The rest of him was too blurry to make out.

"So is that Bible helping? You've had your head in it since we took off."

"I don't know. The guys found it in Max's apartment; it's just that I don't think it's his. Someone made all these notations all over the passages in Genesis, and other places, but they're all in German.

"I had to ask a woman in the PR department to translate as much of it as she could before we left but... You've talked to Max, if even for a short time. Do you know at all if he could speak German?"

"Couldn't say. But, hell, Steiner is a German name, isn't it?"

"Hold on a sec." David consulted the notes he made of Hasline's channeling session. He circled a paragraph on the notepad before paging through the Bible. He found the passage in question then he called up another document on his laptop.

He matched up the pages with the translation from German. "Check this out: 'I see the creature's deeds and I can not comprehend his brutality,'" he read. "'All I am certain of is that he is an imposter. He is a trickster spirit that spans the ages, a dark angel that sits on the shoulder of man. He will rule again, unless someone stops him. He believes it is his destiny, and he may well be right.'

"That's just one of a bunch of random quotes and thoughts. Most of them about this 'imposter.'"

David brought the video of Hasline back up on the computer screen, fast forwarding to a spot well into Hasline's channeling session. He unplugged the headphones, turned the sound down to a whisper, and let it run forward.

"The old gods are gone," Hasline droned. "It is time for the new gods to reign. The imposter fears the new gods. He fears The Nine."

"Who is this imposter?" Bud asked.

"Not sure, but I'll bet Max knows."

11

The Friday morning before the Unity Council's big show was a hectic one for the San Luis Valley. The caravans had been arriving all morning, along with the colorful Native American contingent, in preparation for Sunday's events. The sudden influx of people and vehicles was throwing the normally pastoral high-alpine valley into chaos.

Just shy of New Jersey in size, the San Luis in south central Colorado could be accessed by only four main highways. All of which had seen a constant flow of traffic since sunup. A flow that had been exceeding not only Hector's expectations, but the expectations of the news teams following the main convoy since Hector's speech in Arizona.

Panicked calls to affiliates in Denver and Colorado Springs brought helicopters that had taken to buzzing the lines of incoming travelers, contributing to the growing mayhem and spreading the images of the valley across the world.

Both the modest airport outside Alamosa and the bus station on Main Street were steadily adding to the invasion and providing a late boom for what would have been a meager tourist season.

The main street of Alamosa was no more than ten or twelve blocks long, with the rest of the town clinging to that one strip of commerce. Every block of shops and museums was crawling with Unity Council migrants and Native Americans celebrating their return to the sacred valley.

A steady flow of traffic stretched from that bustling center north on Highway 17 past Mosca, which was no more than a few gas stations on the side of the road. And Hooper, which didn't even have a gas station, consisting only of a convenience store and a post office.

Less than a mile up the road from there was the turnoff to the two hundred and fifty acres the Unity Council had chosen for its auxiliary headquarters. That intersection was the scene of a traffic snarl that was causing backups that stretched a good mile, north and south, on Highway 17. Meanwhile, the freshly paved access road from the highway that cut straight into the center of the property was at a standstill.

The Unity Council outpost at the center of it all was five stories high and circular, and essentially still under construction. The entire circumference of each floor of the bright red brick structure had been lined with tinted windows only a week before. While inside finishing crews were still hanging wallboard and painting offices.

Enormous Native American meeting tents had been erected all around the headquarters, amid a long row of offices standing opposite the building, forming a small main drag in front of the HQ that was clogged with crowds of people.

Adjacent to the main street, an enormous amphitheater had been created by heaping earth up into a broad semicircle and covering it with lush, green sod. Short bleachers were being assembled along the ridge of the arc that would provide clear views over the seating on the lawn. A fully arrayed stage was being erected in front of it all, with a gigantic screen mounted on scaffolding that stood behind a podium and a long row of tables.

Radiating out from the central action were acres and acres of campsites. One at a time, orderly streets were being created by crews of men and women assembling army surplus tents, spaces occupied by the incoming cars, trucks, and RVs spread out beyond there.

On another part of the property, individual camping tents were springing up everywhere, creating a colorful patchwork that complimented the rich Native American decorations adorning the Pow Wow tents.

Mary brought her cup of coffee to the fifth floor window of the building for a look over the masses of people below. Positioned directly above the front door, the employee break room offered a bird's eye view of everything south, east, and west of that location for miles, including the deadlocked access road, the mounting traffic jam at the highway, and distant Alamosa.

Sheila joined Mary in marveling at the eclectic assortment of people descending on the Unity Council property.

"All the buses from L.A. are in," Mary said. "I know they had a bunch of elderly people on them. I hope they have enough help down there."

"They do, Mary, trust me. I approved the payroll."

The buses from most of the neighborhoods in Southern California were lining up south of the strip of offices on the main drag. Migrants were disembarking there, into a tumult of people. Men and women in yellow windbreakers were leading the somewhat bewildered arrivals to their tents.

On the main drag and around the Pow Wow tents, the families who had already gotten settled were mixing with brilliantly-dressed Native Americans celebrating their trip to the valley, with activists – young and old – representing the various causes which had come together to form the coalition.

"I'm glad we got in early this morning," Sheila said. "It seems like it just went crazy in the last few hours."

"That's it, isn't it?" Mary said of the cloud covered Mt. Blanca in the distance. "That's where they're hiding out."

"People have taken to calling it Mt. Doom. Blanca Peak is bigger than all the rest of the mountains, and those mountains are huge! Have you heard the stories about it?"

"We've only been in the valley for a few hours and you've got stories?"

"According to the Indian legends, the 'Star Seed' people came to this world through Blanca, like some kind of dimensional doorway. It's been sacred to a lot of tribes for a long time."

"That's pretty wild. The place looks about as dangerous as it probably is, too."

The mist whipping off the still snowy mastiff made Sheila momentarily shudder. "No one at the Unity Council happened to mention that this valley is a hotbed for UFO and paranormal activity, did they?"

"Nope. So it's UFOs now, is it? This morning it was the haunted house that finally burned down 'mysteriously.' Where are you getting all this?"

"Nancy in the relocation department was reading this book by this guy, Chris O'Brien. Apparently this valley was the first place an animal mutilation was ever officially reported."

"Seriously? There haven't been any human mutilations, has there?"

"No, but someone was saying a rancher down south toward the New Mexico line lost two bulls just last week. Cost him thousands of dollars."

"Wow. You think that's why the CIG chose this place?"

"I don't know, but we're talking Bigfoot sightings, El Chupracabra, ghosts; it's all going on out here. Barely twenty miles to the north is where good old Alfred Packer went to eat people, he was like one of the few people in the country that have ever been convicted of cannibalism."

"You know what? Maybe I don't want to know about some of this history."

"Are you kidding me? I've been asking why I haven't ever heard about this place before." Sheila peered into the clear blue sky outside the windows. "It's supposed to be a beautiful night, clear as a bell. After we take the kids over to the Pow Wow – they're having dancing and storytelling, so cool – we were going to this spot just outside camp where people will be getting together to watch for UFOs."

"That sounds like a full night."

"You and Sara are coming, Sara already told Heather as much. Besides, this way we can keep our eye on you."

Mary shrugged. "You would think I'd be used to it by now... UFOs, huh?"

"You can't blame them for wanting to see something mysterious." Something in the sky caught Sheila's attention. "Nobody has any mystery in their lives anymore. Except for maybe what their credit score is; that's a damn state secret."

"What are you looking at?"

"Look at that jet, look at the trail it's leaving." Sheila pointed out the high flying jetliner and the uniformed, continuous white streak it left in its wake.

"Yeah, it's called exhaust. They say it's going to kill us as bad as what comes out of the tailpipes of our cars, so what?"

"OK, I started timing right now." Sheila marked the time on her watch. "Actually, the white streak is condensed water vapor, at least that's what it's supposed to be."

"Wait," Mary said, noticing another jet. "Look."

The women watched through the window while the aircraft Sheila spotted slipped into the distance and a second one cut across the first plane's contrail at a right angle.

"Look at that," Sheila said.

A third aircraft appeared and cut a path across the second plane's trail forming a partial checker pattern.

"What the hell is going on up there, Sheila?"

"Apparently this goes on all the time. They call them *chem*trails." She looked at her watch again. "Now see, they say the trails will linger for way too long and then disperse into a thin cloud layer."

As Sheila predicted, the precisely laid pattern, instead of disappearing completely due to the clear and dry conditions, dispersed into a haze that hung over the valley.

"I'll be damned," Mary said. "I wanted Sara out of L.A. over the smog as much as the earthquakes. Then we come out here and look at this."

"The scuttlebutt is that it's either weather control, you know, like a nastier version of cloud seeding, or population control, like an aerosol tranquilizer, or both."

Mary laughed, patting her shoulder. "Always gotta go for the most paranoid option, don't you Sheila."

"Hey, they put fluoride in the drinking water, right? And one of the oldest 'antidepressants' on the market is over 90 percent fluoride, right? They're drugging us and poisoning us all the damn time anyway."

Mary smiled politely.

"You saw it, Mary. Those didn't even look like regular commercial jets. Nancy was talking about how a bunch of concerned residents from the valley are calling for people to get together and demand to know what they're spraying."

An artificially created fog settled in the high atmosphere over the area.

"My God, how long have they known?" Mary said.

"Known what?"

"That the air was going to start killing us. From the content we put on the website, and the presentations for Sunday, apparently it's a lot longer than you and I've been alive."

"I was watching the *Beverly Hillbillies* one morning after the kids went to school. I just love that Jed Clampett. He's one big old laid back dude, reminds me of my Leonard. But I was knocked out when I realized what the episode was all about.

"It seems the Clampetts got it into their heads that they wanted to do something about the smog problem in Los Angeles. So this oil tycoon and his family decide to go to Washington DC and give Nixon 95 million dollars – their whole fortune – to help solve the smog problem."

"I've never seen that one, I loved that show though."

"I didn't know whether to laugh or cry considering the episode had to be from the '60s, at least, if not older. It was in black and white. Then Jethro decides he's going to outfit their old truck with an electric motor and then they'd drive to Washington. He just couldn't find an extension cord long enough."

"Are you serious?" Mary said. "When was this made?"

"Before I was born and I'm forty-two, a Gen-Xer. I mean, how long have the Baby Boomers known? How about their parents? How long have the older generations known there was a serious problem? Forty years? Fifty years? There's just no excuse.

"I figured it up; 95 million dollars would be over 500 million in today's money. Think a half a billion dollars would help change something?"

"It'll take a lot more than money."

"That chemtrail crap could be one of their classically stupid-assed reactions to a problem they knew was coming all along. The other option is even worse than that."

"Don't say it, Sheila, you paranoid woman you."

"Population control. I'm telling you, Mary. The government thinks we're all going to go crazy when the climate goes really bad, that we'll riot and tear this country apart."

"I don't know, maybe they're right."

"Well yeah, anybody would riot when you leave them to die in a hurricane or an earthquake. You were in L.A. in '92, and a natural disaster didn't even start all that."

"That was one dangerous city during those days. I was young... I remember feeling so helpless, the feeling of lawlessness was terrifying, and we didn't even have any problems in our neighborhood. Just think about that happening in cities all over the country at the same time."

"The Unity Council sure considers it a possibility."

Sheila turned her back to the window. "Do you realize that after Northridge, and after all the scientific warnings, it took Len and me years before we realized that we had to leave. What was that all about?"

"Sixty deaths, 600,000 people homeless," Mary said with a shudder. "The actual quake only lasted for seven seconds; the ground shook for only fourteen seconds. But it ended up being the costliest earthquake in California history, and it wasn't even on the San Andreas Fault."

"And it happened in 1994, why the hell didn't we move before now? If we're being honest, Leonard and I could have afforded to move any time since then. He could have transferred to another police department. Not like some of these people who've been thrown out of their jobs and homes. We were lucky, or so we thought."

"Denial is a very powerful thing."

"But we've moved now, baby... with a vengeance!"

Mary walked back toward the door to the hall. "That's a fact."

The ladies shared the elevator with a mix of construction people and Unity Council medical staff on their way down to the first floor. They stepped off the elevator into a reception area that smelled of fresh paint and hummed with people.

A parade of travelers was being guided through the lobby by several of the medical staff; their destination was the medical facilities on the fourth floor.

Minding their coffee, Mary and Sheila navigated through the commotion to the broad hall that circumnavigated the entire building, looping past Mary's office, behind the elevators, and back to the other side of the reception area.

Mary swiped a key card to open the door to the climate-controlled room where the Unity Council's computers were being kept. She immediately consulted her laptop, to ensure all was running properly.

Four computer servers were positioned in the corner, their fans humming steadily twenty-four hours a day. A security door to the outside allowed the easy delivery of equipment.

Amiable campers and migrants wandered around outside the windows that lined the server room, unable to see into the office due to the tinted glass.

Mary took her seat behind her laptop with a determined expression.

"Stay the hell out of my bank account young lady."

Mary giggled. "I traced the hacks that took the website offline the first time through like twenty different servers and dummy IPs, all the way to this weird foundation." She consulted her notes. "It was called the... oh yeah, here it is, the 'Americans for Integrity and Justice.'"

"Yeah, right... integrity and justice. What you wanna bet it's just a bunch of tight-assed white people getting together to bitch about everybody who isn't white and tight-assed?"

"Their website went on and on about the Unity Council's 'socialist agenda to take over the country.' Apparently they're pretty freaked out about it."

"Bunch of fanatics. Len said that the guy they had planted in your IT department started raving about 'The End' after they busted him. Talk about an apocalyptic cult. "

"I'm still not clear on how they found out it was him. He sure covered his digital tracks."

"Yeah, Len pulled one of his 'closed mouth' routines again on that when I asked him."

"Well, they won't be getting into our business again. We made sure of it."

"But?"

"But this Intra-Guard lead Hector gave me. I traced that to a server farm in DC, a government server farm."

"And?"

"The domain was a dot-gov. And the agency name was the Continuity in Government. I found this online. It's their public website."

"What does it say that they do?"

"Get this: 'Civil Integrated Group: a small group of consultants specializing in urban and suburban emergency management scenarios for the purposes of planning and reaction assessment.'"

"Try saying that two times fast," Sheila said. "But that's not the Continuity in Government."

"As far as I can tell, this is a think tank that contracts for... I think it said, 'various government agencies.'"

"It could still be a coincidence."

"Not with them both using the same server farm in DC. That's too close."

"What the hell is a server farm?"

Mary pointed to the corner. "That's basically a server farm, just a really small one. I told Hector and he gave me this sign-on from something called the Intra-Guard."

Sheila flipped her blonde hair spitefully. "The Intra-Guard, sounds absolutely fascist."

"Actually, it is pretty weird. Hector said there are over twenty thousand of them, corporate and professional types and I guess they think they're all special because they get these 'exclusive' terrorist and disaster warnings."

"Being in-the-know. That kind of crap can be like a drug to some people."

"Yeah, but most of the 'bulletins' I've read are just stupid reports about unattended baggage and mystery packages. As far as I can see, none of them have panned out at all."

Sheila smirked. "You just imagine some buttoned-down, Wall Street tight ass all giddy over being able to log onto his 'special' and 'exclusive' website to get 'inside' information about a bag of underwear somebody forgot on the subway?"

"If everyone in the country has been living on fear for the last ten years, these people are mainlining it." Mary clicked through that week's Intra-Guard dispatch.

"Some people just aren't happy unless there's some kind of drama going on."

"Or there's someone to hate. According to these secret bulletins, some guy named Max Stiner is the most dangerous man in America."

"You didn't see your picture on there, did you?"

Mary laughed then got serious. "Hey, that's not funny."

"Did getting into this network of weirdos get you any closer to the CIG?"

"In a way."

"Could you be a little more vague?"

"I hacked the Intra-Guard website and sent the webmaster an email," Mary finally admitted.

"In for a penny, in for a pound, huh?" They exchanged sly grins.

"It was just spam, but it included a specially engineered worm. I'm waiting for him to send it to the spam folder. That'll cause the worm to go into a mail server that's shared with the CIG. Then it'll burrow deep into their system. Hold on," she said, typing on her laptop.

The cyber security department in Masterson's Eastern Shore Complex may have been quiet, but the CIG computer technicians who had averted Billy's hapless unauthorized attempt to access CIG servers were keeping a watchful eye on their charge. The alarm that sounded sent them flying to their computers.

"What the hell is going on?" one said. "Is it her again?"

"No, this is an attack!" the other said.

"No way! There's no way anyone gets this deep into our system!"

"Well somebody has!"

The first technician took steps to cut off Mary's access to the CIG's most sensitive data. "It's a seriously modified worm. Here, I found it, I'm quarantining it now."

"I'm ready to run a code comparison," the other tech said.

"Do that while I track this sucker down. I'm tracing now."

A racket of keyboards and typing fingers ensued. "I've got him all over the place. He's using servers in Europe, Eastern Europe... OK, hold on..."

The tech's monitor was tracing Mary's Internet trail on a map around Europe and North Africa until the red line sprung off of the African continent toward America. It terminated in Washington DC.

"Oh, this one thinks he's cute. The trail ends at the FBI cyber crimes division."

"Clever, we're definitely talking an elevated skill level... Uh oh, check this out."

The tech joined his colleague in front of the monitor. "It's finished analyzing the code in the worm. It found a match."

"I'll be damned, Mary Jenkins."

"It's the White Widow herself."

"She was a legend."

"She was a crusader, a total old-school white hat hacker. You can't buy this type. And she's almost too good to completely shutdown."

"The White Widow, man do I remember her. She swiped a bunch of internal stuff from some animal testing labs in the '90s. It was before the World Wide Web. But she posted it all over the bulletin boards they used back then."

"Yeah, and there ended up being some congressional hearings over the stuff she took, too. She was what? Twelve?"

The tech blushed. "The White Widow... Nobody in the wannabe hacker world knew what she looked like, but we found out when she got caught that she was our age. She was just a kid, like us. Man, did we crush on the White Widow."

"You better get the General on the horn."

The CIG's computer technicians went about confidently eradicating Mary's worm.

Back in Colorado, Mary was sporting a self-satisfied grin.

"It worked," she told Sheila without looking up from the computer screen.

"What?"

"The worm I nailed them with was a kind of data scoop and I designed it to replicate and hide, for awhile anyway. It copied all the files on that server it could before they found it. It accessed a commonly used Internet connection to upload the information to a virtual hard drive I have on a server overseas."

"That's sneaky. Damn, girl, are you a little pissed or what?"

"If we don't find out about what we're up against, we don't have a chance."

Mary performed several more diversionary maneuvers, taking extraordinary measures to mask her trail, before she recovered the data and severed her connection with the Internet. She sent all the information to a standalone hard drive that could be disconnected from her system and destroyed at a moment's notice.

She finished by staring at the photo of Sara's last birthday party on the computer screen. Her head was spinning with a combination of pride, anger, and dread.

"Are you OK? You look a little out of it all of a sudden."

"I snagged a couple hundred gigs of data on that one."

"Wow, just like that?"

"I wrote the worm to be a low risk way to gather info on different computer systems. You know, don't stay long enough to do any damage, just get the data out and give up, or self-destruct, if necessary."

Sheila was looking over her shoulder while Mary accessed the portable hard drive and called up a directory of filenames, her only means of identifying the random cache of information.

She clicked on files with names like "SEC payroll," and "WRC hard goods register."

"These are database files," Sheila said. "Looks like you robbed them blind."

"I want to check each file for viruses and tracking code before I launch one. Hector needs to hear about this, like right away."

"Yes, he does. But this is going to take some time."

It was late morning on the day of Mary's arrival in the valley before Carlyle regained consciousness. Draped in a black silk robe and carrying a mug full of coffee, he had to step over half-naked bodies on the way to his redwood deck. The aftermath of a drug-fueled orgy.

Ever resilient, Carlyle had left his cohorts passed out all over the living room of his lavish mountain home; his focus had already shifted to his next job. He sat down at a table in front of a panoramic view of

Taos, New Mexico.

The sumptuous breakfast before him had been laid out by servants who knew how to stay invisible. The charts and reports he was about to study had been delivered by an old friend.

He took a deep breath and closed his eyes, letting the pristine New Mexico air inflate his lungs and the sun shine on his face.

Carlyle considered the research he performed for his rituals as important as the rituals themselves. Each time he learned something new, another approach, or another bit of arcane information he could use in the commission of future "jobs."

After a drink from his cup, he went to work reviewing the charts of solar flare activity, the tables of geomagnetic readings for the area around the Unity Council's San Luis Valley headquarters, and the geological surveys of the valley floor.

Finally, he lingered on a carefully compiled list of sacred and sinister places between Taos and the Council's valley base.

The ravishing Cameron came out onto the deck, naked but for a blanket over her shoulders, her hair loose and crumpled. She curled up in a chair across from Carlyle as she plucked a strawberry into her mouth.

"Another satisfied customer?" she asked.

"Indeed, as usual your services are comprehensive, to say the least."

She noticed he was reading the list of sacred places she herself had prepared. "I suggest Arroyo Hondo first," she said.

"The Penitentes," Carlyle read.

"They were a fundamentalist Catholic cult known as the Brotherhood of Blood that lived in the valley."

"Am I reading this right? Over the course of three hundred years they went from flogging themselves with whips during Good Friday services to *real* crucifixions of willing brothers of the cult?"

Cameron sampled a croissant. "There's something about self-flagellation and human sacrifice in the name of your God that will tear a hole in the veil anytime."

"What else?" Carlyle asked, continuing down the list.

"The house on River Road. It's outside Alamosa."

"Two owners killed their wives and then committed suicide," Carlyle read from the summery. "And three other owner's just plain committed suicide?"

"There were other mysterious deaths as well," Cameron said. "Then the place burned down in '93. But I have the GPS coordinates. I went out there and dowsed the exact spot years ago, for another client."

"Like I said, comprehensive."

"You really should be focusing in on a target already. Sidereal time won't be optimal, and that's just the first of the conditions that won't be favorable on Sunday night. You sure you don't want me close? They have people you know."

"I know all about their people. I'm better than all of them put together. That includes that Indian."

He opened a folder of satellite photos of the Unity Council grounds in the San Luis Valley. The third one was taken from directly above the building. "What's that look like to you?" he asked Cameron while tapping on the photo.

"That's a propane tank, a big one."

A serpent's grin marked Carlyle's satisfaction. "We need to know who has that office right there. Where are those building specs?" He picked through the folders on the table. "Here we go. It had a preliminary directory." He ran his finger down the list of names and departments until he came to the correct one. "Of course, it's the computer room. Hmm who's in charge of that?"

"There's an employee roster there," Cameron said.

"Ah, there she is. One Mary Margaret Jenkins, we have a winner."

Even though the Front Range of the Rocky Mountains was still miles away, Curtis had been catching glimpses for over an hour. But despite the occasional appearance of Mt. Evans dead ahead, and Pike's Peak to the south, he and his passenger were still faced with the mind-numbing distance of grass covered plains.

"Damn, man, is this shit flat as a pancake until it runs smack into the mountains? I'm an East Coast boy, never seen anything like that."

Max was curled up in the backseat of the sedan, the history textbook open in his lap on top of the *Epic of Gilgamesh* translation. "Yeah, it's pretty abrupt. I was stationed at Ft. Carson for training for two months back in the '90s. It's all military and country folk when you go south of Denver. At least it was back then."

The gleaming summit of Pike's Peak was momentarily visible to their left once again. The sight struck a chord with Max, and not because he had been stationed near there. It was another 14,000 foot mountain he was recalling.

A series of lone trailer parks flew by, the first indications that the weary men had finally reached the outskirts of Denver. Curtis saw the speedometer go from a sustained eighty miles per hour, to seventy, to sixty-five, until he was jockeying for an opportunity to change lanes around the growing pockets of slower moving traffic in the right lane. Then they came around a bend and Denver came into view.

The mountains rose from foothills to peaks behind a dense group of skyscrapers that marked downtown Denver. The rest of the metropolis overflowed the shallow valley that stood between the foothills and the plains. A brown haze hung over the extent of the valley, obscuring what could have been an impressive vista.

Curtis took the wheel with both hands when trailer parks began to give way to industrial parks, and he suddenly found himself in hectic city traffic.

"You know how we're supposed to get to the HQ?" Max asked.

"I have the address. I looked it up on the Internet back in Ohio. But someone was supposed to come get me from the bus stop. I know it's close to Colorado Boulevard and the Denver City Park."

"That shouldn't be too tough to find..."

"Look!" Curtis said. "Colorado Boulevard. I'm getting off here."

"Which way, north or south?"

"South, it's like Manhattan, the numbers get lower when you go south," Curtis said.

Both Max and Curtis were back on guard at the stoplights as they worked their way south, casing the morning commuters and delivery drivers.

"That's it, that's the City Park," Max said.

"It was just south of here. I'll go around."

The turn west along the south edge of the three hundred and thirty acres of trees and grass was still blocks away by the time they hit the beginning of the traffic jam. Two of the three southbound lanes of Colorado Boulevard were clogged with vehicles trying to make the right turn around the corner.

A red light changed to green overhead but nothing moved. A stressed young man in a bright yellow windbreaker that read "UC Staff" shot out from the curb to knock on the passenger window.

"Have you signed up with the relocation program?" he asked.

Curtis was caught off guard. "Well, kind of, I–"

"If you haven't, we're going to need you to head down to the San Luis Valley. We have plenty of room for you down there and we can get you relocated. Do you need gas money, is your car running OK?"

"No, wait, listen; I work for the Council. I've been talking to Hector. You have to call him. Tell him Curtis is here with Max Stiner."

"This is twenty-seven," the young man said into the phone over his ear. "He's here; tell Hector that he's here. We're on Colorado."

"Think they knew we were coming, Curtis?"

"Look at this mess."

"Is this the rental you guys got in St. Louis?" the young man asked, taking instructions from Hector over the earpiece.

"This is it," Curtis said.

"Hector wants me to get this out of the line here and park it. Somebody will take it to the rental car place later."

"What about us?" Max asked from the backseat.

The young man looked up and down the block several times before answering. "Hold on, we have someone coming."

"They better be some serious ass whoopers because–"

Two of Ben's plainclothes agents converged on the area. Both the agents, one with a brown crew cut and a shorter Asian woman that joined him, wore bluejeans and t-shirts, but sported military demeanors.

"These two will get you over to the headquarters building."

Max and Curtis paused for a moment, sizing up the Unity Council agents.

"Better grab your stuff and hop out before they start moving again."

The two men sprung out of their respective doors, bags in hand. They followed the agents out of the street and into the park.

"Damn, what's going on here?" Max asked.

The ribbon of pavement that trailed through the park was lined with the vehicles of Unity Council migrants, most having picnics and waiting to hear from a Unity Council employee. More men and women in yellow windbreakers were moving among the picnickers to disseminate information.

"You guys got your hands full out here," Curtis said.

"People are unpredictable, that's for sure," the female agent said, her watchful eye searching the large patches of grass between the ribbons of pavement. The male agent moved behind Max and Curtis, his hand on the pistol under his windbreaker.

"I'm Kimberly and he's Jason."

Curtis looked Jason up and down casually, before checking out Kimberly marching in front of them. "Feel safer, Max?"

"As long as they don't work for that psychotic maniac on my ass, I feel a lot better."

"We just can't believe you made it," Jason said. "The CIG has some pretty nasty people working for them, they're killers."

"Yeah, and we bitch-slapped them up and down I-70, too," Curtis said, grinning at Max.

The agents laughed.

"That you did," Kimberly said. "And you're lucky to be alive."

Their walk took them across the southeast corner of the park, where the traffic had been backing up all morning. The jam ran west to where the Unity Council headquarters building overlooked the Steele Street entrance into the park. Police officers were in the intersection, directing the flow of traffic.

Many of the vehicles that were unable to turn left down Steele – due to the crowds – were continuing down to the next corner of the park and circling for another try.

The agents kept their eyes on the waiting vehicles as they hurried their charges through the bottleneck into the crowds that had spilled out of Unity HQ onto Steele Street.

Unity Council employees were working from the curbs on both sides of the approach to the intersection, quickly counseling the occupants of the waiting vehicles and if possible sending them past the packed parking lots of the Unity Council building.

The 1950s office high-rise sat at the end of a block of 19th century brownstone homes, and climbed eight stories above the old neighborhood. Its woefully inadequate parking lot took up the rest of the block along 17th, as well as the end of the next block across the alley.

Unity Council personnel manned barricades at the entrances, letting in only the most desperate of the arrivals and letting out Unity Council-led caravans of those that could make it safely to the San Luis Valley.

"They're backing up," Curtis said.

"We're trying to redirect them," Kimberly said. "But it's kind of getting out of hand."

Max and Curtis found themselves taken aback by the scene they walked into. They couldn't help but let down their guard with so much happening on the gridlocked street and the block around the headquarters building.

Their escorts remained vigilant. Jason and Kimberly tightened up their formation, with one taking Max and the other taking Curtis.

"Is Ben here?" Curtis asked.

"They're on their way," Jason said. "But Hector is here and waiting for you guys upstairs."

"Any intel you can give us will really help," Kimberly said.

They plunged into the throng in front of the building. An extended row of tables spanned out near the narrow cement stoop of the building, where more Unity Council staffers were assisting weary travelers.

"There wasn't supposed to be anybody coming to Denver, was there?" Curtis asked.

Kimberly cleared the way. "Excuse me, please," she said, tapping on shoulders. "No, this wasn't the plan. If all these people were signed up with the relocation program then they would know exactly where they were going."

"And they wouldn't have shown up here," Jason said.

After diplomatically navigating the crowd, Kimberly flashed her badge at the bouncer-like men at the door, their t-shirts printed with the well-known tag "event staff."

The lobby of the building was lined with more tables that were staffed by more counselors, working with even more unexpected visitors.

Max and Curtis walked through a room where every ethnic group seemed to be represented, all obviously destitute. Many were homeless where they came from. Others were working-class poor from cities along the West Coast.

"You always figure your life sucks," Curtis said. "...until you see folks that have it worse."

They passed more hulking event staff at the elevator. They were unable to take their eyes off the scene outside the elevator doors until they closed shut. Kimberly selected the sixth floor button.

"They had you come out here to do what now?" Max asked.

"To help coordinate," Curtis said.

"Then it sounds like your life is going to get pretty interesting here, pretty quick."

"See, you didn't have to go rubbing it in and all." Curtis cinched his bag up over his shoulder.

The elevator door slid open with a ding to reveal another spacious office that was alive with activity. Hector's nerve center was arrayed with maps of the state and the country on the walls. Desks and worktables lined the entire room, including the windows at the far end of the space.

Hector emerged from the bedlam with a gracious smile and an extended hand. "Curtis, man I'm glad you guys made it here alive."

"Everyone keeps saying that," Max said.

"It's been a while, Hector," Curtis said as they shook. "You really helped us out on the road with that rental car. How's Maria?"

Hector sized Max up as he reached to shake his hand. "She's great. She'll be here Sunday. Hope you understand why we couldn't send anybody," he said. "We've been hopping out here."

"Yeah, we get that now," Curtis said.

"You guys have been on the road for days," Hector said. "Kimberly, could you get these two settled upstairs please? Get cleaned up and we'll send some people to talk to you about what's been going on lately. Sound good?"

"Sounds good to me," Max said.

"Curtis, thanks for stepping up and helping with this situation," Hector said. "Can we talk a minute?"

"Sure, no problem."

Kimberly led Max and Jason to a stairwell beside the elevator while Curtis remained in a huddle with Hector.

"So you just met him on that bus two days ago, right?" Hector asked quietly.

"Max? Yeah, man. I mean, yes." The concern on Hector's face began to concern Curtis. "Hector, why are you asking about Max? You know he's the victim here, right?"

"We just need to make sure that he isn't really working with the CIG, instead of running from it."

"What?"

A man rushed up to Hector and presented something for him to sign. "It's no stretch to think the CIG put out a bulletin that they knew we would see, sent Max out there on his own, and waited for us to step in."

"Damn, is this the world we're living in?" Curtis asked. "I just want to know if I should be thinking like a secret agent, because I don't have a lot of experience with that."

Hector came as close as he ever did to a look of disapproval.

"Look, man, I respect that it's your job to think three steps ahead of everybody, all the time. But Max is cool. I know it for a fact. Hell, that CIG dude came dressed up like a cop and hauled him straight off. There was nothing I could do but ram his ass off the road. That wasn't a show, that little bit of action went down for real."

Hector assessed the resolve in Curtis's eyes. "OK. Fair enough," he said. "I would have you on a clipboard coordinating counselors right now, but I need you to stay with him. Until Ben clears him, and we have some idea of what is going on between him and Masterson, we need you to stay close to Max Stiner and keep an eye out."

"I'll spy on the dude for you, Hector, but that's only because I know he's straight up. And I also know for a fact they want a piece of him."

"Any idea why?"

"You wouldn't believe it if I told you."

"I don't know, after today, I can believe a lot of things."

Curtis headed toward the stairs. "Like?" he asked.

"Like the possibility that people might actually be waking up out there."

"We can work with that," Curtis said before the door closed behind him.

Kimberly and Jason had led Max to the floor where the offices had been made into break rooms and sleeping quarters for the many Unity Council employees in the building. It was now in the process of being turned into emergency overnight accommodations for incoming travelers.

With Jason waiting at the door, Max got the use of one of the bathrooms, his first opportunity to really clean up in days. He stepped out of the shower surprisingly invigorated, considering how little he had slept.

He recognized the high as the same high he had been riding since his first near miss with Masterson's agents. It was the same manic anticipation of life threatening danger that had kicked in the moment he felt the searing heat of Kuwait on his skin twenty years prior.

Max dried himself and dressed listening to the hum of people and activity, for some reason it set him at ease. Although the nagging sense that he was still far from his final destination persisted, and robbed him of the satisfaction Curtis was feeling at that moment from the ostensibly simple accomplishment of making it to Denver alive.

He ran a comb through his scraggly mane and collected everything back into his bag, a final check in the mirror before he opened the door. He was greeted by Jason's mammoth frame.

"You guys watching me or something?" Max said with a chuckle.

Jason's silent smile was accommodating. And that was about all.

Max thought about it a moment then smiled as well. "I guess I can't blame you."

"David wanted to talk to you, if you feel up to it?"

"What about Curtis, they putting him to work?"

"He'll be down after he gets a shower."

The fourth floor was another operations level, with relocation counselors hard at work on telephones and computers. Jason took Max through the main room to a hall that led to a series of small offices.

Bud was the first thing Max saw when Jason opened the door. He was hanging one of David's outlines on the office wall opposite where David was working at his new desk.

"It's you!" Max said. "Damn, Bud, I thought you were dead! And that it was *my* fault!" He shook Bud's hand thankfully.

"It'll take more than a couple of piss-ant spooks to kill me," Bud said.

"Thank god for that. What the hell are you doing all the way out here?"

"I was going to hop a bus back to New York and keep my head down for a while. Then I heard from my super that there were some agents sniffing around my apartment building. It's looking like I'm not going to be able to stop watching my back until you're dead." Bud's face was deadpan. "... or we figure this shit out."

"I vote for the last one," Max said. "I'm sorry, man. It's my fault you can't go home."

"Max, I'm David, we're all really glad you made it–"

"Alive?" Max said while shaking David's hand. He looked over David's shoulder, to the vague photo of Masterson on the wall.

"That's him! That's the sonofabitch I've been seeing!" He sidestepped David and the desk to put his hands on the picture. "How did you get this? Who is he?"

David saw all that he needed in that moment of recognition. "That's what we needed to talk to you about."

Max put his hands on either side of the photo as he searched the fuzzy pink blob that was Masterson's face. "He's real, I knew it. I knew he was real. He's military too, isn't he? I've just had the feeling that he's military."

"By title, maybe," Bud said.

"Have a seat, Max," David said.

"No, just tell me!" Max frantically searched the rest of what David had been able to hang behind his desk. He turned to the outlines that Bud was arranging on the opposite wall. "What is his name?!"

"Masterson, General Masterson, OK Max?" Bud said. "Now relax, you have to relax."

Max was too agitated to sit; all he could do was pace and contemplate the name of his tormentor.

"Who is he? Army, is he army?"

"That's a complicated question," David said.

"It's not complicated! Just tell me who he is!"

Jason opened the door slowly. He waited for David to wave him off before pulling back into the hall.

"Max, just sit down," Bud said. "We don't know each other from Adam, but I almost took a bullet for you. And I don't like any of this any better than you do, but these people have been trying to get to the bottom of why. So maybe we can go back to our lives."

"Yeah, no thanks." He reluctantly sat.

"You were in the army?" David said. "Is it possible you met him? Were you ever assigned to any kind of top secret work?"

"No, no, I was a grunt."

David unpinned the photo of Masterson and placed it in front of Max. "Are you sure?"

"I'm sure." Max took the picture in hand.

"Well then, Max. Why?" David took his seat behind his desk. "General Masterson is one of the most secretive individuals in the world. He's a presidential adviser and the head of one of the most powerful top

246

secret organizations in the government."

"He's what?" Max said.

"Think four star general," Bud said.

"In charge of a black project that has complete operational authority," David said. "And he gives new meaning to the word compartmentalization. So it begs the question as to how you could even know the man exists."

Max jumped up to the window, looking to the park and downtown Denver, then to the snowcapped mountains beyond. "Dreams, OK? I've been seeing him in my dreams." He waited for the ridicule.

Instead, David removed the Bible Ben and John found in his apartment. "I figured as much. This is yours."

"What the hell? This was my grandfather's. You people have been in my apartment?" He thumbed through the frayed collection of thoughts and dreams and scripture.

"They hit your place too," Bud said.

"Our people grabbed what they thought would help find you after the CIG agents left. I've been doing my best to read it, Max. I hope you don't mind."

"It's all in German. I got it with a bunch of other stuff when my aunt died. My parents were already gone. They were pretty old when they had me. That was pretty much the last of my family."

"I thought maybe it would give us a clue as to your connection with Masterson."

"Why in the world would it do that?" Max asked.

"Let's just say, it rang certain bells with certain people who are sensitive to these kinds of things. Or rather the notations inside it rang bells. And considering other information we've received... Do you speak German?"

"No, I took Spanish in school, why?"

"Because we need to track down the 'imposter' and kick his ass!" Bud said.

David paged through the Bible. "So you tried to read this? I mean, you've handled it?" He rose and stood in front of the tight collection of outlines.

"I've 'handled' it sure. But I just put it away because I couldn't make head nor tail of it."

David considered Max's responses in relation to the outlines. "We have past lives. We have memories of somebody *else* that lived in the past, usually an ancestor. We have telepathic communication from a human, a spirit, or even an alien. And any of those can take place out of time."

"I couldn't just be going nuts?"

"Then I'm also going nuts," Curtis said from the threshold to the office. "Because I saw it just like you." He closed the door behind him.

"Masterson doesn't put out an unprecedented nationwide call for your capture if you're just some loon," David said. "Up until they caught up with you in New York, Masterson's people had been working from a general description. It wasn't until his team laid eyes on you that they were able to make a positive identification. No, there is something passing between you and him. Somehow, at some time, your lives became entangled, and those kinds of entanglements can defy time and space in their expression."

"What do you mean general description? They didn't jack up anybody else did they?"

David took an uncomfortable look at Bud.

"Tell me no one else was hurt by this maniac because of me!"

"We counted twenty-six men nationwide before your encounter in New York."

"That mother fu...! What happened to them? Where did he take them?"

"They're dead, Max," Bud said, when it appeared David couldn't say the words. "He's a murderous piece of shit that needs to be taken out. Now what are you going to do about it?"

"I'm going to kill him with my bare hands!"

"Curtis, Hector speaks highly of you, my name is David."

"What's up, man? Can you help him?"

"You said you also saw it. What exactly did you see?"

"It was... it was a dream, on the bus. But it was so real that I was sweating from that damn desert."

"What desert? Just exactly what did you see?"

"Dudes flying around in UFOs telling humans what to do. Way back before Jesus."

David reached for a notepad. "Are we talking 'flames and smoke shooting out' UFOs, or 'fly around with no sound' UFOs?"

"I like this guy already. Flames and smoke, big time."

"And Masterson?"

"He was riding the rocket," Max said.

"See, that sounds like the Ancient Astronaut theory," David said as he went back to his laptop. "Bud, we didn't bring any of those outlines. But I guess I could have someone take some pictures of that section in my office in Philadelphia."

Max and Curtis joined Bud in front of the wall that was slowly being papered over with black and white placards.

"What's all this?" Curtis asked.

"It's my lame attempt at meta-analysis," David said. "It's a standard technique for the investigation of varied and complex subjects, and a complex subject is exactly what Masterson is.

"With all the supernatural phenomena swirling around him, and his own limited use of psychics, we're having a problem figuring out just exactly what's been going on with him. Max, there's good reason to believe that you know what it is, even if you don't realize it."

"Where is it, Max?" Curtis asked.

"What?" David asked.

Max dug into his bag for the translation of the Gilgamesh epic. He placed it onto David's desk, laying the textbook on Mesopotamian history beside that.

"There's my book. It's overdue now."

"Sorry, Bud," Max said, distracted by all that was happening.

David skimmed through the translation of the Gilgamesh epic, more interested in Max's many notations and paragraphs than the text itself. He knew the story well.

"You know it's funny," David finally said. "Almost every time someone is talking about an ancient civilization, or about the first civilization, it's always Egypt. The various Brotherhoods just love Egypt. But the birth of Western Civilization took place in Mesopotamia. I've found it uncanny how often that's overlooked."

"Yeah, they overlook it," Bud said. "Then they conveniently overlook the fact that kingship was also born at the same time and in the same place."

"Are you saying you think this was the catalyst?" David asked Max.

"All I know is that this all started right around the time I started reading that. Since then I haven't been able to let it out of my sight."

"You can trust me on that one," Curtis said.

"It was the first work of major literature in the Western World," David said. "The first epic poem, the first real hero myth. *Beowulf, Arabian Nights, King Arthur*, they all have their roots in the Gilgamesh epic."

Bud scoffed. "Sniveling odes to kingship, all of them!"

David just grinned. "Epics like this one and the Mahabharata, for example, they demonstrate how long our writers and sages have been showing us the error of our ways. These ancient works of literature delved into the deepest aspects of the human condition. And they did it way early in our development. Unfortunately for that development, the human condition was, and still is, steeped in kingship."

"So that's what set Max off?" Curtis asked.

"For generations the *Epic of Gilgamesh* was as much a ritual book as a hero myth..." David said, fascinated by Max's notations.

Max took one of the chairs in front of David's desk, thinking not about the Gilgamesh epic, for the first time in some time, but about the twenty-six men that may have died in his stead.

"The Continuity in Government," Bud said. "Where's Orwell when you need him?"

"*1984*," Curtis said. "Good flick, depressing. Course full on *1984* can't happen here. Too many guns in the good old U-S-of-A. They could only come up with that kind of shit in a country where everyone doesn't have guns that spit bullets. I can't count how many bangers I know who have 'choppers.' Those are AK-47s."

"The same guns that were killing us in 'Nam," Bud said. "The only thing that makes the militia guys up by my cabin reach for their rifles quicker than the taxman is the 'gubment' coming for their guns."

"Well, the Continuity in Government isn't just about oppression," David said. "It's about Armageddon. Masterson's tapped into a foolproof way to control people. The whole subject runs straight into our subconscious."

"Me and Max have been talking about how we're a generation just waiting to die. We got it on the brains. That's why all our best movies are about it."

"*Your* generation?" Bud said. "We were diving under desks because the world was blowing up when we were just dumb kids in school. Remember that shit, David? Air raid drills for when, not if, they dropped the bomb."

"I remember," David said, his head buried in the Gilgamesh translation.

"And we never questioned it either. We never once jumped up and said 'this shit is stupid.'"

"Post-apocalypse movies," Curtis said. "And we already have the big ones. You know, like *Mad Max* and *Terminator*."

"*12 Monkeys*," Max said.

"Nice," Curtis said. "That's a 'whacked out lab tech releases a virus that almost wipes out the whole world' apocalypse. Great sci-fi."

"There's all those zombie movies," Bud said.

"*28 Days*," Max said. "*Resident Evil. Dawn of the Dead.*"

Curtis grinned. "Gory 'zombies take over the world' apocalypse."

David tore himself away from Max's book for a moment. "*Zardoz*," he said.

"What the hell?" Curtis said.

"It was a bit before your time, the '70s, I believe. Sean Connery and, what was her name? A stunning European woman... Charlotte Rampling, that's it.

"Zardoz was the name of the god that ruled a bleak, post-apocalyptic world. A world where primitives roamed outside of an energy shield that protected a city full of pampered and basically immortal elite.

"Zardoz was this massive hollow head that floated around this wasteland demanding sacrifices. Good stuff."

"See, that sounds like some hot '70s sci-fi, right there," Curtis said. "They made some great shit in the '70s."

"It was," David said. "Sometimes I think that's what the 1 percent believes – the ones who accept that climate change is real, anyway – that their money will somehow buy them an ivory tower somewhere. Where they'll live safe from the effects of climate disruption, while we suffer and die outside."

"What was that dragon one?" Max said.

"*Reign of Fire*," Curtis said. "Yeah, nice. 'Dragons burn everything to ashes' apocalypse. Nice heads up, Max. They got real creative trying to wipe us all out with that one."

David paged to the first lines of the *Epic of Gilgamesh*. "'He saw secret things and revealed hidden things; he brought intelligence of the days before the flood.' One of the reasons Gilgamesh was so powerful was because supposedly he knew what had gone on in the days before the apocalypse. An apocalypse that everyone seemed to know for a fact had happened."

Bud read through the outline on the wall entitled: "Controlling Armageddon."

"That's right here," David said. "'The Hopi believed this was the Fourth World, because the Third World had been destroyed by a great flood and fire.' These people were on opposite sides of the planet and they were still hung up on the end of the world."

Max had been listening to the conversation burning a hole in the photograph of Masterson with his furious glare.

"More people will get hurt trying to protect me," he said. "...because he won't stop. The dreams won't stop."

"What are you saying?" David asked.

"That I didn't come out here to find you. I came out here to find him."

"Then you came out here to die," Bud said.

"Curtis, I thank you for risking your life saving me like you did, but you should have just let them take me."

"That's crazy, man."

"What about all those guys that died in my place? I'm supposed to just let that go? It's not going to happen. Where is he?"

"From what they are saying," Bud said. "As far as the government is concerned, where he is doesn't exist."

"Think secret foreign prison, but right here in the U.S.," David said.

"Nobody is going to give a shit if you disappear into a place like that," Bud said.

"They can't get away with that, can they?" Curtis asked.

David crossed his arms and leaned against his desk. "We're hoping to expose the conspiracy. That's the only weapon we have: exposure to the world. Telling their secret to whoever will listen. And Hector is making sure that's going to be as many people as possible. We have to keep you safe until that happens."

"That won't stop the dreams," Max said. "That won't stop him."

"Then we also have to get to the bottom of your connection with him."

"Did that help?" Max pointed to his notes in the Gilgamesh translation.

"I need time to study it. Meanwhile, you might want to checkout that outline, in particular." He pointed to the placard that read: "The Nine Phenomena and Masterson."

"He's right about that, Max," Bud said. "You have to show him the video."

Max hoisted himself up from the chair.

"There are two men coming tomorrow who could shed some light on things," David said. "Ben has his ways, and by all accounts his son is quite amazing. I can't wait to meet him."

"The head ass whoopers are gonna make their appearance," Curtis said.

"I can't be hypnotized. Someone has tried before and it didn't work."

David finally closed the Gilgamesh translation. "From what I understand, their approach goes way beyond hypnotism.

12

Mary and Sheila hadn't spoken in hours; they were both hunched over their respective computers digging deeper into the organization known as the Continuity in Government. Worried looks were exchanged between the women, the same worried looks they had been exchanging off and on since Arizona.

"These spreadsheets," Sheila said. "This thing is a monster, hundreds of millions of dollars a year. They're stashing shit in places all over the country. Food, water, weapons."

"Yeah, but none of it's a smoking gun. These kinds of records will prove that the CIG exists, that's about it. I'm cool with dumping it all online. Get rid of it."

"Then it's up to Ben and Hector to prove what the CIG is really up to."

"My God, Sheila, look at this. There are no names here, but you can tell that at least two of them are in Congress."

"There's gigs more data to sift through but we should go."

"They're after all these people. What, am I on the list too? Sara? I can't stop thinking about Denise." She touched the necklace with just a little more reverence than before. "Honestly, I don't know that it's safe to be around me right now."

"Leonard will be there and he won't let you out of his sight. Hector said they would be sending someone, a specialist in this kind of thing. Otherwise we have to make it look good until they make their move. Besides, from what Ben was telling Hector, it could be more dangerous for you and Sara to stay cooped up here all alone."

Mary crossed her arms and squeezed tightly. "One thing has definitely come true: leaving California sure didn't solve all my problems. I wish I knew what to do now."

"If you think about it, we've already basically risked our lives on the Council knowing what they're doing. Len and I were talking and we agreed that it's time to see this through."

"I know; you're right," Mary said, unclenching a bit.

"We were just glad Sara hit it off so well with Heather and Michael," Sheila said with a reassuring smile. "It's kept them all busy. Otherwise Heather and Michael probably would have half killed each other by now."

A series of firm knocks on the security entrance to the hall cut through the persistent background noise of the computer fans.

"I'll get it," Sheila said.

The door was opened by one of Ben's more impressive security agents, his assault rifle at the ready. He let in a tall woman in her late twenties, with dark hair and pale skin. She gave Mary a gracious smile before setting a large valise down on the table where Sheila was working.

"Hello, I'm Jan. I'm heading up the medical department... I was supposed to see you about a laptop."

"Yeah, uh, yes, I have it right here," Mary said. She didn't mention that she had been too preoccupied to have it ready. "If you have a few minutes, we'll get you set up. Have a seat?"

Mary pulled out a chair from the worktable on her way to a cabinet in the corner. "We have wireless Internet set up around the building. I just have to configure your system to pick it up."

"Computers," Jan said with a wrinkled brow. "It's just not right that something so useful can be so damned confusing and complicated."

"My first computer teacher told me a long time ago that computers aren't logical," Mary said. "People think they should be logical because they're machines, but they aren't because they were created by people."

"All I know is that they can be more trouble than they are worth," Jan said. "Until you need one to save a life, then it's hard to remember what we did without them."

"People make jokes about how the Y2K thing was a bust," Mary said, trying to stall. "But nobody ever says anything about the thousands of programmers who had to work for years to make sure the whole thing didn't fall apart, over one digit in a date. Talk about illogical. If you could work code back then, you cleaned up. I got pregnant with my daughter barely two years later but I wasn't too worried, I had saved a good nest egg."

Jan was drawn to the one way windows and the people outside.

"They said they would hang curtains," Mary said. "But I don't mind it, as long as they can't see in."

"I would have said it was just temporary. But the way people have been pouring in, I'm waiting for that laptop to submit the paperwork to set up another clinic. The one we have going now is almost at capacity and the hospital in Alamosa is too."

"Yeah, it was supposed to get quiet after Sunday," Mary said.

"Girl, don't you know it's never quiet in the old San Luis?" Sheila said.

"Jan, this is Sheila, she's in charge of accounting."

"Nice to meet you, Sheila. I just came from Denver and it's turning into a madhouse up there too."

"Are you serious about the clinic?" Sheila said. "Because if so, I'll have some people get on it right away."

"I discussed it with Hector. And he talked it over with the other Council reps. We knew there would be a dire need for medical care among the people passing through this weekend, but this has been something else. And they can't redirect them from Denver fast enough."

Mary shut down Jan's laptop and gathered up the power cord. "How many more people are they expecting?"

"They haven't been able to count. They've been too busy just trying to get people clear of the headquarters building before they start having problems with the police, and of course, the press."

"We've kept the website up since the hacks. Easier now that we aren't leaking vital information. We updated the homepage and told people not to come, to call first. But if the phones keep going out I don't know what we'll do."

An awkward silence ensued as Mary finished packing up Jan's laptop.

Jan looked out the window a moment longer. "So, Ben filled me in on the situation. He sent me to help, if I can."

"What 'situation' is that?"

"Technically, Denise works for me."

"*You're* the 'specialist' they were talking about?" Sheila said.

"I guess you could say that." Jan took out a small notebook and a pen. "Mary, how have you been feeling?"

"I'm fine, so far, anyway."

"Have you experienced any dizziness or disorientation?"

"Nope, I'm tired but I feel OK. Scared as hell, nothing new there."

"I know you're scared. Believe me, we have everybody on this."

Sheila shutdown her laptop and collected her things. She sneaked a few looks at Jan before finally giving in to her curiosity.

"So, Jan, you being the resident specialist and all, I have to ask... seen any UFOs yet?"

"Sheila's got us heading out there later on tonight," Mary said before Jan had a chance to respond.

Jan's fine features lit up. "Oh man, I started hearing accounts of people's experiences here in the valley when I got to Denver. We're getting a database going."

"I heard it started with the workmen who broke ground on this very building," Sheila said. "The skies at night around here are insanely gorgeous. And when it's not overcast with clouds, real or the other kind, it's so clear."

"It's like you can see straight into the Milky Way itself," Mary said.

"The *other* kind of clouds?" Jan asked.

"Chemtrails," Sheila said. "People aren't sure what those bastards are up to, but you know it can't be good."

Jan fingered through a collection of files in her valise until she came to the one entitled "Chemtrails." She laid it open on the top of the bag, turning to the summary page. "One of the first things they want me to do is look into the health effects of some of this stuff that's been falling to the ground after they see these chemtrails."

Mary placed the computer in a carrying case. "There's stuff falling from the skies after these things?"

"In some cases. At least that's what the report says. I'm waiting for a briefing from our climate scientist on it."

"It's not dangerous, is it?" Sheila asked.

"Couldn't say about the long term effects because long term studies are hard to find, but short term symptoms include nausea and headaches."

"Well hell," Sheila said. "You can get some of that from the pollution in L.A."

Mary handed the computer bag to Jan. "You were right, Sheila. It never is quiet in the old San Luis."

Jan slung the computer over her shoulder. She placed the file back in her bag.

"Well, I love it out here," Sheila said.

"Because you ended up in the middle of Weird Central."

"I've been hearing about the strange goings-on in the San Luis Valley for years," Jan said. "Why do you think I agreed to come out here? When Ben called I was psyched."

"Ben hired you?" Mary asked.

"I knew him in Phoenix. Did you know this was where the first official animal mutilation was reported in 1967? It wasn't a cow, either. Actually, it was a horse."

Mary returned to her desk to gather her things. "Sheila mentioned that," she said. "I know I don't like the sound of someone cutting up animals and leaving them for dead."

"With bloodless, laser-like incisions? I know how incredible that is, trust me. And in all the years since it's been happening not one suspect has ever even been arrested, much less convicted."

"Len was talking about how crazy that is," Sheila said.

"And they've tried too. Cattle ranchers have been losing stock for years, that's real money to them, and no one has been caught? Damn right that's crazy."

"I thought everyone decided it was the government doing tests downwind of old nuclear test sites in Nevada?" Sheila said.

Jan nodded. "That has always been a plausible explanation, but then why don't they just buy the stock undercover, or better yet just take them? Why draw attention to themselves by bringing the carcasses back? Sometimes even leaving them dangling in the highest branches of trees?"

"So just to confirm," Mary said. "No reports of unexplained *human* mutilations, right?"

"None that were returned anyway," Jan answered cryptically; she gave the ladies a keen wink.

"How did you get into all this stuff?" Sheila asked.

"I've been watching UFO and paranormal videos for years. This little video store around the block from my house had a big section because the owners were into it. Then I got into the books.

"Plenty of it was either whacked-out New Age crap, or cranks and kooks just trying to make a name for themselves. But I always suspected there was more to it than just that. Then I met Ben and he proved to me that there was so much more."

"We were able to help him out earlier," Mary said. "They're fighting for this family out in DC. He helped me too. And I've never even met him face-to-face."

"It sounds funny being a physician, but one thing I learned in eight years of medical school, and then four years knowing Ben Spiritdancer, is that science doesn't, and possibly can't, explain everything. Whether my analytical mind likes it or not, whether the establishment likes it or not, that is the case."

"The AMA is going to come after you for talk like that," Sheila said. "They have microphones everywhere."

"They can be a spiteful bunch, alright. And at one time I enjoyed pissing them off, but now there's no point. It's like the cattle mutilations. People say it's BS, and scoff at the researchers who talk about it, but when I was in a store down in Alamosa, I saw a poster on the local bulletin board offering a reward for information on whoever is doing it. There are bulletins about the chemtrails too. These are real things affecting real lives."

Sheila and Mary paused on their way to the door to look Jan over.

"I like this girl," Sheila said. "Hey, you want to go out with us later to where they've been watching for UFOs?"

"I need to get this other clinic together but I think the idea was that I would stay close to Mary, just in case."

"Sure, you can join me and Len. We're going to be eyeballing Mary while she eats."

"That sounds like tons of fun," Mary said with a roll of her eyes. "Actually, I would like to hear more about Ben."

Jan grinned fondly. "Talk about a guy that attracts weirdness. Then he introduced me to David, and I've been talking to him online."

"Don't think we've met him," Sheila said.

"We were going to meet up at the cafeteria tent at five," Mary said, locking the door to her office behind them.

"Sounds good," Jan said.

"We'll have dinner and then check out the sparkling San Luis Valley nightlife," Sheila said.

"Sounds like a plan," Jan said.

Back in Denver, inside David's office, Max was slumped in a chair in front of the wall of flawlessly printed outlines. Bud stood beside him, arms crossed skeptically, as they both struggled to assimilate the improbable subject matter before them.

David had been hunched over his laptop and the videotaped channeling sessions of Hasline that Chris found in Hasline's clinic. He had already astonished Max with the footage and left he and Bud to ruminate on what they had seen while he combed the channeling sessions for clues.

"So, First Sergeant," Max suddenly said. "Why did you really come all the way out here? You could have gotten a lot farther from danger than you are now."

Bud didn't look up from the outlines. "The big picture."

"I'm serious; you could have bailed to your cabin, or anywhere, just disappeared for a while."

Bud backed up until he could lean against the window sill. "Paine talked about it all the way back when he was slamming religion in *The Age of Reason*. There's a couple of ways the priests from the Big Three Cults control the people. You got mystery, you got miracle, and you got prophecy. Whoever is behind The Nine has been getting some serious mileage out of all three of those."

"I'm just finding it hard to believe that Masterson is really into all this."

"Well if he is, he isn't the only one. And I don't know about you, soldier, but I don't like the idea of that one bit. Mix in some kingship and you got the way of controlling us all."

David turned down the faint audio coming from the speakers on his computer. "No, he most definitely isn't the only one, either."

The door opened slowly. "Hey, what's going on in here?" Curtis asked as he closed it behind him.

"Just watching some home videos," Max said. "I think Hector called you away before you had a chance to catch this particular freakshow."

Curtis took an incredulous look. "Who's the strung-out stiff?"

"Dr. Stanley Hasline."

Max read from one of the outlines. "'He's President of the Canadian Psychiatric Association, President of the American Psychiatric Association, graduate, Johns Hopkins, Primary research scientist for General Masterson. He pioneered several procedures for the erasing of human identity and the replacement with altered personalities through the use of drugs and torture, also pioneered research into paranormal abilities such as remote viewing, remote influencing, and telepathy.'"

"What the hell kind of mad scientist is this guy?" Curtis said.

"The worst," David said. "He's the fully accredited, highly respected kind."

"'His experiments in the occult can be traced back thirty years,'" Max read. "'He's involved with the recent channeling resurgence and manipulation of 2012 mythology.'"

"And as we can all see," David said. "He channels The Nine, personally."

"Who the hell are The Nine, now?" Curtis asked. "I missed that too. Somebody has to get some work done around here." He gave Max a playful nod.

David directed their attention to the outlines. "It's a damn complicated issue."

"No shit," Bud said.

"Well, what the hell has he got to do with the CIG?" Curtis asked.

"I guess you have to say that it all started back in the early '50s," David said. "That was when this ex-Army intelligence officer and paranormal researcher named Puharich brought this man from India named Vinod to his research center in New York.

"The story goes that Vinod psychically contacted an entity that said it was one of the nine main gods of Egyptian mythology. They were called the Council of Nine."

Max focused in on the outline. "Let's see, there are Atum, Shu, Tefnut, Geb, Nut, Osiris, Isis, Set and Nepthys,'" he read.

"In the mummy cults of Heliopolis, they were the nine gods that came together to create what they called the Great Ennead, or godhead," David said. "Then the entity speaking through Vinod also said that he was an alien circling the Earth in a spaceship."

"Yeah, right," Curtis said. "You got your movies all mixed up. You don't get possessed by aliens."

"Again, it's complicated," David said. "It goes back to the 1600s and the first magician-spy John Dee... Dee was legendary. Supposedly, he and another buddy of his, over the course of a few days, channeled the entire system of Enochian magick. It's supposed to be the ultimate in magickal systems. Not to be attempted by the novice."

"That Enochian shit was on *Supernatural*," Curtis said. "You watch that? It's sweet."

"Then there was this shady woman who lived in the 1870s by the name of Madame Blavatsky," David said. "She started channeling this hyper racist doctrine she called *Theosophy*. That and some other occult garbage eventually became the underpinnings of the Nazi philosophy.

"They downplayed the mysticism and occult influences on the Nazis at the Nuremberg trials because they didn't want people to know just how far it had all been allowed to go.

"In fact, Blavatsky's patently evil philosophy – along with a bunch of nonsense from this woman named Alice Bailey – became the basic background beliefs for most of the Austrian-Bavarian-German brotherhoods of the last hundred and fifty years."

"So they didn't all sit in the same room," Bud said. "They just all read the same books?"

"Books supposedly written by other-worldly entities and channeled by magicians and psychics." David brought up a document on his computer, a timeline he had been compiling of occult history. "Magician-spy Aleister Crowley's Scarlet Woman channeled Horus in 1904," he said. "And later, after the infamous 'Cairo Working,' Crowley made contact with a nonphysical entity called Aiwass. The story goes that that entity dictated *The Book of the Law* to Crowley. It became a sacred book for occultists around the world.

"Then in 1918 he was supposed to have made contact with Lam. His sketch of that entity looked enough like the classic grey alien that later, after alien abductions started to get publicized, people started saying that what he had contacted there was extraterrestrial.

"Then Jack Parsons, one of the founders of JPL – the Jet Propulsion Lab – hero of American rocket science since the very beginning, and devout Crowley follower by the way, he used to dress up in robes and call himself the antichrist. His Scarlet Woman standing by his side. They said he had contacted so many spirits that they haunted his house. His 'Babylon Working' in the California desert was rumored to have opened a doorway to another dimension.

"Now, that's where Puharich comes in. I mean the man wrote a book called the *Sacred Mushroom*, among others, OK? He was out there.

"He started out in the Army Chemical Division when they were getting into LSD research and worse. He was obsessed with using whatever means: drugs, the occult, science, to make contact with entities he knew had to exist, because he knew about Crowley and the Cairo Working, and about John Dee, and Blavatsky, and many others."

"So were they faking?" Bud asked. "Or are they all just crazy? Was Puharich running some kind of sick-ass experiment?"

"Not unless he's lived for well over a century," David said. "And he's dead now and people are still being contacted by something."

Bud read from the outline detailing all David had learned about The Nine phenomena, in relation to Masterson in particular. "Government project in mind control and individual con-artists, aliens, trickster spirits, a combination of all.'"

Max got impatient for a moment. "OK, all that went on back then, but what does that have to do with now, and what does it have to do with Masterson?"

"Good old Hasline is Masterson's oldest associate; still alive, anyway," David said. "It's reasonable to assume that Masterson is either behind all this, involved with all this, or at the mercy of all this. None of these prospects are good considering that he has declared war on the Unity Council.

"And considering that the whole channeling thing has been gearing up all over again, it's the manipulation of 'The End of the World' and Masterson has made that his business."

"He's not the only one on that, either," Max said.

"Oh there have been millennial panics before. But I believe that this time there has been a very real effort to manipulate Armageddon, at least what people believe to be Armageddon. And that effort is from more than one source, for more than one reason."

"For what? To sell books?" Bud said. "OK, it's a shitty, cynical thing to do but–"

"It's true; a lot of it is just about selling books. Or about being the one that everyone runs to when they're afraid of what's coming and their faith is shaken. But it's far more cynical than that.

"Prince and Picknett got into all this in *The Stargate Conspiracy* right before the turn of the Millennium, when it was all heating up.

"The theory goes that something or somebody has been trying to create a new religion by hijacking, first the occult movements of the distant past, then the Metaphysical and New Age movements of the more recent past. And now they're gearing up for the new date of Armageddon, December 21, 2012."

"No, really?" Curtis said. "I don't think anybody here has ever heard of that before."

"Yeah, it turned into a big thing, didn't it?" David said. "Well, it seems that during the '70s,'80s, and '90s, when The Nine were giving full-fledged seminars about metaphysics and the coming millennium through different channelers, other researchers were piecing together the Mayan calendar and the Long Count.

"One of those researchers cooked up his own theory and decided that the calendar, or at least a very important part of the calendar, ended on August 16, 1987.

"You younger ones may not remember, but that was the day of this global New Age event called the Harmonic Convergence. Millions of people across the world got together to meditate at the same time. And it was timed for the end of this particular Mayan cycle. That's when the idea of 2012 got out to a wider audience, the supposed end of the calendar all together.

"Then the guy turned around and announced that he was Valum Voltan, a wizard-channeler channeling an ancient Mayan king named Pikal. He started his own cult that spread worldwide. All based on a calendar system – supposedly Mayan – that was flawed.

"Then New Age writers and researchers started getting involved, some of the same ones that were influenced by The Nine before the turn of the millennium, and all of a sudden the world was ending on December 21, 2012."

"It is, they made a movie about it," Curtis said with a completely straight face. His warm grin soon appeared, though.

"That one doesn't count as post-apocalyptic," Max said. "That was a disaster flick."

"Of course, the Mayans never said that the world will end. The whole 'entire world ending' scenario is a linear, Western, concept. A concept completely alien to a people who lived their lives in cycles.

"That doesn't mean we all aren't very concerned about the sunspot activity peaking during this period, something that with their deep understanding of astronomy the Maya could have very easily known about. We lose enough satellites and it sure would feel like the end of the world to a culture addicted to their cell phones."

"Awe, but I thought that was when it was going to happen," Curtis said.

Max laughed. "What? When we go from *1984* to *Mad Max*?"

"Damn right. Been waiting for that one. Didn't you know? That's all us kids have to look forward to now: crossbows, mohawks, and shoulder pads. Very tight!"

"The calendar just goes into another cycle of 13 Baktun, another age in their system of timekeeping. It's predicted to be a very turbulent

Baktun, but not the end.

"But the lengths to which some people went to make the Millennium the end of the world, and now 2012, well, more than one scholar has written about apocalyptic religions and the power they can have over people. This is one that has millions of followers, one way or another, but doesn't really have a name.

"So, on January 1, 2013, what cosmic conjunction will become the new date of Judgment Day? What ancient prophecy of doom and destruction will we be hearing about then?"

"Well hell," Bud said. "With global warming, all they have to do is keep pushing back Judgment Day until we all shrivel up from the heat and die. It's a goddamn self-fulfilling prophecy."

"That's what I've been saying," Curtis said. "We've got it bad for 'The End.'"

"OK, so they get some New Agers all fired up," Max said. "They sell a bunch of books and DVDs, and then disappoint them when nothing happens, so what?"

"OK," David said. "So a few gullible people spend a little money and do some soul searching, so what, right? But what if those people being manipulated aren't buying DVDs and going to lectures, what if they're policymakers, and heads of corporate empires, and influential scientists, all proceeding on the idea that not only is Armageddon inevitable, but they are the chosen ones to survive it."

"We just had eight years of that," Bud said. "They're called the Right-Wing Fundamentalists, just itching for the Rapture, and they haven't gone away either."

"That's the thing about this high-jacked New Age movement," David said. "Many embrace it, or elements of it, like a religion. Many hang on the words of these channelers like it's gospel.

"We know about the Christian Fundamentalists joining with the Fundamentalist Jews to make sure the Third Temple of Jerusalem gets built, so that Jesus will return."

"Yeah," Bud said. "And the Christians conveniently leave out the fact that all those Jews that don't convert on Judgment Day end up burning in hell when Jesus shows."

"No, that isn't mentioned," David said. "We know about the Fundamentalist Muslims itching for the end of the world, the Western world anyway.

"But this channeling thing has been underground for a hundred and fifty years, and when it does surface, it's been among the secret ranks of government and science, or in the form of the feel-good New Age movement, a massive, global movement."

"A hundred and fifty years?" Bud said.

"I believe it's much longer than that," David said. "I believe it goes all the way back to the beginnings of the Big Three Cults..."

A natural pause in the conversation had all of the men either intently reading the outlines or watching the video of Set/Hasline.

The words "Sleeping Prophet" caught Max's eye. "'Edger Cayce,'" he read.

"They called him the 'Sleeping Prophet,'" David said. "But there is some doubt about his prophesizing."

"Damn, there's like a hundred shows on the cable history channels about that guy."

"No doubt he's a favorite, Curtis," David said. "He would go into this sleep-like trance and be able to diagnose people's illnesses. He even came up with treatments that medicine at the time hadn't thought of. This was around the turn of the 1900s. He did so many 'spot on' diagnoses that that particular ability was well documented."

"People think he saw the future?" Max asked.

"Or the past," David said. "That's part of The Nine story. During the whole pre-millennium panic there were these researchers, writers, and even scientists who believed some prophecies and perceived signs were saying there would be this great discovery on the Giza plateau. And that the discovery was going to coincide with the year 2000.

"They believed there was an Atlantean Hall of Records under or around the Sphinx, a repository of knowledge from before the Flood. Possibly even the lost Chamber of Thoth, the Egyptian god of sciences and building. And of course, what's supposed to be in that chamber is the fabled *Book of Thoth*."

"Let me guess, some king or priest locked the info away," Bud said. "Where only the Brotherhood could get to it?"

"It turned out that nobody could get to this cache of knowledge," David said. "Not until it was time, the momentous turn of the Millennium to be precise. At least that was what The Nine were telling the people who were channeling them. The thing is some old occult and Masonic legends were also telling the same story.

"When Cayce started prophesying in the '40s about how Atlantis would be found in 1968, no one questioned that he was really seeing it, because he had such a good track record as a psychic. When he said the discovery of an Atlantean Hall of Records at Giza would usher in a new "Age of Enlightenment," many of the people challenging the theories of establishment Egyptology wanted to believe it was true.

"For the occult secret societies, and then later the scientists and researchers investigating the paranormal, finding Thoth's Chamber and the *Book of Thoth* was supposed to hold the keys to all the mysteries of alchemy and magick stretching back through the Brotherhoods all the way to the Mystery Schools of ancient Egypt."

"Talk about the ultimate payoff," Curtis said.

"A complete vindication of their alternative theories. There was only one problem: most of it wasn't true."

"That is a problem," Max said.

"Most people don't realize that Edgar Cayce wasn't just a simple country hick with the uncanny ability of diagnosing diseases. His father was so high in the Masonic order that he could found lodges. That was a privilege.

"The sons and daughters of such backgrounds, the people who live in the world of the Brotherhoods, have a wholly different perspective on human civilization, and on history itself.

"Their mythology and their religion are often based on the history and mythology of the rest of the world, but more often they hold secrets hidden from the rest of us. And their perspectives are skewed by those secrets.

"The problem is that they're convinced that their perspective is the only perspective that matters. It's called Synarchy, government by secret society." He gestured to another outline.

"So the idea is that Cayce wasn't seeing the past or future but telling a story from his particular mythology?" Max said.

"None of his prophecies came true?" Curtis asked.

"Depends on how you look at it," David said. "A group Cayce set up before he died started getting an influx of money and influential people leading up to 1968. Then during the year he said Atlantis would 'rise,' the group was able to send an expedition to Bimini and discover what's called the 'Bimini Road.' It's a long structure under the waters of the Caribbean that appear to be manmade. Now, did his prediction come true, did Atlantis rise, or did his disciples make it come true?"

"Sounds like cheating to me," Bud said.

"It wasn't cheating if he got it right," Curtis said.

"He did cite Bimini by name all the way back in 1940," David said. "No obscure riddles and such. But then pilots had been telling stories of seeing structures in shallow water around the Caribbean since the late '40s anyway."

"You mean like buildings?" Max asked.

"Walls, roads... Then on the Giza Plateau in the years leading up to the turn of the Millennium, Cayce's group was one of many secretly digging for an Atlantean Hall of Records, basically Thoth's Chamber... Then there was a plan to cover the Great Pyramid with a gold capstone in a huge ceremony on New Year's night 2000. You know, like the one on the dollar bill."

"See, that shit's also all over the cable history channels too." Curtis fished out a dollar from his pants pocket. He spread it out on David's desk.

"See that?" David said. "The infamous pyramid with the 'All-Seeing Eye' for the capstone?"

Curtis smirked. "Sure, that's the Brotherhood flipping us all off. Everybody knows that by now."

"Well just imagine the Masonic and occult significance of restoring that capstone, for real, in Egypt, at the turn of the Millennium. Do you think that maybe it might usher in the 'New Order of the Ages,' like it says right there?" He pointed to the words printed in Latin underneath the pyramid on the Great Seal.

"Talk about a Brotherhood wet dream," Bud said.

"But that's not the whole story," David said. "It turns out that the man who got Roosevelt to put the Great Seal on the dollar bill like that was Henry A. Wallace. He was the Secretary of Agriculture at the time, before his term as Vice President."

"Yeah, they talk about that shit in those documentaries," Curtis said.

"He was a Freemason for sure, you know, like all the conspiracy shows say, like Roosevelt himself. But what most people don't know is that after Wallace was Vice President, he directly supported paranormal researcher Andrija Puharich.

"Wallace is considered a progressive hero nowadays. I know he wrote a particular screed warning against fascism that I found truly inspiring. But he was also deep into a heady mix of Christian fundamentalism, mysticism, and parapsychology.

"You have him on one hand, then you have J.P. Morgan, one of the biggest fascists in history, quoted as saying: 'Millionaires don't use astrologers, but billionaires do.'

"According to the chief of staff of the Reagan White House in the '80s, you have Nancy Reagan's longtime astrologer supposedly dictating the most favorable dates and times for US air strikes and treaty signings."

Curtis scoffed. "Say what?"

"The influence of the occult on our society has been complex, to say the least. Levenda called it 'American Political Witchcraft.' That means – among other things – powerful people, some of the most powerful people in the country, who are into spell books, magick rituals, and, yes, channeling entities from beyond."

"If Masterson is involved in any way with all this, you can bet he's in charge," Max said.

"So what happened at the pyramids?" Curtis asked. "I haven't ever heard of the Great Pyramid having a gold capstone."

"I guess when it all got out the Egyptian government cancelled that part of the ceremony. But needless to say there was some serious Brotherhood machinations going on during that little episode."

David pointed out the relevant outline. "See, Prince and Picknett make a good case that Cayce wasn't the first person with some real psychic abilities who has been influenced by the underground lore and history of the Austria-German-Bavarian secret societies.

"The Brotherhoods," Bud said with disgust.

"Lots of those guys were Synarchists," David said. "They believed without reservation that it was not only their duty, but their right, as members of secret societies to rule everyone else. It was the natural progression from that stubborn old kingship that had been hanging around for so long."

"Damn," Curtis said.

"So does any of this ring any bells with you?" David asked Max again.

Max shook his head without looking his way, so David turned to Curtis. "How about you?"

"No, couldn't say. It's the wrong, what do you call it, it's the wrong mythology. Max's head is in Iraq; at least that's what they call the place now. They used to call it Mesopotamia back then."

"And the Flood," Max said.

"Max, post-apocalyptic movies," Curtis said, trying to lighten the mood. "Go!"

Bud and David were shoulder to shoulder in front of the outlines, listening to Curtis.

"*Star Trek*," David said. "The entire storyline, including *Enterprise*, takes place after a series of devastating wars."

"Nice," Curtis said. "Wouldn't have thought of that one. Every earthling in *Star Trek* was living in a post-apocalyptic world."

"*Death Race*," Max said, still sullen.

"Good one," Curtis said. "They remade that one, but did you see the original '70s version? Had the guy from *Kill Bill* in it, *Kung Fu* Carradine."

David looked at his watch. "Ben and John should be coming today, if they can get out of DC. We need to talk to them about this. With their experience, I'm sure they know way more about the 'how' of your connection to Masterson. Maybe that can be the way to figure out the 'why' of your connection.

"They're supposed to be bringing a whistleblower, someone very close to Masterson. I'm anxious to hear what he was able to discover."

"You really think they can help?" Max asked.

"Ben Spiritdancer is the head of security for the Council. He was a police lieutenant and he has some very interesting skills. His son though, John, is very special."

David pointed to an outline high in the right corner of the wall full of outlines. "See the government remote viewing programs? Well he came out of the RV programs that came after Star Gate and Grill Flame in the '90s, since 9-11, even. He was involved with stuff so secret that it didn't even have a codename. Basically it involves operational quantum neurology, remote viewing, and remote influencing."

Curtis slapped his hands together. "Hell yes, I wanna meet someone named John Spiritdancer!"

13

Billy and Joan held hands in front of Phil's flower-draped coffin surrounded by dozens of fellow mourners. Billy wore the same black dress she wore to the White House, with her crimson hair tamed by a ponytail and her lips painted red. Far too preoccupied to cry, she was clinging to Joan for support.

Wearing a hastily purchased black suit, Peter hovered protectively behind the ladies, a pair of dark glasses partially obscuring his swollen and lacerated face. He radiated guilt, but like Billy, he was far too distracted to dwell.

Phil's oldest associates had assembled in the center of a patchwork of graves that sunny morning, to say goodbye to their friend and try to come to terms with such a bizarre end to such a well respected man. The clamoring reporters and camera crews being held at bay by the front gates of the cemetery only served to remind them of just exactly how bizarre that end was.

Phil had worked his entire career with presidents and policymakers – with Washington elite from every branch of the government. When all was said and done, only his most beloved employees and associates were willing to mourn him publicly.

His family attorney, his longtime assistant, and the woman who had cleaned his house for years, were all there for Phil. Then virtually every aid and agency worker he had ever supervised during his career had shown up, at least those who had heard of his death in time.

He had been abandoned by the most powerful people he knew, as the loyalty of those he had led was unshaken. And to an extent Billy still felt the same, though his confession to her had raised doubts she never thought she would have had about the Phil she knew and loved.

The priest from a parish Phil had recently started frequenting took his position at the end of the casket to begin the eulogy:

"A child is born on this Earth, innocent and perfect, filled with uncorrupted belief, truly a wondrous creation of God.

"He or she is then plunged into the world. Which as we all know can be a lonely and uncaring place. They struggle to make a life, to love one another, and maybe, as in the case of the departed, to help mankind. The dreams of a child, the dreams of a young man or woman, can become lost in this world of temptation and greed.

"Every morning we wake up, we go to the mirror, and we find another piece missing. We look into our hearts, and we see that another dream has died. Time will ravage what the strain of living spares. But when we meet our Creator, we must be able to say that although the struggle seemed constant, the journey was also quite wondrous.

"Honestly, I didn't have the privilege of knowing Phil Simmons for very long. But in the course of our talks, it was clear to me that his greatest dream was of a society that embraced its fellow humans in times of need, as well as times of plenty. It is a dream that has yet to be realized.

"Still, we are certainly closer, thanks to Phil Simmons's tireless work and his genuine devotion to the world. May he rest in peace."

Gradually people filed by the coffin, dropping flowers as they passed. The mob of reporters gathered at the cemetery gates erupted when they saw the services had ended.

Billy whispered to Joan then turned away from the gates, with Peter in tow. He led her by the arm in the opposite direction. They strolled silently through several rows of gravestones, out of sight of the reporters.

"My wife, she's over here." Peter pointed to a large gray stone at the end of the extended row.

Peter groaned as he kneeled to remove some leaves from around the gravestone. He carefully wiped off the soiled marble and traced the chiseled letters of her name with his hand.

"You loved her very much."

"Not enough to be around when it mattered," he said. "But then, I guess none of that matters now."

"No kids?"

"She couldn't from the beginning. In the end, that was what killed her, ovarian cancer."

"I'm sorry, Peter."

"Me too, Billy, for a lot of things, but especially for what I did to him."

"You were probably one of the few mainstream reporters he ever respected."

"He knew they would send me after him."

"Probably."

"But he sure underestimated you."

"Oh, darlin', I think somewhere down deep he knew that I would never drop this, not when I found out the truth."

"The truth," Peter said with a defeated chuckle, leaning against the gravestone unsteadily. "Your friends are playing a very dangerous game."

"You don't have to tell me. But one thing I've learned during my years in disaster relief is that, within reason, special circumstances call for special responses. And we are alive."

Peter smiled through the pain of his cracking bones when he rose. He slowly removed his glasses, letting the sun shine on his battered face. "We're alive alright. And it definitely was a special circumstance." He took a parting look at his wife's grave. "Are you ready?"

"As I'll ever be."

The pair walked arm in arm back toward the front gates and the waiting reporters. The sight of Billy with the man who allegedly drove her friend to suicide sent the reporters into a frenzy of speculation.

Security guards hired for the occasion had to force the gates open before they could clear a path for Billy and Peter to a waiting limousine. The car doors slammed as it eased away, scattering the reporters and the camera men that had engulfed the vehicle.

The limousine got clear of the cemetery and onto a major thoroughfare without incident, but they hadn't made a clean getaway. Two CIG agents were shadowing at a distance.

The late model sedan in which the agents rode was unremarkable, like all the surveillance vehicles the Continuity in Government utilized.

Meanwhile, behind the tinted windows and bulletproof doors, the backseat of the car had been removed and replaced by a console of surveillance equipment that almost completely encircled the operations officer seated at its center.

Satellite access and an onboard uplink allowed the driver to follow the limousine on a television monitor in real time, without having to keep visual contact, the images being simultaneously relayed back to command at the ESC.

The CIG agent behind the wheel shadowed his target onto the freeway, and off again, keeping less than a mile away from the limousine at all times. This went on until, through the camera overhead, the operations agent watched the limousine disappear into a parking structure adjacent to a shopping mall.

"We've lost visual on them," the ops agent said.

"Can you get a tap into the security cams?" the driver asked.

"Doing it now... Hold up, it says that the system is down for repairs."

"Down for repairs, yeah right."

"This smells like a secret meeting. We let them pass that confession on to anybody who matters and they won't be the only ones who end up dead."

"I'm going in," the agent said as he turned the sedan into the parking structure, immediately searching for the limo. He caught the red streak of a tail-light just as it went around the corner and pursued.

The ops agent jumped to attention when an urgent message appeared on his main computer screen. The entire system in the surveillance unit seemed to be taken over by the alert, ensuring that the ops agent respond in a timely manner.

"Satellite contact with the target has been lost," the message read. "The General will be contacted in two minutes."

"Will have eyes on target in sixty seconds," the agent typed back.

The driver speeding through the tight rows of cars was sending the sound of squealing tires echoing through the cement structure. He launched up the circular ramp to the levels above, having to pin the steering wheel to three o'clock until he came out one floor up. He raced toward the door to the stairs and parked.

"I'll confirm which floor they stopped on and get this directional on them," the driver said as he jumped out, a miniature microphone in hand.

"This could be the best chance we're going to get to take the targets out. And I won't even worry about getting a sanction for whoever they're meeting. Take them all out. Get pictures for the General and maybe we can get the hell off his radar ASAP."

His gun ready, the agent cased the area like a police officer, cracking the door to the stairwell before bounding up the steps to the entry onto the next floor. He was cautious when he opened the heavy metal door, careful to stay hidden while he searched the second level for the limousine.

Just then John swung down from the landing above and planted both his feet into the man's back. The agent went flying through the door head first, onto the cement. John had him cuffed and blindfolded before he could recover.

The ops agent in the back of the CIG surveillance unit was becoming suspicious after his cohort had failed for the third time to respond to his calls for a status report. He was weighing the ramifications of reporting to General Masterson when he felt a gun barrel press against the back of his head.

"You even twitch and you're one dead boy," Gina said, reaching through the window.

"You got him?" Ben asked over the transmitter in her ear.

Gina rendered the agent unconscious with the touch of a taser to his neck. "Give us a sec and we'll be ready to move out."

Chris showed up to help her heave the agent out of the rear of the vehicle. He propped him up in the passenger seat; cuffs went onto his hands and ankles. Gina leaned back into the electronics bay to type a quick message into the computer the agent had been working on.

"Target reacquired, in pursuit," was all it said, just enough to appease command.

The computer system returned to normal operation and one of many bulletins about Max Stiner flashed across the screen. Chris caught a glimpse of it as he was climbing into the electronics bay.

"That's Stiner?" he said.

"Yep, another psychic, like your wife. He also got too close to Masterson and now they want him too."

"Then he's dead. Just like Erica."

"No, he isn't, because we've got him. He's safe with us now and we're going to help him. In fact, you're going to help us help him."

Ben came tearing back down the circular ramp in the limo. Gina allowed him to get all the way out of the parking garage before she fell in behind.

"Oh yeah, I almost forgot," she said. "Check around back there for an instrument panel marked camouflage."

"Got it," Chris said after a quick search.

"Engage that main switch."

Chris did as instructed which caused a curious electric smell to waft through the air.

"What did I do?"

"Watch." Gina nodded to the hood of the car.

The change was almost imperceptible, at first. But gradually the polished white paint began to lose its sheen, before fading to a dull beige. Every inch of the painted surface of the car grew darker until it was finally a deep brown. A lustrous finish soon returned, to complete the transformation.

"Sonofabitch," he said.

"It's special paint. You apply a charge and the pigments change. Great for deflecting suspicion when they're following people, to be able to switch it up once and a while. Works on the non-pros. It's SOP to change up after getting that close to their target."

To the satellite above, and the agents at ESC command who were monitoring the feed, the CIG team was back to tailing their target at a safe distance. The new paint color only went to sell the charade.

The limo got well away from the mall into another part of town before showing any signs of stopping. ESC command followed the car into an older Virginia neighborhood onto a block that was lined with parked cars. Mourners from the funeral were showing up and trailing into Joan's house.

The limo stopped long enough for Peter and Billy to get out then it proceeded to the end of the block and parked. Inside, Ben was behind the wheel in a chauffeur's uniform, coordinating the operation. John was in the back watching over the agent he had subdued in the garage.

"He didn't get a chance to lock us out, did he?" Ben asked Gina over the transmitter. She was just parking the surveillance vehicle under a canopy of oak trees around the corner from Joan's home.

"No, we're good, Ben."

"And the satellite?"

"I'm looking at the feed right now," Gina said. "They don't have eyes on me, just you."

"Then I'll call our hacker and get him on it," Ben said. He dialed another number and waited for a response.

"How can I help?" was the answer.

"I was expecting somebody else. Is this Mary?"

"Yes it is. Is this Ben?"

"Considering the threats against you, we've had concerns about you being involved with anything dangerous. And this could be very dangerous."

"It's the least I can do..."

"Look, Mary, I don't want you feeling obligated or anything."

"Honestly, it's not that. I want to help."

"If you're sure, OK then. We're going to set up an encrypted remote link from one of their mobile surveillance units. It should give you access to their security network. Their mobile network, anyway."

"That I can do, let me know when you have the hardware hooked up. I assume you know what you're doing on that one."

"You assume correctly. I'll call you back when it's done. You almost ready, Gina?" he said into the communicator in his ear.

Chris climbed out of the electronics bay so that Gina could squeeze into the ops chair and go to work setting up their own satellite uplink. She connected it to one of the ports on the console.

"I'm ready here," she told Ben.

"With that thing, we'll get his family out. Then we'll get Graydin, as well."

"If he isn't dead already," Gina said.

Masterson was hovering behind his desk when the guard brought Graydin in, handcuffed and bleeding. He immediately launched the audio file.

"I'm sending you this, Billy, because I'm a coward. I've worked for your respect for so long that I couldn't stand in the same room as you and admit what I am about to admit. I just couldn't do it. They're coming for me, I know it, and I want you to know a few things before they do. First, for the past five years–"

The clip ended after barely a few seconds, Graydin had recognized the voice immediately.

"I'm sending you this, Billy, because I'm a coward–"

Masterson kept hitting repeat then stopping the file at the same place every time.

"I'm sending you this, Billy, because I'm a coward–"

Though he was bruised and battered, Graydin presented a cool, emotionless face. He glared defiantly while Masterson taunted him.

"I'm sending you this, Billy, because I'm a coward–"

"My family, where are they?"

"I'm sending you this, Billy, because I'm a coward–" was the answer.

"Where is my family?!" Graydin dared to look Masterson directly in the eye, something few people ever did. He was surprised by what he saw.

"There have been complications," Masterson said. "And it was your job to deal with complications. Instead, you get tracked down by the very media asset you were supposed to be controlling! And now what began as a minor security leak has turned into a goddamned sieve of classified information!"

"What's happened to you?" Graydin asked, honestly bewildered. "The Masterson I know would have already wasted me and gone for dinner."

Masterson shoved his chair under his desk then snatched up the remote control to the bank of televisions behind Graydin. He changed the channel on one of them to a closed-circuit feed. A narrow view of a

Washington DC motel room appeared on the screen. Ann was sitting on one of the beds with her two children drawn close. Her expression of terror was obvious through the grainy video.

Graydin refused to give Masterson the satisfaction of reacting. He knew what came next. After the threat came the deal. He needed to be sharp if he was going to save his family.

"I reported the contact," Graydin said.

"I believe you reported that he saw you on the street and you evaded him. But the reports I get indicate a conversation of some length. And then your family mysteriously disappears to this motel here."

"He followed me into the alley. At the time I wasn't cleared to kill him."

Masterson took a long, exhausted look at Graydin's family. "Sometimes you can control your destiny and sometimes it controls you."

"I followed procedure in this situation."

"Did you?"

"When cornered and authorization to eliminate has not been given, disinform and disappear. I wrote the damn manual on it."

"Then why did you try to run?! Just exactly what did you tell him?!"

"Nothing he could prove!"

"Unless he's got corroboration." Masterson hit at the keyboard once again.

"I'm sending you this, Billy, because I'm a coward—"

"You own the goddamn press! Corroboration doesn't mean shit anymore!"

"You're right. But you know the protocols as well as I do. Your life was forfeited the moment he made unauthorized contact with you. Your family, well, they could be looked after. They still have a chance. You don't want them to end up classified: 'guaranteed fatalities' do you? That's what the troops call them nowadays, isn't it?"

"How can I be sure?"

"If I make a promise of protection I have to honor it, now don't I? Or the troops will stop trusting me, and we can't have that."

Graydin shook his head sternly. "I told you not to turn that voodoo nutcase on Simmons before we knew what he had. But you knew better, you're half losing it, but you knew better. Too bad he didn't have a spell that could read the guy's mind before he helped him blow his own brains out!"

Masterson hit repeat. "'I'm sending you this, Billy, because I'm a coward—' The reporter and Simmons's oldest friend were at the funeral together, arm and arm," he said.

"Big surprise!"

"I'm sending you this, Billy, because I'm a coward—"

Phil's guilt-ridden voice hung in the air while Graydin's mind worked at lightning speeds to come up with the best way to use what he knew to buy his family's survival.

"If they are working on some story," he said. "I know where he would be hiding out. I followed him there once when I was setting him up for the operation. It's an old house in his wife's mother's maiden name. If he's hiding out, it will be there. Now, let my wife and children go."

"I know all about that place! I warn you, by the time I get through with them they'll wish they did drown in a flood or a hurricane!"

Graydin balled up his fists, fighting with all his strength the urge to turn on Masterson and inflict some damage before the guards could step in and stop him. He maintained long enough to look his old boss over once again.

Graydin had met Masterson in person less than twenty times over the years. Every time the General was short, dismissive, and hostile, giving Graydin little insight into the man. He was certain, however, that he had never seen Masterson that frayed and distracted.

"It's true, isn't it?" Graydin said. "Look at you, how long has it been since you slept?"

"Do I look like I'm in the mood for your questions? Stay on topic before you make this situation any worse."

"You really are coming apart, aren't you? I mean, I've heard the talk but–"

"What talk?! What talk have you heard?!"

When Graydin didn't answer immediately, Masterson leaned in to smack his face. Even Masterson's bodyguards were surprised by his momentary loss of cool.

"I said what talk have you heard?!"

Graydin's accusing look reminded Masterson of Erica, and of Max. He turned away from him and the guards to pace behind his desk, trying to regain his composure.

"It's going to be hell when the climate goes critical," Graydin said. "But I wouldn't want to live in the world you'll create after, that will be worse."

"It will be just like it is now," Masterson said. "That's the point. We maintain the status quos. Oh, it'll be on a much smaller scale, of course. More exclusive, let's say."

"Yeah, right."

The complete lack of emotion with which Masterson deliberated on whether his family would live or die sparked, in Graydin, a feeling of indignant rage. It was a feeling the veteran operative was not used to experiencing. All the questionable things he had done to the parents of other children in the name of survival came rushing back. And with those memories came a wave of guilt.

"I've seen so much death, so much brutality," he said. "...working for sick fucks like you, in and out of the government. And for what? You're all the same.

"You use terror and violence like just another tool. You play on everyone's worst fears to keep your power. But it's all just an illusion, isn't it? That's your biggest secret: that your power is an illusion."

"I don't have time for illusions. I have a country to save. And you can be damn sure there isn't anyone like me."

Graydin took what he assumed would be the last look at his oblivious children, then his panicked wife. "No, there isn't anyone quite like you," he said. "You have the advantage of playing your little game at the most important time in history, don't you?

"The Commies, Islamic terrorists, the big bad black man waiting around the corner, they were all great threats. You got a lot of mileage out of them. But they were lies. This one is real, isn't it? Climate change really could kill us all.

"But your 'dream' of total control after the worst of it starts is only in your head. I see that now. You're going to look out the window one day and find yourself surrounded by the people you've been tormenting all this time. Then you'll be the one afraid."

"You're right about one thing. The threat is real this time. And so is the salvation I offer."

"Maybe, back before Maxwell J. Stiner."

"I seriously suggest you don't say that name again!"

"What did he do to you?"

"You just couldn't keep your mouth shut could you?! Now I'm thinking that your family has to die!"

"You know what happens when they stop believing that you can save them?!" Graydin said, appearing to let his anger get the best of him. "That's when you become unnecessary, obsolete!"

Masterson set upon Graydin with another slap across his rebellious face. Graydin continued undaunted in his prodding.

"No wonder they're all talking about how you're losing it! About how that's the only way all that shit could be happening behind your back!"

"What's been happening behind my back?! Who! Who's saying that? I'll kill them! I swear I'll kill them all! But I'll kill you and your entire family first!"

"If you want to know what I know, then I want your promise that Ann and my children will be safe!"

Masterson huffed and puffed in front of Graydin. "I'm trying to decide whether the information would be worth changing my mind about making an example out of you all!"

"And miss hearing about Hasline?"

"*What* about Hasline?!"

"Has he mentioned getting any 'messages' from the Pleiades lately?"

Back in Colorado, Mary was hard at work patching into the mobile surveillance unit Ben and his team had commandeered in DC. Sheila walked in as she was finalizing her preparations to take control of the computers in the vehicle.

"What happened?" Sheila asked.

"They need help out in Washington." Mary pressed return and a tactical display appeared on the screen of her laptop.

"What are you doing for them?" she asked.

Mary clicked through various links leading to status reports and surveillance photos of both Billy and Peter.

"Who are they?"

"I don't know who they are, but they're in trouble. The CIG is after them just like that Stiner guy. Ben's out there and he's trying to get them out."

"Ben Spiritdancer?"

Mary tapped the secure feeds beaming into the surveillance vehicle and stumbled across the video coming from Ann's hotel room. It took only a few seconds of viewing the video feed for them both to realize that something was terribly wrong.

"Those are kids. My God, Mary, what's going on out there?"

"That woman looks terrified."

Mary's phone rang. Ben was on the caller ID.

"How'd it go?" he asked.

"I'm into their mobile surveillance network. Check your laptop; I need to send you something."

"Go," Ben said. Mary patched through the feed from the motel. "Can you pinpoint where this is coming from?" he asked.

"No, but I have access to the locations of the other mobile units operating in DC right now. There's only one that's currently near a motel. That looks like a motel room, right?"

"Yes it is, Mary, excellent."

"The signal is sitting right in front of 936 Tennyson. Are they going to be OK? What's going on out there?"

"They're going to be just fine now, thanks to you."

"It's OK."

"Any chance you have access to their main computers? We need to find the father of that family."

"The surveillance network for these mobile units is cut off from the main system by password. It's to avoid situations just like this from leading to a total breach. That's what I would have done."

"If a life wasn't on the line I wouldn't ask this, Mary, but I have to, can you crack it?"

"This is high-end government encryption, Ben. If I run any of my password detection programs, they will know. In fact, I'll bet if you input the wrong password more than twice, the hardware in that surveillance unit will shutdown. For all I know it will self-destruct, these people are obviously nuts."

"So no hit or miss?"

"That's it, one shot, maybe two, and we're done."

"And if we could get that password?"

"Then we're in. But you better do it quick; they keep serious track of those vehicles."

"We're on it, thanks Mary. Gina will be going after those kids right now."

"They're kidnapping kids... Hector wasn't kidding about these people, was he?"

"They're doing what they're doing so deep in the shadows that right now, we're the only ones who can stop them. We'll be getting back with that password. Nice work."

"I realize you're busy, Ben, but I need to know...."

"Shoot."

"You obviously took what Denise said seriously."

"Yes, I did, but we have people like her who will do absolutely everything they can to protect you. Beyond that, I won't make any promises because I can't."

"These are the same people after me?"

"Yes, they are, we're certain of that now."

"Do you really think you can stop them?"

"Again, no promises, but I know it's possible. And on national television too, if all goes well."

"OK, Ben, thanks. Be careful, please."

Ben nodded to John in the back of the limo. John went into action by wrestling the bound CIG agent he subdued into the backseat and laying him down. He went into a pouch on his belt for two sprigs of a dried plant. He took hold of the struggling agent.

"You can torture me, but I won't tell you anything! He'll do way worse if I talk."

"Don't sweat it, Frank, this is just something to relax you, won't hurt a bit."

The agent clenched his teeth, attempting to wrench away. The struggling ceased, however, when John found a pressure point under the man's jaw that forced him to open wide. John pushed the plant into his mouth before tearing the second sprig in half and swallowing one of the pieces. The other piece went back into his pouch.

"Ready?" Ben asked.

"Ready." John lay down in the seat adjacent to the agent, their heads almost touching. "Pop, you'd be dangerous if you could do numbers."

"I can't do it all, Son. You're going to have to earn your money sometime. Gina, I'm coming to relieve you. Did you get the address?"

"I got it," she said over the transmitter.

"I'll have what we need soon enough," John said.

Ben got out of the limo with his chauffeur's hat in place and walked up to Joan's house. From above, he looked like a driver in need of a bathroom. Peter met him at the front door.

"How's it going in here?"

"Well, I can tell you one thing, they certainly loved him."

Billy was on the couch in the crowded living room comforting Joan while she wept. Billy looked up from her grieving friend and nodded to

Ben.

"I shouldn't be here," Peter said. "I can barely face these people."

"We have to keep you two together or they will send another surveillance unit," Ben said. "We have our hands full with one."

"I'll stay here until they start showing up."

"Fair enough," Ben said.

Ben took off his hat and black jacket on his way out the backdoor. He cut through the backyards of Joan's neighbors, while the agents at the CIG command center saw only the dense canopy of trees that sheltered most of the block. He had to traverse a ten foot fence and duck a particularly territorial dog on his way over to the waiting surveillance vehicle, but he made it without being detected.

Gina jumped out to meet him. "Is John doing his thing?"

"They'll be out for a few," Ben said. "How's he doing?" he asked, pointing at Chris in the rear of the sedan.

"I don't know, he's pissed. They killed his wife and he wants revenge. He's as dangerous as you get right now."

"Take him with you, would you? Maybe having a hand in getting those kids out will help his mental state."

"Yeah and it could get us all killed if he flips out or something."

"He's not going to flip out, trust me. He infiltrated Hasline's clinic and got out with some serious information, all without getting killed. We need to channel his grief or he will do something stupid that will disrupt our plans."

"I don't like working with amateurs. The drop car is just around the block. We'll get them out."

Ben opened the rear door to let Chris out. He led him out of earshot of the CIG agent in the front seat.

"Look, I know you want blood right now, but we need your help."

"I know, she told me. The family of one of those bastards, right?"

"We don't judge children by what their fathers do. If we can get them out of CIG hands, then we will. But that bastard, if we can find him before Masterson has him shot, it could blow the lid off this whole thing. He's the ultimate whistleblower."

"If he lives and you turn him over to the Justice Department, he's dead. He won't see the inside of a courtroom."

"He will if his face is plastered all over the international press before we let anyone official anywhere near him."

"How are you going to do that?"

"On Sunday the television news will do it for us. We just have to get as much proof as we can before then. Graydin is proof, and I guarantee that if we save him and his family he will cooperate."

Chris became sullen, refusing eye contact. "None of this will help me put Masterson in the ground."

"You and I both know that that isn't going to happen. You got as close as you will ever get to Masterson in Hasline's clinic. These are real things you can do to bring them down, and at the same time help other people who have been victimized by the CIG. You're just going to have to trust me that after Sunday, the name Masterson will be a household word. And after that, he will be finished."

Chris agonized in front of Ben, shaking his head stubbornly, his eyes full of tears.

"You don't understand, you just don't understand..."

"Let me see..." Ben looked Chris up and down, to confirm what he already knew. "It's guilt, a guilt that's smothering you."

"Don't try to read me," Chris said, crossing his arms. "I used to hate it when she would do that."

"No you didn't. It was one of the things that drew you to her. Her ability to understand other people. Her ability to sympathize with other people."

Chris broke down momentarily but Ben persisted.

"You came from a family that didn't communicate. So really expressing your feelings didn't come easily. You loved the fact that so much passed between you two without words."

Chris turned away. "It was my fault. I was the one that told her about the project. Damn it, I encouraged her to join."

"The weather prediction project? Chris, how could you have known?"

"It was supposed to help people, to save lives. The climate's too unstable for computers to predict. Fault lines and volcanoes are overdue to blow all over the country. A project aimed at predicting natural disasters that result in the loss of life before they happen? She was sold the first time she heard about it."

"Of course she would be. It's not your fault or hers."

"Then she met that sonofabitch Hasline. She knew that day that something was wrong. She stayed in to find out more about the monster behind it. So she could tell it all to someone at something she called the Unity Council. I didn't know what the hell she was talking about. Then she disappeared."

"It's time to make it right. It's time to do what your wife wanted. And that's not for you to throw your life away. Will you help us?"

Chris relented, temporarily relieved by his admission to Ben. Gina joined the men and indicated for Chris to follow. He did so without a word. They used the trees to avoid the satellite until they were around the corner.

Ben was getting into the rear of the surveillance vehicle just as an alert lit up the screen on the instrument panel. An urgent request for a status report appeared, followed by a text prompt.

Ben got into the ops agent's seat behind the banks of computers and closed his eyes. He ran his hands over the arms of the chair, the keys of the keyboard.

He opened his eyes and concentrated on the blinking prompt. He spontaneously typed out a quick report in the distinct style of the ops agent tied up in the front seat.

Back inside Joan's house, Peter was busy keeping his distance by lurking awkwardly in corners. Billy broke away from her friends to join him.

"It's OK, you know, Peter. They don't blame you for what happened to Phil."

"They don't know that it was all a lie."

"Maybe, but he was involved with the CIG. Which one is worse, stealing money from climate refugees or being involved in a conspiracy to let them die?"

"You can't be too hard on him. I know what it's like to be in over your head, with people who are more ruthless and murderous than you can ever imagine."

Billy dabbed Peter's shell-shocked face with a handkerchief she took from his suit pocket.

"You look beat, literally and figuratively."

"Didn't sleep much last night; needless to say, I had a few things on my mind."

"You mean you didn't get any sleep on a cot hiding out at a safehouse?"

"I doubt I'll be getting any sleep until after Sunday."

"Amen to that." Billy watched the room. "I haven't seen some of these people in years."

"They all obviously loved him very much."

"Not one elected official. Not one stooge from the Administration."

"It's for the best."

"Did you call them?"

Peter parted the curtains of the front window in time to catch the first television news broadcast truck speeding up to Joan's house.

"They're here," he said.

Billy nodded to Joan, who broke away from the woman with which she had been talking to dial the police on her cell phone.

Outside, two of Phil's larger mourners met the news team at a small fence at the edge of the property. They took up positions at the gates that prevented the crew from coming onto Joan's property.

A second and third broadcast truck arrived, forming a barrier between the unbroken lines of parked cars on both sides of the street. More vehicles arrived with more reporters, all of which began to clog the sidewalk in front of Joan's home.

"Did you enjoy getting back at your buddies in the press?" Billy asked.

"Let them see what it feels like to be manipulated."

"It's almost time." Billy opened the closet door behind Peter. She slung her backpack over her shoulder and handed Peter a small bag of clothes. "The other bathroom is down the hall to the right," she said.

"I'll meet you in back," Peter said. "We better get going before this place turns into a madhouse. I hope they were able to get what we needed."

Just outside the tinted windows of the limo in which Billy and Peter arrived, a bevy of frantic reporters and their support staff were jockeying for the best place to confront the mourners on their way out of Joan's house.

John woke in the rear of the luxury vehicle, the CIG agent still unconscious nearby. He crossed his legs and employed his measured breathing. He stretched his arms, his neck, extended his legs, and touched his toes.

"Yeah, Pop, we got what we need," he said over the transmitter in his ear. "His access code is 4-3-9-7-Alpha-Sam-2-8-3. It's only good until the next code rotation at the end of the shift. That's in an hour and a half.

"It should give us access to tactical data. And information on current operations they're involved in right now. But it won't give us much more. He doesn't have clearance, none of the field agents do."

"That's OK. It's almost time to move out. Billy and Peter should be just about ready to move."

"That's a roger."

Hard at work at her desk in the Unity Council Headquarters, Mary was familiarizing herself with the CIG's tactical computers. Armed with the code from Ben, she was careful not to raise any suspicions by first clicking on several routine updates and bulletins. She checked a duty roster and confirmed the next day's assignment for the subdued ops agent.

While all that was going on, she surreptitiously gained access to an administrator's directory and used it to look at the reports from other operatives in the Washington DC area. Sheila leaned in over her shoulder to skim the terse, condensed reports of clandestine and often heinous deeds.

"My God, Mary. What the hell kind of morally reprehensible psychos are we dealing with here with this CIG? First kidnapping children, now this?"

"Probably costs billions of tax dollars too."

"What are we looking for?"

"All I know is that they're going to kill the guy. His codename is Graydin. His real name is Parker. He's those kids' dad."

"Look at this."

"Yeah: 'Have leverage on target, moving to next phase,'" Mary read. "What do you suppose that means?"

"Blackmail, Jesus, they're blackmailing and manipulating people all over Washington."

"How many of these 'targets' are politicians?"

"Stop! Look, scroll back."

Mary rolled the pages on the computer screen back to a report that was short and sweet: "'Subject being transported to site N for disposal,'" she read. "Unless they're 'disposing' of more than one person today, that's got to be him."

"They may very well be, look at all this, Mary."

Mary got Ben on the line. "Site N, somebody is being taken to site N, for 'disposal.' I can fish around for the location of site N but—"

"There won't be any addresses in there. When was the time of the report?"

"Twelve minutes ago."

"Damn, we're already too late. Do you have an ID code on that report?"

"Yeah, but no name."

"Can you access the vehicle assignments for today?"

"Yeah." Mary called up a duty roster. "Here we go."

"Can you tell what vehicle was assigned to that ID code?"

"Yeah, vehicle 492."

"OK, now, can you locate the transponder signal for 492?"

"Of course."

"Can we track that signal?"

"The only way is with that surveillance unit, and once you go off grid, they will know."

"It's a chance we have to take. Thanks, Mary... So, should I tell Hector that we need to look for a new head of IT?"

Mary paused, but only for a beat. "All I know is that we can't let these people get away with this. Period."

"No we can't. I'll be in touch."

Ben hung up the satellite phone. "Site N, any idea?" he asked John over the transmitter.

"It's over near the Potomac," John said from the limo. "They get verbal briefings on rotating safe houses every shift."

"Come on, we have to take this," Ben said.

"Thought we were ditching their vehicle."

"It's the only way to track him."

"Then this could get interesting."

He tested the plastic restraints on his prisoner and made sure he had gathered his father's laptop before opening the rear door of the limo. He locked the door and slammed it shut. The agents at the SEC watching the satellite feed caught only a glimpse of John before he disappeared into the growing crowd of reporters blocking the road.

"You get those kids clear, and I'll take care of the guards," Gina told Chris.

"Are you sure they're in there?" he asked.

Gina squinted through a pair of binoculars at a distant hotel. A muscle-bound man in a windbreaker and jeans circled a black cargo van in front of the door she was interested in, confirming that they were in the right place.

"If things get weird, just grab them and run, understand?"

"Look at him, he's huge, and there's got to be at least two, you sure about that?"

"I'm not worried about them. But I won't have time to worry about any of those kids getting hurt."

Gina could almost feel Chris's mind working as he stared at the van, and the CIG agent on guard.

"You with me here, or what?" Gina's firm tone jarred Chris. "Because if you are, that means you do exactly what I say."

"I'm with you," he said. "Just give me the opportunity and I'll make sure they're safe."

"And don't look back, understand?"

"Got it."

Gina put the car in gear when another CIG agent – burdened by several suitcases – emerged from the room. He and his partner finished loading the luggage into the van and visually swept the area for threats before one of them waved to the door of the hotel room. Ann emerged fearfully from the room with her two children staying close to their mother.

Her diamond tennis bracelet and the kids' overpriced children's wear suggested an upper middleclass family on a weekday outing. The heavily armed killers accompanying them weren't taking them to ballet lessons or karate class though. They were being "relocated" to a place the General deemed fit. Ann knew enough about her husband's work to know that that could be very bad.

A squeal of tires challenged the combat instincts of one of the agents as they were about to herd everyone into the van. He decided to perform a final security sweep of the parking lot, moving to the end of the van for a wider angle of the area. The moment he cleared the end of the van, he was sideswiped by a speeding car. The vehicle grazed him and knocked him to the ground, but didn't kill him. The other agent ran to his injured partner's side near where the car screeched to a stop.

The agent felt his unconscious partner's neck for a pulse. "What the hell!" he yelled. He stomped to the driver's side of the idling car, his pistol in hand. He was surprise when Gina jumped out, her beautiful face locked in a convincing expression of shock.

"Oh my God! I didn't even see him!" she shrieked. "He just jumped out from behind the...! Oh God, please tell me he's OK. I was late for work and– Oh no! I'm not insured!"

Gina raved on, eventually convincing him that she was a genuinely devastated Washington D.C. professional. His suspicion eased enough for him to slide his pistol back into his belt.

"Just settle down," he said.

The agent was too busy patronizing her to react when Gina drew her automatic pistol from behind her back and fired two shots. One went through the meat of the agent's left thigh; the other grazed his right calf. She lunged toward him and snatched the pistol from his hand on his way to the ground. He landed flat on his back.

"Treacherous bit–!"

"Don't say anything I'll want to make you regret." She threw the agent's weapon deep into the parking lot.

Chris had already jumped out of the back. "We have to go!" he said to Ann. "The cops will be here in minutes!"

"No! My husband! What about my husband?"

"Your husband is dead, but you can still live!" Chris said.

"No, he can't be!"

Gina made her own security sweep of the parking lot as she rushed to where Ann and her two children were frozen in fear.

The agent Gina shot was struggling with his hemorrhaging legs. "He's dead all right and if you go with her, the General will track you down and kill you all! Count on it!"

His threats paralyzed Ann. She knew he was not exaggerating.

"You should be more worried about what he's going do to you when he finds out you couldn't even hold on to a woman and two kids," Gina said. "He's real hard on failure, from what I hear, anyway."

"We have to go," Chris said.

She looked to Gina for some sign as to what to do.

"Trust me," Gina said.

Ann hesitated for a second more before pushing her children toward Gina's car.

"Our things!" she said.

"No time! Move! Move!"

"I'll get them!" Chris said. He threw as many suitcases as would fit into the open trunk and slammed it shut.

"You're dead!" the wounded agent yelled. "He's gonna find you!"

Gina got Ann and the children into the backseat and strapped them into seatbelts. She climbed behind the wheel, expecting Chris to join her in the front seat. She looked for him in the rearview mirror but caught only a glimpse of the door to the CIG van closing with a slam. Red brake lights came on when Chris started the vehicle and began backing out.

Gina jumped back out to see that the agent she had hit with the car was gone. Chris was speeding away by the time she realized he had dragged the agent into the van and was running with him. Fast approaching sirens prodded her back into the car.

"What the hell did he do with my partner?!" the bleeding agent yelled after them. "You're dead! He's gonna kill you all!"

Gina was barely able to drive them all out of the parking lot ahead the authorities' arrival. After performing a series of evasive maneuvers through the swelling Washington DC traffic, she charted a roundabout course toward the airport.

Ann and the kids kept low during the ride. "Is it true?" she finally asked.

"As of right now, we believe your husband is alive," Gina said, keeping an eye on the traffic. "We have our best people on the situation. But right now what you need to worry about is your kids. We're getting on a plane out of here, if our people can follow then they will."

Ann's gratitude was preventing her from protesting. In truth, she hadn't expected to see her husband again after the agents found them. She held her children tight. Gina could see through the mirror that they were worried.

"Look, kids, it's going to be OK," she said. "We're going to head out to the mountains for a while. I have some friends that are going to do their best to get your dad back and they'll fly on out behind us if they can, OK?"

Ann's son and daughter were trying to maintain brave faces, feeling the adults' fear and tension. It hung in the air while Gina negotiated the Washington streets to a less public side of the sprawling international airport, where private flights were taking off.

She turned into an outlying parking lot according to the plan, and only a few minutes behind schedule. Peter suddenly appeared while she was looking for a parking spot, waving her down. He directed her into the space beside a car in which Billy was sitting. She opened the passenger door so that he could get back under cover as quickly as possible.

They spoke through the open windows. "There aren't any cameras in this lot, we made sure," Gina said.

"No, but look." Billy pointed through the rear window, past the chain link fence, to where private jets and prop planes were loading for departure. Ann ducked down so that Gina could point the binoculars toward the area. Flashing lights and people in flack jackets could mean only one thing.

"Looks like ATF and ICE, they called out all the stops," Gina said.

"What do you mean?" Ann asked. "What does this mean?"

"It's OK. We have a backup. It won't be pretty, but we have a backup."

"Wait a second," Billy said. She dug her cell phone out of her backpack and dialed through all the text messages she had been receiving since Phil's death. She knew she had seen an offer of condolence from an old friend, not of Phil's, but of hers.

"I have a friend," she said. "He has a jet now, the number he texted me from was the same office number he's always had. He'll to fly us to Denver, if we'll pay his fuel."

"Can you trust this guy?" Gina asked.

"I've known him for almost twenty years," Billy said. "But I can't call him either."

"That wasn't a yes."

"We don't have a choice," Peter said.

Gina deliberated a moment. "Either way we have to get the hell out of here."

"His hanger is at the Humboldt Airfield, it's−"

"A few miles north, I know, we scouted it for the op. Follow me to a place were we can leave that car and we'll all go in this. I'll call Ben and

John."

"Will do," Peter said. He turned the engine over and eased out of the parking space. Gina did the same, then led them out of the parking lot. She rang Ben's satellite phone.

"Yeah."

"Our transportation is blown. You've got feds crawling all over."

"Can you get to the alternate airfield?"

"Billy says she has a friend with a plane."

"What do you know about him?"

"That she's known him for a lot of years. But then she knew Simmons for a lot of years too."

"Check it out. We're about to intercept the transport. How's Chris doing?"

"Oh, you'll love this, right in the middle of the grab he took one of the guards and drove off in one of their vans."

"He did what?"

"I couldn't go after him, he's gone."

"If he hadn't taken one of their agents I would agree but this isn't good."

"That man wasn't going to stop until somebody put him in the ground next to his wife."

"I know, I know. We better move on these guys. We'll get back to you."

"Tell John not to go get himself shot, would you?"

"Check out the airfield and this pilot, and let us know if it's our way out."

"I'm on it."

Ben stowed the satellite phone in his jacket so that he could brace himself as John cranked over the wheel of the commandeered CIG surveillance vehicle. Two of the tires came off the ground at one point.

The ops agent in the passenger seat was trembling, his eyes opened wide as silver dollars. Ben watched from the electronic bay in the rear of the sedan while John weaved through traffic at an alarming speed. Each near miss drew a smile from John and a terrified cringe from the agent.

"Hey, look Tommy, no eyes!"

Eyes closed, John steered the speeding car around two others, slowed behind a waiting truck until it was clear and then passed it clean. Tommy was frantic until John finally looked back at the road.

"Quit showing off, Son. The signal is right up here, we can't be more than a few minutes out."

"Great, so what's the plan?"

"Still working on it."

"We let them get to the site there could be more agents to deal with. And a lot more security."

"I know that."

"Well hell, Pop, if they're following procedure, then Graydin's stowed in a relatively safe place. He might be able to handle a small crash and survive."

"A *small* crash? Seriously?"

John blew between two slower moving cars without hesitation and with mere inches for clearance. "Hey, he'll live," he said with a wink to the now manic ops agent beside him. "I can't guarantee he'll be ambulatory, as they say, but his mouth will still work. Hector will still get what he needs."

"Yeah, maybe...after an extended hospital stay." Ben turned to the agent. "Does that sound good to you, Tommy?" The stunned man shook his head quickly. "No, Son, Tommy says that's no good at all."

"Well you need to come up with something better real quick. Because they're just up the block here."

"They're armor-plated, these transports, a PIT probably won't be easy."

"But we're armor-plated too, aren't we Tommy?" John said.

The agent shook his head frantically. The blinking green dot on the display was now down to half a city block away.

"They should be just up here," Ben said.

"Slowing down." The agent let out a very loud sigh of relief. "Relax, Tommy, this will all be over very soon."

"There!" Ben said.

The vehicle the CIG agents were using to transport Graydin to the place of his execution was as bland as the surveillance unit John drove in pursuit. The extended sedan wasn't too new or old, white in color, and besides a dent from a mishap in a parking lot, left to add to the authenticity, it was in no way remarkable to anyone.

"What do you think, Son?"

"If I can get close I may be able to do something. But it could be dangerous."

Tommy's frantic reaction confirmed John's suspicion. "Tommy says that they're very heavily armed," John said.

"Hey, this is your idea."

With that John veered out of his lane and accelerated into oncoming traffic. He took less than a second to anticipate which way the cars would turn, avoiding a succession of head-on collisions before turning back into the correct lane behind the CIG transport. He waited for another car to pass before zooming along side the transport.

Over Tommy's frenzied protestations, John persisted in trying to get a direct look at the driver. He matched the transport's speed, almost allowing him to see into the front seat. The tinted rear window of the other surveillance unit rolled down. Ben expected to be able to see into the backseat but couldn't.

"Look at that," he said.

"Holographic shade," John said. "Thought that was still in development."

There was no sound when a hail of heavy caliber bullets erupted from the rear window.

The armor on the surveillance unit was protecting Tommy and Ben from harm, for the moment. The windows in the vehicle were cracking and splintering, being whittled down by the persistent gunfire.

"Oh this is fun!" John said. "Feel that blood pumping, Tommy!?"

The agent shook his head, pleading through his bounds for John to stop. Meanwhile the bullets spewing through the holographic shade were peppering the agent's side of the car over and over.

A small corner of the glass finally gave way letting several rounds through. They riddled the dash. John snatched Tommy away from the torrent before he was hit. Ben yanked the agent the rest of the way over the seat and into the electronics bay.

"We can't take much more of this!" Ben yelled.

"I know, I know," John said, his forearm dripping blood from a bullet graze. "I just need a second."

Despite the gunfire that continued from the darkness in the rear of the sedan, John made one more attempt at getting close. He successfully locked eyes with the driver of the transport as the rear window protecting the electronics bay was ready to give into the relentless barrage. The power of suggestion did the rest.

John pointed to the empty lane in front of the CIG driver and mouthed the words: "Watch out for that truck!"

The driver instinctively stomped on the brakes and cranked the steering wheel, in a panicked effort to avoid an obstacle that wasn't there. The momentum sent the top-heavy vehicle sliding into the curb then spinning into the air. The hulk bounced off its reinforced roof and continued rolling through a grove of bushes, down an embankment.

"Wow, he really bit at that one, didn't he?" John said, looking through the rearview mirror.

"Yeah, he really did, Son. Think Graydin's still alive?"

"Only one way to find out." John executed a daring u-turn on the fast moving expressway and sped back to the scene of the crash. He shot across traffic, over the curb where the CIG vehicle launched down the embankment. He left the car running while he hauled the now half-catatonic ops agent from the passenger seat.

"Cops are coming," Ben said.

"I'll get him out and meet you two mile markers down."

Ben climbed into the driver's seat. "What if he's hurt?"

"There's plenty of cover here, we'll make it."

Ben turned the vehicle around and waited for an opportunity to merge with traffic. John led the dazed ops agent down the embankment before they were spotted by the concerned citizens stopping to help.

Ben was back in traffic and looking for the mile marker, his satellite phone rang.

"Thank god you're still alive," Mary said. "Are you still in that surveillance vehicle? Because if you are, I think you better get the hell out of it."

"What's going on?"

"I was poking around in the system on that thing. A countdown just started, I think they know that particular unit is off the grid."

"A countdown to what?"

"I don't know, complete shutdown? Complete implosion. I told you they would have a failsafe. That's what I would do."

"Why don't they just activate it then?"

"Frequencies can be hacked. Personally, I wouldn't ride around on a bomb that could be activated by a smart hacker."

"Just shut it down, you have total access to the system, don't you?"

"That's the point of a failsafe. It's an independent system. To prevent smart hackers like me from deactivating it. When the vehicle goes out of its daily operational area without clearance, things get dangerous."

Ben dropped back out of traffic at the second mile marker down from where the CIG transport crashed. "How long do we have? We don't have a lot of options for another vehicle right now."

"I have no access to that system. There's just no way to tell. Get the hell out of there, Ben."

"We will but we can't leave this thing if it's going to blow, somebody could get hurt."

"I have an idea; let me check the map of where you are."

Ben looked up to see John running toward the car with a bloodied and unconscious Graydin slung over his shoulder. Ben flung open the passenger side door, clearing the way for John to throw him into the front seat.

"We have to move!" Ben said. "This thing is rigged to blow!"

"Shit," John said, turning back to the crash down the road.

There the CIG prisoner transport had come to rest on its roof at the bottom of the embankment, with both doors hanging wide open. A highway patrolman that had just arrived on the scene called back the concerned citizens who had already descended on the wreck.

"There's blood but there wasn't anyone in there," one of the bystanders said. "It started smoking so we got away."

The patrolman began climbing down the embankment. "Wait shh...shh.. do you hear that?"

All those gathered heard a banging coming from the trunk.

"Someone's in there!" one of the men said.

The banging became violent until the trunk lid fell open and Tommy came tumbling out of the padded cell inside. The CIG agent was unharmed but frantic. From his knees he was trying to warn the patrolman and the others away, the gag muffling his cries. He finally got the strap out of his mouth.

"Get back! Get away from here!"

The patrolman saw the restraints on Tommy's wrists and the handcuffs hanging inside what was obviously a specially designed transport cell. The patrolman's first instinct was to rush to the rescue, which he attempted to do, until a fiery explosion blew him back onto the embankment.

It engulfed the wreck, then Tommy, and burned white hot. More explosions ignited at several locations on the chassis that began to melt through the metal frame itself.

Ben was still close enough to hear the explosion when it went off, a reminder of what would happen to them if they didn't act quickly. Graydin lay unconscious and bloody in the passenger seat while John recovered in the electronic bay, tending to the graze on his arm with a salve from his pouch.

"How long has it been since you worked with REGs?" Ben asked.

"It's been a while but random event generators were actually pretty easy to influence."

"There's a solid-state timer counting down somewhere on this vehicle. Can you buy us a little time?"

"I've messed with timers but never shut one down. I could mess with this one until it blows us up."

"According to Mary, it could blow up at anytime anyway and we can't just leave it here, people might get hurt."

Finished tending his arm, John spun around in the chair, his back to the oncoming road. Ben was back on the satellite phone to Mary.

"Take a right up at the next block," she said. "You're close!"

"I'm going to need your help, Pop."

"OK, get ready."

John began, as always, with his breathing. While he concentrated on his lungs and diaphragm, he closed his eyes and braced himself on the instrument panel. His breathing grew faster and faster.

"Imagine the bomb, Son, strapped to the undercarriage beneath us."

John concentrated on his father's voice. "Go!" he said once he had that firmly in mind.

"Now imagine the mechanism on the detonator," Ben said. "Corner!" he yelled as he guided the vehicle around the last corner before their destination.

"Imagine the circuitry inside the detonator, Son. Imagine the electronic signals alternating back and forth, on and off. You can control those signals. You've done it before, you can do it now." He looked at his watch. "We're coming up on 13:47 sidereal! It's all in your favor!"

In his mind's eye, John could see the arc of electrical energy that went from one circuit to another in the detonator. He could imagine being able to randomly short out that arc and break that connection, thus disrupting the ability of the timer to properly count down.

"Better hurry, Pop!" John's eyeballs were darting around behind his eyelids.

Ben activated the windows that weren't too damaged to roll down. "Hold on!"

The people in the CIG vehicle felt a minor lift when Ben hit the cement lip at the edge of the lake, but it sent them a good twenty feet into the lake. Water came rushing in immediately upon landing.

Ben unbuckled Graydin and hoisted him through the driver's side window, into the water.   "Come on, Son!" He towed Graydin's motionless body clear of the swamped vehicle.

John moved to the window, all the time concentrating on the timing mechanism on the bomb, and the countdown. He launched himself out of the driver's side window just before the vehicle exploded behind him. His dive was perfect and left only his boots exposed to the blast. He surfaced beside Ben and Graydin.

Ben paddled behind after John took Graydin by the neck like a lifeguard and leaned into a backstroke. He had Graydin well away by the time the park goers gathered at the edge of the lake to gawk at what was turning into a fireworks show on the water.

Even the submerged parts of the surveillance vehicle were being melted by high temperature explosives, which were burning with such intensity that they were creating clouds of steam from the lake water. Clouds that masked their getaway.

Graydin's bath was reviving him. By the time John was hauling him out of the shallow end of the lake, he could almost form words.

"Who are you people?"

"We aren't your former employer, that's for sure," John said. "Can you walk? You have to help us get you out of here."

Ben reached the shallows where he was able to stand. He ran up to John who was helping Graydin out of the water and took the other shoulder. Graydin was responsive but still deadweight.

"We have to get you out of the city," Ben said. "You're gonna be our deep throat."

"I don't say a word until my family is safe," Graydin said, his head bobbing from side to side. "And I don't go out in the open. I'll record a statement, but I won't–"

"Stop making deals and help us get you out of here!" Ben said.

The stern tone got through Graydin's aching brain and inspired him to try to walk. Dripping wet, the trio stumbled through a crowd of bewildered picnickers, into a packed parking lot.

Ben fished out the satellite phone from his drenched jacket. "We're alive, Mary. We have to move now, but I just wanted to let you know. Thanks." Ben tapped the transmitter in his ear. "Can you hear me Gina?"

"Got him?"

Ben tightened his grip on Graydin with a nod when John disappeared into the lot.

"How's it look?" she asked.

"We got him. How's it look out there?"

"I don't like it worth a shit, but the plane will fit us all, and we have no other options."

"Where?"

"Humboldt Airfield."

"Got it."

Less than two minutes later John was driving back toward the men in a stolen car. "I took an older one."

"Great, Hector won't be as pissed when we have to compensate the owner."

"Cost of doing business."

On the other side of Washington DC from the airfield, Chris ripped a black hood off the bleeding head of the CIG agent he had captured, blinding the man with a flashlight pointed directly at his eyes.

The agent moved enough to test his bounds; his wounded shoulder prevented a struggle. He detected the darkened room and laughed uneasily.

"Looks like someone's seen too many spy movies."

"Are you one of the ones?!" Chris yelled from the shadows.

"What the hell are you talking about? What the hell is this? I was hit by a damn car today! I need a hospital!"

"Did you do it?!"

"I'm an FBI agent and they'll be looking for me!"

"No they won't. People disappear from the Continuity in Government all the time, for all kinds of reasons."

"The what? I don't know what you're talking about. Like I said, I am an agent of the Federal Bureau of Investigations and you are committing a federal crime here."

Chris jammed the barrel of his automatic pistol into the agent's already bruised cheek. "Oh yeah, and what kind of crime is murder?! Did you do it? Were *you* the one that killed her?!"

The agent turned his head away grudgingly. "I've never killed anyone."

"We both know that's not true! The question is whether it was you who killed my wife!" He cocked the hammer of the pistol. "Every house on this block is in repossession. That means no one will hear or care when I blow your brains all over that wall!"

"I don't even know who the hell you're talking about!"

"Erica Brown! Sergeant Erica Brown!"

The agent's face immediately went blank. His manor softened and his eyes began to dart around evasively.

"You know something. What do you know?"

"That was the General...," he finally admitted, actually more concerned at that moment about the Masterson situation than Chris's revenge.

"I know who gave the order! Are you the one who pulled the trigger?!"

"He did it himself, OK! Everyone knows he did that one himself."

Chris doubled over as if he had been kicked in the stomach. The agent had merely confirmed what he already knew but now he was forced to accept it. He stumbled out of the shuttered up dining room into the empty living room.

For days Chris had been convinced that his wife did indeed reach out to him with a message of love right before she was killed, so convinced that he had committed a string of felonies. But the entire time he was assaulting the innocent and kidnapping the not-so-innocent, he held out hope that somehow, at the end of it all, he would find her. It took hearing the truth from a genuine agent of the Continuity in Government to make it painfully real.

Erica's final moments played over and over in his head. He was in tears and raving to himself by then.

"I'm sorry, Erica! I let you down! I let you down!"

He went to the kitchen, to a shaving bag that held a vial and a syringe. He prepared the amount his intelligence friend had shown him, careful not to let his trembling hands waste what little of the precious truth serum he could acquire. After cleaning himself up a bit, he went back to the dining room.

"I told you what you wanted to know. You know damn well I'm not lying. Now let me go."

"Now you're going to tell me everything you know about the Western Range Complex and something called the Aries."

The agent shook his head. "Not a chance in hell."

"I thought you might say that."

Chris deftly inserted the needle into the agent's neck.

At Humboldt Airfield, Billy hopped spryly around in front of Hank's desk, charged from the events of the day. She hadn't seen her old beau in over ten years, they hadn't been involved for longer than that. There was a marked difference in how they were aging.

Hank's old baseball cap hid a receding hairline and his gut hid his belt buckle, though his deep black eyes were still as piercing as Billy remembered.

"All those times in the Congo when I convinced you to fly supplies in, when it was so hot that no one else would do it. I seem to remember that with enough persuasion of the green variety, you always did the right thing."

"Red, the money wasn't that good and you know it. You know why I always came through for you."

"Is that the same flannel shirt you wore the day we broke up?" she said.

Billy recognized in Hank's toothy smile the boyish charm that endeared him to her all those years before.

"So how many people we talking here?"

"Eight, can you get us to Denver? We'll pay when we get there."

"Let me call about a flight plan," he said. "DIA is always busy, but there is an airfield just south of town in Centennial that can handle jets."

"We can't give names, Hank."

"Don't have to with this kind of flight, just the number of passengers.

Don't tell me Miss Goody-Two-Shoes is in some kind of trouble?"

"Just let us know when we can leave."

Billy cut through the hangar where Hank's passenger jet was maintained. Hank's mechanic was performing his preflight inspection on the craft.

Ann and the kids were waiting in the car outside. Peter stood by the driver's side door.

"Where's Gina?" Billy asked Peter.

He waited for her to get close enough for him to whisper. "She said she was going to do some reconnaissance."

"He's filing the flight plan now." Billy perked up for the kids. "Your dad is on his way and we're going to take a plane trip. Then things will calm down a bit, promise."

Billy's pleasant accent and determined smile set the children at ease. Their mother wasn't so easily placated.

"Where is my husband? We aren't getting on that airplane without him."

Gina stepped out from behind a nearby shed. "They should be here any minute now," she said.

The visceral roar of a jet engine drowned out all conversation and drew everyone's attention to the cockpit. Hank could be seen there putting on his headphones and preparing for the flight to Denver.

The kids were awed by the jet coming to life; Ann was prepared to dig in. She got out of the car to confront Billy directly and noticed another vehicle appeared at the gate to the airfield. Gina was certain it carried John, Ben, and Graydin.

"That's them! We have to go now!"

"I need to see him!"

Peter loaded up with two of the three bags from the trunk. Billy was able to get the other, along with her backpack. They headed toward the rear entrance of the aircraft.

The moment John brought the stolen car to a stop it became clear to Gina that he had been shot. "How deep?"

"It's just a graze. Don't start."

"For a guy that can almost walk through walls, you sure get shot a lot."

"Nice to see you too partner."

Graydin fell out of the passenger side into Ann's arms. She and the children supported him while they lavished him with hugs.

"You've seen him, now we move!" Gina said to Ann.

She looked to her husband, who nodded in agreement. With the help of his family, he hobbled toward the waiting jet. Ben, John, and Gina kept watch from behind until the entire family was loaded and they were certain no one was following.

"What about this pilot?" Ben asked before he boarded.

"He'll get us to Denver," Gina said. "Or I'll give him a timeout and I'll fly us there myself."

"You can fly this?" Ben asked.

"You kidding? In her sleep," John said. He secured the hatch behind them, which let Hank know they were clear to go. He steered the jet onto the runway and accelerated into a flawless takeoff.

To be continued...

Hands of the Maker

Book II

The exciting conclusion is now available at Barnes and Noble and on Amazon!

Visit: handsofthemaker.com for more!

All of the authors mentioned in the story have written books presenting their theories about everything from conspiracy to black magick to alien visitation.
Visit: www.handsofthemaker.com
for more on those subjects and suggestions for further reading.